A Vengeful Shade

BOOKS BY KIMBERLY GRYMES

Aevo Compendium Duology Series
Young Adult Science-Fantasy

Isoldesse
Fawness
The Red Umber Forest (a companion novella)

◆ ◆ ◆ ◆

Three Shades Trilogy
Young Adult Dark Fantasy

Shade of Light
A Vengeful Shade

◆ ◆ ◆ ◆

The Four-Week Story Prep Workbook:
A Brainstorming and Outlining Workbook for Fiction Writers

A VENGEFUL SHADE

Book Two in the Three Shades Trilogy

KIMBERLY GRYMES

Tractor Beam Publishing

ISBN: 978-1-9652250-11 (paperback)
ISBN: 978-1-9652250-28 (hardcover)
ISBN: 978-1-9652250-35 (special edition hardcover)
ASIN: B0D53KCXPC (Kindle eBook)

Cover Design and Interior Formatting by Kimberly Grymes
Character Artwork by Yves Muench | Fiverr.com/creatyves
Map by Angeline Trevena | Step-By-Step Worldbuilding
Chapter title page illustrations were created with images from Canva.com and/or DepositPhoto.com

A Vengeful Shade is book two in the Three Shades Trilogy.
Genre: Dark Fantasy
Age Category: Young Adult (14+)

Trigger warnings: Medieval fantasy world violence including death, battle scenes, and torture through mind infiltration.
Light Romance. All scenes are appropriate for teen readers 14+ years.

Tractor Beam Publishing
P.O. Box 261, Rose Hill, KS 67133

For more information visit https://kimberlygrymes.com/

To Chloe,

You are crafty, creative,
and full of imagination.
In the end, you are perfectly you,
and I wouldn't have it any other way.
I know you're destined to do amazing things,
now and always.
I love you, baby girl.

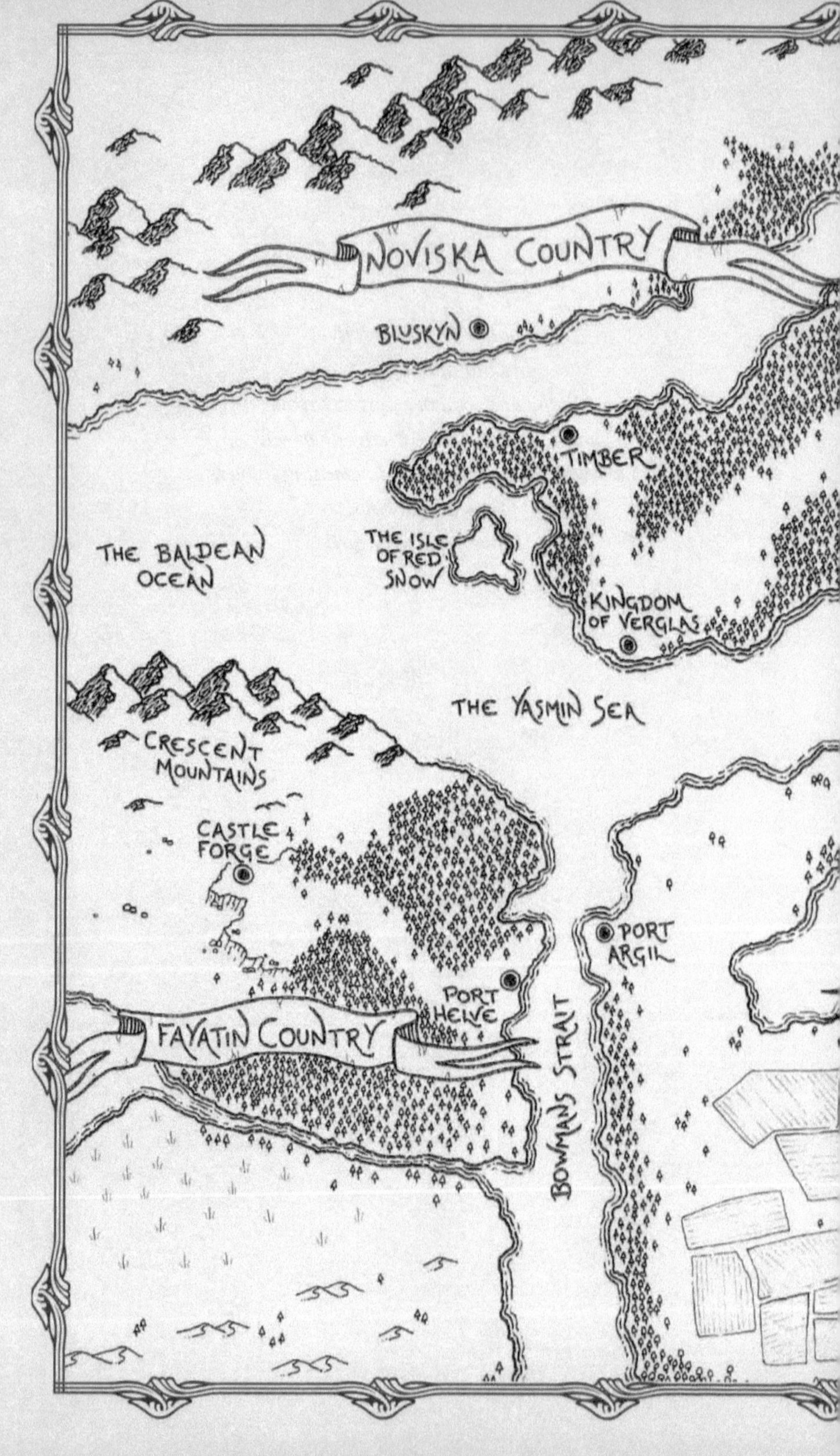

NOVISKA COUNTRY
BLUSKYN
TIMBER
THE ISLE OF RED SNOW
THE BALDEAN OCEAN
KINGDOM OF VERGLAS
THE YASMIN SEA
CRESCENT MOUNTAINS
CASTLE FORGE
PORT ARGIL
PORT HELVE
FAYATIN COUNTRY
BOWMANS STRAIT

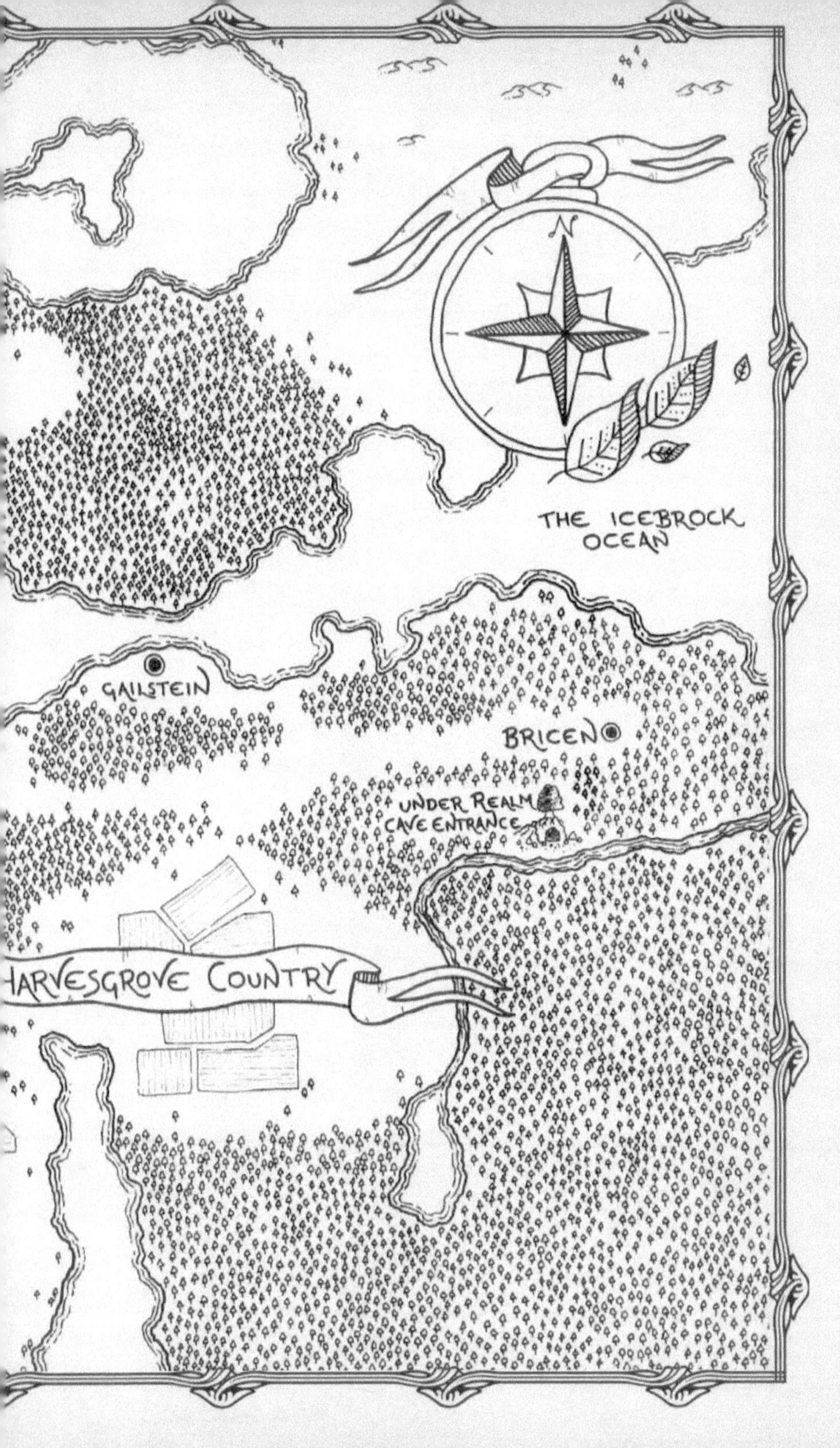

THE ICEBROCK OCEAN
GAILSTEIN
BRICEN
UNDER REALM CAVE ENTRANCE
HARVESGROVE COUNTRY

PROLOGUE

MARCELLUS

We have not lost.
Not yet.

Brushing away several strands of pale hair from my queen's face, I lean closer and press a hand to her cheek. I'm instantly met with a chill that prickles my palm. Ignoring the rough edges of her cracked skin, I close my eyes and concentrate. With a gentle nudge of my ability, I stretch the sinews of my mind out through my fingertips and into her resting thoughts. Or at least, I try to breach her mind, because Instead of being thrown into a sea of memories and a torrent of thoughts like in every other mind I've breached, I find nothing but an infinite space of darkness. All that remains is a glass sphere, floating in the void. No matter how hard I push, I cannot break the mental confinement Adele constructed. I'm helpless to free my queen from reliving the memory of the moment she was banished from the Starlight Realm.

Through the transparent cage, Merigoth screams as she faces the giant mirror Adele added to the memory. The second my queen's cries die after she runs off into the forest, there's a subtle flicker, and the scenario resets. Merigoth, then known as Loralai, crawling on her hands and knees, begging for help from three female angels. Their wings are vibrant and healthy while Merigoth's infected wings are poisoned and dying, falling to the ground until there's nothing left but bones. And when the moment comes that the angels turn her away, I want to cry out and tell her she doesn't need them. That she has me.

As I face the mirror again, her screams pierce my heart, fueling my desire to make Adele pay for what she's done.

I withdraw from Merigoth's mind, feeling the heavy stretch of my reach reeling in through the tips of my fingers. Opening my eyes, I tell her, "I promise you that I will make her pay for her treason. You were the one betrayed by the angels. You are the one who has suffered all these years, afflicted with demon poison from a battle you fought in their stead. They should've healed you and revered you as a hero."

A chorus of deep moans resonates from outside this temporary bedchamber, drawing my gaze to the ominous tunnel opening. The Reborns are growing restless.

I pluck a burning candle from a nearby candelabra, its once-gilded surface now mostly covered in rust, and cross the small cavern to relight other candles that've snuffed out. More groans fill the tunnel, and I try not to think about the needs of the Reborn right now. I'll deal with them later. Before leaving, I drag the edge of the blanket up over Merigoth's shoulders, knowing how drafty these mountain passages can get after nightfall.

It took a few months to learn to navigate these dark tunnels, but now I'm quite familiar with which way leads to a dead end, or to the Reborns, or to the outside. I have no desire to check in with the Reborns or that menace Alister. Without Merigoth's presence, he's getting more and more defiant. He's not like the others—obedient, witless soldiers—and I imagine it's only a matter of time before he tries to kill me and take control of the Reborns.

But I won't let that happen.

I will maintain control.

And when I find a way to free Merigoth from her prison, she'll take the throne and rule not just this realm, but all of them.

Soft light breaks through the darkness ahead. I can no longer hear the moans and groans deriving from the cavern deep beneath the mountain. With each step forward, my heart grows colder, my patience wears thinner, and my skin hums with vengeance. As I approach the cave opening, a gust of cold wind sweeps by, carrying a flurry of snow. The sun rises over the tops of a forest full of pine trees. Folding my arms behind my back, against the fur-lined coat I obtained from a local villager, I scan the frigid world before me, swathed in snow, and smile.

Adele thinks she's won.

She has no idea what's coming for her and everyone else in this pathetic realm.

CHAPTER 1

ᴀDELE

My life in Bricen has been a dream come true. Ever since Rune closed off the doorway to the Under Realm, the village has had time to recover and grow. Yet here I am, running through the woods after a new threat. Not how I was expecting to start my day, but it's not the worst way to start one either.

It began when Elijah snuck into my house early, before sunrise. He was careful not to wake Selene in the bed next to mine, and when I finally woke up, he told me about the intruder he saw sneaking around the village while everyone was asleep. I should've been annoyed or angry at the early morning hindrance, as normal people would be, but what I felt was quite the opposite. What I felt was excitement.

When it comes to the darkness within—which I now often refer to it as my *reach*, since that's what Mum calls it when she's healing or helping people—I haven't had the opportunity to use my ability for judgment nearly as often as I did while living at Castle Forge. It's been a difficult transition, but a worthy one for sure. Over these past few months, I've devoted much of my time to fitting in and living a normal life here in Bricen. I've even managed to change how people perceive me, turning their fear into respect. But it's a lie I'm not sure I'll be able to uphold for much longer. I thought I could control the darkness, like Mum, but it's growing fiercely, and soon, I won't be able to contain it.

My thoughts veer from this morning's wake-up to now, where we're racing through the wooded area, pursuing the audacious thief who dares to steal from Bricen. With each step, a dark and longing hunger drives me forward as the darkness within craves an overdue release. This poor soul picked the wrong village to pilfer.

"Adele!" Elijah's voice carries through the early morning mist enveloping the forest. Despite my dislike for running, I press on, skillfully maneuvering between the trees, ignoring the fatigue in my legs and the icy air filling my chest with each breath. "Do you see anyone?" he shouts from somewhere to my right.

The stranger moves quickly, keeping a discernible distance ahead. Their choice to run through the woods, rustling leaves and snapping sticks, instead of using the road makes them easier to follow.

"Adele? Where are you?"

Ignoring him, I slow my pace to a jog and search for signs of which way our thief went. More sticks snap, and I spot a line of swaying branches, most likely disturbed from someone sprinting past. With a predatory smile, I continue my pursuit in that direction.

A familiar *caw* echoes from behind me, and a few seconds later, Valor soars over my head, joining our chase. She releases another loud call before veering right and disappearing into the gray morning haze. Trusting my feathered friend, I follow her lead, making a sharp turn. My foot slips on the frozen ground, and I nearly lose my balance. A curse escapes and I quickly recover, bracing against a tree and pushing off with one hand. The prickle of the rough bark through the leather of my glove lingers on the palm of my hand.

If this chase had happened a few months ago, I would've easily gotten lost. However, in recent weeks, I've spent most afternoons out here reacquainting myself with the forest. The days exploring the grounds brought back fond memories of me, Kit, and Elijah playing in these woods. I also discovered many of the well-trodden shortcuts and hidden spots, along with places to avoid.

Ten weeks ago, I never thought I'd be here, surrounded by everything I've ever wanted. The love and acceptance from those who truly care about me, the unexpected reunion with my mum, who I thought was gone forever, and the empowering sense of freedom to live life on my terms all contribute to my happiness. And then there's Selene, my dearest friend, who has yet to return to Castle Forge because she, too, is busy living her best life—free from her uncle's authority and the constraints of noble society.

Bricen is my home, and I'll do whatever's necessary to protect it—from perilous dangers to petty thieves trying to steal from us while we sleep. A threat is a threat in my eyes, no matter the situation. The miscreants out there who choose a life of harming others, disrupting the peace, and depriving people must learn the error of their ways—a lesson I'm more than willing to bestow.

Slowing to a stop, I steady my heavy breathing and listen for the trespasser. An eerie silence descends, as if I weren't chasing anyone at all. He…or she…has to be out here somewhere. I don't like how close we're getting to the road, because once they're out of the forest, it'll be difficult to track them.

"Adele!" Elijah's calls out again, followed by the crunching of dead leaves. His voice is close. The intensity of the situation makes my heart race. If Elijah stumbles upon the thief, he could either startle them into fleeing or put himself into danger. On the upside, Kit's out here somewhere too, and she understands the rules of a successful hunt. Hopefully, she'll intercept her brother before he gets too close.

My insides tense when he calls for me again. I'm about to break my silence and shush him when Valor caws from somewhere in the mist above. It isn't until she stretches her wings and flaps them that I spot her dark form perched on a thick branch in a tree a few paces from where I stand. Trevor's instructions resurface in my mind. *If she flies, then all is safe. If she remains perched, then it's best to wait because danger lurks.*

She's not flying away, which means the thief's still close by.

Silently, I ease into a squat, praying to the stars I haven't been spotted. My attention remains on the shrouded trees straight ahead, and with deliberate care, I remove one glove and tuck it into the front of my leather vest. Seeking warmth, I shelter my bare hand under the protective layer of my winter cloak while I wait for their next move.

Out of the corner of my eye, I spot a fleeting shadow slipping out from behind one tree and swiftly disappearing behind another. Instinctively, I flex my fingers beneath my wool cloak, anticipation rising as my mind hungers to stretch its powerful reach and bring the criminal to their knees. I steady myself on the balls of my feet, ready to spring into action at the slightest sign of their advance. But then, off to my right, Elijah yelps and emerges from the fog, stumbling over an exposed tree root. The trespasser takes advantage of my friend's clumsiness, except instead of fleeing, they run toward Elijah and throw their full body weight on top of him.

"Elijah!" I hurry to catch up with their tumbling forms. The echoes of Valor's *caws* fill the forest, repeating one after another, similar to the chiming of Bricen's old alarm bells. "Get off him!" I grab a fistful of cloak along the collar and give the woolen fabric a harsh tug, tearing it from their body. Both arms swing out wide in response, causing a dagger to slip free from their hand. The blade takes flight, then lands on the ground before spinning off into the dense underbrush. Getting a good look at the intruder—a man—I can see he's not much older than my friends and me. Shoulder-length dark hair conceals most of his face, and the second he gets to his feet, an arrow whistles through the woods and pierces into the trunk of a nearby tree, level with his head. He doesn't stop to question where the arrow came from and takes off running.

I start after him, only to stop when Kit calls out, "Adele! Let him go! Elijah's hurt!" My boots slide along the frigid ground, and I regain my balance before glancing over my shoulder at Kit. She's kneeling by her brother's side.

Elijah's brown eyes are open to their fullest as he gasps for air, his back arching off the forest floor. His newly knitted scarf has partially unraveled from around his neck, hanging off one shoulder. He presses one hand to his chest while flailing the other in the air until he finds Kit's arm.

"I can't let him get away!" is all I say before turning and leaving her to aid Elijah. I don't need to listen for his escape route any longer. We're close enough to the road that I know where he's heading.

I emerge from the forest and climb up the small embankment, which is covered in dead grass, to reach the road. Two individuals on horseback are there, waiting with an extra horse in tow. Our thief hurries over, grabs the reins, and climbs up, then settles into the saddle. The two riders immediately take off, while Bricen's trespasser turns his horse so he's facing me. It's then that I see he's not just a random, petty thief. There, on his white shirt, over his collarbone, is an embroidered insignia featuring a big black *F* with blue stars encircling it.

Fayatin.

The blue stars indicate that he's not from Castle Forge. General Onica assigned different star colors to the lords who governed the divided regions of Fayatin, and blue stars represent the southeastern coastal region, controlled by Lord Houfston at Castle Nautica. General Onica used to refer to it as "Castle Fishrot," not only for the horrid smell coming from the marina, but also because of Lord Houfston's selfish reputation.

I'm standing less than ten paces from him, cold air prickling at my bare hand. I could try to lunge for him—try to pull him off his horse. But I don't.

"Why are you here?" I shout over the low fog, now thinning out with the rising sun.

Wavy hair frames his face, hanging low over his forehead and hooding his eyes. What I didn't notice before was the burn mark along his jawline, trailing his neck. There's something menacing about his stare, and when he smirks at me, I know my gut is right.

"Did that little chase amuse you?" I ask, taking one step closer. "Why don't you get off that horse and tell me why you're really here?" He doesn't respond or look away. "You couldn't possibly be afraid of a girl, especially one with barely any brawn."

That causes a reaction. His smirk spreads into a wide smile. "Oh, you don't know, do ya? Your secret is out, you vile creature. All of Fayatin knows who…and what…you are. The infamous Fayatin Interrogator; a spawn of evil and the bringer of death!" He then clicks his tongue and pulls hard on the reins. Before riding off, he shouts, "I'd watch your back and sleep with one eye open, if I were you!"

Lost in thoughts about the man's ominous threat, I slowly return to Kit and Elijah. I barely notice the sun rising in the east or the mist disappearing as the new day begins. It isn't until I reach my friends, right where I left them, that I realize the morning fog has completely lifted. Elijah stands talking to Kit in a spotlight of sunlight streaming through a break in the treetops.

Kit's gaze finds me, and with a pointed finger, she storms over, yelling, "He could've died!"

"He wasn't going to die." I step closer and only stop when I see Elijah's pained expression.

"You don't know that!" she continues, her tone sounding like her mum's back in the day after finding ourselves into some trouble.

"Getting the air knocked out of you won't kill you."

"That's not the poin—"

"Hey, I'm okay," Elijah says, cutting Kit off. He rubs a hand against his chest, while reaching for Kit's forearm. "We'd better make our way home before Sara and Lauren notice we're gone." Without waiting for her, or looking at me, he walks away, stepping over the tree root that tripped him earlier. I don't regret my decision, but I do feel bad he's in pain.

"It's not always about the win," Kit snarls before jogging to catch up with her brother.

I resist the urge to argue, allowing them to stew in their anger. They'll understand once I explain that if I hadn't caught up to the man, we wouldn't know about the Fayatin soldiers in Harvesgrove. Or at least I hope they forgive me. I'm still getting accustomed to the idea of considering others and not just myself. My focus at Castle Forge was always on my own well-being. Selene was undoubtedly important, but I didn't have to worry about how my actions impacted her. She was under the protection of her uncle, Lord Caldridge. That was why I told her to stay in Fayatin after I escaped.

Taking a minute to calm my nerves, I kick a few rocks, thinking about the rest of my day. One of the rocks rolls under a nearby bush, and as I stare at the long, waxy leaves, recognition stirs. Crouching low, I part the branches, allowing a clear line of sight to the ground. Then, using my shoulder to hold aside the foliage, I reach down and sweep my gloved hand along the dirt until I find it—the dagger the Fayatin man held during his attack on Elijah. As I pull my hand out and stand tall, I bring the weapon up to eye level, and I see my reflection staring back at me in the sharp, polished steel.

Now, I have proof that the Fayatins are in Harvesgrove.

Tucking the Fayatin dagger into the waistband of my pants, I head toward Bricen. I'm hesitant to show Mum because I can't imagine she'll be thrilled to know we've got Fayatin men lurking in our woods, but we made a promise to tell each other everything—no more secrets.

CHAPTER 2

ᴀDELE

Two villagers push open the double doors to the front gate of Bricen's massive barrier wall. Kit and Elijah are nowhere to be seen, so I assume they're already inside. Knowing Kit, I suspect she'll drag Elijah straight to Aunt Lauren's cottage to have his injuries assessed. Now that everyone in the village knows Lauren's an angel from the Starlight Realm, she's taken on the additional role of village healer alongside Mum. Though, while Mum heals the mind, Lauren aids the body.

"Morning, Adele," a man says, helping two young boys prop open one of the oversized gate doors. He leans on his crutch, trying his best to help the boys secure the gate. The man, whose name I can't recall, was one villager who almost died from the demon attack. Thankfully, Rune saved them all with only a few drops of her blood.

"Morning," I reply with a small smile. The boys helping the man shout their good mornings as well, their voices blending with the metallic creaking of the swaying gate door.

My people skills have also been slowly improving these past few months. Selene reminds me often about the significance of acknowledging the villagers by initiating some form of interaction, such as greeting them or making eye contact. Now, my stellar talent for remembering people's names is truly a sight to behold—or would be, if only I could actually remember them for more than a fleeting moment.

Besides this morning's Fayatin encounter, things around here have only been getting better. Once the Shade attacks stopped, Bricen had the chance to heal. We've even welcomed new residents. The abandoned houses near the front gate are now occupied by two families with children, a widower who loves gardening, and two young brothers with blacksmith experience. They were more than agreeable to helping us revive the old smithy. I don't deserve such a happy life, not with everything I did for the general, but I'll take it regardless.

Continuing along the road, up toward Goslings, I pass the smithy where the brothers are heating the forge. I offer a small wave to Nathaniel, and he waves in return with a smile too big for this early in the morning. The broad-shouldered man standing next to him turns to see who Nathaniel is waving to, and when our eyes lock, the man's lips purse and his brows pinch. Shaking his head, he returns his attention to stoking the fire. Nathaniel grabs his coat, hops over the low fencing that encloses the smithy, and jogs over to me.

"Hey there. Where ya coming from?" he asks, keeping pace with me. Unlike most men who grow their hair out for the colder season, he maintains longer length on the top and shears the sides. He pulls the soft leather edges of his coat across his chest, covering his exposed shirt beneath.

"Don't you have blacksmith work to do?"

He breathes into cupped hands, warm air escaping between his fingers. "Yeah, but—uh, I was hoping to run into you today—"

"Yeah, why's that?" I ask, wanting to move this conversation along.

"Could you slow down, so—uh…I can talk to you?" he politely asks, reaching out but not touching my arm.

I stop and face him. He's slightly taller than me, sparing me the need to strain my neck to meet his gray eyes. As I look at him more closely, I notice the flush on his earlobes, along the tip of his nose, and across the tops of his cheeks. Why doesn't he grow his hair and beard out during the winter like other men? I want to ask, but engaging in small talk with people I hardly know isn't something I'm comfortable with.

"Right," he says, then begins breathing hard through his nose. His hands go to his waist, but they don't stay there long, as if he's unsure of what to do with them. After clearing his throat, he asks, "I was wondering if you'd like to sit with my brother and me tonight…during supper?" He pauses to swallow whatever lump has formed in his throat. "You and Selene."

Narrowing my eyes, I try to understand his intentions, which would be so much easier if I could reach into his mind.

"Selene too?" I ask, assuming it's her company he's truly interested in. When he doesn't reply, the muscles in my jaw tense. It was a straightforward question, yet he says nothing. Instead, he glances over my face, as if searching for a secret hidden in my features. Then, his curious gaze dips, and I clasp my hands behind my back. It wouldn't be the first time someone wanted to get a closer look at the Shade girl's hands, but his attention doesn't continue past my chin.

This is getting awkward, and now he's got me wondering if there's dried drool in the corners of my mouth or something stuck in my teeth from last night's supper. Trying to be discreet, I wipe my mouth with the back of my glove.

As if awakening from a daydream, and suddenly becoming aware that he's staring, Nathaniel blinks several times before taking a step back, putting some distance between us. He gives me an apologetic smile, his gray eyes finding mine again. He's got an intensity in his stare that I can't explain, unlike the others who regard me with either fear or curiosity. This is something different—an expression I've never seen before.

"Nathaniel." I say his name with a hint of concern because I don't know why he's not answering my simple question. "Are you okay?"

After a moment, he gathers himself, standing taller and nodding as the words finally tumble out. "Sorry. Yes, of course. Selene too."

Hesitantly, I give him an answer. "I guess we can sit—"

And then, before I can finish, he claps his hands and exclaims, "Shining stars!" His face flushes, a fresh heat of red blending into the already rosy parts. Walking backward, a little bounce in his step, he confirms, "Well, then… Brandulf and I will see you two ladies later tonight!" He spins and hurries to the smithy, where his brother waits with a scowl.

Continuing on my way home, I repeat his brother's name in my mind—*Brandulf*. I'm going to have to remember his name if we'll be eating with them tonight. The echoes of clanging metal and distant chatter from the smithy fade as I round the side of Goslings and head out across the Green. The open common is still mostly dirt, speckled with a few stubborn patches of dead grass.

Across the way, Selene stands in the open doorway to the home given to us by Mum and Lauren. It's conveniently right next door to Elijah and Kit's place. My friend leans against the doorframe with a thick wool blanket wrapping her shoulders, her favorite pale blue dress peeking out from beneath. Even with long sleeves, that frock isn't weather appropriate, something I've explained to her more than once. A slight breeze catches the ends of her dark hair, blowing them across her pale face, and she tightens her hold on the edge of the blanket.

When I reach the threshold, I ask, "What are you doing out here? It's freezing! Get back inside."

She draws a hand from beneath the blanket and points to the cozy cottage at the top of the low hill. "I just saw Kit and Elijah go into your mum and aunt's place. What happened? And why aren't you with them?" She retreats into the open room of our home, her movements guided by the dim light of the dying fire.

Before removing my cloak, I quickly take two logs from the small stack, noting I'll need to chop more wood before it gets dark, and make my way toward the fireplace. "Selene, it's almost as cold in here as it is outside! Why didn't you throw more logs onto the fire?" I set them inside the hearth, and the weight of the fresh wood crushes the charred remnants of the previous logs, sending a plume of gray ash up into the chimney.

She flops on her bed, the wooden frame creaking at the corners. "I wasn't thinking about the fire, Adele! You gave me an unbelievable fright when I woke up and you weren't in your bed. My thoughts went straight to someone kidnapping you in the middle of the night!"

I was aware of Selene's dramatic nature during the countless years we spent talking through the iron fencing of my secret courtyard at Castle Forge, but it wasn't until recently, while living with her, that I truly understood the extent of it.

"Well, someone did sneak into the house and take me, but it was Elijah. And the 'taking' part was more me willingly going with him."

"Oh, what for?"

"There was a thief meandering about the village that needed to be dealt with." It's best not to add more concern by telling her that the thief wasn't a thief at all but a man from Fayatin. I lower myself to her eye level, gently placing my gloved hands on top of hers where they rested on her lap.

With tenderness, I explain, "I know you adore your life here in Bricen, but you're still relying too heavily on Agnes, me, and the others. If you want to live freely outside of Castle Forge, then you need to be more independent. How are you going to survive on your own if you can't even add wood to a dying fire?"

The room falls into a quiet and tense hush. Selene's gaze remains fixed on the fire, the fresh wood slowly being consumed, crackling, and casting a warm glow throughout our cozy house. I stay in a crouched position before her, giving her time to mull over my words in the silence.

Eventually, the blanket slips from her shoulders, and she turns her gaze to me. "I thought things would be different. I guess I never fully grasped what living outside the castle really meant."

"It's not like your uncle's adventure books."

Shaking her head, she softly agrees. "No, it's not. And I imagine that Captain Roksana Bruiser's life at sea is way harsher than life on land."

I can't help but chuckle at the thought of Selene trying to manage a life on the rough seas. "I'm guessing you're right."

"Do you think she's real?"

The turn of conversation is a familiar habit, and I often wonder how Selene can finish anything when her mind is always thinking of anything else but the task at hand. Obliging her with the answer that would please her most, I say, "I believe so. I even think General Onica had a meeting with her once. She's a strong and beautiful woman, with a loyal crew."

Her eyes go wide, and she slips her hands out from beneath mine to clasp them tightly. "Oh, Adele! Why have you never spoken of this before?"

"I didn't want to get your hopes up... But enough talk about a life at sea. You need to focus on your land legs, and life here in Bricen."

Selene's adjustment to a simple life hasn't been easy, but she's trying. Not only for me, but because she has always yearned for a free life. I think she's realizing there's no "in-between." Either you live the noble life where others take care of you, or you live the simple life where you must learn to take care of yourself. Then there's Captain Roksana Bruiser's way of life—but I won't even bring that up again, or we'll be talking about pirate adventures all day and into the night.

Not wanting to discourage her from continuing her efforts at a free life, I tell her, "And there's nothing wrong with trying new experiences. How else will you know if this is the life for you?" I stand, my knees cracking with the abrupt motion, and remove my heavy cloak. After shaking it out, I hang it on a wooden peg by the front door. "Don't forget you're not alone with living in unfamiliar territory. This is all new for me too."

With my back to her, she whispers, "I know." Her bed groans, followed by leather shoes shuffling across the hardwood. When I turn to face her, she's standing close by. Before I can react, she snatches the dagger from my waistband, her fingers nimble. With a foxlike swiftness, she darts across the open room, putting our small dining table between us, and giggles with amusement. I try to retrieve the weapon before she realizes what she's taken, but it's too late. Her laughter dies with a sharpness that matches the steel in her hands.

"Selene, I can explain," I say to get ahead of the dire mood setting in.

She spins to look at me, the skirt of her blue dress twirling from her abrupt motion. As she unsheathes the dagger, a smooth metal *sching* cuts through the tension building in our small cottage. Pointing the tip to the ceiling, she inspects the weapon. Then her gaze slides in my direction. "Where did you get this?" Her tone mixes anger and fear, as if she's caught me in a prank, though she knows what I've taken is anything but humorous. "Adele, I asked you a question. Where did you get this dagger?"

"I can explain," I say, holding out an open hand. Hesitantly, she sheathes the dagger and sets it on the table rather than in my hand.

"That's Fayatin steel." She points to the weapon. "Are there Fayatin soldiers here?"

I pick up the dagger and return it to my waistband. I didn't intend for Selene to see it, only Mum, Elijah, and Kit. Maybe Aunt Lauren. But definitely not Selene. "There was a Fayatin man, but he's gone."

"Why didn't you tell me right away?" Crossing her arms, she narrows her eyes at me. "And what do you mean by 'gone'?"

"I didn't kill him, if that's what you're asking." The painful sting of her question serves as a constant reminder that, no matter what, she's aware of the demon blood harbored within me and how it'll forever carry a certain level of influence. I wonder who else has come to this conclusion, always keeping their guard up around me in case—well, in case I give in and become the monster General Onica molded me into. It's my biggest fear, and the reason I don't indulge the cravings of my reach. Feed it once, and it'll only want more.

Selene cuts through my thoughts, throwing both hands into the air. "Well, how am I supposed to know what you do out in those woods?" She storms over to the fireplace, grabs the iron poker, and starts stabbing at the logs.

I would never admit it out loud, but the strain between us has grown more and more over the months, and I don't understand why. I mean, it's Selene, for stars' sake. She was the one person who anchored the goodness in me all those years while I was locked up at Castle Forge. And even though my circle of trusted friends has expanded to include Elijah, Kit, Mum, Aunt Lauren, the crows, and of course Rune, Selene will always be the closest thing I have to a sister.

Yet something between us has changed, and I don't know how to fix it.

To diminish the tension, I offer a bit of the truth. "I'm sorry I lied. The intruder was a Fayatin man, but not from Castle Forge. His insignia had blue stars."

Selene straightens and rests the poker against the stone hearth. "You're telling me a Fayatin man traveled all this way from Castle Fishrot?"

I try not to chuckle as Selene's lips twist in disgust while saying *Fishrot*, as though she actually just ate a dish of spoiled fish. I nod, and she continues, "You think Lord Houfston sent some of his men to find you?"

A fast rap at the front door cuts into our conversation. "I didn't get the chance to ask him."

As I lift the iron latch and open the door, Selene asks with urgency, "Well, what's our plan? He's probably still out there, right?"

Kit stands outside on our small porch. Behind her, the wind has picked up, causing the ends of her knit scarf to flap around her neck.

"Hey," I say, and move aside so she can come in. A gust of cold air sweeps inside, and I quickly shut the door, unwilling to lose any more of the warmth we've gathered from our still-growing fire. Bricen has yet to see snow this winter, but if the temperature remains this cold, I imagine we'll see the dreaded white stuff soon enough. And I loathe the snow even more than I do running.

Kit unwraps her scarf just enough for her mouth to show, then with a snarky tone tells me, "Elijah's going to be fine, in case you were wondering."

"What happened to Elijah?" Selene interjects, her brows pinched as she swiftly looks from Kit to me.

Of course I care, but I'll not revive the argument that losing your breath won't lead to death. "Where is he now?"

"Home, resting," she says, then sighs. With a hint of curiosity replacing annoyance, she asks, "So, did you catch the guy?"

I pull out the dagger and show it to Kit, then tell her everything I relayed to Selene. When I'm done, Kit sighs. "This isn't good."

"No, it isn't." I return the dagger to my waistband and walk over to my bedside. My fingers wrap around the familiar grip of my favorite bow as I take it down from its spot on the wall. I was grateful when Selene's uncle had it sent to Bricen with her trunks of belongings back when she decided to stay in Bricen. Shouldering my quiver, I throw out a suggestion about what to do next. "Let's do a quick border check. Maybe set some trip wires so we know if someone's been in the area."

Kit nods. "We can string up a few of the alarm bells. Elijah and I have them stored away in our old hidey-holes. I'll grab them and meet you at the front gate in ten." After Rune closed the doorway to the Under Realm, Bricen didn't need so many alarm bells. We kept a good number up, especially the ones attached to the roofs.

"Good thinking." I grab my heavy cloak from the wood peg and put it on, fastening the buttons along the front. "While you do that, I'm going to go update Mum and Lauren."

"What about me?" Selene asks.

She means well, but there's not much she can do in this situation. Then again, leaving her alone to stew about the dangers lurking in the woods may not be the best choice, either. "How about you come with me to Mum and Lauren's? I'm sure Lauren could use some help kneading fresh dough for tonight's supper." Mentioning supper reminds me about my talk earlier with our new blacksmith. "Oh, I ran into Nathaniel this morning, and he invited us to sit with him and his brother, Randulf, during supper tonight. I told him it was fine with me. I hope you don't mind."

"Brandulf," Kit corrects, a grin forming.

"That's what I said, Brandulf," I grumble, ignoring Kit's smug expression. After clearing my throat, I continue telling Selene, "I think Nathaniel was particularly interested in sitting with you, so I took the liberty of saying yes."

Selene smiles, and it warms my heart to know our quarrel has faded—for the time being. Grabbing her winter cloak, she says, "Oh, Adele. You have so much to learn about reading people on the outside." Then, after she's swapped out her leather shoes for high boots and wrapped her knit scarf around her neck, she adds, "It's not me he wishes to be near. But we can talk more about that after you and Kit are done securing the village. For now, yes, I think I'd like to help Lauren bake some bread."

CHAPTER 3

RUNE

I'm not running away.

I'm taking a well-deserved break, allowing myself a moment to gather my thoughts and restore my emotional balance. Ten minutes. That's all I need. Soaring higher, I eventually stop and hover directly over our once-pristine home, the capital of the Starlight Realm, Stellara. My wings beat in a familiar rhythm as I stare out at the horizon, beyond Stellara's borders, toward the distant mountains. I try and come up here at least once a day to appreciate the view…and our freedom. I inhale a deep breath and hold the fresh air in my chest while letting the troubles weighing me down slip from my mind.

Up here, it's just me and the open sky. No one following me around and asking questions I don't have answers to or burdening me with new problems to solve. It's a refreshing break from constantly masking my exhaustion.

When a giant cloud drifts closer, I seize the moment. One powerful sweep of my wings and I coast forward, letting the warm air caress each feather. Picking up speed, I fold my wings against my back, streamlining my body, and spear myself into the cloud. A refreshing cool mist envelops me as I soar through the center. With a tilt of my head and shoulders, I steer myself up and out of the cloud. Emerging into the sunlight, I lift my chin and bask in the warm rays. Being up here, flying through the clouds and over the city, has me feeling like my young self again, the angel I was before Merigoth's attack.

I despise thinking about the years I spent under Merigoth's enchantment and Marcellus's manipulative control. However, it serves as a reminder that angels aren't invincible. That we can be captured, brainwashed, and even killed. For nearly a century, she controlled us, stealing our free will and concealing our wings. Yet, I always sensed something was amiss. When we were sent to the Human Realm, the stars would often distract me, though I never knew why. Now, I understand. My mother, the North Star, ruled alongside the East, West, and South Stars here in the Starlight Realm. Those shimmering dots in the night sky were my saving grace, stirring my curiosity and allowing me to question my existence, offering temporary relief from Merigoth's enchantment.

Hovering high in the sky, reluctant to return to the daily task of restoring our beloved city, I think back to how my wings tried to break free each time I used my special ability to open a new doorway. If only I had endured the pain beyond that task—the intense push from beneath my spine—I might've found freedom earlier and saved hundreds of lives from being sacrificed to the demon spirits of the Under Realm.

I shake the dreadful thoughts from my mind because there's no point in dwelling on things we can't change. We can only focus on what's in front of us, despite the seemingly hopeless endeavor of restoring our realm's capital. Stellara is too far gone to be rebuilt by less than thirty angels. We need more help.

Gradually, the cloud I speared through passes by, revealing the city below, which is covered in a vibrant green landscape. It's not just nature that has reclaimed the once-pristine Stellara, but time as well. Layers of dirt and grime cover nearly every inch not overtaken by plant life. It breaks my heart to see Stellara in ruins. From up here, I can see every building and their decaying stone exteriors. Even the walkways and roads are cracked and broken, showing their age.

Stellara is our home, and I won't give up on it, nor should any other angel. One day, it will be restored to its former glory, though I fear that may not happen in my lifetime.

I glide over the city, taking in the extensive damage caused by Merigoth's attack. Those who managed to survive the fight and weren't captured to serve Merigoth fled the city, abandoning it for fear she'd return. Or at least, that's what most of the angels have told Evander. He and I both agreed that sending out a child born from one of the former Star leaders would encourage angels to come back, reassuring them it's safe. Nevertheless, despite his best efforts, he has been unable to convince the angels residing beyond the city border and in other realms to return.

Warm air rushes against my face, and I continue to circle high over the city. Silently, I count the days Evander's been gone—eighteen days. It often feels as if I've forgotten something or misplaced a valuable trinket whenever he's away. Anxiously, I anticipate his delay is because he's successfully found angels willing to come home and they need time to pack their belongings. I'm not sure how much longer I can maintain this hopeful demeanor.

Catching my attention, a few angels fly low over the south side of Stellara. Being this high has its advantages. The first time I flew this high was with Evander when we were children. Due to our limited experience with extended flights, it was unsafe for us, with our young wings, to fly any higher than two stories. Evander's mother, the West Star leader, caught us up here, and instead of turning us in to my mother, she made us promise that we'd never put each other in danger ever again—that we'd take care of one another.

Something changed in Evander that day. The way he looked at me, and continues to do so, I knew he'd always be there for me. Even during our time in the Under Realm, when our minds weren't our own, he always remained close by.

"Rune!" a distant voice calls to me from below.

Cringing, I send a silent plea to the stars for a few more moments of peace, but the angel spots me and veers right with a sharp tilt of her black wings.

Flying toward me, she shouts, "Rune! There you are!"

As the distance between us closes, I raise my voice against the tailwind—"Gianna, whatever it is…it can wait"—and continue soaring past her.

It doesn't take her long to swing around and catch up to me. "We've been looking all over for you."

I didn't think I was away for that long. Hesitantly, I side glance her way. The concern wavering in her eyes and her hands clutched at her stomach tell me something's wrong. Knowing I have a duty to uphold, I give her my full attention. My mother was the North Star of this realm, and as her daughter, I have a duty…a responsibility…to protect the angels of this realm. To always be here for them.

Though, I wouldn't say *no* to a visit to the Human Realm. I'm overdue to see my friends, Adele and Elijah. Hopefully, they're further along than we are with rebuilding and regaining a sense of normalcy.

Breaking my thoughts, Gianna reaches me, stopping within speaking distance. Her wings beat, holding her in position, a dark contrast to the bright blue sky.

I raise a curious eyebrow at her. Gianna and Evander are my confidants, the two angels whom I can freely discuss mostly anything with. Together, the three of us oversee the daily activities of our small community. Despite Gianna not being a daughter of one of the Star leaders, she is a cherished friend, possessing powerful healing abilities and a bluntness I often wish I had.

"Before you drawl on about how you need more alone time, I came to tell you Evander's returned." And before I can respond, she adds, "He's been injured."

My heart sinks, and I quickly ask, "How bad?"

Hands still balled at her stomach, she shakes her head. "He can still walk. Thankfully, he managed to escape before they could cause any major harm."

"Take me to him," I say, before diving toward the city. A tear slips free because I don't know how I would go on without my dearest and closest friend.

We land outside the south library, the designated meeting hall for whenever we gather to share news or announcements with the community. Before the attack, all news and announcements were publicized at the Stars Council building located in the central district of Stellara.

The south district of Stellara remained unscathed by the attack, making this area the best place to live. There was no fire damage to these buildings and their structures remained stable, even though the bordering forest, with its relentless overgrowth, had reclaimed most of this sector. The removal of vines, weeds, and unruly shrubs posed the most significant challenge during our initial cleanup efforts.

As I ascend the front steps of the south library branch, I cautiously navigate around drops of red blood staining the stone treads. Gianna graciously holds open one of the ornate iron doors. This was one of the first buildings we cleaned up after returning home. Since the windows and doors were intact, the invasive vines growing along the stone exterior hadn't made their way inside. But there was still a lot of cleaning and dusting to do.

Immediately after I step into the open space, my eyes lock onto Evander, who sits at one of the elongated tables in the center of the room. He's facing the back of the library while one of Gianna's apprentices applies a bandage to his left wing.

"Evander!" I call out, and he winces while trying to turn my way. His name resonates up into the cathedral ceiling. I hurry to his side. As I get closer, I'm suddenly taken aback by the overpowering smell of blood in the air, and my breath catches when his battered face comes into view. He offers me a weak smile, which does little to settle the unease stirring inside me. My fingers hover over the deep purple bruise marring his left cheek, and then the small bandage covering a wound over his eye. Gianna's apprentice continues to bandage his wing, and as she secures the cloth, his wing flinches, releasing a reddish-brown feather. It drops to the stone floor and lands on top of a few others, which sit in a small pool of blood.

"What happened?" I ask, my voice a mixture of concern and fury. "How did you not sense the attack coming? Why didn't you fly away?"

I could've asked a dozen more questions, but I stop when Gianna offers him a glass of water. He takes it, and while drinking, he reaches out and holds my hand. There's a heat beneath his skin, as if he too is furious with the situation. Then, with the tip of his finger, he subtly traces a circle in the center of my palm. A secret signal shared only between us.

My lips purse in understanding. I look to Gianna and her apprentice, Val, and thank them for tending to his injuries. Then, gesturing with a glance to the front doors of the library, I add, "Can we have a moment alone, please?"

They both nod, but before leaving, Val places an amber jar on the table and looks to Evander. "You'll need to reapply this salve to your wounds later this evening. Come see me if you need help." With a tender smile, she leaves us alone, following Gianna outside.

The moment the iron latch on the library's door clicks shut, I settle into the chair next to his. "Tell me exactly what happened."

He rubs his forehead while shaking his head. "I shouldn't have gone north alone." His bruised hand glides upward, fingers threading through his wavy brown hair. Evander was one of the first angels to have his hair reappear after returning home. Along with our wings and heightened senses, our hair was also taken from us, concealed and bound by Merigoth's enchantment and Marcellus's manipulation.

A smear of blood marks his forehead and mats part of his hair. I grab a clean cloth from the table and reach for his hand. "Your hand," is all I say as I clean the wound, occasionally soaking the cloth's end in the warm bowl of water, already tinted red.

"Start by telling me where the other angels are. The ones you visited in the Human Realm." I open the amber jar and apply a small amount of the salve on the gash crossing the bottom of his palm. He averts his gaze, and I ask again, "Where are the other—"

"There are no other angels, Rune!" he confesses, and then tries to pull his hand away, but I've got a firm hold on his wrist. His shoulders slump in defeat and he lets me continue working, wrapping his hand with a clean bandage. His angst weighs heavy as he mutters, "I'm sorry. I failed you, Stellara, and our mothers."

I let the silence linger before securing the end of the bandage. With one hand gently placed on top of his injured one, I tell him, "You did not fail me, this city, or our mothers. No one is to blame but Merigoth. She did this to us—to our people and our home. And she will pay for her crimes."

He tries to sit taller, but then flinches and grabs one shoulder. His expression twists and I wish I could do more for his pain. Gianna must've done all she could've to heal his physical wounds, which all the blood on the floor tells me were extreme. But she doesn't possess the ability to numb the mind, offering a break from the pain while healing. That power belongs to the Songwielder family—to Merigoth's lineage.

With a shake of his head, he utters, "No angel would return with me. I visited over sixty angels, some living within a reasonable distance of one another while others chose to live together in one home. Every single one of them would rather pretend to be a human and live in that realm than return home, fearing another attack by Merigoth."

Their fears are understandable. Some days I worry about another attack too, but I don't share this with Evander. "They need time. We have records of where they are, and we'll continue to check in on them every so often." My words are the complete opposite of the anger and disappointment that fills me, but I don't want my friend to feel any more somber than he already does. "Each visit we can praise our progress and reassure them that the city is safe. One by one, they will return."

"You don't know that."

"I don't, but I have to hold on to the hope that Stellara will return to its former glory, and that includes having the city filled with angels again." With a deep sigh, I hold his gaze and ask again, "What happened?"

He exhales a deep breath, wincing and pressing a hand against his ribs. "I was in Verglas, visiting a group of angels. They have a small nursery on the outskirts of the kingdom where they grow herbs and other potted plants. The harsh winters in Noviska Country make growing things difficult, so the angels there all have affinities with nourishing the soil."

"Groundwielders," I say, confirming their ancestral ability. We could use one or two of them here, but again I hold my tongue and let him continue.

"Yes, Groundwielders." He takes another sip of water. "One of them had heard a rumor while delivering some fresh herbs to the Verglas castle about an isolated village up north under attack."

Standing, I say, "Villages are attacked all the time in the Human Realm. It's not our place to get involved in their politics."

"You don't understand. The villages weren't being ransacked or burned and the people not killed. Rather, the men were being rounded up and taken."

"What for?" I ask, hoping for a response that involves a human dilemma, such as a rivalry or a territorial conflict.

He winces as he reaches over and sets the glass on the table. "I'll give you one good guess, but first let me finish. The reason the attacks were being brought to the king's attention was because the people who were taken would return weeks later and randomly attack other local people. They were said to have soulless eyes and dark red veins along their temples. One man escaped and rode straight to Castle Verglas to inform the king."

Every word Evander said made me think of one thing…but I refuse to acknowledge it. I refuse to say it out loud.

"Rune, you and I know exactly what happened to those villagers. I needed to go north and see for myself."

Just by looking at his injuries, I know his story isn't going to end well. "You're right. You shouldn't have gone alone."

"Well, I did. And I don't even know how the brute snuck up on me. This massive man…no, not a man, but a—"

"No! Don't say it. Because it's not possible." I move to the table and lean over it, my hands gripping the edge. "This can't be happening," I mutter. "I closed the doorway between the two realms."

"You closed a doorway. There must be another one."

My fingers tighten over the wood. My muscles impulsively siphon power from my heightened senses. "I promised the angels here they were safe." The edge of the wood table buckles and splinters from the increased pressure of my hold.

"Hey, we will deal with this. Together."

Lifting my gaze to the dingy ceiling of the library, I release all my frustration and rage that's been bottling up in one giant, fearsome scream as my wings extend to their full span. Each hawklike brown feather bristles with energy.

Will we ever be free?

As I draw in my wings and gather my composure, Evander continues, "There's something else you should know."

I pinch my eyes closed, uncertain if I can handle any more bad news. Without waiting for me to look at him, he adds, "There's something off about that village. I can't quite put it into words, but I was unable to fly, and my extended senses were somehow blocked."

Now I open my eyes and look at him. "Blocked?"

"Yes, blocked. As I approached the village, something in the air changed—like an invisible haze that blocked my senses and numbed my wings." He inhales a deep breath, presses his hand to his ribs again, and then as he releases the air, tells me, "Either Marcellus has learned some new tricks, or there's something else at play here."

Marcellus. That vile man has to be involved. If the Reborns have found a way into the Human Realm, then I'm sure he's the mastermind behind it all. And I know he wasn't the one who attacked Evander. One touch from Marcellus and Evander would've fallen under his control.

The library doors burst open, and Gianna runs inside. "Is everything okay? I heard Rune scream from three houses over and hurried to make sure you're both all right."

I know we can trust Gianna. She's taken on a leadership role with Evander and me, even though her bloodline is not one of the ruling Stars. I sidestep away from my injured friend and face the healer. "I need you to stay here with Evander."

He gets to his feet, then curses under his breath while hobbling closer. "You're not going there alone."

"Going where?" Gianna asks.

As I brush my hand through my shoulder-length hair, I firmly state, "I must witness the situation with my own eyes." I hand Gianna the amber jar of salve. "Stay with him."

She nods, but Evander steps between us, his back to me. "Gianna, I need you to heal my ribs. I think they're broken."

"You're not coming with me," I protest.

Over his shoulder he says, "Yes, I am. Otherwise, I won't tell you the exact location of the village in question."

"What village?" Gianna asks, but no one answers her.

"You need to stay."

Clutching his side, he winces as he faces me. "And I say you're not going alone."

"Going where?" Gianna tries again, but again, we don't answer.

"Damn it, Evander," I curse, then crane my neck over his shoulder to look at Gianna. "You'd better heal his hand too. I'm not sure I wrapped it tight enough."

"He can't fly," Gianna tells me.

"He won't."

I'm already regretting this decision.

After tending to Evander's broken ribs and the cut on his hand, Gianna insists he shouldn't go anywhere, or try to fly again. I don't disagree, but Evander made it clear he wouldn't let me go alone, especially if Marcellus is involved.

I stand aside as Gianna aids Evander in concealing his wings for the journey. With her hands delicately placed on his shoulders, they focus in complete silence, weaving their intentions into the fabric of reality. The veil that will keep humans from seeing his wings flickers, making his wings fade and reappear several times before their efforts finally take hold. Normally, manipulating our heightened senses or concealing our wings is an effortless task. However, with Evander's injuries at the base where his wings connect, and along the humerus bone, he's unable to tap into the ethereal network of strings that control our senses and wings without assistance.

After Gianna steps away, I tell her, "I'll need you to oversee the community in our absence."

While making her way toward me, she takes a moment to push back a few stray strands of dark hair from her face. "I wish you'd let me accompany you or at least tell me where you're going." Then in a softer tone, she confides, "He's in no condition to be traveling. You might need me."

"I do need you—here." I pull Gianna in for a hug, and whisper, "Don't let anyone know of our absence. There's plenty to do to keep everyone preoccupied and busy." Leaning away, I reassure her and say, "We'll be back by nightfall."

"So late?" she asks.

With a smile, I say, "Since we're out, I'd like to stop by Bricen and say hello."

A smile spreads on the petite angel's face. "Oh, is that right? Someone in particular you're hoping to see?"

"Maybe," I say, hoping to lessen her concern about us leaving.

Her smile almost drops, but she's quick to maintain it. "I'll watch over everyone here until you return. Please be safe." She gives Evander's arm a gentle squeeze before leaving the library.

Once we're alone, I try one more time to persuade Evander to stay. "Are you sure you want to come? I'm only going to scout the area. Not to engage."

"It's not you I don't trust," he answers with a groan. "What concerns me is how something in the air affected my senses and prevented me from flying. If you get cornered or pinned because of whatever magic he's using to hinder our abilities, well, I can't lose you to Marcellus."

His gaze lingers on mine, and an unsaid proclamation wavers in his trembling eyes. Even though he's never explicitly revealed his feelings for me, they are evident at this moment. At one point in my life, I would've welcomed his affections. My mother would've been thrilled to know of a match between Evander and me. However, things are different now. These past few months, after our liberation from Merigoth's enchantment, those feelings have changed. Despite my knowing that he's the one I'm supposed to be with, my heart remains dedicated to someone else, someone whom I'm forbidden to ever be with.

But the matters of my heart aren't the priority.

An awkward silence lingers in the air between us. Then he breaks it, saying, "Rune, you must know—"

"How are your ribs?" I blurt out, cutting him off. Focus on what's important, like discovering if Marcellus is truly in Noviska, rebuilding our city, and persuading the angels living outside our realm to return home. Those are the priorities. Not love. Now is not the time for him to express his feelings. He's endured enough, and I don't want to add a broken heart to his list of wounds.

Understanding crosses his face. He lifts his chin, and a muscle along his jawline tenses with a slight twitch. With a reserved tone, he answers, "The pain in my ribs is gone. I almost feel like myself again, except for my wings." The bandage wrapping his wing pinches between reddish-brown feathers.

This is a bad idea.

He's going to get himself killed.

But I know his mind is set. So, I step closer and clear my thoughts in preparation for him to show me where I need to open a doorway to. Before we begin, I tell him, "This is our home, and I refuse to let Marcellus, or anyone else, take it away again."

His stony expression softens. "You have a loyal heart and will make an excellent North Star leader."

I nod, knowing neither of us are officially Star leaders yet. Another decision we made together. We promised the angels living in Stellara that we'd focus on rebuilding the city before turning our attentions to the formalities of politics.

He raises both hands, and his warm skin presses into the sides of my face. We've done this a hundred times before, so I don't need to instruct him to focus his thoughts solely on our destination. The visual of the snowy world appears in my mind as clear as if I were looking at it through my own eyes. When I nod, he slowly withdraws his hands.

"Okay, let's go see if we can find Marcellus."

CHAPTER 4

RUNE

The temperature drop is noticeable, but not uncomfortable. After I close the doorway, we stand in the Human Realm, our boots sinking in the snow up to our ankles. No village in sight. Instead, we find ourselves in an open field with rolling hills, circled by a vast forest of pine trees. Under the cloudless sky, the sun's rays reflect off the snow, creating a blinding white landscape. Needing to adjust my heightened vision, I concentrate on my eyes, reducing the intake of light. The change gradually takes effect, and I blink until they've adapted. When the adjustment is complete, I turn and ask, "Where's the village?"

Blinking, he surveys our surroundings. "I'm not sure where we are. I showed you the village. So, what happened?"

Good question because I don't know how we ended up here. The village was there before we stepped through.

Turning in place, my boots kicking up the powdery snow, I search for signs of where to go. Behind us, tall pine trees with sparse branches border a short mountain range that seems to be within walking distance.

"That mountain was northwest of the village," he says, pointing to the left before trudging toward the edge of the forest.

I follow behind, and we make our way across the wide-open land. Sweeping my gaze over the bordering line of trees, I keep watch for any signs of movement. The constant rush of wind dies once we've cleared the rolling meadow and enter the calm hush of the forest.

"Do you need to rest?" I ask, brushing off the snow clinging to the tops of my boots.

"No, I'm good," he says, walking on ahead, gauging which way to go. I'm impressed with his steady pace, knowing he's out here with an injured wing.

Not wanting him to get too far away from me, I jog up and stay in his shadow. After a few attempts at striking up a conversation and him shutting me down, I focus on the unknowns we're heading toward. Like, how long have Marcellus and the Reborns been in Noviska? Do they have Merigoth with them? Did they find a way to wake her from Adele's mental prison? How was Marcellus able to numb Evander's heightened senses and keep him from flying? If Marcellus isn't here, where is he—still in the Under Realm? Maybe one of the Reborns wandered off and somehow ended up here. I hope that's the case, because I can handle one Reborn nuisance.

Concentrating, I tug at the invisible tethers to my senses. They seem fine, so I double-check and test them out by focusing more energy on my hearing. Instantly, I hear faint voices coming from north of our direction. Drawing back, letting the energy return to its equal flow, I shout over the howling wind, "There are people somewhere ahead of us."

The second I've said it, we walk around a large tree and get the first glimpse of the village. It's the same one he showed me in Stellara before we traveled to the Human Realm.

He points slightly off to the right, between two slender trees. "Do you see the stone monoliths over there?" Next, he drags his hand through the air toward another stone sitting at the front of the village. "And there? There are a few more out of sight from here, bordering the front side of the village."

I've seen monoliths, and if that's a monolith, it's a minuscule one. The Starlight Realm has monoliths four times as tall an hour south of Stellara, bordering the shadow lands. Those monoliths are more of a warning to travelers, letting them know they're about to cross over into the part of our world that the sun doesn't reach. These tapered rocks don't appear any taller than either of us. "You mean that narrow-looking boulder?"

"Come on, this way," he quietly says. "And stay close."

The closer we get, the more I see he's right when its tapered top with a flat front becomes apparent.

Significantly smaller than Bricen, the village boasts only six or seven weathered stone houses, each quaintly spaced out across the front half of the settlement. Snow blankets the wood-slat roofs, icicles hanging delicately from the eave overhangs. The sight of dark smoke billowing from every chimney brings a sense of relief—a reassuring sign that the villagers are keeping warm inside.

Nestled at the rear of the village is a large stone building, presumably their communal meeting house or great hall. A tall watchtower connects at the side, rising high over the treetops. When I spot movement along the battlements, circling the tower's top, I duck low behind the trunk of a nearby tree and call to Evander. "There's someone up in the tower."

His gaze lifts, and he nods. Checking our immediate surroundings, he waves for me to follow, and I do. Weaving between trees, we approach the edge of the village. It isn't until we're a few feet from the monolith that a strange pressure builds in my ears at the same time as everything gets brighter. My skin prickles and the hairs along my arms rise beneath my sleeves. Suddenly, my shirt feels too thin and my leather jacket not long enough.

Evander stares up into the blue sky, his hand shielding his eyes from the blinding light while he asks, "Do you feel it—the block smothering our heightened senses?"

"Is that what's happening?" I concentrate on my eyesight, eager to test this blockage. Focusing, I attempt to redirect the tether of energy in my core that controls the output levels. These levels are used to adjust and extend my senses' range. Right now, I want to enhance my eyesight, allowing me to get a better idea of what's happening at the top of the watchtower. Connecting to that part of myself is typically an effortless maneuver, but I'm currently experiencing some difficulties in doing so. My vision hasn't gotten any better. If anything, the world around me continues to grow brighter. Whatever is dampening our ability to heighten our senses is invisible—a mystical force that we haven't experienced before. The effects don't hurt. Rather, they leave me feeling weak and vulnerable—like a human.

"I don't know what it is, or where it's coming from," Evander says, his attention focused on searching the village homes.

My steps are sluggish, and when I reach the monolith, I lean against it while surveying the village. It's then I notice more stone monoliths placed every ten or so paces, surrounding the front half of the village. I'm going to assume they continue all the way around the back. Turning my attention to the well-trodden path stomped out in the snow, I see that it winds through the center of the village, ending at the front steps of the communal building.

"We're going to need a closer look," I tell Evander. "This time, you stay behind me. If we encounter any threat— human, Reborn, or Marcellus—you take cover. You're no good to Stellara if you're dead." He opens his mouth to protest, and I shut him down. "Don't argue with me. I want to be done with this quickly."

I'm fairly sure I won't be able to fly, but I need to try. My wings quiver beneath the veil I enabled before we left Stellara. If there are villagers in those homes with the smoke streaming out of the chimneys, then they're about to see an angel for the first time. Releasing my wings from their concealment, I silently pray to the stars that we'll be able to escape safely from whatever situation awaits us.

I'm about to test my wings but don't get the chance to because Evander falls into the snow. I rush over to his side and crouch next to him. "Did you slip?"

Shaking his head, he rubs his nose. "I walked into a wall."

Standing and helping him to his feet, I search the air along the path. "What wall?"

He doesn't bother brushing the snow from his clothes and walks past me, one arm out. The palm of his hand presses flat against…against air. "Here," he says. "It's here but it isn't here."

I approach and reach one hand out. Sure enough, my hand finds the barrier. It's the strangest thing I've ever encountered. There's nothing but air, yet it's solid.

A loud groan resonates through the cold air from behind us.

We both turn. Making its way through the forest is a line of people, men and women, walking toward the village. Instead of dashing off to hide, I conceal my wings. It takes me twice the effort to shroud them from sight. We slowly back away from the path, our boots trudging into deep snow again, giving room for the incoming procession. I immediately regret our decision to stand by and wait when I notice the man leading the line has an unhealthy tinge to his light brown skin. He cocks his head in our direction, revealing tiny red veins sprouting out along his skin around his black eyes.

A Reborn.

The Reborn's attention returns to the path in front of him, and he leads the humans straight into the village, their gazes vacant and mesmerized. That can only mean one thing…

"Ah, I was wondering when you were going to show up." The man who stole everything from me steps out from behind the last Reborn, trailing the procession. I almost didn't recognize Marcellus in regular clothes. He's wearing a long, fitted, dark brown leather coat, the hems trimmed in fur. And boots—actual leather boots. Most of his face is covered beneath a hood attached to a short fur shawl draping his shoulders. "It's good to see you again," he says in a nonchalant tone while removing his hood and revealing his shaved head. I have a sudden urge to run my fingers through my hair for reassurance that I'm still me.

He takes a step off the path and into the fresh snow. Instinctively, I release my wings, huffing deep breaths from the overexertion.

A sinister smirk lifts onto his face. "Are you not well, Rune? Is something…" He pauses, then emphasizes his next words with a hint of amusement. "…affecting you?" He rubs his thumb across the tip of each finger, as if he's checking for dirt under his nails. Then his gaze slowly meets mine.

My heart pounds inside my chest. If I fly away…and that's *if* I can fly away…that'll mean leaving Evander to the mercy of Marcellus. That's not an option. While my eyes remain fixed on Marcellus, I whisper to Evander, "Get ready to run."

"Just say when," he answers, and shuffles back a few steps, giving me room.

All I need to do is cause a distraction. Enough time for Evander to get out of here. Taking a step closer, I say with a seething tone, "You'll never hurt me or any of the angels ever again. I swear to it." Then, with a forceful sweep of my wings, I lunge upward—except my feet don't leave the ground. Instead, my body falls forward, plunging face-first into the snow.

My hope for a distraction falls short, and panic seizes me, sending my heart into a frantic rhythm. Evander's shouting, but all I hear are the soft crunches of someone walking in the snow. The weight of whatever enchantment Marcellus is using grows more burdensome, making it almost impossible to roll over. But I do. My hand slips on the packed snow beneath me as I scramble to put some distance between us.

This can't be happening.

Not again.

One simple touch and it's all over.

He crouches, mere feet from where I lie, then whispers, "It's not you I want."

I don't get the chance to respond. From behind, Evander dives over me and slams his body into Marcellus. The two men tumble, rolling and kicking up snow as they fight. I hurry to my feet, needing to help Evander. Thankfully, he has Marcellus's arms pinned to the ground, deep in the snow. Marcellus thrashes about, wafting white powder up into the air.

"Run!" Evander yells. "I can't hold him much longer!"

"No! I won't leave you!"

"You saved me once," he says. Marcellus's arms and legs go still, his stare focused on Evander as my dear friend continues, "And I trust you'll find a way to do it—"

My friend's words are cut off when Marcellus rotates his wrist and twists his hand free from Evander's hold. Then in one swift motion, he brings his hand up and touches Evander's cheek.

"No!" I scream and my knees buckle, but I quickly regain my balance. I'm torn between charging forward or running and saving myself.

Evander releases his grip on Marcellus's other arm, and both men get to their feet. They're covered in snow, but only Marcellus brushes clean. He then narrows his menacing brown eyes at me. "You won't be saving him this time."

"Let him go!" Tears stream down my face, freezing against my heated cheeks. "Please! You've already taken so much from us!"

Inhaling a deep breath, as if trying to reel in the anger boiling inside him, he takes a step closer, to which I don't react. If he wanted me under his control, he would've done it by now. And my suspicions are proven right when he says, "I'll make you a deal. Bring me Adele and I'll return Evander to you."

Evander stands perfectly still, with the familiar blank expression we all wore during our time serving Merigoth.

Every part of me trembles with anger and fear because I can't win this scenario. Either I lose Evander, or we lose Adele. But in order to buy myself time to figure out what to do, I tell him, "Fine. I will bring her to you, but you have to promise me you won't hurt him."

Marcellus pulls out a leather string from his pants pocket. The ends are tied, and there's a small leather pouch hanging from it. After putting the necklace around Evander's neck, he tucks the pouch, and whatever's inside it, beneath Evander's shirt. When he turns his attention back to me, his wicked grin returns. "I can't make you any promises." Then, with a swift motion, he plucks a single feather from my dear friend's wing. Evander doesn't react. Not even a wince. He only stands there, oblivious to the world around him, ready to do Marcellus's bidding.

More tears escape, and rage takes over my thoughts. I would kill this man right here…right now…if I could. "You're a monster!"

Releasing the feather, he says, "I may be a monster, but at least I've accepted that. Adele lives among the humans, pretending to be one, and it sickens me."

I want to tell him she's not a monster. It's not the blood in their veins that makes someone a monster, but their actions. Adele has hurt people in the past, but now she's more humane than many humans in this realm. Her heart is good, and she will always protect those she cares for. Unlike Marcellus, Adele would never give in to malevolence.

Tsking, he turns and walks toward the village. I don't know how, but Evander stays by Marcellus's side, able to follow him into the village. Glancing back at me, Marcellus shouts, "Don't keep me waiting too long, Rune!"

CHAPTER 5

ADELE

"That's the last one," Kit says, double knotting the rope she's strung along the forest ground. When she steps away, I use the toe of my boot to push against the trip wire, which pulls on the bell hanging from the tree branch above. Once the bell settles, we collect our things and make our way toward the road.

"Ten is good enough, right?" she asks, slinging the large sack over her shoulder. Metal clangs inside the bag from the impact of hitting her body.

I'm tempted to say *no* and that we should string up the last two bells, but my stomach grumbles. Shrugging, I say, "I guess we'll find out. I'm hungry, so let's head back and see if Lauren has any leftover bread or porridge." The old bells were carefully spaced out around the outskirts of the village. They were positioned deep enough in the woods that a person wouldn't be directly outside Bricen's barrier wall if they stumbled, but near enough to alert the villagers.

"Hey, about earlier," I say, breaking the silence of the trek home, "I wanted to tell you that if Elijah was in real danger of dying, I would've stayed. You do know that, right?"

Kit trudges on. Her gaze focused on the ground.

While we traverse the woods, the distant cawing and the crunch of leaves beneath my boots add to the natural soundscape of the forest, providing a sense of security. Eventually, Kit takes the lead while I linger behind. My thoughts circle back to the Fayatin man from Castle Nautica. He was here with at least two others, but were there more? Was Lord Houfston among them? With General Onica dead, could the lords of the divided regions be vying for regency? If so, Lord Houfston likely wouldn't leave his stronghold. But then what else could've brought them here?

After stepping out of the forest and onto the road, Kit waits for me to catch up. She adjusts her knitted scarf around her neck, and when I reach her, she says, "He's all I've got left. And, well…" Her words trail off, and her expression looks tense, as if she's trying to not punch something. "I can't do *this* without him."

I shoulder my bow and it hits my quiver, jostling the arrows stored inside. "What are you talking about?" But then, I remember my earlier question in the woods. "Oh, you're talking about Elijah."

It was only a few months ago that Elijah experienced the same sorrow after Kit was taken by the Shade. With a simple touch from Marcellus, he was able to take control of her will, bending her to his commands. In those dark days, he led Kit and others to the Under Realm, where they were offered up as sacrifices to Merigoth's demon spirits. A haunting memory resurfaces—when one of the demon spirits outside Castle Forge overtook Alister. My stomach churns, and I'm unable to tear my thoughts away from replaying the scene. I remember the black smoke forcing its way into his body through his mouth, killing him from the inside, and claiming his body for its own use. Alister became a Reborn.

Thank the stars he and Marcellus are trapped in the Under Realm. I almost died twice in one day at the hands of them both.

Kit's hand smacks hard against the outside of my arm.

"Ow! What was that for?"

"You need to pay attention."

I stop along the road, furrowing my brows at her. "Pay attention to what?"

Metal clinks as Kit adjusts the bag on her shoulder. "I've been talking to you. About how hard it's been for Elijah since we lost our mum and Alya. That I don't know what I'd do if I ever lost him."

Quickly, I respond so she knows I'm listening. "You're not going to lose him. I swear by it." My mind has been all over the place lately, and I don't know why. I used to be better at keeping my focus. With an apologetic smile, I tell her, "Hey, I'll do better. It's just my head has been hazy these past few days."

"Are you out of your sleeping tonic?"

I shake my head. "No. I made a fresh batch the other night." As we continue down the road, I add, "I'm just tired, that's all." We round the corner, and Bricen's barrier wall comes into view. The gates are open, as they always are now during the day. "Actually, if you really want to know, I was thinking about the day Marcellus took you, and how your brother was ready to fight every Shade that crossed his path to get you back."

She brushes away a stray brown curl that has slipped out from under her woolen hat and takes a deep breath through her nostrils. As she lets the air out, she nods to show her understanding. "You know, he was lucky you were here." After a few steps, she adds, "I'd be dead if you hadn't come to Bricen."

"Yeah, well… I should've come sooner."

"You're right. You should've," she says with a straight face, and when I shoot her a surprised look, she cracks a smile and chuckles. "Life unfolds as the stars choose, Adele. We can only do our best in the moments given to us. And we should be grateful for every moment until the end."

Nudging her with my shoulder, a gesture I would've never done a few months ago, I say, "I don't recall you being such a philosopher when we were kids."

"Times have changed."

I can't argue with that. My life has had one altering moment after the next these past eight years. From innocent kid to captive, to torturer, to escapee, to protector. Mum would love to have me be more of a healer than a fighter, though, but that's a battle she knows she won't win. My training to heal people hasn't gone as well as I hoped these past few months, and because of that, I prefer to stick to protecting the village.

As we get closer to Bricen, we can see more people bustling about inside the village. Mum and Lauren deemed it safe enough to leave the gates open during the daylight hours about a month ago, around the same time when Rune and Evander last visited. During their brief stay, Rune shared that their home was in ruins, and they believed it would take a significant amount of time for things to go back to how they were before.

Despite the trauma of Merigoth's enchantment, Rune's unyielding determination, enduring optimism, and refreshing straightforwardness persist. Qualities of hers I admire. Though that wasn't always the case, especially after she told me the truth about my origins as one of the three original Shades, born in the Under Realm with Merigoth's demon blood in my veins. I think at that moment I hated her more than I did General Onica. Adapting to my new reality has been a gradual process, and though I'm not entirely at peace with my origins, I'm actively working on it.

As Kit and I enter the village, the day falls into its routine. Villagers mingle outside, children play, the blacksmith brothers work on their tasks, and... *Is that Rune outside of Goslings?*

"Hey." Kit slaps me on the arm, and I flinch at the sudden contact. She points straight ahead and asks, "Isn't that your angel friend?"

Then, off to the right, I notice Aunt Lauren and Selene carrying baskets of bread toward the tavern. Shifting my gaze back to Rune, I see her talking with Mum and Elijah. The fact that Rune is visiting must bring joy to Elijah. Since her last visit, he's been asking at least once a day when we think she'll return. With her here, I feel more hopeful about my chances of making amends for leaving him this morning.

As we approach, I notice Rune's face becomes tense, her jaw tightening. She's completely focused on their conversation and unaware of Kit and me approaching until we are right beside them.

"Adele," Rune says with a forced smile. She opens her arms but waits for me to give her the okay to proceed. After I've nodded, she pulls me in for a hug. I return the gesture, but only with a few quick pats, while her arms squeeze tightly around me. When she releases me, she turns and gives a polite nod to Kit, and Kit returns the greeting.

Elijah's standing next to me, and I offer him a pleading grin, hoping he sees it as my apology. He does and smiles back. Thank the stars Rune stopped by.

Then Mum cuts in, getting right to business. "How long are you planning on staying?"

In the past, things have gotten a bit heated between Rune, Mum, and Aunt Lauren, so I imagine Mum is hoping to avoid rekindling that tension.

"Are you here for a friendly visit or to lecture Lauren again about how she needs to return to your Starlight Realm?" Mum crosses her arms, shooting a quick side glance at Lauren and Selene approaching.

Rune narrows her sharp eyes on my mum, then shakes off her annoyed smirk by widening her smile. "Neither." She looks my way and says, "We need to talk."

"Let's go inside and talk in private," Mum suggests, then heads up the front steps of Goslings.

Rune follows, as do Elijah and Kit. Aunt Lauren and Selene come up next to me just as everyone's heading inside. Mum is positioned in the doorway, with the dim interior of the tavern looming behind her. She calls down to us, "Lauren, you and Selene might want to check on Magdala. Her mother was here before Rune arrived and said Magdala's fever has returned."

I imagine it also gives Lauren a reason not to come inside and avoids the unresolved argument. Making sure my bow is secure on my shoulder, I take the basket full of bread from my aunt. Selene steps forward and stacks her small basket on top, then with a genuine smile she asks, "I can stay if you need me to?"

"Thank you," I answer, momentarily glancing up to Mum, who is subtly shaking her head, "but why don't you help Lauren out with Magdala? I'm sure Rune's only here to pay us a quick visit and update us on her progress in the Starlight Realm."

Aunt Lauren tugs at Selene's wool cloak. "Let's go see how the little one's doing." Selene obliges and follows. My aunt's kindness fills me with gratitude as she places one arm around my friend's shoulder.

I carry the two baskets of bread up into the tavern, then set them on the bar counter at the rear of the room. Inside,

Mum, Rune, Elijah, and Kit stand around the table farthest away from the front door. I weave my way around the other round tables, over to stand between Rune and Kit, and rest my bow against the side of the table.

"And you tried to enter the village from other vantage points?" Mum asks, her vexed expression matching Rune's tense one. She's not the same woman I knew as a kid; someone who never spoke a harsh word or took an angry tone. Now, she's all about doing what's best for Bricen, which means she's compassionate yet cautious, and not afraid to be stern when it comes to the safety of the villagers. Despite successfully containing the threat from the Under Realm, she remains concerned about potential dangers approaching Bricen's gates from other sources.

"We didn't have time to try," Rune answers. There's a faint redness lining her lower lids. Before I can ask what they're talking about, she continues, "Sara, there's some kind of strange mystical enchantment preventing my kind from walking or flying in or around that village."

Mum's lips purse into a tight line while she rubs at her temple. Kit jumps in and asks, "Can someone please bring Adele and me up to date on what's going on?" She removes her woolen cap and unwraps her scarf from around her neck, then sets them both on the table.

Before we get an explanation, the fire in the tavern's fireplace flickers as a winter breeze sweeps in from the front door. Mum steps aside and addresses the villager, who after I turn to see, is Nathaniel. "We're in a private discussion. Whatever it is, it can wait."

Nathaniel slightly bows his head and stammers out his words, "Oh, right… Well, was hoping to talk to Adele about—"

"Later!" Mum bellows, then in a calmer tone, she says, "Please, Nathaniel… Later."

My attention snaps from the blacksmith to Mum. Something's not right. I quickly intervene before any resentment blooms. Bricen can't exactly lose its blacksmiths.

I approach him and gesture to talk outside. Once we're on the porch, I say, "Now's not a good time. If you're wondering where Selene is, I believe she's tending to Magdala."

"Oh, no. It's okay. I, uh—was hoping to talk to you about something. I mean, it's not important-important but kind of important." He shrugs and tucks his hands under his arms, looking everywhere but at me. "I guess it can wait until you're done in there." He finally lifts his head, our eyes meeting. "Brandulf thinks I should keep my distance, and—"

"Brandulf?" I ask, unsure of who he's speaking of.

"My brother." He quickly looks out over the porch railing toward the smithy, where Brandulf is hammering something on his anvil. Hot iron sparks fly off of whatever he's working on. Turning his attention to me, Nathaniel continues, "My brother doesn't know I've left to come and talk with you. He thinks I should keep my distance, and I probably should, but I can't seem to follow orders." With a smile, he tries to downplay his staring. "It's never been a strong quality of mine—following orders I don't agree with."

"Well, that's something you should work on. Being able to follow orders is a basic skill required for any community to maintain order."

He laughs and nods. "You are not wrong on that." His feet shift and his body doesn't seem to want to stay still. "I like how forward you are, Adele. You're not like other girls."

Why is he staring at me like that? And what does he mean, he likes how forward I am? He can't mean he's interested in me romantically—can he? Heat blooms beneath my shirt. Moving away, I sidestep closer to the tavern door. "I should get back inside," I mutter, avoiding his eyes.

He says something about finding me later, but I don't catch the end. I'm too focused on getting inside and closing the door. Selene was right. I need to get better at reading people on the outside.

"What did I miss?" I ask, hurrying to return to my spot next to Kit. Rune's visit, that's what I need to focus on. Not Nathaniel or how he's interested in me—me—not Selene.

"Adele, did you hear Rune?" Kit nudges me with her elbow.

"What? No." Looking to Rune, I catch Mum sighing while rubbing the bridge of her nose.

Rune looks hesitant, but then after taking a deep breath, she says, "It's Marcellus. He's in the Human Realm, and he's taken Evander."

CHAPTER 6

ADELE

There has to be a mistake.

"What? How?" My gaze shifts from Rune to the people surrounding the table, eventually settling back on Rune. "You closed the doorway, didn't you? And we would've noticed if Marcellus or the Reborns were roaming the woods."

Groaning, I step away from the group and go to stand in front of the large window at the front of the tavern. A chair blocks my path and I push it aside, knocking it to the ground with a loud clatter.

"Adele," Mum calls, but keeps her distance, "there are other doorways leading into this realm."

"If a Realmwalker—" Rune begins, but is cut off when Elijah asks, "What's a Realmwalker?"

I don't return to the group, but I do pay attention to what Rune has to say.

The angel's voice softens, something I've noticed she does mostly when talking with Elijah, and she explains, "I'm a Realmwalker—an angel that can open doorways between realms, over distances, or through objects. Every angel possesses an inherited ability. Some abilities are more abundant among the family lines, while some, like mine, are less. If I recall correctly, there were only two other families besides mine that had Realmwalker traits. But I can't be sure. It was a long time ago. Our numbers aren't what they used to be." Then, rubbing her arms, she tells us, "I believe I'm the last with this ability."

"So, if something happens to you…" Elijah's question trails off.

"If something happens to me, then there's no way to travel between our two realms."

The room falls silent, as if we're all trying to process what it would mean if something were to happen to Rune. Outside, I spot Aunt Lauren talking to one of the villagers. She sees me from the road and waves. Rune is the only angel in the Starlight Realm that I'd want to see. But looking down at Aunt Lauren, I can't help but wonder how she, or any others, would feel about never being able to return to their homeland. They'd be stuck here forever, whether they wanted to be or not.

Rune shifts her tone. "I believe your Trevor was both a Realmwalker and an Ultralinguist. The latter is someone who can basically communicate with anyone and anything. Hence his strong connection with the crows. I also believe that even though Realmwalkers are forbidden to leave a doorway open, it occasionally happens."

I can't believe this is happening. Will it ever end?

"Adele," Rune calls to me.

I don't turn to face the group, but I do shift my gaze from out the window to over my shoulder.

"He'll release Evander, if…"—desperation creeps into her voice—"I bring you to him."

"Of course," I say under my breath, then return to staring out the front window. Loud enough for everyone to hear, I say, "He still can't free Merigoth from the mental prison I constructed." Out along the road, villagers smile and talk to one another as they go about their day. For a fleeting moment, I envy their trivial problems. Their main worries revolve around daily tasks and minor concerns in maintaining the village, while we're the ones having to face the life-threatening dangers. I shake off the feeling, because deep down inside, I don't know who I would be without my demon-blood abilities. *Could I live a normal life if ever given the opportunity to take away that part of me?*

"Adele," Mum whispers, now standing by my side. "You can't go to him, you know that, right?"

Nodding, I shift my attention from those outside to her. "I won't do it." Then, shifting my boots along the hardwood, I turn to the group. "I refuse to let Bricen, or any village in Harvesgrove, return to that state of suffering. Merigoth cannot be allowed her freedom."

Mum wraps one arm over my shoulder, and I quickly brush her attempts to comfort me off, stepping closer to the table. My heart pounds inside my chest, beating like a battle drum, waiting for me to decide our next move.

Marcellus is in the Human Realm, and he has Evander.

And now, he wants me.

Letting out a groan, I shake my head in frustration. Feeling overwhelmed, I find myself uttering the words, "I don't know what to do." Usually, I berate myself for making impulsive decisions, but right now, I'm starting to think that I actually prefer those rash choices over the daunting task of devising and planning. There are so many uncertainties surrounding the situation, making it incredibly challenging to come up with the right course of action.

Kit leans on the edge of the table, arms folded over her chest. "Rune, you said angels aren't able to get into this village Marcellus has taken over?" She answers with a nod, and Kit continues, suggesting a course of action. "What about me? Can a human enter the village?"

Rune furrows her brows as she carefully considers the question. "I believe so. We did see two Reborns leading a line of humans into the village. They had no difficulties walking past the snow-covered monoliths—the point at which we were met by an invisible force preventing us from going any farther."

"Snow? Where exactly is this village?" Elijah shifts his weight to the other leg. I miss seeing him in that worn red scarf, but since giving it to Rune, he now wears a knitted scarf gifted to him by Magdala's mum. It was one of the many gifts she gave us and Aunt Lauren for rescuing her daughter from General Onica's sword. Elijah wears his new scarf all the time. It drapes loosely around his neck now, with the thick brown yarn blending perfectly with his skin.

"The village is in Noviska," Rune explains. "North of the Kingdom of Verglas."

I cringe when the word *Noviska* leaves her mouth. The Kingdom of Verglas and the castle grounds with its ice sculptures and winter foliage is truly a wonderous sight, but the frigid temperatures and the number of fish they eat has me wishing never to live in the snow-covered country. Traveling there under General Onica's thumb was always a miserable and cold endeavor.

Pushing aside my dislike for the northern country, I stare at the grain lines of the wood table and wonder aloud, "Why would there be a doorway between the Under Realm and Noviska?"

Mum lowers herself into a nearby tavern chair, muttering soft words as she presses her hands to her face. "Oh no… It can't be."

Whatever she continues to mumble is indiscernible to me, but not to the angel with heightened hearing. Rune tucks a short strand of brown hair behind her ear and asks, "Why do you believe this to be your fault? You don't possess the ability to open doorways between worlds."

I move past Rune and lower myself in front of Mum with a slow and deliberate motion. The room falls quiet, except for the sound of the fire crackling in the fireplace. Eventually, her glossy eyes find mine, and I grip the chair's arms tightly while adjusting my crouched posture. "Mum, what is it? Why are you upset?"

She finally snaps out of whatever reverie consumes her thoughts, and she stares at me, a tear breaking free and falling onto her lap. "This is my fault. The doorway—I begged him to help me get my freedom. To open a passage between our worlds, giving me a way to escape the Under Realm."

"Who, Mum? Who did you ask to help you?"

"Trevor." More tears fall and she quickly wipes them away. After a few sniffles, she continues, "We'd met a long time ago in the Under Realm. You wouldn't remember," she says, stroking the side of my face. "You were only a baby."

Her hand is warm against my cheek. She's the only person I'll allow to touch my skin, and it's because I know she can handle herself if my reach ever extends into her mind. When Merigoth injected her blood into Mum, to help aid the pregnancy, her human body also changed. She insists we're more human than demon, but that doesn't change the fact that we're part demon—and who knows if one day we'll be more demon than human. A day I fear more often than I should.

Mum sweeps her long blonde braid over one shoulder, and with a softer, lifted expression she begins, "Trevor was a young man—an explorer between realms—wanting to visit other worlds and help people."

Ever since Mum returned from her imprisonment in the Under Realm, she's been reluctant to tell me more about her life before Bricen or how she escaped the Under Realm. I've asked many times since she returned what happened all those years ago, why she left Marcellus behind, and what happened to the third Shade child. I don't even know if it's a brother or a sister. No matter how many times I asked, she'd always say *One day I will tell you everything. But that day is not today. There's no reason to dwell on or revisit the past. The memories of my failures are for me to bear, not you.*

Well, it looks as if that day has come.

"You knew Trevor before you came to Bricen?" Elijah asks, pulling up a chair to sit in. He leans forward and rests both elbows on top of the table. "He never said he knew you."

"I imagine he thought I was dead."

"Why don't you start by telling us how you met," Kit suggests, leaning against the bar counter at the back of the room.

Mum nods. "I'd never met anyone so energized and full of life." A smile spreads, as if she's happy to reminisce. "It was purely a coincidence how we met. He could've ended up anywhere in the Under Realm, but fate led him straight into my bedchamber. Naturally, I was frightened when the doorway appeared, but as soon as he stepped through, my heart instinctively knew he posed no danger. He explained who he was—an angel from another realm—and how he traveled from realm to realm, looking to help those in need. And I was definitely in need of his help.

"Over the next several weeks, we became friends, then…well, more than friends." A flush bloomed across the tops of her damp cheeks, and I was tempted to stop her from delving too deep into the details of how close she and Trevor became. But thankfully, Mum spared us the details of whatever memories were playing out in her head. "Once

Trevor realized who Merigoth was, the banished angel Loralai Songwielder, he strongly expressed that we keep our friendship a secret. He told me the story about her deceit and betrayal of the Starlight Realm."

What is she talking about—deceit? From what I saw while entrapping her, Merigoth…or Loralai…seemed to be the one who was betrayed. I stand and step away, giving Mum some space to retell her story, and glance over at Elijah. He seems to share my confused expression because he was there in the throne room with me, watching Merigoth's memory play out, and it wasn't Loralai who betrayed the angels. In fact, she was the one afflicted and needing help, begging for aid to heal her from the demon blood poisoning her body. The three angels who stood before her refused to help and instead banished her from the Starlight Realm.

In that moment, I actually felt sorry for the demon queen.

But that didn't stop me from trapping her in a secure mental prison. Looking back now, I wonder if she chose that specific memory for my benefit. To share the truth about that day, especially if the truth everyone else knew was skewed into painting Loralai as the enemy.

For now, I don't argue Mum's story. I've been waiting weeks for her to open up about the day she escaped.

I return to my earlier position next to the front window, except this time I don't look at the bustling villagers outside. Instead, I lean my back against the windowsill and listen to Mum continue her story.

"Our rendezvous gave me hope that one day I'd be free from Merigoth's custody and live a happy life with Trevor and my children..." Her voice trails away as if she's imagining that world she once so longed for.

Mum has changed so much from the person I knew as a child. Watching her sit there, looking so vulnerable and worn down by time, I suddenly realize how little I actually know about her. She has always worn a smile, hiding behind her role as a mother—a role I once believed was solely about loving and guiding one's children through life. Now I understand that being a mother is much more—it means being a protector. Sometimes, keeping secrets and putting on a smile are strategic methods of being an effective guardian.

Knowing that's not how the story ends, I ask, "What happened next?"

With a heavy sigh, she shakes off whatever thoughts consume her mind. "We devised a plan to escape. Except on the day I was supposed to leave with you and your siblings, things didn't work according to plan." Her smile falls flat, and her eyes tremble as if the memories are hard to bear.

"And?" It's not me who asks, but Rune. She seems to be just as curious about what happened all those years ago as the rest of us.

Mum straightens in her chair and clears her throat. "Trevor opened the doorway from the Under Realm to Noviska. What happened after I escaped through it is irrelevant. The point is, it was never closed. Trevor never returned. It wasn't until years after I settled into my new life, here in Bricen, that our paths crossed again."

The room falls silent. They've accepted Mum's decree as the final say in the matter. I, however, do not. Pushing off the wall, boots pounding against wood planks, I come around her seat to face her. "No. That's not all. What happened after you left the Under Realm? What happened to the third Shade baby? Why did you leave Marcel—"

"Adele, stop!" She jumps to her feet and gives me the same scolding look I used to get whenever I ran off and played after she specifically told me to stay inside the house. "She's gone, and I will never forgive myself for what happened. I have to live with that." She pushes the chair away, wood scraping wood, then heads for the front door. Before she leaves, she turns to the group and sternly says, "And you're not going to Noviska, Kit. It's too dangerous. We'll think of another way to rescue Evander." Kit opens her mouth to protest, and Mum quickly shuts her down. "I said no!" Then, with a wide swing of the tavern's front door, a gust of winter air sweeps in, causing the hairs on the back of my neck to rise. The chill leaves the second Mum slams the door shut.

Even though I'm frustrated that she didn't finish her story, I focus on the two words that stand out in my mind: *She's gone.*

I had a sister.

I've always considered Selene to be like the sister I never had—but I do have one. Or had one. Even though I don't know what happened to her, rage builds in me, igniting a fury that awakens the part of me I've worked hard to keep suppressed. My reach tingles beneath the skin of my fingertips, wanting to hook its tether into someone. Closing my eyes, I focus on the air filling my lungs—how it streams in and then slowly flows out. After a few more calming breaths, I open my eyes. Kit and Elijah quietly exchange words while Rune, arms crossed and a distant look in her eyes, gazes into the flickering flames of the fireplace.

Kit breaks the silence and leans over the table, both palms pressed flat against the wood surface. "So…" She aims her question at Rune. "Angels can't get into the village, but you mentioned humans can?"

Our angel friend looks to the front door, and I know she's replaying Mum's instructions not to even consider going to Noviska. With a deep sigh, she steps closer to the table and nods. "It appeared so."

Straightening, and resting one hand on the pommel of her short blade, Kit says, "Well, then it's decided. It's our only option, regardless of what Sara wants. I'll sneak in, assess the situation, and then return without anyone ever knowing I left."

"You can't go." Elijah twists in his seat to look up at his sister. "Sara will have your hide if you go—"

"What other choice do we have?" I cut him off. "Besides, my mum isn't exactly thinking straight, is she? It's the best plan we've got with the amount of time we have before something happens to Evander." I move to Kit's side. "I'm coming with you."

Kit doesn't argue, only nods and gives me that famous mischievous smile I remember from when we were kids. Mum should know better than to argue with Kit, especially once she gets an idea in her head.

"It's settled. Kit and I will go to Noviska and scope out the village. We won't engage, and we'll keep our distance from Marcellus and the Reborns." The idea of facing danger again has me anxious to get going, even if it means walking through deep snow and facing frigid headwinds.

Nudging her brother in the upper arm, Kit offers him some reassurance. "In and out. I promise." Even though he appears unconvinced with his pursed lips, rigid posture, and crossed arms, he gives her a nod anyway.

We turn to Rune. The angel stands like a statue, deep in thought. As she takes a deep breath through her nose, her shoulders loosen and she exhales, nodding in agreement. "I can't say it's the best idea, but you're right—it's the only one we've got. Evander and I went to Noviska with the same intentions—to find Marcellus and send him back to the Under Realm—which, of course, didn't happen. Our time there wasn't as in and out as we'd hoped. My point being… Don't underestimate whatever new magic Marcellus has harnessed. It's powerful."

"You didn't know what you were walking into," I reassure her. "We'll be careful and stay out of sight."

Knocking a fist against the wood tabletop, Kit says with determination, "Uncovering the source of this new magic will be the key to how we save Evander." She then locks eyes with me. "Getting inside the village is the only way to get answers. It's not up for debate. We have to go."

She's not wrong about there being no other choice. If we stick to the shadows and only observe, then I'm confident we'll find the answers we're looking for. It's a good plan.

One I'm ready for. The darkness within jolts, seemingly just as eager for some excitement as I am.

"Sara is going to lose her mind when she finds out," Elijah grumbles, rubbing a hand through his short curls.

"Then let's make sure she doesn't find out." As Kit turns to leave through the back door, she says, "I'll be right back. I need to grab a few more weapons."

I quickly add, "Be sure to dress warm. It may be cold here in Harvesgrove, but up there in Noviska a person will freeze to death in a matter of minutes if they're not properly protected with enough layers."

Kit nods in understanding before disappearing outside into the afternoon bustle of villagers, leaving me alone with Rune and Elijah. It feels as if we've gone back in time to when it was the three of us trying to save Bricen. "Will you be joining us?" I ask Rune.

She rolls her neck and shoulders, bristling her brown feathers. "No. I need to see something in the Under Realm."

"You're going to look for Merigoth?" I narrow my eyes at her, surprised she's all right with returning to the place that held her captive for so long. Hesitantly, she nods and immediately I know I'm mistaken. She's not at ease with returning. Her fears are evident from the way she stands, her body rigid and tense. "If she's awake…" My words trail off, because we both know if the Queen of the Under Realm is awake, she won't hesitate to enchant Rune or anyone else.

Stepping closer, she reaches for me but halts before her hand can touch my arm. "I trust you and your abilities. You, my friend, are a formidable presence. And I don't believe

Marcellus would be going through all this trouble if Merigoth were free."

"So, if she's not in the Under Realm, then we know she's in Noviska," Elijah points out, then stands, his chair sliding across the wood floorboards. "It's a good plan, and I want to go with you."

"It's too dangerous," Rune explains.

"I can handle myself. And I'm the stealthiest one in our village."

I recall this morning's chase and how he was most definitely not the stealthiest one from our party. His confidence is admirable, but his desire to be closer to Rune confuses me. This isn't the ideal time to spend time with her. Plus, even if Merigoth remains unconscious, the demon spirits could try and claim his body, turning him into a Reborn. "Someone needs to stay here and keep an eye on my mum."

The front door slowly creaks open, and Lauren pops her head in. "I didn't mean to eavesdrop. I was looking for your mum." She comes inside, closes the door, and says, "I will keep Sara busy so you can help Evander."

I shift my weight from one leg to the other, turning myself to face her. This new side to my mum can get quite scary if pushed the wrong way. I wouldn't want Aunt Lauren to be the one to bear Mum's anger if she finds out where we've gone.

"Are you sure?" I ask, double-checking.

Aunt Lauren nods. "You have to promise me that you won't engage with Marcellus. That you're only going there to observe the grounds and what he's got going on up there."

"I promise."

"And if he does see you and tries to claim your will—"

I finish her train of thought and say with confidence, "I will end his life."

She looks over my shoulder, first to Rune and then to Elijah. "And you two promise to watch out for one another?" They both nod. Lauren moves past me and approaches Rune. "I know you and I aren't exactly seeing eye to eye right now. Not with you persistently sending Evander to request for the angels of this realm to return to the Starlight Realm to help rebuild Stellara."

Bitterly, Rune responds, "A conversation for another day."

"Yes, my thoughts exactly. My point being that these humans are my family. They are my priority." The two angels stare hard at one another, and I almost worry someone's going to throw a punch. Aunt Lauren eventually breaks the silence. "You will respect my home, my family, and my wishes to remain with them."

Unexpectedly, Rune levels a finger inches from my aunt's face. Her words tremble as she yells, "You are an angel! And this is not your home!"

Her eyes are glossy. I know one blink will release the tears building up. I've seen that look too many times before. It's the look of those begging for their life, just before I end it. It's the look that says, *I can't take it anymore.* It's the look of someone bottling everything up, praying to the stars they won't break.

But Rune doesn't give Aunt Lauren the satisfaction of seeing the tears fall. She turns her pointed finger from my aunt to herself. "We are your family." Then, without waiting for a response, she pivots away and storms out the back door of the tavern, toward Trevor's shed.

We all watch, and when the door slams shut, Lauren faces us. "She's trying to hold onto the old ways—her mother's way of life. If she truly wants to rebuild Stellara, she'll need all the help she can get."

"But you said you wouldn't return?" I ask, unsure of where Rune will get more help if the angels living in the Human Realm won't return.

"I'd go and help," Elijah says. "If she'd have me."

Lauren offers him an encouraging yet small smile. "She would never let you or any other being that's not an angel cross over into the Starlight Realm. It's forbidden in the laws created by our ancient ancestors. Laws that need to be amended to reflect current times."

"Well, then that's something Rune will have to come to terms with." I can see the hurt on Elijah's face. Hopefully, one day Rune will see how change can be a good thing. That it's possible to have the best of both worlds. Resting a hand on the outside of his shoulder, I tell him, "She knows where to find help if she truly wants it." He smiles, accepting the hope I offer behind my words.

My aunt turns and adds a few logs to the dying fire, then says as she brushes her hands clean, "I have some extra fur coverings and a heavier cloak that you can borrow." I follow her out of Goslings, unsure of what to expect in the next few hours. All I know is that we're about to venture up into the one place in the Human Realm I loathe more than Fayatin— the snow-covered country of Noviska.

CHAPTER 7

ADELE

Walking through one of Rune's doorways feels like stepping into another room. There's no unusual sensation or disorientation, but with Noviska being a land of snow and ice, there's a significant temperature drop.

While waiting for Kit to come through, I take a moment to double-check my two daggers are secure beneath my winter garb. Before leaving, Aunt Lauren provided me with a sleeveless tabard that looks more like a narrow blanket with a hole in the center for my head. She claimed it would provide an extra layer of warmth over the thin fabric of my tunic and leather vest. She also insisted I borrow a leather belt with a dagger sheath hanging off the side for better access to my weapon. My trusty blade that I've had for years, which I normally tuck into my waistband, fit perfectly. Then, in place of my normal cloak, she offered me her special double-layered woolen cloak that drapes across the front and buttons at my right shoulder. And to keep my legs warm, she wrapped each leg from the knee down with fur coverings. The Fayatin dagger I found this morning hides beneath the right one, tucked in my boot.

It wasn't only the chill in the air that changed, but also the landscape. It's been a long time since I've seen snow. The overwhelming brightness of what stretches out before me adds to my sense of dread, knowing that we have to navigate across the open field. For stars' sake… Why Noviska? I hate snow.

Rune, still standing in Goslings, shouts through the passage, "This is as close as I can get you." The edges of the round doorway shimmer like molten silver. Lauren and Selene are there too, standing off to the side behind Rune. Their attention is focused on the frigid northern land.

"Are you sure about this?" Selene questions, rubbing her arms as a gust of wind carrying flakes of snow whirls into the tavern. "Can't someone else go?"

Squinting from the light reflecting off the snow, I change the topic, hoping to lessen her concern. "I can handle myself. Besides, think of this expedition like one of Captain Roksana Bruiser's adventures. She always returns to her ship and crew, unharmed, and with treasures to share."

My aunt gives Selene's arms a gentle squeeze, reassuring her that everything will be fine. Then, she unloops her arm from my friend's and steps closer to Rune. "Remember, you're not to engage. Only assess the situation and then promptly return home before anyone sees you."

"Where's Mum?" I ask, surprised she hasn't discovered our plan yet.

"I sent her to tend to a hole beneath the barrier wall."

My muscles tense and I shuffle through the snow, toward the passage. "A hole? Did something happen? Is there an intruder?"

Lauren holds up a hand, her palm facing out. "No. Calm yourself. I dug the hole as a means of distraction, but with Sara's efficiency, it will be filled in no time. You need to hurry and get back."

"In and out," Kit reassures my aunt, coming up from behind and walking through the doorway. The second she's through, the snow reaching well above her ankles, and standing next to me, she shields her eyes. "This is Noviska? I'll never curse at the winter weather we endure in Harvesgrove ever again."

"Agreed. I wouldn't want to trudge through this every day."

"You have three hours left of daylight," Rune informs us. We both turn to her. Elijah stands at Rune's side. "I'll reopen the doorway at sunset."

Kit and I both nod.

"Watch each other's back," Elijah says.

"You too, little brother. Stay close to Rune, and don't get yourself killed," Kit counters before lifting her scarf higher over her mouth and nose. She wasn't thrilled to hear that he was going with Rune, but she knows he would jump at any chance to spend more time with the angel.

Shuffling through the calf-high snow, approaching the passage, I say, "I know you're able to defend yourself against the Reborns, but he can't." I gesture with a quick glance to Elijah. "Alister...the Reborn version...is not like the other Reborns. He's stronger. If anything happens to Elijah, if he dies, I'd hate to resort to violence, because I consider you a friend, but..." I don't finish the sentence, hoping she understands the weight of my implication.

"I will protect him with my life," Rune promises, pressing a fist to her chest, right over her heart. As she lowers her hand, an unexpected flush crosses her cheeks, and she flashes Elijah a heartwarming grin.

"Thank you," Kit says from beneath her scarf.

"So be it," I say, holding Rune's gaze. "The fate of your life is tied to his."

She straightens her shoulders, which causes her wings to rustle gently. Then, with her chin held high, she declares, "You have my word that I will put his life before my own." With a softer expression, she says, "Adele, you can trust me."

I inhale a deep breath of icy air. "Right. Well, then... I guess we'll see you in three hours."

Rune points to a break in the trees lining the open field we're standing in. "Head in that direction, keeping the mountain on your left. You'll find the village within the hour."

Stepping away, Rune raises a hand to close the doorway, except before she does, a loud *caw* fills the tavern. Two black crows dart through Rune's passage and fly up into the clear blue sky of Noviska. Bright sunlight momentarily blocks my view until I see them circling, soaring toward us.

"Selene!" I yell. "You were supposed to keep them away! I don't want to risk them getting stuck here."

"I did!" she retorts with a shriek. "I told them to stay in the tree by our cottage."

"Oh," Elijah sheepishly says. "That might be my fault. I don't think I closed the tavern's door all the way."

"Elijah!" I can't help the annoyance and concern lacing my tone.

"I'm sorry!"

Sighing, I reel in my annoyance and say, "Just make sure the other two—" I stop mid-sentence, recalling how Trevor said they aren't able to travel into the Under Realm…or maybe it was that he didn't want them *going* into the Under Realm. I can't remember. "Just make sure the other two don't go with you."

"They won't," Rune promises. We exchange silent goodbyes and good lucks with a few curt nods and subtle hand waves before the tavern flickers from existence, leaving Kit and me far from home.

"The crows?" Kit asks, her mouth still covered by the fabric of her scarf. She's searching the sky for my feathered friends.

"They'll be fine. It's our departure that concerns me. They'd better stay close and be ready if we need to flee in a hurry." I spot the two black silhouettes disappearing behind the treetops ahead of us. Before leaving, I specifically spoke with all four, instructing them to stay put. I guess I don't have as much influence over them as I assumed. One of them is Valor, I'm sure of that, but I can't tell who the second one is or why they came.

Turning, I lift the edge of my scarf up over my mouth and nose and start our trek through the powdery snow, keeping the mountain on my left. "Let's go. I've no desire to stay in this freezing country any longer than needed."

Our pace through the open field is slower than I expected. In some spots, the snow is so deep that it almost reaches our knees. Once we do cross the threshold into the forest, we stop to catch our breath beneath the towering canopy of pine trees. My concerns about our time constraints lessen as the snow lightens and the ground levels out. The fur along our legs is sodden with wet snow, the ends clumping together, resembling sharp daggers.

We don't rest for long and continue forward, keeping the mountain on our left. Despite the freezing conditions, beads of sweat collect on my skin beneath the many layers. Every so often, I unbutton Aunt Lauren's winter cloak and let it hang open for a short relief. Kit does the same and unfastens the top buttons of her surcoat. It's a long leather coat with high slits along the sides, giving her access to the shortsword strapped at her waist. It's a sturdy garment, and I'm tempted to barter one from the neighboring village's seamstress.

The crows make an appearance every so often as we walk through the forest. I'm still unable to make out the identity of Valor's companion. I'm guessing it's Serafina since she favors Valor as company over Barclay and Olive.

Kit lowers her scarf, and as she exhales, a visible cloud of warm breath escapes her mouth and dissipates into thin air. Her voice is slightly winded when she asks, "Have you figured out Olive's gift yet?"

I unraveled my scarf some time ago, letting the ends hang from my neck. "No. She's being quite secretive about it, too. Did Trevor ever mention anything to you or Elijah about the crows and their special talents?"

She shakes her head. Tight brown curls peek out from beneath her winter cap. "I assumed they were messenger birds. If he wasn't tending to the village, he was with those birds. He'd often send out messages with one of them wearing that little leather pouch around their neck."

That's interesting, and now I'm curious to know who Trevor was sending messages to. "That was probably Barclay. He has a talent for finding people. I don't know how he does it, but he's yet to fail whenever I've tested him. He just knows where they are."

"And Valor," she states, rather than asks, "is your scout."

"She is. That bird has a keen sense for danger."

"What about Serafina?"

"Serafina is a sneaky thief and has an eye for shiny trinkets." It was Serafina who stole Selene's hairpin during our first encounter. Looking back, I believe the crows wanted me to follow them—to find the cave with the Under Realm doorway. "I'm sure Olive will reveal her hidden talent when she's good and ready."

Suddenly, Kit stops, throwing an arm out in my direction. She slowly lowers her hand closer to the hilt of her shortsword. I react, bracing into a defensive stance as I survey the area, watching for movement from behind the tree trunks. The forest is silent, except for the occasional howl of wind.

With a hushed tone, I ask, "What is it?" My hand mimics Kit's, hovering over the hilt of my dagger, which hangs from my belt.

With two fingers, she points straight ahead, then takes cover behind the closest pine tree. The second I spot the flutter of green fabric, I duck from sight. After crouching to one knee, the fur wrapping my leg pressing into the snow, I peer out from behind the trunk. Two cloaked figures with hoods concealing their faces walk in our direction. I pivot in the snow and press my back against the tree trunk. Soft mutters grow louder as the figures continue to come toward us. When I look at Kit, she presses a finger to her lips while slowly unsheathing her shortsword.

My power rustles within me, as if waking from a nap, hungry and ready to be fed. It stretches its reach from my mind down through the muscles of my arms, overriding my brain's command to withdraw my dagger. One at a time, I remove my gloves, and then I reach beneath my cloak and through the sides of the tabard, tucking them into the front of my vest.

Kit gestures to the approaching figures, and I nod. We cautiously peer out from our hiding spots. The two figures are no longer walking toward us, and have veered off to our left, in the direction of the mountain.

Kit says something, but I can't hear. So, staying low, I run over to her and say, "I think we should follow them."

She rolls her eyes. "That's what I just said." Using the trees for cover, she waves for me to follow. The two cloaked figures aren't in a hurry, so trailing them is easy enough. It isn't long before stone structures come into view. The mountain that was to our left is now within walking distance set off behind the quaint village.

We keep our distance as the two figures enter the village. There's no sign of any people milling about, but they're in there somewhere, because every house in the village has a stream of thick smoke rising up from within its chimney.

"Come on, and let's hope we're able to get past whatever invisible barrier Rune was talking about." We move quickly and cautiously toward the village, taking cover behind a tall rock with a tapered peak and a flat face. Thankfully, it's wide enough to conceal both Kit and me. Glancing around, I spot other rocks similar in structure, circling the settlement's outer boundaries.

"These must be the monoliths Rune mentioned." Kit runs a finger along the symbols carved into the front. "I've never seen symbols like these."

From somewhere ahead of us, a door groans open and then slams shut with a forceful *bang*. We both move to look past the stone monolith and into the village. Behind the stone houses sits a large communal hall. Attached to its left side is an enormous tower that stretches high enough to see over the treetops.

Kit holds her blade close. "I'm going to guess that's where we can find Marcellus."

We both watch for movement at the top of the tower. A few heartbeats later, someone appears along the battlement. A man with a limp, wearing a linen shirt and a simple brown arming cap over his head. The long laces of the headpiece are not tied and dangle freely. It's an oddity that he's not wearing any other winter garments. He continues behind the stone battlement before reappearing again.

"Do you see him?" I ask Kit.

She hums in agreement, squinting at the man. "Something's off about him," she notes.

"Yeah, he's not wearing any winter garments." Then I see why. His attention is suddenly captivated by something in the woods, and a deep, primal moan escapes his lips, reverberating through the air and carried away by the Noviska wind among the trees. "A Reborn."

Kit repeats my words, a slight tremble in her voice. "A Reborn."

My friend has always been fearless, never backing down from a challenge or adventure. When we were kids, she was always on the move, often getting into trouble for going too far or being a bit reckless. I can't say how much she's changed over the years because I wasn't here, but I do know something changed in her after she was taken by Marcellus. Every time I try to talk about her time in the Under Realm, she stubbornly maintains that there is nothing to discuss—that's she's fine, and the past is in the past. Yet, it's evident that something still bothers her from the way she quickly shuts down the conversation and the hurt in her voice. I should've considered this back at Goslings when we were devising this plan. As tough as Kit is, I fear she may not be ready to face Marcellus or the Reborns.

A loud *caw* fills the air and Valor lands on one of the other monoliths a few yards from where we hide. Then another crow lands next to her. Now that she's close enough, I can see I was right—it's Serafina.

"You're not supposed to be here," I scold.

"He's still up there," Kit whispers, watching the top of the tower.

"Valor, fly up to that tree," I say, pointing off to my left, "and let us know when it's safe to enter the village."

She releases a *caw*, then launches into the air. Serafina quickly follows. At least they're staying together. That gives me hope they won't get lost.

When the Reborn guard disappears behind the battlement again, Kit pushes my shoulder, urging me to go, but I shake my head. "Valor hasn't given the signal to move yet. We wait until she says it's safe."

"There's no one—" she starts, but stops when a man's voice fills the frigid air.

Every muscle in my body tenses, and I shrink to the base of the monolith. I can't make out his words, but I recognize that voice. It's Marcellus. Not even my sleeping tonic has been able to keep him out of my dreams. The nightmare of him spearing me in my shoulder replays, except the ending is different. Rune doesn't save me. He wins and I lose. This time his grimy, calloused hand reaches my face, and my screams slowly die as he takes control of my will. His victorious laughter is the last thing I hear before startling awake.

The mere thought of losing everything with one swift movement of his hand against my skin leaves me momentarily frozen with fear.

"Hey!" Kit nudges me in the arm. "What does the bird say?"

Forcing myself to shake off the lingering fear from the thoughts of my nightmares, I ask, "What?"

"The birds, Adele! What are they saying?"

"They don't *speak*," I say with a hint of sarcasm. My friend's shoulders sink and she shakes her head at me, then points to my two feathered friends. Glancing up, I see Valor and Serafina waiting, perched wing to wing in the tree above. "It's still not safe to go."

This time when Marcellus speaks, it's eerily closer. "Make sure everything is ready! Tonight, our queen wakes and I want everything perfect!"

"This is a bad idea, Adele." The outside of Kit's arm pushes against mine as she settles in the snow next to me. "We need a plan," she whispers.

My leather gloves are still tucked inside my vest from when we saw the two hooded figures. I reveal my hands from under my cloak, then raise them and say, "If he appears from around the corner and spots us, you run as fast as you can, away from here, into the forest."

Her jaw tenses, and through tight lips, she emphasizes each word when she says, "You. Cannot. Fight. Him. You will lose, and then what am I supposed to do?"

"Thanks for that confidence."

Kit leans in closer, her words barely above a whisper. "We're only here to observe and look for—" When we hear Marcellus speaking again, we both go perfectly silent and still, like rabbits trying to hide from the prowling wolf.

For the next several minutes, we remain still, and I pray to the stars Marcellus can't sense our presence. With my back pressed to the monolith, I keep my attention fixated on Valor. She's all that matters. If she flies, then we make our move…depending on her direction. Out into the forest means run for cover. Toward the tower means all is clear, and we can head into the village.

The cold air chills my unblinking eyes as I silently count the pounding beats of my heart.

One.

Two.

Three.

And then… Valor takes off, and my mind screams to move—to run.

CHAPTER 8

ADELE

We bolt out from behind the monolith and run. I head to the closest house inside the village, kicking up snow with each step. There's no good place nearby to shield me from the lookout guard, so I press on, keeping low while trying to find cover. Three houses in and I spot two large barrels along the stone wall exterior. With haste, I slide to a stop and wedge myself behind them. I notice my breath matching the rhythm of my racing heart, the icy air drying out my throat with every inhale.

Once settled, I take a moment to assess the area. Heavy smoke billows from every chimney, yet there are no signs of villagers. Not a single mark in the snow other than the one well-trodden path leading to the gathering hall.

A chorus of squawks grabs my attention as my two feathered friends soar by, then land on the roof across the way. They shuffle about, causing snow to cascade off the shingles to the ground, directly onto Kit's head. My friend stumbles forward, almost toppling out from her hiding spot behind a two-wheeled wooden cart. At some point, she lost her winter cap. I'm guessing it must've fallen off during our sprint. After brushing her head clean, she glares at the birds perched on the roof. Dark brown curls spring loose from where she's tied her hair, framing her face in disarray.

"Psst," I call softly to her. When she glances my way, I mouth the word *sorry* to her, a playful smile tugging at my lips. A chuckle bubbles up despite my efforts to contain it. I know this isn't the right time, but it feels nice to laugh with someone besides Selene.

Kit waves two fingers in the direction of the hall, and I settle my amusement and focus on our task again. Quickly, I raise a closed fist, telling her to stay. Then, I point to the crows still perched over her. We don't move until Valor moves.

The passing minutes feel like hours, and it isn't until I hear Marcellus's voice that I understand why my feathered friend remains perched. "Tell your master," he commands with authority, "that I request his presence. And he better not come empty-handed this time."

A pair of individuals dressed in dark green cloaks hurry along the path, their hoods serving as blinders, which gives me confidence they didn't take notice of our presence.

Then, when a heavy door slams shut, Valor and Serafina launch into the air toward the tower. I swiftly emerge from my hiding spot and follow the crows. Without hesitation, Kit follows suit and is soon running by my side. It doesn't take long for us to reach the bottom of the front steps of the hall. The overall building size is comparable to five or six houses put together, while the watchtower looms over us. Thankfully, there's no sign of that Reborn patrolling the battlements. Before ascending the stone steps to the front door, Kit tugs at my elbow and waves for me to follow. We slip into the shadows where the stairs meet the exterior wall, then huddle in the secluded corner. Crouching low, we take a moment to strategize our next move.

With a pursed look and a shake of her head, Kit whispers, "I don't have a good feeling about this. We don't know what's on the other side of that door."

She's not wrong, and I silently weigh our options. "We can't leave without knowing what he's up to."

Stabbing her shortsword into the snow, she lets her words spill out in a rush. "This feels like a trap."

"You're right. It could be." My fingers are turning pink from the cold, so I draw out my gloves. I slip them on, then remove my trusty dagger from its sheath, gripping it tight in one hand. "Though, from what we just overheard, I'm guessing Marcellus is focused on getting ready to meet with whoever this 'master' is."

Kit's expression slowly relaxes, and she flexes her free hand while clutching the hilt of her shortsword tighter with her other. "Okay, then." She inhales a deep breath before asking, "Do you think *she's* in there?" A hint of foreboding laces her tone.

"Who? Merigoth?" I shrug, because I don't know if she's here or if she stayed behind and they're using the doorway to travel between the two realms. We'll know more about what's going on in the Under Realm once we've all returned to Bricen. "In and out," I say, reminding Kit that we're going in, finding out what Marcellus is up to, then getting out with no one noticing us. "You ready?" I adjust my grip on my dagger, and the second she nods, I guide the way over to the wide steps leading up to the front door.

Climbing two steps at a time, we race to the top, and I promptly seize the iron ring door handle and pull. With an eerie *creak*, the weathered door, adorned with massive black metal hinges, slowly opens enough for us to slip inside. Before it shuts, a familiar pair cries out as if to say, *Wait for us*. Valor and Serafina fly inside and immediately land on top of a tall cupboard hutch.

Daylight departs the moment I close the door, the latch locking shut. Inside the front room, there's a long and narrow space with a lively fire burning in the fireplace at one end. The glow reaches the opposite end, where a wide archway cuts into the entry room. Back over next to the fireplace is a smaller archway that is significantly darker.

I step closer to a shallow table in front of the hearth and hold a fist up to the birds. Their low chirps grow quiet, and I tell them, "Stay here." They both lower into a nesting position atop the hutch, their black feathers blending in with the shadows.

"Now what?" Kit says, surveying the room.

With my dagger, I point to the smaller stone archway opening closest to the fireplace. "You take a gander at what's in there." I slide the tip through the air and point to the larger corridor. "And I'll see what's down this one."

She doesn't argue and moves around the table, past the fireplace, and down the dark corridor while I cautiously check out the other.

The corridor is twenty paces, opening up into a large meeting room. A murmured conversation from within the main hall is enough for me to know this is as far as I go. It's not worth being seen. Right as I'm about to turn back and look for Kit, I catch sight of a narrow gap in the wall. It's barely noticeable, blending in with the glow of the standing candelabra holding three candles. Shuffling closer, I get a quick look to see what's inside. It's a stairwell, going up. It must lead up to the watchtower.

One foot after another, I retreat into the entry room. When I unexpectedly collide with someone, I swing my arm, dagger in hand, ready to defeat whoever snuck up on me. Thankfully, Kit is alert and redirects my swing with one swift push of my arm. It's a move she's gotten good at whenever we spar on the Green behind Goslings.

After regaining our composure, we stand in silence and listen, hoping our fumble didn't alert anyone to our position. When all is clear, I narrow my gaze and ask, "Well, what did you find?"

"The corridor leads to an empty storage room. There is a spiral stairwell that leads to the lower level. Oh, and there's a door to the outside."

I store that information away in case we need it for later. "I think I found the stairwell to the tower."

With a heavy sigh, Kit smirks and says, "We've come this far. Let's check out the tower."

Nodding, I add, "It's a colossal risk. And if we get caught…" I don't finish. We both know what'll happen if Marcellus gets his hands on us.

Kit takes the lead, then looks over her shoulder and says, "We can't go back without knowing what he's planning."

My gaze shifts past her, down the hall. "No, we can't."

Wings flap from behind us, and I look up at the two birds hiding on top of the cupboard. Valor briefly has her wings spread wide before settling next to Serafina again. Shrugging, I tell Kit, "Valor says it's safe to go." Though, I don't actually know if that's what she meant.

Kit shakes her head and says with a low chuckle, "You're a terrible liar." She slaps me on the shoulder before stalking forward. "Come on, let's get this over with."

Adjusting my proximity allowance has been a process over these past few months. Wearing gloves eases any concerns about accidentally hurting someone, but it doesn't erase them entirely. I trust certain individuals, like Kit, enough to allow physical contact, but only because they understand they should only touch my clothing and not my skin.

As we reach the stairwell, the conversation ahead grows louder. Beneath the layers of winter garb, my heart races at what awaits us up these stairs.

I send a silent prayer to the stars that fate is on our side.

We follow the spiral path up, then stop at the first landing. To our surprise, there's a small balcony overlooking the hall below. Keeping low, we move into the balcony's shallow cove and peer over the edge. On the opposite wall, a few windows let in streams of sunlight that illuminate the room. Below, the stone floor is bare except for a single high-back wood chair set in the center—where Marcellus sits. When he rises, arms spread wide, both Kit and I duck farther behind the stone railing.

"Master Ebenus!" Marcellus's voice resonates up into the open cathedral ceiling, where heavy beams span the width of the meeting hall, and also up, supporting the pitched roof.

Both Kit and I cautiously peer over the stone balcony again. With long strides, a man wearing a deep green garment enters the hall. Two robed figures wearing the same verdant hue follow close behind. His cloak resembles more of a regal vestment than a mere hooded garment like the others, its edges adorned with intricate gold embroidery. Completing his ceremonial ensemble is a long stole that gracefully drapes to the man's knees. He wears a fur cap, and from this angle I can't see his face.

"Marcellus," Master Ebenus greets him, matching my brother's volume, his hands concealed within the bell-style sleeves of his robe. "I said I would return in the morning. Why do you summon me now?"

"Something's come up." Marcellus waves for someone we can't see to approach. The clergy-looking man and his two followers turn in our direction. However, instead of looking up, their eyes are fixed on something below us. I gasp when Evander steps out into the open, then walks over and stands next to Marcellus.

Kit clutches the edge of the balcony. "We can't leave him here," she whispers, her eyes mirroring the dread I feel for our angel friend.

"Right now, our task is purely observational. Afterward, we'll regroup and decide our plan of attack. You heard my aunt… We're not to engage." Marcellus continues to talk to Master Ebenus while Evander stands close by, his expression resembling a cold, unmoving stone. His vacant eyes lack any awareness. Despite the guilt swelling in my core and the wish to save him, I tell Kit, "We stick to the plan."

"Where is the girl?" Marcellus asks, stepping closer while craning his neck to look behind the tall, poised man.

Though this man appears to hold much power among those in green hoods, he steps away from Marcellus, keeping a maintainable distance between them. It appears this Ebenus person is fully aware of Marcellus's touch. With a gutsy tone, he answers, "She's safe."

"I made it extremely clear that you were to bring her to me."

"Yes, you did," Master Ebenus answers. "But we agreed to wait until the morning, and after you provided me with an ample supply of demon blood."

Who is this man, and how does he know about the existence of demons? I wonder.

Kit shares an uneasy look with me.

"Bring me the girl, and I'll give you something better," Marcellus bellows. "Something worth more than a few vials of blood."

There's a long pause before Master Ebenus answers, his drawn-out words exposing his curiosity. "I'm listening."

Marcellus swings out an arm, beckoning Evander to come closer. When he does, Marcellus continues his pitch. "You give me the girl and I'll give you a living angel. One you can do as you please with. Pluck his feathers, drain his blood, study his existence… I don't care. I only want the girl, and I want her now."

Master Ebenus sidesteps so he's standing in front of Evander. "Angel, you say? When you asked for a protection ward against angels, I merely thought you were delusional. I mean, I've heard stories of humans with birdlike wings, but never thought them to be real." The man drags a hand along Evander's reddish-brown feathers.

From our view up on the balcony, it's easy to see Marcellus slyly moving closer, and I fear this situation is going to get violent at any moment. The man in the ornate green cloak isn't paying attention as Marcellus comes up from behind, stalking his next victim. Both Kit and I watch with intensity as Marcellus reaches his hand around the man, grabbing him by the neck from behind. The man's arms immediately drop to his sides, and he slowly turns to face Marcellus.

"You may not touch my angel. What you can do is return to wherever it is your encampment is hiding and bring me the girl." With a dramatic flair, Marcellus abruptly loosens his grasp. When the man doesn't move, he yells, "Go, now!"

Master Ebenus nods, but oddly, his attention wavers when heavy footsteps enter the great hall. The cult leader spins and steps aside, letting the incoming man approach Marcellus. The second I see the man I came to know and hate those eight years at Castle Forge, I sink to the stone ground behind the balcony wall. I take a moment to remind myself that *thing* isn't Alister. The Fayatin man's soul is gone, and his body now belongs to the Reborns.

"I think it's time to go," Kit whispers. "I don't think there's anything else to know. Marcellus and that monstrous Fayatin man are here. Let's get home and devise a rescue plan."

I agree. Even though we don't have any knowledge of Merigoth's whereabouts, who that man in the green cloak is, or what girl Marcellus is after, Kit is right. We need to leave.

We're about to get to our feet when a girl in a green cloak, her hood covering her head, makes her way up the tower stairs. She comes to an abrupt stop when she sees us. "Hey, what are you doing—" is all I let her say before lunging at her, dagger in hand.

CHAPTER 9

RUNE

The silence filling the tunnels of the Idle Tombs only increases my fears that the situation in Noviska is much more dire than we expected. I don't want to be here in the Under Realm any longer than we have to. I wish I could level this mountain and leave it in ruins, just as Merigoth did to Stellara.

I haven't seen or heard a single demon spirit while soaring through the labyrinth of tunnels beneath Merigoth's castle mountain. None of the Reborns either. Typically, their cries and groans are a constant presence, resounding from within and creating an eerie cacophony that fills the air.

I land at the prison entrance and continue on foot to the throne room, where Elijah waits. With my wings tucked against my body, I swathe them in an invisible cloak as I step into the open cavern. I adjust my internal tethers, releasing the extra energy I used to enhance my eyesight while flying through the dark tunnels of the Idle Tombs, returning it to normal levels.

Merigoth's throne room is dimly lit, with only a handful of torches flickering against the walls. There's also an overlying glow of red throughout the space, a result of the magma coursing beneath the stone surface, revealing itself through cracks in the floor and along the walls.

With long strides, I approach Elijah where he sits and waits. He quickly rises, and his gentle smile brightens in his typical optimistic manner. I've missed that smile these past few months. "Did you find anything?" I don't detect any fear or unsettlement in his tone, which surprises me since it wasn't long ago that he was shackled to the throne room wall.

"There's nothing down there. No demon spirits. No Reborns. Even the torch lights are out." His shoulders sag and his head drops. I give his shoulder a quick squeeze, hoping to improve his mood. "Thank you for coming with me. Your company is always nice."

Lifting his gaze, he finds my eyes and stares into them. "It's been too long since you've visited. I didn't want to miss out on spending time with you."

"Even if it's a trip to the Under Realm?"

He shifts his feet and looks up into the high cavern ceiling. "I don't know what you're talking about. This place is great."

"Your humor always makes me smile," I say with a soft chuckle.

He fidgets with something metal in his fingers. Beneath the grime, something glints red along the top of whatever he's holding.

Curious, I ask, "What did you find?"

Holding up the trinket, he rubs one of the red stones clean and says, "It's Adele's hairpin."

I recall the vibrant red stones glinting in the sunlight during our trek to the cave by the river. I also remember wanting to wear something so beautiful in my hair. How naïve my thoughts were, then. I mean, I knew that my mind wasn't fully under my control, but the level of responsibility I had was absolutely nothing compared to what I have now. Elijah continues to use his thumb to wipe the thin layer of charcoal-gray dust off the three red stones. I won't mention how it's most likely remnants of human bones crushed over the years to form Merigoth's throne.

"I think she'd want it," he says, turning the hairpin over in his hand.

While he may consider his find a triumphant result from our visit, I hold a different viewpoint. We have bigger priorities than worrying about lost trinkets. We should be more concerned that there's nothing here. None of the sleeping holes outside the mountain castle are occupied, the caverns inside are devoid of life, and the Idle Tombs have been left empty, which means one of two things. The Reborns and demon spirits have scattered elsewhere beyond the mountain, or Marcellus has regrouped them and hidden them away from me.

Turning away to face the decrepit throne, I simmer down the rising heat of anger brewing in my core. The last thing I want to do is lash out and belittle his positivity. But this is not a win. Not even close.

"Rune," he calls, pocketing the hairpin. His voice is soft, as if he knows not to agitate me. "We haven't had a moment to connect and catch up on things."

"Look, I understand you came along to spend more time together, but honestly, now is not the time," I say over my shoulder.

He comes around and stands in front of me. The dry heat makes his short curls stick out with a slight kink. It's hot, and his shirt is soaked with sweat around the collar and under his arms. Reworking my internal tethers, I listen to his heartbeat. His body is struggling in this realm; I can hear the strain in his breathing and heartbeat and worry he may pass out if we don't get back to Bricen soon. This place isn't meant for humans.

"I think we're done," I tell him, then raise a hand to open a doorway to the Human Realm, but he reaches for me and grabs hold of my fingers. The contact sends shivers along my spine.

He lets go as I lower my arm and asks, "What about the doorway to Noviska? The one Marcellus is using to travel between realms."

"What about it?"

"Well, don't you think we should try to find it? Then you can close it?"

We should, but I'm not sure we have enough time to explore all the tunnels in the Idle Tombs. "We should report back to Sara and open a doorway to Noviska so Adele and Kit aren't waiting in the freezing weather. The best plan of action would be to regroup and think of a new plan to get Evander away from Marcellus."

He nods, but then it shifts into a shake. "I disagree. I mean, I do agree," he says, wiping the beads of sweat from his brow, "but I think we need to learn as much as we can here before leaving. We haven't been here that long. I think we can spare the time to look for that doorway."

Sighing, I challenge, "No, Elijah. There's nothing here, and we'd only be wasting valuable time. We have to get our priorities straight!" I don't mean to be harsh, but like the never-ending list of problems I have to deal with in Stellara, it's all about managing the important issues first.

"Okay, my apologies. I didn't mean to upset—"

"I'm not upset!" I shout, then realize my reaction was too loud. Stars, why am I lashing out at the one person who doesn't deserve it? And the more I think about it, the more I realize he's right. We're going to have to locate that doorway at some point. Calmer, I concede, "All right. I'll look again. Fifteen minutes, then we leave."

As I enter the tunnel, he calls out, "Rune! Wait!" His boots hit the stone behind me. He's trying to keep up, so I slow my pace.

"Please, you need to wait here. Going deeper into the mountain isn't good for you," I say, waving at his weakened state. "I can search the tunnels much faster alone."

"No. I'm coming," he insists. "I don't like sitting alone in this place."

I assumed he had no concerns about returning, but I was wrong. Nodding, I say, "Fine. But we're not staying long. If we don't find anything in fifteen minutes, we're leaving, and I'll come back and search again later."

We start walking, the light fading behind us as darkness consumes our path. I reroute more internal energy to my eyesight, and the tunnels brighten with my special night vision, casting everything around me in a pale blue glow. "Stay close to me," I say, reaching back to take his hand. He doesn't hesitate and holds on firmly. His breathing is growing more ragged, so I distract him with my thoughts. "I don't think the doorway would be outside the mountain. The Reborns might have accidentally discovered it here in the Idle Tombs while digging. There's a specific tunnel Merigoth forbade anyone from entering. It's a few levels below her bedchamber."

When we reach a fork, I point to the right. "That way leads to Merigoth's chamber, and this sloping path to the left will take us to the Idle Tombs."

Still holding my hand, he lets me guide him through the dark tunnel, winding into the depths of the mountain. His breathing becomes erratic, and I'm torn between stopping and returning to Bricen or continuing on a few more minutes to try and find this doorway. After a few minutes, he stops and grabs the front of his tunic and beats it against his chest, trying to waft fresh air beneath the fabric.

"You better not pass out on me," I tell him.

"Don't worry, I won't. I just need to rest for a second."

While we wait for him to catch his breath, I offer him an apology. "Elijah, I can't thank you enough for your friendship, and I'm sorry if I'm being difficult. I've been under a lot of pressure back home, and now this… Well, it's all a bit much."

He pushes himself off the wall and moves closer to me, taking a few shallow breaths before speaking. "You are always welcome to take a break and visit me…and, uh…" He tries to correct himself, his words breathless and faint. "Adele and Kit…and—and everyone else in Bricen." His hand starts to slip from mine, but I hold on tight, not letting go.

A smile spreads, and it feels good. I need more enjoyable moments like this. "I'll try to keep that in mind."

After descending one more level, I stop along the path because I feel it. A tear in the realm—an old one—that draws me in. Leaning toward Elijah, I tell him, "We're close. I feel its power nearby."

"Oh, good," he says. Sweat stains ring the collar of his tunic and under his arms. One would think the deeper you go beneath the mountain the cooler it would be, but not this mountain and not in the Under Realm. The stone surrounding us radiates heat, a reminder of the magma coursing through the mountain like veins beneath the skin.

"We need to hurry," I say, draping one of his arms over my shoulder and letting him lean into me for support. With each step, the energy from the doorway becomes more palpable, signaling that we're nearing our destination.

"Maybe I'll just rest here for a minute," he says. "You go ahead and scope out the doorway and then come find me after." When he tries to slouch against the wall, I immediately raise him up and keep him upright; his body is easy to carry.

"No, I'm not leaving you here," I insist. "We're almost there."

"Okay," he slurs, his head bounces about like an intoxicated human who had one too many at the tavern. I'm about to continue forward when his knees buckle from under him.

"Hey! Careful there." I quickly grab him and lift him upright until he's on both feet. Once he's stable, we proceed forward together, while I carry most of his weight. Rounding a tight bend that spirals downward to another level, we're instantly met with a soft white light. "We found it," I say, then look at Elijah. With his eyes barely open and his breathing ragged, I'm not sure how much longer he'll last before passing out. Gently, I help him rest against the tunnel wall while I gauge the realm doorway. The surface ripples like water along a peaceful lake. It's dark on the other side, which concerns me. Normally, whatever lies beyond is visible. I can't be sure if this passage leads to Noviska or another destination.

Crouching in front of Elijah, I explain, "I'm going to go through and see what's over there. Then I'll come right back and get you."

With a shallow breath, he presses a hand to my face. "You're so pretty." His eyes are half-closed, drowsy-like. "Have I told you that yet? I keep meaning to, but—"

My insides flutter and I want to hear more of the things he keeps meaning to say. I want him to know the things I cannot say out loud and should never say out loud. I hate that we can never be together. Our future is one of friendship and friendship only, no matter the love I hold for him in my heart.

I take his hand in mine and remove it from my cheek, then squeeze it and place it on his chest. "Let's talk more later," I say, offering him a smile to show appreciation for his kind words. "First, I need to make sure this doorway leads to Noviska." Looking him directly in his sleepy eyes, I say, "I'll be right back. Stay here."

He nods with a weary smile. "I'll stay. Maybe take a quick nap."

Slapping his face, just enough to stun him awake, I instruct, "No sleeping! Stay awake!"

He stirs with alertness, sitting up a little higher and adjusting his spot on the rocky floor. "Right, sorry—no sleeping!"

"I'm literally just going to walk through and make sure it's safe before bringing you over, okay?"

He nods, his eyes open fully, staring at me. With a sluggish wave, he urges me to go. "But hurry, because I don't know how long I can stay awake."

I get to my feet, then approach the doorway and step through. Instantly, I'm met with an icy chill in the air. I'm standing in another dark tunnel, one enclosed by rough rock walls. It leads to my right and left. I must be in Noviska, and this must be the doorway Marcellus used to escape the Under Realm.

Time to get Elijah. I turn to face the doorway, where I can see Elijah's on the other side, slumped against the stone wall. Now that we know where the doorway is and leads to, we can relay the information to the others.

I take a step to cross over, except my foot hits a solid surface. Pressing my hands to the surface, I'm met by an impassible barrier. Panic strikes and my pulsing heart feels too small for my chest. Using my fists, I bang desperately on the doorway.

"No!" I cry, and continue to pound my fists against the rippling surface. "No!" I need to get to Elijah! I have to get through!

My thoughts are chaotic, and it's hard to focus on what to do while he's sitting right there, slowly dying. My forehead rests against the doorway while tears collect behind my eyes.

After a few moments, I stand tall, not ready to give up on him, and try again. Praying to the stars, I press both palms to the surface and concentrate. I focus on the energy that helps me open doorways, except I can't feel anything. There's no energy, no internal tethers, nothing. My gaze shifts to the ceiling of the tunnel. I must be beneath one of those insufferable monoliths…or whatever it is blocking our abilities.

Looking at Elijah again, I start to shout and yell for him to wake up. But he doesn't. His eyes are closed, and his body lies still.

CHAPTER 10

ADELE

We both lunge for the girl in the green cloak. Kit goes straight for the girl's mouth, covering it with a hand while forcing her to back away from the open balcony. A small shriek escapes as the girl stumbles in the stairwell, her foot catching on the bottom of her green cloak. Kit steadies her with a firm grip, ensuring she doesn't fall.

Her hood covers most of her head with only a few honey-blonde curls peeking out from the edges, framing her face. Standing before her, I raise my dagger to eye level. Her trembling eyes widen, focused on the sharp steel aimed at her head. "Try to run or scream and you die. Do you understand?"

Her attention shifts from the weapon to me, and she frantically bobs her head in understanding. She tries to speak, but Kit's hand muffles her words. Only after Kit and I exchange a silent glance of approval does she slowly remove her hand from the girl's face.

"I won't scream." She tugs on the edges of her hood, making sure it's in place before asking, "Who are you? And how did you get in here?" Her voice carries both worry and a strong sense of urgency.

"Not here." I point down the spiraling stairs. If we're going to talk, we need a more private spot to do so. Kit nods and grabs the girl's arm, ushering her between us. Once we've reached the narrow corridor, I lead us toward the entry room where the crows wait. From behind us, Marcellus's boisterous voice, filling the great hall, fades.

With haste, we make our way into the storage room. A faint scent of aged wood and damp stone lingers in the crisp air. Kit wasn't wrong about the bare shelves lining the walls, their emptiness echoing the bleakness of this place. It's too cold for spiders, so no cobwebs cling to the corners. At the rear of the room, three large barrels are pulled out, creating the perfect hiding space behind them. The light from the fireplace in the entry room only reaches halfway into the storage room, leaving the rest shrouded in shadow. The only other light comes from the sizable gap beneath the side door that leads outside.

Kit shoves the girl onto the cold stone ground behind the barrels. It's safe to assume that she's not going anywhere, squeezed between the barrels and the wall.

She stammers as she scoots along the floor, backing into the corner. "Is it coin you want? I-I can get you coin or food or—or weapons! You're pillagers, right? Just don't hurt me, please!" She holds the edge of her hood close to her face, as if shielding her eyes will protect her.

I kneel before her, and she peers out from behind her hood. "We have no intentions to harm you, but if you try to scream or run, then any harm that befalls you is of your own doing. All we want is the girl. Whoever Marcellus is after. Give her to us." Marcellus seems to be going out of his way to obtain this girl, and my gut is telling me she's somehow connected to the Under Realm or Merigoth's demon bloodline. Why else would he want her? "Tell us where the girl is. I won't ask again."

A part of me wishes she'd test my patience, because I'm more than happy to find the answers for myself.

Her gaze darts between me and Kit, and something changes in her demeanor. She straightens against the stone wall at the same time the fear that trembled in her eyes moments ago sinks away, replaced with an intense protective stare. "Sayen has endured enough pain for two lifetimes. I'd rather suffer the consequences from your blade than surrender her to you."

"And what do you think will happen when your master hands her over to Marcellus, huh?" I hold my blade in one hand, resting it on my knee. I don't mention how her master no longer has a say in the matter and will bring Sayen to Marcellus. The man lost his free will the second Marcellus's hand touched him.

"Do you know who Marcellus is?"

She stares at us with confused eyes. After a long moment, she says, "He's like all the rest, wanting the power coursing through her veins."

Now this piece of information has my attention.

"Your friend is as good as dead if handed over to Marcellus," Kit seethes from behind me.

The girl's mouth slowly drops open, then with a whimper, she exclaims, "No! He won't kill her. Master Ebenus wouldn't allow it."

"Master Ebenus is gone," I say. "Marcellus has the ability to take control of a person with a single touch." I raise my gloved hand, spreading my fingers wide and then slowly clenching them into a tight fist.

She nervously gulps and repeats, "Master Ebenus is gone, but not dead. Rather, his mind is under this man Marcellus's control?"

Both Kit and I nod.

"And he will do the same to Sayen?" The protective stare she aimed earlier has softened.

"Yes. Marcellus is a dangerous man," I say, drawing out each word, stressing the weight of the situation.

Her gaze lifts to Kit, who confirms, "It's true. One touch and your mind isn't your own any longer. You lose all sense of the world and fall under his control. Take it from me, kid, it's not anything you want to experience."

If I'd known the consequences of his touch when I first arrived at Bricen, I would've done more to protect Kit from Marcellus during their encounter at Goslings. For stars' sake, if I'd known years ago that a banished angel turned demon was kidnapping villagers, sacrificing them to demon spirits, and transforming them into Reborn soldiers for her own army of vengeance, I would've escaped Castle Forge much sooner.

"Will you take us to the girl now?" I ask. We need to hurry before Master Ebenus leaves.

"What will you do with Sayen if I help you?"

"Protect her from Marcellus." I will not lie to her, yet I don't have to tell her the full truth either. We will need her as a bargaining piece if we're to save Evander.

"You won't harm her?"

I shake my head, and to show some good faith, I sheathe my weapon. "And if Sayen is happy here with you, and your master, then—"

"We're not!" she blurts, scrambling to her knees while holding the edge of her hood, and then leans in closer. "We never asked for this life. Neither of us, but especially Sayen. We were bartered for coin and forced to serve the Order."

Kit's boots scuff along the stone. A bitter tone laces her voice when she asks, "Your parents traded you off like livestock?"

"No. Not exactly. We're what you would call 'lost and claimed children.'"

I inhale and hold the air in my lungs, trying not to let the memories of my "lost and claimed" experience resurface. After slowly letting the air slip free, I say, "I'm familiar with the barbaric merchant-line."

"You are?" Kit quietly asks, trying to keep this conversation private.

I say over my shoulder, "It's how I ended up in Fayatin."

"Oh. I'm sorry." She pounds a fist against the wall and grumbles a string of curses. "What kind of people take children and trade them off for coin?"

Now is not the time to ponder the answer to that question. Shoving the memory away about that tragic day eight years ago, I refocus on the unfortunate soul before me. "I'm sorry you and your friend were taken and forced into this life. I know what that's like."

"We're orphans," the girl says, "but a kind family took Sayen in, and she's wanted nothing more than to return to them. To let them know she's not dead."

"And you?" Kit asks. I personally think we should focus on finding Sayen and get back to the field where Rune might be waiting.

"My parents died a few months before I was taken. Sayen found me scrounging for food and let me hide in her family's barn. It's my fault we were taken and sold to the Order. I asked her to—"

I interject with an exasperated sigh, cutting her off mid-sentence. "I really would love to get to know more about you and Sayen, but time is not on our side. We must be going."

A loud *caw* comes from the adjacent room, and both Kit and I take cover, ducking low next to the girl behind the barrels. My friend reacts, immediately covering the girl's mouth again. She tightly clasps one hand over it while holding a dagger at the girl's throat. Cautiously, I peer out from around the side of the barrel, my face pressed against the cold planks. A powerful scent of rotting wood and rust fills my nose.

At first, I think Valor is mistaken, but then I hear it. Boots pounding against stone grow louder, and seconds later, a grumbling Alister storms into the storage room. I quickly look away, squeezing my eyes closed, willing the memory to stay locked away. But it's too late. That moment when he was choking the life out of me resurfaces and replays in my mind. Being that close to his face…seeing the void of evil from within those black eyes…we wouldn't have a chance against him. He's too strong and would snap our necks before anyone could escape.

After a few calming breaths, I open my eyes and find the girl staring back at me from beneath her green hood. Kit's hand still clasped over her mouth. I slowly shake my head and press one gloved finger to my lips, praying she understands the seriousness of what will happen if we get caught.

Thankfully, she nods. Then she narrows her gaze at me, as if she sees the tremble not only in my eyes but in my entire body. I don't peek out from behind the barrel to see him. It's better not to see death coming than to watch it storm toward you. And if he sees us, that's exactly what will happen. Death to all of us.

But his pounding boots fade, and I turn to see the last of him disappear down the stairwell.

I release the air from my lungs, then tell the girl, "We can't stay here. So, you're going to take us to this Sayen girl. Right. Now."

Kit lowers her hand, allowing the girl to speak. Swallowing nervously, she musters up the courage to negotiate. "I'll only agree if you promise to take me along."

Aunt Lauren would kill me right now if she knew we were deviating from the "just going to observe" plan. But then again, if this girl turns out to be the third Shade child, I think she'll overlook our defiance. Plus, taking the thing that Marcellus wants will hopefully buy us more time to plan a proper rescue mission to save Evander.

I make the decision without considering Kit this time. "Fine. You bring us to Sayen, and we'll take you both with us to a safer place."

"I don't know about this, Adele," Kit chimes in.

"Adele? Your name is Adele?" There's a hint of surprise in her tone, which does pique my curiosity. But we don't have time to talk any longer. We need to get to Sayen.

I sheathe my dagger and step out from behind the barrels. "And yours?"

The girl stands and says, "I'm Aleksandra."

"Well, Aleksandra, you promise not to cause problems? And to tell us all about your little cult?"

Aleksandra narrows her eyes and replies, "And you—do you promise no harm will come to Sayen or me?"

"You have my word that neither of you will be harmed." Then I quickly add, "Unless, of course, you force our hand."

"Adele, I'm still not sure—"

"It's fine, Kit. I think we have an understanding," I say, holding Aleksandra's gaze.

There's a brief pause before the girl agrees. "We do." She points to the side door. "We can go out that door. Our camp isn't too far from here."

"I'm assuming Marcellus doesn't know where your camp is?" Kit asks, moving to open the side door.

"He doesn't. Master Ebenus raised a concealment veil over our encampment using a unique method of imbuing, just as he has prevented any angels from entering or using their abilities in the village of Bluskyn."

Kit leads the way out the side door. I whistle for Valor and Serafina, and they come flying out the door and up into the trees. Closing the door, I step out into the deep snow. There's nothing on this side of the meeting hall but forest. We follow Aleksandra toward the line of trees that border the rising mountainside, leaving the village—which now has a name, Bluskyn—behind. I swear to the stars that if this girl is lying or walking us into a trap, it won't be Marcellus or her master that she needs to fear—it'll be me.

We trail behind, letting Aleksandra take the lead. Her vibrant green cloak billows out around her as we race through the woods. She slows to a stop when we reach a large clearing, the edges of her cloak settling against her body. Off to our left, the sun has begun its descent behind the mountainside.

"Is your campsite nearby?" I ask, looking to the sky and spotting a thin trail of smoke, yet unable to locate its source.

"We're here," Aleksandra answers, leaning against a tree to catch her breath. She slaps a hand to the trunk, pointing out a row of symbols carved into the wood.

Kit comes over and traces them with her finger. "They're the same as on the monoliths surrounding the village."

"Almost." As Aleksandra slides her fingers over the line of symbols, she lingers on the last symbol. "This one means 'veil,' or 'conceal.'" She steps away, her boots pushing through the ankle-deep snow, and waves for us to follow.

When she holds out her hands to us, I shake my head. "That's not the best idea. Me touching you."

Her brows pinch, and she cocks her head. More golden-blonde curls pop out from beneath her hood. "Why?"

"Never mind that," Kit cuts in, saving me from having to lie to the girl. Kit moves from my side by the tree over to Aleksandra. "How do we *see* your camp?"

She stretches her arms out from beneath her cloak and gestures for us to take hold of them. "You just need to be in contact with someone in the Order."

"No skin?" I double-check.

"No," she answers with a raised eyebrow.

The girl turns and waits for us. Kit and I exchange cautionary glances before striding over and each resting a hand on Aleksandra's shoulders. Instantly, an enormous circular tent appears in front of us. My gaze trails over the massive canvas structure. It's as big as Goslings.

Kit gasps and then bellows out a laugh. "Whoa! That was amazing!" Kit exclaims, then skips ahead, leaving us where we stand. She comes to an abrupt stop, then turns to us with a scowl, her initial excitement completely gone. "Hey! Where'd it go?"

Aleksandra looks over her shoulder at me. "You let go too soon."

I nod and move in step with her, and we approach Kit. My friend returns her hand to Aleksandra's shoulder, and the tent must reappear because her eyes go wide with awe again. Aleksandra explains, "Once we're past the camp threshold, you can let go. And remember, stay quiet. If anyone sees you, they will attack."

Keeping one gloved hand on Aleksandra's shoulder, I survey the campground. The unguarded entrance suggests that the symbols hiding the area are enough to protect it. Off to our right are a few wooden crates stacked up against the side of the tent between the taut ropes holding up the structure. A thin layer of snow blankets the tops of both the crates and the ropes. This tent isn't like other tents I've seen when traveling with General Onica. This one features a roof that's more like a low dome than the traditional apex peak in the center. The brown canvas material blends in well with the surrounding tree trunks and the overcasting shadow from the mountainside. It's a good strategic location.

Vibrant green banners with decorative gold filigree flank the tent's wide opening, which greets us with a mysterious darkness. The two iron braziers flanking the entrance have blazing fires, yet they don't help reveal what's inside. I squeeze Aleksandra's shoulder and ask, "What can we expect in there?"

Without stopping, she whispers, "Not much. Should be fairly quiet without Master Ebenus around. The only ones inside will be Sayen and the cohorts guarding her." Then, a few paces from the entrance, she halts and points to her right. "Everyone else will be at the novice campsite, fifty paces east, preparing the evening meal. Master Ebenus prefers to dine at sunset."

"Well, he won't be returning to dine," I say and urge her to keep moving with a gentle nudge. She complies and the three of us walk in sync toward the tent's entrance. "Remember, he's not himself and will follow Marcellus's orders to retrieve the girl."

"How many guards?" Kit asks.

"Four."

"That doesn't seem so bad," Kit says under her breath. "We can handle four guards."

Once we're inside, Aleksandra says, "You can step away now."

Instead of snow, the packed dirt along the ground is covered by ornate rugs. Kit circles the inside of the tent, checking the contents of a few large nearby trunks while I take note of the heavy oversized curtains hanging on the tent walls to my left and right. "What's behind the curtains?" I ask, reaching for the fabric to see for myself.

"I wouldn't go behind there!" Aleksandra warns. "That one leads to the master's private space, and this one"—she pivots and gestures to the opposite side of the tent—"is where Sayen and I reside."

Kit closes the lid of the trunk, then steps to the curtain and raises the edge to peer behind it. She releases the fabric and shakes her head to me. We both look at Aleksandra.

"If she's not in there, then they have her out back," she says, moving past us toward the slit in the tent. She pulls one side open and peers out. I come up next to her, careful not to get too close. I'm still wary that this whole rescue might be a trap. "There," she says, pointing between the pine trees, across the enclosed space. "She's been chained to that tree over there."

I find her exactly where Aleksandra says she is, a petite figure crouched on the ground, bound to the tree trunk with black iron chains. But what really catches my attention is how the outdoor space appears to be an entirely different landscape than that of Noviska. The tent walls encircle the ground level, leaving the top open to the blue sky above. That's where the similarities between what's outside and in here end. In here, the springlike temperature and lush grass have my mind spinning, trying to understand how something like this can even exist.

Closing the flap, I ask, "How is that possible? There's no snow."

"Master Ebenus prefers the warmer conditions. Just as he used his skills to imbue our encampment with concealment, he also knows which symbols to combine and that allows him to change the season. By carefully selecting certain magical symbols and infusing the magic into certain objects, he can do many wonderous things."

As Aleksandra describes the outside conditions, Kit decides to sneak a look for herself. When done, she releases the canvas flap and says to me. "There are four guards out there. They're sitting around a small fire about ten paces back from a large wood table that's set for dinner."

"Before we engage with the guards, what exactly is a *cohort*?" I ask.

Aleksandra retrieves a leather string from around her neck. Hanging at the end is a small vial, half the length of my finger. She tugs hard at the string until it snaps free, then holds it out in front of us so we can see the vial better. "A cohort is someone who has proven themselves to the master—and upon doing so, they are bestowed this gift."

Kit takes the vial in her palm while carefully examining the contents of the vial. "What is it?" The thick dark liquid clings to the sides of the glass, moving sluggishly along the surface.

"It's a mystical power that gives those who ingest it temporary unearthly abilities and strength."

I can't help but meet Kit's gaze, as we are most likely both thinking the same thing—demon blood. I'm also happy that for once, my impulsiveness didn't get the best of me, driving me to rush out there and confront the guards. If these cohorts down the contents of one of these vials, then we might be in some serious trouble. Aleksandra drops the vial to the ground and slams the heel of her boot onto it hard. The glass shatters and the dark liquid seeps into the fibers of the rug.

"It's the bane of…Sayen's existence." The girl's eyes tremble and turn glossy, as if she's holding back tears. "We can't leave her here."

"And we won't," Kit says with a surprising amount of compassion. "No one should be locked up against their will."

"Thank you." Aleksandra wipes her eyes, then secures her hood over her head. After she inhales a deep breath, she tells us, "We should hurry. The others will be here soon with dinner for the master, and for this evening's prayer session to the Under Realm."

Kit and I exchange surprised looks before simultaneously calling out to Aleksandra to wait a minute. She's about to sneak out into the center of the tent, but stops and holding the edge of her hood, she hurries over to us. "What is it?"

Brows furrowed, I ask, "Did you just say you have a prayer session in which you *pray*—to the Under Realm?"

CHAPTER 11

There has to be a connection between that realm doorway and this cult. Marcellus's presence in Noviska isn't a coincidence.

"Adele!" Kit shouts, jarring me from my thoughts. She's standing in the tent's entrance, staring at me. "Forget the girl. We need to leave. Now."

I pivot and look at Aleksandra. "Is your master from the Under Realm?"

"You know of the Under Realm?" Her brows pinch closer beneath her green hood.

We don't have time for this. I remove my glove, ready to obtain the answers for myself. But Kit comes up behind me and rests her hand on my arm. "No, Adele. Don't."

"Why not?" I snap back, then quickly add, "She's hiding something, and we need to know exactly what's going on here!" I lean closer, the muscles along my jaw tensing as I whisper, "This is who I am." A weight lifts as the words slip free, but the reprieve is short lived.

"No," she says, her hand dropping from my arm. "That's who you used to be. You are not that person anymore."

And this is exactly what I've feared these past few months. That those closest to me fear my ability—fear me. They wouldn't understand the turmoil of my inner darkness I battle with daily, another good reason they haven't learned about the nights I sneak out and prowl the forest for thieves and miscreants.

I curse under my breath while securing my glove over my hand. Then, I slide my dagger free from its sheath and hold it to Aleksandra's throat. "Tell us. Is your master from the Under Realm?"

But the steel tip doesn't instill the fear I hoped for. Instead, she narrows her brown eyes at me. Her attention dips to my hands, then rises back to my face. The curiosity in her eyes remains as she answers my question, "I don't believe he is." After a long moment, she takes a step backward and lifts the flap of the tent. "Now, can we help Sayen before Master Ebenus shows up and we're outnumbered?"

She's not wrong. Time is running out.

"We can't trust her," Kit says, inching closer to the entrance. A brisk gust of snowy air sweeps into the tent.

I face Kit. "I don't think we have a choice. If we leave now, we won't know why Marcellus wants the girl."

Kit presses the heel of her palm to her forehead, as if needing a moment to evaluate the situation, then eventually gives in, dropping her hand from her face with an exasperated sigh. "I suppose you're right." She draws her shortsword from beneath the tails of her leather coat and returns to my side. Clutched in her other hand is a small knife. Knowing we need every weapon available, I hold up my gloved hand to Kit. Her gaze momentarily flickers to my hand then to the outdoors before her lips purse. After a brief hesitation, she nods, giving me her silent blessing.

Moving closer to the rear opening, I remove my gloves and tuck them under my cloak, into the front of my leather vest. With dagger in hand, I tell Aleksandra, "Lead the way."

As we round the corner, we suddenly find ourselves in the heart of the tent, and it's even more astonishing than the glimpse I caught earlier. I've never seen grass this green and lush, or wildflowers with so many colors. Contained within the inner tent sanctuary are three pine trees. Each tree has branches spanning from the top all the way to the ground, and to our benefit, the trees are perfectly spaced out. Their proximity to one another allows us to see the guards sitting around the fire while also shielding us from their sight.

We discreetly proceed toward the outdoor dining table, our footsteps muffled by the soft grass. Each seat around the long wooden table is arranged with a complete formal place setting. The plates, silverware, spice jars, and platters glisten under the sunbeams, reflecting the polished steel. Something sweet fills the air, and for a second, I believe it to be the wildflowers, but then I see the plate of pastries at the other end, closer to the head of the table. The place setting at the head of the table stands out from the others with its extravagant display of solid gold, creating an atmosphere of luxury and significance.

"Where's Sayen?" I ask, crouching low behind one of the tall dinner chairs.

Aleksandra quietly stalks to the other end of the table, scanning the area before pointing to her friend still shackled to one of the trees.

"Which guard will most likely have the key?" I ask, then pick up one of the gold dinner forks. My fingers seldom have the opportunity to explore and feel outside of the gloves. The combination of the metal's warmth from the sun and its smooth gold surface creates a pleasant feeling that I'll use to remember this moment. Not even General Onica had such lavish dinnerware.

Aleksandra answers my question about which guard will most likely have the key, but I'm distracted by the loud *caws* that suddenly fill the air. I squeeze my eyes shut and clutch the utensil tighter in my hand, wishing Valor and Serafina had stayed put outside of the tent. Their black forms circle over the enchanted grounds before landing in one of the nearby pine trees.

I curse under my breath, as the four guards have also taken notice of the crows.

"Is that a bird?" a broad-shouldered woman asks, her husky voice matching her towering frame. She stands and removes her hood, revealing her brown hair that's tightly pulled back, resembling a horse's tail. She continues to search the branches of the pine tree.

To her right, a slender man gets to his feet and also draws back his green hood, exposing thin, straggly black hair and a pale scalp. He appears much older with age spots framing his face. With a nasally voice, he asks the woman, a hint of annoyance in his tone, "Better question is, how did they find our camp?" The two Hoods across from them remain seated but are also looking up at my feathered friends. I can only hope they know what they're doing flying in here.

"Rhoda," Aleksandra says, pointing across the tabletop to the brawny woman. "She'll have the key hanging either around her neck or from her belt. Watch out for her right hook. She once punched a man so hard he lost most of his front teeth."

I narrow my eyes. "Thanks, I think." I've no plans to lose any teeth today, and time is ticking. Best to get this over with. Maintaining an arm's length between us, I lean closer and tell her, "Just be ready when we throw you the key."

Aleksandra nods and sneaks off to get closer to Sayen. She stays low, using the shadows provided by the setting sun and towering pine trees. Once she's reached her friend and is safe, I shuffle closer to Kit and ask, "Are you ready?"

Kit stops rolling her neck and shoulders and turns her attention to the four Hoods, who are still engrossed with the crows finding their secret camp. "I've never killed anyone," she confesses.

Not the response I was expecting, and my brain abruptly stops strategizing our attack. I'm not sure what reply she's wanting…or needing, because we both know I have.

"Not even when we fought the Fayatin soldiers on the day General Onica invaded Bricen?"

"I made sure to only wound, not kill."

I'm impressed by her ability for restraint during battle. For now, I offer her some honest advice. "Then don't start today. You're one of the best fighters I know, and the smartest. Besides, we only need to retrieve the key and get Sayen out of here. No one needs to die."

Lips pursed, she nods, and we step out from behind the table.

"Excuse me," I politely call out, a smug grin helping me play the role of cocky thief.

The two Hoods standing and staring up into the tree, searching for the crows, turn their gazes on us. The two who are still sitting also shift in their seats to our direction.

"How did you get in here?" the skinny man standing next to Rhoda asks. His voice has a childlike pitch that cracks as he speaks. He narrows his enraged gaze on us, tiny creases pinching in the corners of his small eyes.

"Not sure. We just happened to stumble upon your camp. And lucky we did," I say with a mischievous laugh. Nudging Kit with my elbow, I continue playing the role of thief and say to her, "Looks like we've found ourselves a real treasure with this lot." I hold up the gold fork so the Hoods can see me admiring their belongings. A small chuckle comes from Kit, and I'm glad to see her mood has lightened.

Suddenly, I turn my attention to Rhoda as she drapes her cloak back over her shoulders, revealing a large iron key hanging from her neck. I run my tongue over my teeth and recall Aleksandra's warning about Rhoda's right hook. This lady has the same build as Trevor—the old Trevor—when he was a strapping huntsman, and I have no doubt she can do more damage than merely knocking some teeth out.

The woman's pudgy lips curl up at the corners. "I don't know how you got in here, but you won't be leaving alive."

The two seated Hoods jump to their feet and come at us first. Even though the darkness within is itching to be released, I refrain from revealing my ability. Instead, I patiently wait for the first Hood to reach me. And when he does, he doesn't hesitate to lunge forward and take a swing. I skillfully duck under his arm and deliver a precise stab with the gold fork into his side, just below his armpit. When he screams and tries to remove it, I strike a forceful kick to the side of his knee, causing him to crumple onto the grass. Then, with a swift motion, I slam the pommel of my dagger hard against his temple, knocking him out.

As I straighten, Kit comes and stands next to me. Her attacker is sitting on the ground, scooting away while he clutches his ankle. Blood spurts out from between his fingers, spilling onto the grass. Facing the two remaining Hoods, I whisper to Kit, "I thought you said you didn't want to kill anyone today."

"And I didn't," she says, her gaze also fixated on the two remaining Hoods. She adjusts her grip on the dagger while raising the shortsword in her other hand, then centers her feet into a defensive stance. "He has a choice to continue trying to fight me and bleed out, or to stay put and tend to his severed tendon. The choice to live or die is his own."

The scrawny man tsks at us. "You two are either well-trained thieves or excellent liars." He draws out a leather string necklace from beneath his cloak. The second I see the small vial filled with the dark liquid, I curse to the stars and whisper to Kit, "We can't let him drink tha—" But it's too late. He's uncorked the vial and consumed the contents before I can finish my sentence.

"That's not good," Kit says, worry lacing her voice. "So, now he has powers like you…like Marcellus?"

"I don't know, but I wouldn't let him touch you."

"Right," she says, readying her blades. "I'll cut his hands off before I let him touch me."

"Do whatever you need to do to keep him distracted. I'll get that key." I look to the treetops and search for my feathered companions.

The second I feel the ground shake beneath my feet, my attention shifts from the birds to Rhoda, who's charging straight at me. Kit backs away, giving me room to fight the brute woman, and taunts the slender man to come at her. "You get the key, and I'll handle the creepy-looking Hood!"

Rhoda swings and I duck, then circle to her other side. Heat surfaces in her cheeks, and both nostrils are flaring. She's slow, and I plan to use that to my advantage. Already winded, she struggles to withdraw something from beneath her shirt. It has to be one of those vials. Looking up, I yell, "Serafina!" and within seconds, a flash of black feathers swoops between us.

A piercing scream of pain fills the air as Serafina claws at the woman. Rhoda coughs out a strangled gasp before grabbing the two leather string necklaces from around her neck. Cursing, she scrambles to grab the key clutched in

Serafina's talons. The crow escapes, flying up into the air, still holding on to the key. Rhoda searches her body and then the grass for what I assume is the other necklace—the one with the glass vial. Serafina's loud *caw* causes her to cease her search in time to see the key land in the grass near Aleksandra and Sayen.

"You!" Rhoda seethes, eyeing the two young Hoods with a deep growl. "Aleksandra! Master Ebenus will give you more than a few lashings for your betrayal!"

While my attacker is distracted, I take a quick glance to check on Kit. The creepy old man halts in his advances toward Kit to berate Rhoda. "Finish them, you mindless ogre!" he commands with a shriek, then returns his attention to stalking his prey. Kit patiently waits for him to get closer. She's smart, and even when he yells threats at her—"I'm going to enjoy spilling your blood!"—I know she'll outwit him.

"Let's see you try!" Kit retorts, pointing the tip of her shortsword at his head.

Rhoda releases a battle cry, and swings at me again, and this time I don't dodge her blow. I catch her fist with my hand. The contact briefly stings the center of my palm from her strength, but I recover quickly, knowing she's about to experience a whole other world of pain. In an instant, the towering woman collapses onto her knees, unable to move. Her eyes widen and roll back into her head as my hungry reach slithers through my hand and into her body, seizing her mind. Except, for the second time today, I'm taken aback as I encounter the black void that is her mind, containing nothing more than a heavy oak door. My reach coils around the door handle, twisting and turning and pulling, but nothing happens.

Well, this is unfortunate. Somehow, she's able to block me from accessing her memories.

I may not be able to see her memories, but at least I can keep her in this state. Erecting a prison for her consciousness comes to me as easy as breathing. It isn't until an agonized scream fills my ears that my concentration falters. I recognize the scream. It's Kit. But if I stop to see what's happening, Rhoda will break free. Refocusing my attention on the task at hand, I hurry to finish entrapping Rhoda in her mental prison. It only takes a few more seconds to finish. Then, I release my hand from her fist, and she topples over onto the grass.

Another scream fills my ears, but when I spin to face Kit, I can see it wasn't her who'd screamed. "He's going to kill her," Aleksandra shouts.

Kit's sword and dagger lie in the grass by her feet while she grapples at her throat, struggling to breathe. The scrawny man stands ten paces from her, one hand outstretched in front of him. His bony fingers are clenched, as if squeezing something, yet all I see is air.

"No!" I scream.

Valor also reacts. She swoops down and dives for the man's hand, except before she reaches him, he grabs her with his free hand mid-flight with unnatural speed and accuracy. Whatever was in that vial has given him enhanced— unearthly—abilities. Valor flaps her wings nonstop, desperately trying to escape his hold. Small black feathers cascade to the ground, and I fear she's not going to survive.

As I rush forward to try to save my friends, a stabbing pain pierces my head, causing my vision to blur and my head to pound with agony. I'm unable to walk straight, my feet staggering about. Pressing a hand to my chest, I cry out. Something inside me stretches outward, squeezing between my ribs. I half expect whatever it is to burst free from my body, leaving a gaping hole in its wake. Crashing to my knees, my lungs barely getting any air, I try and make sense of what's happening. Valor's *caws* for help are deafening—the only thing I hear, and I realize the pain in my chest is the tether connecting us. This is what Trevor must've felt that day in Goslings when Barclay was under attack at Castle Forge.

It isn't until the man shrieks, then bellows out a string of curses, that I regain my composure. My vision restores, and the piercing pain within recedes. Slowly, I get to my feet and see Valor is alive, but barely. She's hobbling in the grass, retreating from the man. Kit falls to her hands and knees and greedily inhales the fresh air. Tear tracks line her cheeks.

With a venomous tone, the man seethes, "You are going to regret that!" He rubs his head, and his hand comes away coated with blood. He sneers and turns away from us. His threat isn't meant for me or Kit.

Aleksandra drops the large gold plate and shuffles away. "My apologies," she whimpers, holding both hands up and cowering.

A clump of bloody black hair slips free from his scalp and clings to the front of his green cloak. Bloodshot eyes narrow on Aleksandra. "Oh, I'm going to make sure your death is a slow and painful one." He raises his hand, curling his fingers.

This time it's Aleksandra's throat he's squeezing. She gasps and pulls at the invisible rope strangling her. Struggling to breathe, she pleas, "Nooo, don't…Gregor!"

Inhaling a few deep breaths, still recovering from the effects of Valor's attack, I stagger toward Gregor. "Let her go—"

My words are cut short when the tip of a sword pierces outward from within his chest. Standing behind Gregor, Kit clasps the hilt in her hands as she pushes the blade deeper into his back.

Trembling, she releases the sword, and he falls face-first to the ground. Aleksandra also falls to the ground, gasping and coughing, her green cloak sprawled out around her. One of her hands rubs at her neck while the other holds her hood in place over her head. Her gaze lingers on Gregor's dead body before she looks up at Kit.

Tears stream down Kit's flushed brown skin. Still struggling to catch her breath, she eventually stumbles over and wrenches her blade free. I slowly approach her and stand by her side. We both stare at the blood dripping off the blade and onto the grass. "I had to," she whispers.

She's not wrong, yet an ache pinches my heart. The first one is always the hardest to bear. Hopefully, her spirit won't be affected because this man deserved every bit of pain caused by her blade slicing through his flesh.

Withdrawing my gloves from inside my vest, I slip them back on before moving to her side. Hoping to ease any dread or grief, I say, "He would've killed Aleksandra. In truth, we might have all died at his hand if you hadn't intervened." I reach out and rest one hand on her forearm. This small act of physical contact causes her to abruptly look up at me. There are no pleasantries crossing her face, only recognition. After I lower my arm, she bends down and uses the man's cloak to wipe her blade clean.

I turn to the two young Hoods. Aleksandra gets to her feet, still rubbing her neck, and with a raspy voice thanks Kit before turning to check on Sayen. The girl, the one Marcellus is after, stands there, cradling Valor in her arms.

I approach the girl, who I may have blood ties to, but focus on my injured friend. "You gave me quite the scare there," I say, and gently stroke her feathered head. Barely able to open her beak, she answers with a faint chirp before closing her eyes and resting against Sayen's arm.

"Thank you for looking after her." I lift my gaze and lock eyes with Sayen. I have many questions for her, even though everything I know of her is still only an assumption. But now is neither the time nor the place to be interrogating her.

"We need to go," Kit says with a stern and urgent tone, walking past me.

"Thank you," Aleksandra says, one arm wrapped around Sayen's shoulders. "We owe you our lives." She leads Sayen out of the tent behind Kit.

I glance at the sky. Serafina caws before flying out of the open area and away from the encampment. Taking one last look around, fallen bodies lying in the grass, I withdraw my gloves and slip them on. I have no regrets about leaving Rhoda in her mental prison.

A taunting gift to let my brother know I was here.

CHAPTER 12

RUNE

"Elijah!" I scream as loud as I can, not caring who hears me on this side of the realm doorway. "Wake up!" One fist after another, I pound on the surface that refuses to let me return to my friend. If I don't do something, he's going to die. "Please, Elijah! You need to wake up!"

He bobs his head upright, dazed, eyes blinking as if he's forgotten where he is. Eventually, his gaze finds me. My insides ignite with hope, and I frantically wave for him to come. "I can't cross over!" I yell, but he holds one hand to his ear and shakes his head. He can't hear me.

I continue to wave for him to come to me. With slow movements, he pushes himself off the wall and crawls toward the doorway. When he drops to the ground and lies there, mere inches from the threshold, I gasp, knowing I need to do something. I stare at the doorway, knowing I won't be able to pass through with the will of my power. There's got to be another way—a loophole that allows me to use my gift in a way that the enchantment won't recognize. The answer doesn't come to me. Each second that passes is one second closer to his death.

In a rage, I slam my fist into the stone wall. My skin splits with an agonizing sharp pain, and I clutch my hand against my chest. Normally, a wound like this would heal within minutes, but beneath the monoliths, I'm reduced to the fragility of a human.

Elijah stirs once again, slowly crawling toward the edge of the doorway. He leans against the barrier, unable to cross, and I drop to my knees beside him. Struggling to keep his eyes open, he places one hand flat against the surface of the passage. Ignoring the searing pain, I flex open my hand, causing fresh blood to trickle down my palm. I press my hand against the doorway, lining it up with his.

Our eyes meet, and he slowly nods, as if he doesn't have the strength to speak. The never-ending stream of tears causes my vision to blur. I briefly wipe them with my bloodied hand before returning it to his, which is slowly slipping down the barrier. "No! Hold on, Elijah!"

Then a faint shimmer ripples outward from beneath my palm against the doorway. I shudder at the unexpected sight. On the other side, Elijah's hand has fallen to the ground, and he lies completely passed out, slumped on the stone floor. Drawing my hand back, I examine it to see my blood smeared against my skin. I place my hand to the doorway again, but nothing happens.

I need more blood.

Quickly, I wedge my fingernail inside the wound between my knuckles, causing fresh blood to seep out. When there's a good amount covering my palm, I slam my hand against the barrier. The shimmer returns. I silently pray to the stars while pushing my free hand through, and it works! With a strong surge of determination, I firmly grip Elijah's arm, just above his elbow, pull with everything I've got. Groaning and heaving, I drag him through while keeping my blood-soaked hand on the doorway.

I don't know how or why this is working, but I'm not stopping to question anything until he's safely through.

It's not easy, dragging his limp body through with one hand, but I manage to get him on this side in one piece. After I let my hand drop from the doorway, the shimmering power along the surface fades, and the surface reverts to its original impenetrable window, looking out to the Under Realm.

I crawl over to him, then hover my ear over his mouth. He's not breathing. There's only one way I know to save a human. Ignoring the pain throbbing between my knuckles, I quickly squeeze a few drops of my blood into his open mouth. Carefully, I use my finger to make sure the blood smeared along his lips gets into his mouth.

"Please let this work," I whisper, my gaze searching his face for any signs of life.

After what feels like an eternity, his eyes flutter open and he gasps deeply, the sound sharp and desperate. He exhales puffs of warm breath, each one visible in the chilly air, accompanied by a rapid bout of harsh, rattling coughs that echo down the dark tunnel.

Struggling to sit up and gasping for air, he asks, "Rune, are you okay?"

This has me laughing. "Am I okay?" When he finally sits upright, I lunge forward, wrapping my arms around him. His body is still warm from the Under Realm. I slowly lean away and look him over again. "How about, are you okay?"

"Yeah, fine. I think."

I'm not fully convinced he's recovered, but at least he's alive. "Don't ever scare me like that again, do you understand?"

He clears his throat, the coughing fit dying, and nods. Then, glancing over at the doorway, he says, "Well, at least we found what we were looking for. So, where are we?"

I rock backward and sit on the cold stony ground next to him. "We're in Noviska."

Then, as if a chill runs through him, he shivers while getting to his feet. While asking me about the tunnel we're in, he rubs his hands over his arms. This isn't good. I fear I've put his life in danger yet again, but this time he'll freeze to death. I should've been more adamant about him staying in Bricen.

"What happened to your hand?" He reaches for my bloodied hand, and I don't stop him. His nurturing nature is one reason why I'm so drawn to him.

"It's nothing, really. It looks worse than it is, and it'll heal once we're out of here." I point to the ceiling of the dark tunnel and explain, "We must be beneath the monoliths

Marcellus is using to prevent angels from entering or using their abilities. It also means I don't heal as quickly." There's a long silent moment as he examines my hand before slowly lowering it and letting it go. "It was irresponsible of me to leave you over in the Under Realm. If I'd thought it through, remembering the monoliths and…well, I didn't realize that I wouldn't be able to get back to you. I'm so sorry, Elijah."

"This isn't your fault," he responds, taking a step closer. I want to wrap my arms around him again—to tell him how I would've never survived his death—but those feelings need to remain with me. Besides, he's a good friend and I'm sure that's the extent of how he sees me.

"Hey." His gaze finds mine and forces me to focus my wandering thoughts and give him my full attention. "I consider this a win. We found the doorway, and"—from his pocket, he pulls out the treasure he found in the throne room—"we have Adele's hairpin."

His optimism warms my heart, but it won't get us home or keep him alive. Gooseflesh dots the skin of his neck. With each passing minute, the possibility of his death looms closer—once more. "You're going to need warmer clothes."

He waves a dismissive hand. "I'm fine. It's only a little colder than Bricen's winter season."

"You won't last five minutes when we find our way out of this cave and into the forest."

After getting to his feet, he searches the tunnels in both directions. "Good point. I guess we need to find some extra clothing. Let's go this way," he says, pointing behind him.

"I believe that's a dead end."

He spins on the balls of his feet and redirects his pointer finger in the opposite direction. "Then we go this way."

As we navigate through the labyrinthine tunnels, a surge of optimism eases my tense nerves the moment we turn a corner, stumbling upon a wider passage that seems more inviting. A melodic hum resonates from its depths, hinting at life within. Yet, it's not only the captivating sound that draws my attention. The temperature gradually warms, thawing the chill in my bones with each step. There's also a subtle scent of smoke in the air, suggesting a nearby fire, which is a good sign there are people in the vicinity—people who may have extra clothes we can use to keep Elijah warm. Even I could use the respite from the biting cold now that my state of being is more vulnerable.

We keep a slow and cautious pace. The humming sound becomes clearer and distinct, sounding more like a collective of groans. Throwing an arm out, stopping Elijah along our path, I whisper, "It sounds like Reborns."

We both stand in silence, the darkness pressing in around us. Suddenly, a spike of unease prickles at my skin, my heart racing as if trying to escape my chest. Unable to rework my inner tethers to heighten my hearing or enhance my vision, I find every sound is a lurking danger and every shadow taunts me like a potential threat. Elijah's silence mirrors my own, both of us acutely aware of the lurking presence of the Reborns, their very existence a chilling reminder of the dangers that surround us.

"How many do you think are here?" Elijah asks.

"I don't know, but let's hope not many."

As we continue, the passage narrows, and there's no way we're going to fit side by side. I reach down and slide my hand in his. His skin is icy cold, and I can't tell whether he's shivering or if my touch caused him to shudder. "I'll take the lead," I say, carefully navigating the rough, uneven path beneath my feet.

I catch the faintest hint of light flickering along the edges of the tunnel ahead. Squeezing through another tight gap, I'm glad I shrouded my wings while still in the Under Realm. Otherwise, I might not have fit. It's a slow process, but eventually, I come out on the other side. Letting go of his hand, I cautiously walk the final stretch of the tunnel. With nowhere left to go, I stand on a ledge, overlooking a dark open cavern. The moans of the Reborn fill the air, but I can't see them. All I see are five or six tall rock pillars rising from the darkness, each topped with a giant iron bowl blazing with voracious fire. The space between each fiery pillar tells me the cavern is enormous.

Once Elijah's through the tight gap, he stands by my side at the edge. The collective moans and shuffles of the Reborns echo through the air, intensifying the sense of dread, drowning out my hopeful thoughts. Despite the glow of the fire, it's not enough to see them; its purpose seems to be solely to heat the cavern and prevent the Reborns from freezing.

"How are you holding up?" I ask, keeping my voice low.

"I'd be better if I knew where we were."

"Well, we're definitely beneath that Noviska village." I inch closer to the edge and while holding the wall, I lean outward over the ledge and search the cavern for any signs of another tunnel or entrance, but it's hard to see anything from up here.

Backing up, I tell him, "We can't leave without knowing how many Reborns are down there." I scan the cavern, my gaze landing on the nearest rock pillar. After assessing the distance from our position, I note the pillar's wide, flat surface, offering ample room for someone to move around the ignited iron bowl perched on top. Then, following the rising smoke, I trace its path to where it escapes through a sizable hole in the cavern's ceiling. Every fire has a hole directly above it. Through breaks in the billowing smoke, I glimpse beams of sunlight, which provide enough light for me to see each hole leads into a stone building—like a house. Those must be the villagers' homes with the chimneys Evander and I noticed earlier. The smoke isn't from fireplaces but from the giant brazier-like pillar fires.

A hand presses against my arm, pulling my focus from the cavern. "Hey, let's retrace our steps. There has to be another tunnel leading up and out of here," Elijah urges, gently tugging, but I don't move.

Because I can't. I need to know.

I concentrate on my wings. Whatever magic prevents me from using my abilities or my angel strength and senses, surprisingly doesn't keep me from unveiling my wings. After releasing them, I stretch them as wide as the tunnel area allows me.

"Uh, Rune. What are you doing?"

I try flying but my feet don't leave the ground. *Right, no flying*, I silently tell myself. Looking out at the blazing fire filling the metal bowl, I gauge the distance between here and there. Then, without telling him what I'm planning to do, I sprint forward and launch myself off the ledge with all my strength. It's not the first time I've done this—glided through the air. Evander and I, and a few of our friends back when we were kids, would challenge each other to jump off the north bridge that stretched across the lake, seeing who could glide the farthest. Of course, Evander always won. But I came close to surpassing his distance on more than one occasion.

Elijah's shouts clue the Reborns in to our presence, causing their moans to grow louder. But there's no turning back now. With my wings spread wide, I soar over the cavern and aim for the nearest pillar. It's closer than I expected, and I collide with its jagged side. My fingers scramble for purchase on the rock, and when I find a solid foothold, I haul myself up onto the ledge.

"Are you mad?" Elijah shouts as I roll onto my side. Lying there and catching my breath, I stare up into the flames flickering out from within the iron bowl.

Careful not to slip, I get to my feet and shout across the cavern, "We need to know how many Reborns there are!"

The heat resonating from the fire is enough to scald the skin, so I keep as much distance from it as I can without falling off the edge. When I glance into the bowl, my shoulders dip with disappointment. I hoped for some kindling or branches. That way, I could grab one and toss it over the side, revealing their numbers.

Right. Alternative plan. I search the immediate area. Nothing to burn. Looking down, I see all I have are the clothes I'm wearing. Well, I didn't come over here for nothing. After removing my vest, I set it by my feet and remove my white shirt.

"Rune! What are you doing?" Elijah yells. Looking over my shoulder, I see he's turned away.

"I'm not taking off all my clothes!" I shout, and he slowly faces me again. His modesty and gentlemanly demeanor are just two more reasons I admire him.

With his hands cupped over his mouth, he continues to shout to me, "Then what are you doing? You need your clothes!"

Shifting my focus, I swiftly put on my vest before bundling up the shirt. I make sure most of the fabric catches fire, then toss it over the edge, letting it unravel and fall. The flames cast sufficient light, allowing us to see the cavern in its entirety. There are thousands of Reborns tightly packed together, swaying and shuffling about. The fiery garment lands on a few, igniting their hair, skin, and clothes before nearby Reborns move in to extinguish the danger. With the brief illumination gone, darkness once again consumes their numbers.

I stand there and silently contemplate what we're going to do because there are so many.

"Rune!" Elijah's voice pierces through the cavern, cutting through my thoughts. Glancing over, I see him pointing to his left. Carefully, I step around the iron bowl to get a better view. A flickering glow blooms brighter in a tunnel at ground level. I drop to my stomach, watching intently. At first, one figure emerges, holding a torch. The groans within grow louder until Marcellus commands silence, plunging the cavern into eerie quietude. A few moments later, my dear friend Evander steps out of the shadows, holding a torch. He stands beside Marcellus. His expression is blank as he gazes at the horde. The sight of him makes my heart ache, knowing his life hangs in the balance.

In a commanding voice, Marcellus bellows, "You are Merigoth's Reborns! You owe her everything! And in her absence, you will obey my orders until she's freed!" His words hang in the air, met with a collective moan from the Reborns below. When their enthusiasm subsides, he continues, "Your time to help free our queen is coming. Remain here, and soon you will be free to terrorize and devour our enemies!" The Reborns show their enthusiastic approval by pounding their feet in thunderous applause, making the ground shake and debris cascade from the ceiling. Marcellus turns and walks away, Evander mirroring his commander's movements. Their torchlight becomes dimmer by the second. As they fade into the darkness, I bury my head in my arms, fighting the hopelessness threatening to consume me. It isn't until Elijah's voice cuts through my emotional distress that I pull myself together.

After getting to my feet, I spread my wings once again and launch off the pillar, then soar toward Elijah. My descent comes faster than expected and I fall short, slamming into the stone wall several feet beneath the ledge where Elijah stands. He drops to his stomach and reaches for me. We grapple with each other's hands as I struggle to find my footing. My body sinks and I briefly imagine falling into the horde below, but Elijah grabs my hand and holds tight. Reaching up, I firmly grasp his other hand, and he helps me get up over the ledge.

We lie there on the ground, side by side, staring at the tunnel ceiling, both breathing heavy. "You are mad," he says between breaths. "You could've died!"

"It would've taken a lot to kill me, but yeah—that would not have been fun, fighting off all those Reborns."

Then, with no warning, he rolls over and positions himself on top of me, careful not to put his full weight on me as he takes hold of my face. Our eyes lock for the briefest of moments before his lips press over mine. My heart pounds beneath my leather vest, bursting with a longing I didn't realize I felt. He parts his lips and deepens our kiss. I reach up and over his shoulders, threading my fingers through his short hair. For a moment, the problems of the world vanish, and all I can think about is how I never want this to stop.

But then I recall Evander, and how he may never experience a moment like this with someone who loves him—if we don't save him.

Elijah must sense my distraction for he leans away. Still breathless, he says, "I'm sorry." His gaze meets mine, and all I want is for him to lean down and press his lips to mine again. To make the entire world disappear—his world, my world, every world—and leave us to revel in each other's company, just for a few more minutes. Then we can return to saving our friends.

"You scared me," he says softly, his breath catching in his throat. "I mean, what if you died, I'd never have the chance to kiss you. And by the stars, that's all I've been thinking about these past few months while you've been gone."

His declaration means everything to me because now I know he feels the same as I do about him. I wish I could return the sentiment, but I cannot.

He's human.

I'm an angel.

We can never be together.

Our laws were written to protect our realm and the angels within. I cannot afford to be reckless just because he embodies everything I desire from a partner.

Again, I use what strength I have to keep my tears from falling. "Elijah," I begin, my voice strained as I struggle to find the right words, hoping he can't sense my lie, "I want you to know that I value our friendship, but I don't feel anything more than that."

As soon as he realizes the meaning to my words, he rolls away from me and lies silent on his back. My heart aches for the pain I'm causing him.

With a sigh, he gets to his feet and moves to the ledge. He stares out into the darkness, letting the sounds of the Reborns fill the space between us. I slowly stand as he clears his throat and says, "Right. Again, my apologies." Then, with the best smile he can muster, he walks toward the narrow gap. "We'd better hurry and find a way out of this mountain."

Instead of calling out to him and offering my own apologies, I choose to let the moment pass in silence. I will forever remember the way his mouth pressed against my own. The intensity of his concern for my well-being and the depth of his feelings for me were all conveyed in that single, heated kiss.

A kiss that can never happen again.

CHAPTER 13

RUNE

Ten minutes later, we've discovered a narrow exit from the mountainside out into the forest. I still don't have full control of my ability, so I'm unable to create a doorway. Elijah reaches the opening before me. The sudden rush of cold air forces him to seek protection deeper in the tunnel.

"You weren't kidding. It's freezing out there," he says, teeth chattering. He vigorously rubs his arms.

The frigid weather sends a shiver down my spine as I feel the icy touch on my bare arms, prompting me to release my wings and wrap them over my arms for warmth. I note Elijah's brown skin along his face and neck growing paler by the second. If we stay here too much longer, he's going to die. Shouting over the wind, I suggest, "What if I go to where I can open a doorway, then return with something to keep you warm?"

"Splitting up always ends badly." He looks to the dim outdoors, where dusk has settled. "I can make it."

"No. No, you can't. Your body will go into shock from the freezing temperatures within minutes. Maybe seconds." His lips are losing their rosy color. I need to act quick. "I have an idea. Come here."

He glances over his shoulder, shifting his attention from the cave exit to me, and without protest, he turns and faces me. I open my wings and arch them forward, wrapping them around him. "I don't want to make you feel uncomfortable, especially after—"

"I'm fine," he utters sharply. His eyes look everywhere except at mine. "Just do whatever it is you think will keep us warm."

"Fine. Move in close." He barely moves, and I say, "Closer, and wrap your arms around me." This time, he locks eyes with me, his expression a mixture of skepticism and reluctance. "Elijah. We are friends. I will always be your friend, and I refuse to let you die out here. Now, get over here and wrap your arms around my waist."

He swallows and shuffles even closer, sliding his arms under mine, entwining them beneath my wings. Softly, he asks, "How does this work?"

"I'm not exactly sure," I tell him, trailing my hands over the muscles of his arms and shoulders. "I've only ever heard through stories. Now, don't move and keep quiet. I need to concentrate."

"But you don't have your abilities."

"Do you want to freeze out here?" He shakes his head and closes the space between us. "Then shush and let me concentrate."

With my hands pressing into his back, and my wings enveloping him in their protective embrace, I draw in deep breaths, seeking tranquility in the rhythm of my breathing. Despite everything my mind is screaming about the laws of our land, my heart races relentlessly, betraying the turmoil of my emotions. I probably didn't need him to hold me this tight, but his embrace feels good—gives me hope I won't lose him after rejecting him. Plus, I don't even know if this will work, but I have to try something. Even without my enhanced abilities, I'm still an angel with an abundance of stored energy, three times greater than that of humans.

I concentrate on my breathing. With each exhale, warmth emanates from my body and creates a cozy haven within my wings.

"Whoa. It's working," he says. I feel his body relax against mine. And when his chin rests on my shoulder, his cheek grazing mine, I want nothing more than for his lips to find mine. To know he desires me as much as I do him, even though I know it's forbidden. It's selfish of me to have these thoughts, because in the end it would mean hurting him again.

"This will help keep you warm," I say, caressing the muscles along his spine with my hands, not that I need to, but he doesn't know that. We stand there in silence, letting the heat thaw the chill in our bones. With each passing moment,

I continue to expel more heat from my body. We stay like this until the color has returned to his lips.

Leaning slightly away from him, I say, "I can't be sure how far we'll have to go before I'm able to open a doorway. Are you sure you want to go out there?"

Before he can answer, a holler comes from the woods. We both turn our heads toward the cave entrance. I lower my wings, tucking and concealing them once again, immediately missing his embrace.

"Better?" I ask, and when he nods, I move to the cave entrance and step out into the brisk, fresh air. The sun has disappeared behind the mountain, making it hard to see, but there are definitely people running through the woods. Despite the darkness, I can easily identify the familiar voices that fill the air.

"It's Adele and Kit," I say, turning to Elijah. "It sounds as if they're getting farther from us."

"Here, let me." He gestures for us to swap spots in the cave's narrow opening. He then uses his fingers on one hand to whistle.

Immediately, we hear the voices calling out to each other, then to us. Kit is nearest, and she's shouting for Elijah. He faces me and explains, "It's our special call, for when we're hunting or scoping out danger."

"Clever," I commend.

It isn't long before Kit finds us. I look past her and ask, "Where's Adele?"

Panting, Kit furrows her brows in annoyance when she reaches us, eyeing over her brother. "Where's your coat? You won't survive a minute out here without the proper winter attire!"

"We didn't mean to come without warmer clothing," he says. "We found the doorway between the Under Realm and Noviska, and then ended up getting stuck over here."

Kit shimmies into the cave with us. "We need to hurry. Here," she says and unbuttons her leather jacket.

"That won't fit me," Elijah points out.

"I know. But this will help you." She removes the oversized tunic she's wearing beneath. "I wore two shirts to stay warm."

He doesn't turn down the woven shirt and quickly puts it on. "Thank you."

"How far are we from the clearing?" I ask, glancing out the entrance. The sun has set, but there's still a little light left of the day.

"Five minutes, give or take, that way." She points with one hand, then resumes buttoning up her jacket. "Adele's leading the others. They don't move as fast as we do, so—"

I cut her off. "What others?"

"Two girls. One of them is supposedly valuable to Marcellus." She steps out of the cave and waves for us to follow. "We'll explain once we're all safe, back in Bricen."

I let Elijah go first. Outside, the northern conditions haven't let up and hurl a steady breeze of frigid air straight at us. I call out over the winds to Elijah, "Let me know if you need a moment to rest or get warm!"

"I'm fine, but thank you!" he shouts over his shoulder, keeping pace with his sister. I can't help but wonder if I've permanently wounded our friendship.

Once we reach the open field, he struggles in the higher snow. I test my wings, and I'm able to fly. Not wasting the precious moments we have before he freezes to death, I lunge forward and grab him under his arms and scoop him up into the air. The wind is colder, but we're moving faster. I lower us both to where Adele is waiting with two older girls, green hoods covering their heads.

"Can we get out of here, please?" Adele shouts, the wind picking up, carrying large flakes of snow.

With a flick of my wrist, I open a doorway into Goslings. Elijah, Adele, and Kit hurry through while the two girls in green cloaks stare in awe. "It's perfectly safe," I reassure them. One of them cradles an injured crow. "Quickly, we'll need to get that bird to Lauren."

"Come on!" Adele yells from the edge of the doorway, waving the two girls to hurry.

The one holding the injured crow doesn't move her feet, shaking her head as if she doesn't want to go. The other hooded girl bellows, "Sayen, we can't stay here! Now, let's go!"

The wind is picking up. Eventually, after the one hooded girl practically drags the other girl, they both make their way through the doorway, leaving Noviska behind.

Before I close the passage, Adele calls for her crows. Through the blustery snow, we see a small black figure flying toward us. The crow swoops inside, then lands on the table closest to the fireplace.

After Adele gives me a nod that all is accounted for, I close the doorway. Drifts of snow cover the hardwood floor of the tavern. Turning to the room, I ask, "Everyone okay?" but the question is really meant for Elijah.

Everyone grumbles and catches their breath. Elijah stands by the fireplace. His hands are outstretched, soaking in the heat from the fire burning bright. After all we've discovered, done, and seen, all I care about at this moment is that he's alive.

CHAPTER 14

The fire burns fiercely in the hearth at Goslings. The heat thawing my bones has never felt so good after running through the freezing conditions of Noviska after sunset. I could've sworn my toes had succumbed to frostbite. I can't even imagine what it must've been like for Elijah, traipsing through the snow and bearing the frigid wind without the proper clothing. At least he's alive. I'd hate to end the day with a reckoning on our angel friend.

On the brighter side of things, Mum's nowhere to be seen. I'm praying to the stars she's still unaware of our little trip north. Kit returned from gathering extra blankets moments ago and is passing them out to our two guests and her brother.

While everyone settles in and gets warm, I stare out the front window of Goslings. The sight of the blazing torches lining the road, and the two villagers closing the front gates for the night, fills me with a sense of safety and security. My gaze drifts to the dying embers smoldering in the smithy's forge; the brothers are probably home by now. I'll have to apologize to Nathaniel for missing supper, though if Selene joined them, her company was surely more than enough.

"You should go say something." Kit approaches, then gestures with a hooked thumb to where Aleksandra and Sayen sit. A large woolen blanket drapes over their legs as they huddle together. Both still wear their cloaks, but only Sayen has removed her hood. Elijah sits across from them at the table, talking and finding out more about the Order and their Master Ebenus. Rune stands by the crackling fire, lost in her thoughts. I can only assume she's worried about Evander, still under Marcellus's control.

"Adele," Kit repeats. "You should say something."

Barely turning her way, I ask, "What's to say?"

"She has to be your sister. Why else would Marcellus want her?"

"We don't know that," I counter. Fleeing from the campsite gave me time to consider the fact that I might have jumped to conclusions about her identity. "True, the demon blood from those vials comes from her veins, but that doesn't mean she's one of the three original Shades."

Both Kit and I turn away from Gosling's front window and look our two guests over. Aleksandra whispers something to Sayen. Whatever it is, Sayen appears nervous and afraid, clutching the wool blanket tight. Kit moves from my side and accidentally bumps a nearby chair, which startles the girls. Aleksandra sits tall in the chair, searching for danger.

"No one's going to hurt you here," I say, crossing my arms over my chest. Though, I imagine whatever kind of life she and Aleksandra were forced to live, she'd be right to always be on her guard.

Aleksandra adjusts the blanket over her friend's lap and reiterates my words, "See, we're perfectly safe here."

Slowly, Sayen turns to her friend, offering her a weak smile and an even weaker nod. "Aye, we're far from d-danger." She stutters on that last word, then swallows whatever nervous lump has formed in her throat.

Something's off with these two. The darkness within me stirs, and I know it wants a turn to reach into their minds and find out what they're hiding.

"Can I get either of you some water?" Elijah asks, and when they both nod, he gets up and heads behind the bar along the back wall.

"When can we go home?" Sayen stands from her seat, the blanket slipping off her legs. "If the one with wings can open doorways that easy, then you can surely send me home."

"We don't mean to sound ungrateful," Aleksandra interjects, reaching for Sayen's hand and insisting for her to return to her seat with a gentle tug. "Once Master Ebenus knows we've escaped, he'll search every home in Noviska for our whereabouts. The secrecy of the Order comes first over everything else. No one knows it exists."

Sayen then adds, "To that, she's not lying. He knows of my family. He's threatened them before, were I ever to escape."

Dragging a wooden chair closer to the table, Kit sits and asks, "I thought you said you were 'lost and claimed' children?" The logs in the fireplace crackle as one shifts and falls from its stacked position.

Sayen slowly takes her seat again, readjusting the blanket, and answers with a tremble in her voice, "We are, but…that doesn't mean we didn't have families before we were taken." Her gaze briefly meets Aleksandra's before continuing, "I was an orphan, taken in by a kind family."

My eyes lock with Sayen's bright green eyes. Green—not brown. I take note of her long brown hair cascading over her shoulders. These small details affirm that she is not one of the three original Shades, unless her features resemble more of our father's than Mum's. Marcellus must want her for a different reason.

Kit turns in her seat so her back faces the two girls, and whispers to me, "Are you thinking of sending them home without your mum or Lauren talking to them first? I would advise—"

"Shh." I quickly shut her down. "Let me think."

There's the right thing to do and then there's the thing we need to do. Returning them to their families is the right thing to do, but we need them—as bait—to save Evander. Plus, if Sayen does in fact have demon blood in her veins, I'm not sure letting her out of our sights is wise. We cannot grant her freedom until we assess how much of a threat she poses.

Not wanting to upset or panic the girls, I quietly tell Kit, "They stay until Mum and Lauren talk with them."

Kit dips her head and hums in understanding. "Sara's going to want to know how they got here."

With a depleted sigh, I say, "I know."

I'm about to walk over to Rune, who has been keeping to herself by the fireplace, to ask her opinion when the front door to Goslings swings open. Mum storms in, with Aunt Lauren trailing behind. Without taking her winter coat off, she marches right up to me and looks me over for injuries. Then to Rune, she barks, "What were you thinking? He could've taken her! Then what? Did you even think about what you—"

"Hey!" I interject. "It wasn't her idea. It was ours." I gesture between me and Kit.

Rune slowly walks over. "We needed to do something. I don't know how much time Evander has. Sitting around and doing nothing doesn't help him or us."

Mum purses her lips and brushes a strand of blonde hair that's come loose from her braid behind her ear. "No more secrets. I thought we agreed on this." Now, she's looking at me.

"Yeah, sorry." I didn't mean to lie. Then again, I didn't exactly include her in the plan to observe the Noviska village and Marcellus.

Mum snaps at Rune, "Why didn't you go with them to Noviska?"

"If you recall, Sara, I'm not able to enter the village because of the monoliths. While Adele and Kit assessed the situation with Marcellus, Elijah and I traveled to the Under Realm. We can confirm that the Black Mountain Castle and surrounding area are completely empty. No demon spirits. No Reborns. And no Merigoth."

Lauren rubs at her arms, flour dusting the front of her apron. "Where did they all go?"

"Marcellus has gathered the Reborns in a massive cavern below the village," Elijah explains, handing cups of water to the girls, who sit in silence while Mum scolds us. He then takes his seat. "As far as we could determine, there's only the one tunnel on the main level of the cavern."

Nodding to him, Mum sighs and asks, "How many?"

I'm a little surprised she hasn't taken notice of our two guests yet.

"All of them," Rune answers, shifting her body to face my mum. "There are thousands of them, just shuffling around in the dark."

"That can't be good." Aunt Lauren faces Mum and quietly suggests, "Maybe I should go to Castle Verglas and warn the king and queen."

"Maybe." As Mum turns to pace the room, she finally notices the two girls. She abruptly stops and points to them. "Uh, who are they?"

"Mum… Aunt Lauren…" I swing an arm out toward the girls, pointing more toward the green-eyed girl. "This is Sayen. They are…were…part of a secret cult. Their leader was going to give her over to Marcellus." I pause, then add, "She has demon blood in her veins."

From across the room, Rune strides closer, her gaze filled with fury. "Is she the third Shade?"

Sayen's mouse-like voice asks, "What's a Shade?" but her voice is drowned out by Rune continuing her string of questions about how and why we brought a Shade back without telling her.

Mum moves from the center of the tavern over to the bar counter in the rear, her eyes locked onto the girls.

"We only just returned," I calmly explain. "And we don't know for sure if she's actually the third Shade."

Rune balls her hands at her sides. "How is he doing it?" she demands, aiming her question at the two Hoods. "How is he empowering those monoliths to keep my kind out and block our abilities?"

No one argues with Rune's question. The power we possess—Marcellus, Mum, and I—to access people's minds, manipulate their memories, and influence their free will is not rooted in mystical magic like spells or potions. Dealing with mystical forces, like when that man held Kit's life in his hands from twenty feet away, is uncharted territory for me. How do we confront adversaries who wield forces we can neither see nor touch?

From her seat next to Sayen, Aleksandra explains, "The master imbues, or enchants, physical objects, like the stones outside of the village. He doesn't tell us how or what is needed."

Sayen whispers to her friend, "Tell them about the scroll."

"It's not relevant," Aleksandra dismisses, pushing down the girl's hand tugging at her sleeve.

Then Sayen takes it upon herself to inform everyone by shouting, "He has a scroll that—"

Aleksandra cuts off the girl, taking over and explaining, "We've never actually seen what's on the scroll, but supposedly a long time ago, when the master was still under the Queen of the Under Realm's good grace, he would receive gifts for his loyalty and good deeds. The scroll is the most valuable among these gifts, containing instructions on how to imbue nonliving things with mystical powers. When different symbols are intricately carved into an object, they create unique results."

Kit scoffs, then asks, "So, that's how he's able to keep angels out of an entire village or conceal a giant tent as if it's not there?"

The girls nod in unison. Aleksandra reaches up and adjusts her hood over her head as she continues, "He carries it with him everywhere, so there's no chance of you retrieving it. And like I said, we don't know its contents. There could be ten…or there could be a hundred…symbols."

This "Master Ebenus" character is adding to the difficulties of an already dire situation, becoming quite a thorn in our side. And his connection to Merigoth and the Under Realm remains a mystery. He's not one of the original Shades; that distinction belongs to me, Marcellus, and possibly Sayen. "All this thinking has my brain aching," I say, rubbing my temples. I don't mention how his followers have also taken steps to protect themselves from my reach. That would imply I used my ability while up in Noviska, and I don't need that kind of judgment right now.

Rune shifts her feet and faces me. With an intense look, she questions sharply, "How do you know the girl has demon blood in her veins? Is that why Marcellus was going to trade Evander for *her*? To see if she could wake Merigoth?"

Everyone turns their attention to Sayen. Everyone but Mum, who is staring at the girl's companion. Kit jumps in and explains, "That Ebenus guy had Sayen chained to a tree. She has to be Adele's lost sister; one of the original three Shades. Why else would he secure her from leaving?"

Thinking out loud, I say, "He's using her blood."

"How?" Elijah chimes in, seemingly the only one who heard me, while Aleksandra asks, "Wait, Merigoth is real?"

"She most definitely is," I answer.

With a hint of sarcasm, Kit mutters, "Who did you think you were praying to during your little Under Realm prayer sessions?"

Neither girl reacts to Kit's question. Instead, Aleksandra briefly makes eye contact with Mum before asking me next question. "And this Marcellus person believes Sayen can, what...wake her?"

Pacing the front length of the tavern, I explain, "Yes. Merigoth is the demon queen from the Under Realm, and until recently she had all the angels compelled, with Marcellus's help, to do her bidding. But when Marcellus kidnapped Elijah and Rune"—I gesture to each with a pointed finger—"I went to the Under Realm and faced her, ultimately trapping her in a mental prison."

Both girls sit perfectly still, absorbing every word of my story.

"You are one of the three original Shades," Sayen asks, eyes narrowing at me.

I nod. "And if it's true that you have demon blood running through your veins, then I'm guessing you're also one of the three."

Mum shakes her head. Tears well up in her eyes, causing them to shake and glisten. "I never thought I'd ever see you again. Yet here you are...the daughter I lost." To everyone's surprise, Mum isn't looking at Sayen.

CHAPTER 15

Mum's eyes are glossy as she moves past Elijah and over to the two girls. They both stare up at her, and Mum slowly crouches to their eye level, right in front of Aleksandra. "I named you after my favorite wildflower that blooms in the spring in my childhood village in Noviska. The south side of our home, bathed in sunlight for the longest duration each day, would be covered with the beautiful blooms of the aleksindrias. Their tiny, pale pink petals would curl at the ends, giving them a unique appearance. After you were born, it was the first thing that came to mind when I saw your full head of curls."

"Was that the only thing you noticed about me as a babe—my curls?" Aleksandra narrows her brown eyes, which bear a strong resemblance to Mum's, and inhales a deep breath before saying, "It's been a long time, Mother."

Aunt Lauren, who is standing next to me, gasps in surprise.

I swallow the knot that's formed in my throat as understanding settles. "If you're the third original Shade, then why was Sayen shackled to the tree?"

Sayen's pale skin, affected by the freezing temperatures of the north, has regained a healthy rosy color. Her gaze drifts to her hands, which are fidgeting in her lap.

"I asked her to pretend to be me," Aleksandra explains. "Sayen is my friend, and decoy. Master Ebenus made sure no one, not even those in the Order, knew which one of us possessed the demon blood."

Throwing her hands up and then crossing her arms, Rune releases a frustrated groan. "How is this helping us come up with a plan to save Evander?"

"Rune!" Elijah calls out sharply, his eyes pleading. "Let them have a moment. We haven't forgotten about Evander."

His curtness catches me off guard, and I wonder what happened between them during their trip to the Under Realm that has him reacting so abruptly with her.

Rune turns away, returning to sulking by the fireplace. Elijah shifts in his seat to face Aleksandra. "Go on. Tell us what happened next—after you had Sayen take your place shackled to the tree."

But it's Kit who answers. "That's what you were doing when you found us on the balcony. You'd gone to spy on your master."

Aleksandra nods, her eyes never leaving Mum's.

"What other reason does Master Ebenus have for keeping you away from others?" I ask, curious to know if it's because she has a dangerous ability—one she may not be able to control. If she's a threat to those near her, then I want to know. I will not put the people of this village in harm's way. They've been through enough.

"The master was fearful that individuals aware of my true self would seek to end my life." Aleksandra rests a hand over Sayen's to still her fidgeting fingers. "It's more than just the demon blood coursing in my veins that makes me different."

"What does that mean?" Kit asks before I can.

"This is what she means," Mum softly says. She moves closer and slowly draws Aleksandra's hood off. My jaw drops and Kit mutters something to the stars under her breath. Just above the girl's ears, sticking out from within the large curls of her honey-blonde hair, is a pair of curling black horns. The similarity between Aleksandra's horns and the ones I saw on the head of the Under Realm queen is uncanny.

The sounds of gasps and whispers fill the room, causing Rune to turn away from the fireplace. Her eyes widen in disbelief before narrowing into focused intensity, fixating on Aleksandra. With purposeful steps, Rune closes the distance, her wings materializing and unfurling, their intricate pattern of mottled browns and golds dominating the tavern space.

I quickly step between her and Aleksandra. "No!"

"She's a child of Merigoth!" Rune shouts. "She can't be trusted!"

The tension in the room spikes. Rune is more powerful than anyone here, and I don't want to risk either of us getting hurt.

Needing to ease the tension, I offer her a reasonable middle ground. "You're not wrong. We can't trust her. Yet, we should give her the chance to prove to us that we can."

Rune slowly lowers her wings but does not veil them from sight. "We're treading in dangerous territory…trusting her."

Stepping closer to her, I whisper, "I know. I need you to trust me, right now." Standing tall, I assure everyone, "You have my word that neither she nor Sayen will hurt anyone during their stay in Bricen. They will be under guard throughout their stay."

Though Rune's defensive stance remains unchanged, her feet poised for action, she offers me a tentative nod. "I trust you."

As I pivot to confront Aleksandra, my patience dwindling and my exhaustion taking hold, I ask, "Why did you deceive us?"

She tears her gaze from Mum's and narrows spiteful eyes at me as she says, "If you've lived the life I was forced to endure, you learn to keep your guard up and not trust every seemingly kind person offering to help you escape."

The chair Elijah sits in scrapes along the hardwood as he adjusts his seat. "Was this not the first time you've tried to enlist people to help you get free?" His tone carries more compassion and concern than annoyance or anger.

Sayen's nod gradually changes, her shoulders withering in a somber shrug. "Once they see"—she gestures to Aleksandra's head—"then things usually take a turn for the worse."

"I become a *thing* to gawk at," Aleksandra adds. "Even the kindest person will become a threat, wanting to kill me or worse, trade me like I'm some prized livestock." Her gaze drifts to Rune. "When you opened that magical doorway, giving us our freedom, I knew it was finally over. I owe you my life for saving me and Sayen. Thank you."

Reluctant at first, Rune eventually offers a slight bow of her head and grumbles, "No one deserves to be held against their will. I know that feeling all too well."

Aleksandra looks to Mum again, who hasn't moved from her crouched position in front of her. "All these years, I've waited for this moment. I had a speech planned out about how I would yell and scream and spit at your feet!"

I take a step closer, ready to block her strike if she lashes out.

My muscles relax the second her tears break free, streaming down her cheeks, and she asks Mum, "But now all I want to know is why? Why did you leave me?"

This has Mum on her feet, walking away, crossing the room. She slowly weaves between the tables and chairs in her path until she's standing by Rune at the fireplace. Her gaze locked onto the flickering flames. No one speaks. Everyone waiting to see if she'll actually provide an explanation. It's the part of her story she hesitated to tell us earlier—what occurred *after* her escape from the Under Realm.

She takes a few deep breaths before finally uttering, "I didn't intend to leave you." Relief floods through me, even if she finds it easier to recount the events to the blazing fire rather than the room.

"I'd made a promise to Marcellus that I'd return for him, and the instant I knew I was going to break that promise, my heart broke in two. You'll never know the difficulty I had carrying two babies through the tunnels beneath the mountain. There were no Idle Tombs or carved-out tunnels back then, and I had to manage on my own without Trevor's help. Once I found the passage he'd opened and left for me, I crossed over, returning to a land I hadn't lived in for almost a decade. It was night, and the temperature had dropped to freezing conditions. I didn't know where to go, and..." Her voice fades, as if the memory is too painful.

"What happened next?" I uncross my arms and grip the top of a tavern chair, my anticipation growing as I urge her to finally disclose what happened that day, even if it means dredging up difficult emotions.

She exhales a deep breath and slowly turns away from the fireplace to face her audience. "We would've frozen to death if it weren't for Lukah on his way home. It was a miracle he'd found me wandering the deep snow through the forest, holding two babies."

"Lukah?" I don't recall ever hearing Mum speak of such a man before. Not recently, or when I was a child.

"My husband…and your father," she says, glancing between Aleksandra and me. "At first, I believed it to be a blessing by the stars, him randomly coming upon me in the woods of Noviska. I was such a fool. I like to tell myself that anyone in my situation wouldn't be thinking straight after escaping their captivity."

Old memories resurface from when I escaped Castle Forge, of the poor souls who lost their lives during my escape. Was it survival instincts, or did the darkness within get the better of me?

"Lukah took me and you girls to his cabin. After we got comfortable, he prepared a hot meal for me and warmed up goat's milk for the two of you. We put you both down to sleep, and then he and I talked all night until morning. Seeing him again—alive—was like a dream come true. All those years, Merigoth let me believe he'd willingly chosen to leave our life in the Under Realm, but I knew she was lying. I believed she'd killed him. So, you can imagine my relief to know he was alive and well and reunited with me—his family."

Again, I can relate. I thought I'd lost my mum after the attack on Bricen eight years ago. Every night I would take my tonic and hope for peaceful dreams where I could relive happier days.

"It wasn't until sunrise, after I'd consumed a fresh pot of tea, that my eyes grew weary and I could barely keep them open, and he finally divulged the truth about his orders." Mum takes a deep breath and rubs her forehead, seemingly disappointed in herself for her lack of judgment.

"Orders?" Kit repeats, leaning on the bar counter.

"Yes. Orders. Apparently, Merigoth knew about my plans to escape and made preparations in advance to deal with my insubordination. It appears she'd kept contact with Lukah over the years and enlisted him to guard the doorway Trevor had opened."

"Why would he do that?" Aleksandra asks from her seat across the room. She and Sayen are as entranced by Mum's story as the rest of us.

"I don't know," Mum answers, and by the exhaustion in her expression, I can tell she's telling the truth. "Whatever Merigoth offered him held far greater value than the lives of his wife and children. As I dozed off from whatever he laced into that last cup of tea, he begged for my forgiveness and said even though he'd been ordered to end my life and return the Shade children to her in the Under Realm, he couldn't go through with it."

"But he did something," I point out.

Nodding, she continues, "Whatever Merigoth had given him to bring about a forced sleep, he still used. I lay there, unable to hold myself up. My vision blurred and my words slurred as I begged him not to take our children from me. I remember how his hazy form stood over me, his voice sounding so distant as he promised he wouldn't give me or our children to Merigoth. That he'd hide us all from her for as long as he could."

"But why inebriate you?" It's the first thing Lauren has said since her gasp after Mum revealed Aleksandra's horns. It was surprising to discover that my aunt, known for her immense compassion, never knew what truly led my mum to

Bricen. It is possible that she had some knowledge of Mum's past, but not the complete story.

Silence falls over the room, and I drop my arms from over my chest, hoping there's more to the story. "That's it? He drugged you and you passed out—then what?" I point to our angel friend. "Rune said the angels were taken from the angel realm—"

"Starlight Realm," Rune corrects.

"The Starlight Realm," I repeat with annoyance, because using the proper realm name isn't the point right now. "Merigoth invaded and took the angels over a hundred years ago. The math doesn't add up."

"She's right," Rune agrees. "Stellara's invasion happened after you were gone. And we were there, brainwashed as Merigoth's Shade soldiers for almost a century."

"Timeless sleep," Mum says, then explains, "It's what the girl in the green cloak told me when I finally woke. I don't know who she was or what she meant by a 'timeless sleep,' and I didn't stick around to find out. My thoughts were about finding the girls and getting out of there as fast as I could. It didn't take me long to find your cradles. Except—"

"Except I wasn't in one of those cradles, was I?" Aleksandra finishes.

"No, you weren't."

"And you didn't think to look for me?" Aleksandra stands, the blanket falling from her lap. She moves past Sayen, around the table, out into the middle of the tavern. Her dark horns adorn her head like a daunting crown. "You grabbed her," she seethes, pointing to me, "and left me to grow up without a mother. Do you know what it was like for me? Not only because of these"—her hand shoots up, and she points to her horns—"but because of the harsh conditions and cruelty that come with living in that unforgiving country!"

"I'm sorry!" Tears streak Mum's cheeks, and she steps closer to Aleksandra, only stopping when Aleksandra throws up a hand, leaning away to keep the distance between them.

"You abandoned me and Marcellus. For what? To save yourself?" The sound of Mum's whimpers doesn't discourage Aleksandra from piling on more guilt. "Would you have left Adele behind too, if it meant saving your own skin?"

I can't blame her for being angry. I'd be furious too. What kind of childhood did she have, surviving each day in the ice and snow? Meanwhile, I was here, living a happy life playing with Kit and Elijah, ending each day snuggled up with Mum, listening to her stories with Tato before going to sleep.

With a sniffle, Mum apologizes again. "It was wrong, and you'll never know how much I regret not staying to find out what happened to you."

"You want to know what happened to me?" Aleksandra's voice carries the weight of all her bottled-up pain from over the years. "Well, here. Let me show you!" With a swift motion, she tosses her green cloak over her shoulders, then draws up both sleeves to reveal giant circular scars and welts covering both arms. "This is what happened to the daughter you left behind!"

Mum's eyes go wide, and she clasps a hand over her mouth.

I'm well familiar with the signs of torture, even if the pain I doled out was never physical.

Aleksandra's tears continue to trickle over her faintly freckled cheeks. "Merigoth banished *Lukah*"—she spits his name as if she's bitten into something rotten—"from receiving any more of her blessings or gifts from the Under Realm. If our father hadn't gained popularity among a small group of followers by sharing his diluted blood, granting them unnatural strength and speed, I imagine my life could've been different—perhaps even normal."

"He did what?" A look of horror and shock appears on Mum's face.

"Wait," Kit interjects, waving a hand as she pushes off the bar counter and cuts into the conversation. "Are you saying your father shared some of his blood with humans?"

"Diluted in water, yes," Aleksandra confirms while rolling down her sleeves.

"And drinking his blood," Elijah asks, a look of disgust crossing his face, "gives them powers?"

Aleksandra shakes her head. "No, not powers. It just enhances their physical bodies—making them stronger and faster."

"Lukah is Master Ebenus," I conclude out loud. "I was right—he's using your blood."

Aleksandra faces me, still glaring at me with a look of dislike, but nods. "Once he realized that my blood not only gives his followers supernatural strength and speed, but also mystical abilities, well, you can see how valuable I became to him."

Gesturing to Aleksandra's arms, which are now covered by her cloak again, Kit asks, "So, it's your blood inside the vials? That man up there who…" She pauses, muscles tensing along her jaw. "He was able to strangle me with his mind because he drank a few drops of your blood?"

"Diluted blood," Aleksandra corrects again. "And yes."

Rune tucks a short brown strand of hair behind one ear and asks, "And you're sure they're not working together— Marcellus and this Master Ebenus character?"

A chair scratches against hardwood as Sayen stands. "If you will not allow us to leave, then I'd like to sleep." She clears her throat and adds, "Aleksandra can stay and answer your questions, but I'd like to rest."

Aunt Lauren comes over to the girl and wraps an arm around her. "Of course, dear. And I imagine you're hungry too. We can get you some warm food."

It doesn't go unnoticed how Aleksandra watches with intensity as Sayen hurries closer to the front door. "One moment!" she shouts, then turns to Mum. "I know you believe we are family, but we are not." Her gaze drifts to me. "We may share the same dark blood, but I don't share your interests, especially when it comes to saving one of them." Now, her gaze lingers on Rune. "You may have saved us today, but you are the seed that has sowed my pain throughout my entire life."

She then moves to Sayen's side, looping her arm with the girl's. "You may now show us to where we can rest," Aleksandra tells my aunt.

My aunt doesn't look to my mum for approval, and swiftly opens the front door of Goslings, ushering them both outside. Once they're gone, everyone starts talking at once. Everyone except for Mum.

"It's clear she's not going to help us rescue Evander," Rune says, pointing to the door. "So, now what do we do?"

Taking a seat next to her brother, Kit reminds Rune, "We bought your angel friend more time by taking what Marcellus wants. So, how about you focus on that? Plus, there's a lot more going on than just rescuing Evander."

"This is all too much." Mum sighs, lowering herself into a nearby chair. "Kit was right. We've underestimated the magnitude of this problem."

Elijah leans both elbows on the table and says, "Our task is twofold—saving Evander and ending this cult that thrives on hurting Aleksandra."

I pull up a chair and sit at the table with the others. "And don't forget about the massive horde of Reborns waiting to be unleashed to terrorize Noviska."

There's a collective sigh, and it's Mum who suggests we all call it a night and get some much-needed rest.

After agreeing, I say, "I should check in on Selene, too."

"Good night," Mum quietly says without making eye contact with any of us. She makes her way toward the back door and leaves, closing the door behind her.

"I'm going to do a quick perimeter walk outside of the wall before heading to bed," Kit says, then yawns as she meanders out the front door.

"You're sure this is a good idea, waiting until morning?" Rune crosses her arms over her leather vest, pursing her lips.

Probably not, but what other options do we have? I don't tell her that because I'm too tired to argue or fight with her. Instead, I tell her, "Marcellus has no way to wake Merigoth now that we have Aleksandra here. Evander is an asset to Marcellus, for intimidation and as someone who can carry out his bidding. I think for now, not much will change over the next day or two."

Lowering her arms to her sides, Rune nods. "Yes, I believe you are right. Though, I imagine Marcellus won't hesitate to use Evander to make a point if needed."

"We won't let it get that far," Elijah interjects. "He's your friend, which makes him our friend."

Rune offers him a small smile. Then she says, "Well, if we've got time to spare, I should return to Stellara and check on the angels there. Plus, I believe there's a journal in my mother's study that might offer more insight into Merigoth's past. The symbols on that scroll Aleksandra and Sayen mentioned had to have come from somewhere, and I think her journal might give us some answers. I'll return first thing in the morning with the journal and to discuss our next plan of action."

"Can I come with you?" Elijah blurts out, his voice trailing off as if he already knows the answer will be *no*. "Just for the night? I mean, I'd love to see where you live."

"I already explained to you," she says, frustration clear in her voice, "that only angels are allowed in the Starlight Realm."

I'm not completely oblivious to matters of the heart. I've noticed Elijah's strong attachment to Rune. She's all he's talked about these past few months. It's absurd how tangled emotions can make things. They distract your mind, cloud your judgment, and sometimes lead to disastrous consequences. I can't help but worry about my friend's unwavering devotion to Rune, and I hope he doesn't ever put himself in harm's way because of it.

A yawn comes over me, and I can't help but stretch my arms. It's been a long day, and I'm ready to climb into bed. Looking to Rune, I mutter, "Just let him go with you."

"It's forbidden!" she counters, looking scandalized.

"It's fine. I don't have to go," he says, turning from us.

Crossing my arms over my chest, I glare at Rune. She understands my unspoken gesture and responds with an eye roll. "Fine! But only because it's nighttime and everyone's sleeping. And only if you promise to do as I say and keep out of sight if we do come across another angel."

Elijah instantly perks up, his smile spreading from ear to ear. "I promise." Then he turns to me, scrambling to pull something out of his pocket. "Here, Adele. I forgot to give this to you." He holds out Selene's hairpin.

I rub a gloved finger over the three ruby stones, ignoring the dirt that's accumulated in the metal settings. My heart swells with joy that my borrowed item has found its way back to me. "Thank you." I've never been this emotional about something before, and I'm not sure why. Selene is here with me in Bricen, safe and happy. What is it about such a tiny trinket that stirs up so many emotions?

"If you're coming, then let's go." Rune opens a doorway with a flick of her wrist, and I shout, "Enjoy your time in the Starlight Realm!" as they walk through.

CHAPTER 16

I cross the Green and make my way toward the cottage I share with Selene. Three houses down from my destination, Aunt Lauren steps out from the vacant cottage, then closes the door behind her. She pulls up the hood of her cloak and holds the front closed while walking toward me. The chill in the night air is nothing after spending a few hours up in Noviska, for me at least. I wait until she's close enough to ask, "Why do you wear all this?" With a sweeping gesture of my hand, I point toward her winter garb.

"I've been living among humans for so long it's a habit now." She lowers her hood and glances over her shoulder. "They're settled in for now. I'll keep watch over them tonight."

"All night?"

She nods. "I don't require as much sleep as humans, and your mum has graciously agreed to wake up early and take over."

That makes sense, angels not needing as much sleep as everyone else. As a child, I remember Aunt Lauren staying up late into the night and then waking up before dawn to bake bread for the village. No matter the time of day, she was always full of energy, her smile lighting up the room.

"Thank you. It means a lot to have you watching over them."

"I'm more than happy to help," she says, gently grazing her hand over my shoulder as we cross paths. Her touch has always brought a unique sense of comfort, never feeling intrusive. Even on that first day when I returned to Bricen after a long absence, her embrace took me by surprise, yet it felt familiar and stable. Her presence, not just for me but for everyone she interacts with, exemplifies the value of caring for others. It's her unwavering selflessness that serves as a reminder that simpler, happier times are still within reach.

At the front door of my cottage, I pause, my hand hovering over the iron latch. Then, before my aunt gets too far, I call to her and ask, "Do you think I should check in with Mum?"

Soft moonlight shines through a break in the clouds, outlining the right side of my aunt's body, her dark brown braid trailing over one shoulder. She holds her cloak closed, despite knowing she's perfectly comfortable without it, shielding herself from the winter breeze.

"You get some rest. I'll talk to Sara and make sure she's coping. I have a feeling we're going to have a big day tomorrow, rescuing Evander and getting those two home, and we'll need you at your best." She turns and starts up the small hill toward her cottage. Then, she shouts over her shoulder to me, "Oh, and Valor is recovering well. She's resting, but come by in the morning and check on her."

"Thank you!" I shout up to her. I would ask her more about Valor's condition, but the phrase *getting those two home* keeps repeating in my head. A silhouette walking across the Green catches my attention, and I pivot on the porch, the wood creaking softly beneath my shifting weight. As the figure steps out of the shadows, I can see it's Kit. Moonlight bathes her figure in a soft, silvery radiance.

"Your brother went to the Starlight Realm with Rune," I say.

"Is that right?" She stops on the gravel path running the length of the row of homes. "Well, good for him." Her warm breath comes out in wispy puffs.

Her voice gently stirs the stillness of the calm night as she tells me, "The perimeter is clear and the front gate is secure. I'm going to get some shut-eye, so I'll see you come first light." With purposeful strides, she approaches the front door to her home, next to mine, and quickly disappears inside. Tonight, she'll have the place all to herself since Elijah is with Rune.

When Kit's door shuts, I open my own door and make my way inside. An ease settles within my mind at the knowledge that Aunt Lauren will be keeping watch over our guests throughout the night.

Inside, Selene stands by the hearth, already in her nightgown. She leans closer to the fire, a blanket wrapped over her shoulders, and adds a log to the lively flames. Removing my cloak and hanging it up, I say with a bit of humor, "Wow, look at you…tending to the fire."

"Yes, well… I burned my finger earlier." She stands and rubs the side of her pointer finger.

"Nothing wrong with acquiring a few minor injuries while gaining new skills."

She doesn't seem amused. Her expression turns concentrated, as if she has a secret to confess. I remove one boot and set it by the door, while Selene picks up an iron candleholder and carries it over to her bed, then places it on the small wooden table between our beds. While I'm removing my second boot, she slides into bed, draping her long black hair over one shoulder. She slowly combs her fingers through her hair before braiding it. Then, as she ties the end off, she tells me, "I know you have a lot going on, but I received a letter from my uncle while you were in Noviska."

"What does he want?" I ask, setting my boot next to the other.

She smooths out the bumps along the top of the quilt. "He's arranged a union of marriage for me and one of the Fayatin lords' eldest sons."

My hands freeze over the strings of my leather vest. "Without consulting you first?"

"Not exactly." She doesn't look at me. Instead, her gaze lingers on the long piece of string that's come loose from the quilt. Winding it around her finger, she continues, "Uncle says it's more than we could've hoped for."

Unsure of how to respond, I stay quiet and resume unlacing my vest. The second it's off, I toss it over the back of the chair. "You didn't even consult me before making a final decision."

She shakes her head, unable to hide her guilty expression. "I knew you'd be upset."

I'm not sure if it's the well-tended fire or the conversation that has me sweating, but all of a sudden, I feel the need to step outside and cool off. But I don't. "And the lord's son has agreed to this marriage?"

Bobbing her head, she says, "The Stolkin family is a very reputable—"

I cut her off, my voice pitched higher than I intended. "Vincent? That pompous, greedy—"

This time, Selene stops me by shouting, "Victor. His name is Victor. For stars' sake—when will you learn people's names?" I open my mouth to apologize, but she cuts me off. "I wasn't finished. You will not address my future husband in such a manner." She's no longer cowering and fumbling with her quilt, but sitting upright in her bed. "He's a respectable man, and his father, Lord Stolkin, has raised him proper. He plans to unite the regions and the lords—"

This noble-blood attitude has my insides boiling. "Oh, and I suppose he plans to become the new regent of this united Fayatin," I say with a scoff. Selene's safety has always been a priority. Noble status or not. And there's no way I can protect her over in Fayatin, not when I'm needed here to help save Evander, defeat Marcellus and his Reborn horde, and put an end to the Order.

I stalk away, disappearing around the corner to change out of my shirt and into my long nightgown. Then, after removing my pants, I pull out the hairpin Elijah returned to me and drape the pants over the chair. I set the hairpin on the long table in front of the fireplace, in plain sight for Selene to see. Before heading to my bed, I find my sleeping tonic in the cupboard and take a swig. The lemon extract overpowers the other ingredients, but I don't flinch at the tartness. Instead, the sour taste aids in calming my mind and body, reassuring me that the haunting nightmares will stay at bay through the night.

As I reemerge into her line of sight, she says sympathetically, "Adele, I'm his charge. My uncle is only acting in the best interest—"

"Do not say you…because he is most definitely not thinking of what's best for you." Lowing myself onto my bed, sliding my feet beneath the quilt, I blurt, "I've been the one protecting you and helping you do what you wanted to do—be free from that life."

"Do you even know how killing General Onica has affected everyone over there?" Selene asks. "My uncle writes that the country is in chaos. The regional lords are squabbling over who should be regent, who will settle their broken trade contracts, and who should claim rights to the iron ore mines in the Crescent Mountains. Things aren't going well, and Uncle is trying to maintain order and control."

I will admit, of all the lords I met during my time at Castle Forge, Lord Caldridge was the only man who considered others before himself. He was never in it for the power or the superiority. It's possible that his goal is to improve the dire conditions that General Onica caused in Fayatin.

I lean across the small side table and blow out the candle. A soft glow from the fireplace reaches our beds, barely grazing our faces. But I can see Selene staring over at me. "Adele, I thought I wanted this life. The freedom to go wherever I wanted, to talk to anyone regardless of their status, or to fall in love with whomever I please. But we both know my upbringing has me struggling to adjust to this life."

"Don't you like Bricen?"

"I love this village!" she exclaims, and I can see her smile. Her attention shifts from me to the fire. "Is that my hairpin?"

"It is. Elijah found it when he and Rune went to the Under Realm."

She stares at it for another long moment before lying back, resting her head on her pillow. "Good. Now, I don't have to give you another one before I leave tomorrow."

Fully alert, I sit up in bed and stare at her from across the alcove. "You're leaving tomorrow?"

She makes a *mmhm* sound. "I already told Agnes to pack and be ready."

"Just like that? And what happens when you get to Castle Forge? Your uncle ships you off to get married to *Victor* Stolkin?" I emphasize his name so she knows I know it.

A laugh escapes before she rolls onto her side, propping her head up with her elbow, she asks, "Oh, Adele. Be honest with me. Besides believing Victor's a pompous, greedy, entitled man…do you have any other objections?"

"Honestly, I don't know him personally. I've only ever seen him in passing, and it was long ago when he was still…young."

"Adele," Selene playfully says, "he's still young. We all are! But I do believe he can provide a good life for me."

"Well, his family does reside in the second wealthiest region in Fayatin. His father, Lord Stolkin, oversees the daily activities at Port Helve."

"Aye"—she smiles—"and now you see what I mean by 'a good life' and why I've accepted the offer. They are a wealthy family, and they live very comfortable lives."

We both know I cannot accompany her to Fayatin. Not with Evander's rescue mission and Aleksandra being here, but I offer anyway. "Would you like me to come with you?"

Still propped up on one elbow, she tells me, "You know I always need you nearby, but no. That won't be necessary. You're needed here more than I need your company on my journey to Fayatin. And I promise to send word the moment we reach Castle Forge."

"I'll do you one better. I'll have Barclay accompany you. Then he can fly home once you're safe at Castle Forge."

A tinge of excitement hikes her voice as she says, "Oh, I'd like that very much! I've grown quite fond of the crows' company."

My eyes drift closed, and then I recall the supper I missed. "Selene?"

She mumbles a weary, "*Mmh.*"

"How was supper with the smithy brothers?"

Softly she says, "Nathaniel was sad you couldn't make it. He'd even brought you a gift."

"A gift? What was it?"

She yawns, then rolls away from me. "He wouldn't show me, and only said he'd find you tomorrow. He likes you, and you should pay him more attention. Now, I will be leaving before sunrise and need to sleep. I will miss you, dear friend, but I insist you come to the wedding dated for a fortnight."

"A fortnight! That's so soon!"

"Yes, and now you understand why I must head out as soon as possible."

"You're not even going to say goodbye to my mum or Lauren…or Kit?"

Selene rolls over in her bed. "I will, knowing they'll be up. But you…I will let you sleep. And when you wake, you will know I've left with a happy heart, excited to start my new life with my new husband."

"I will miss you," I say.

The darkness fills our cottage, and for a moment I believe her to have fallen asleep, but then she whispers, "And I you."

I lie there, thinking about all the romance going on. Elijah and Rune…and now, Selene and Victor Stolkin, for stars' sake. What am I missing out on that everyone is so eager to claim? Lifting my hands and looking over my gloves, I can't help but wonder if one day I'll be able to hold someone's hand, caress their cheek, or run my hand along their skin without my reach overpowering me and seizing their mind.

I need to figure out how to control the darkness within so I too can one day experience love.

CHAPTER 17

This was a bad idea—bringing Elijah. If anyone sees him, there'll be serious consequences. They might remove me from leadership, or worse, banish me from Stellara. What was I thinking, allowing him to come?

I increase my pace, eager to get inside and off the dark streets. Elijah briefly lags behind before catching up. Instead of focusing on our path, his gaze drifts to the elaborate stone buildings around us. It's his first time in a city, and I can't blame him for being curious. The Human Realm's progress in structural development is decades, possibly centuries, behind. The Kingdom of Verglas in Noviska is the closest they have to a metropolis.

At least it's nighttime, with only a sparse glow from tonight's half-moon. The shadows stretching across the street from the tall buildings help conceal my friend's presence. If we were traipsing through the southeast sector, where power's restored, chances are we'd be easily detected.

A few paces away, Elijah's voice carries, filled with awe as he marvels at another sight we've passed. "This place is unbelievable."

I come to an abrupt halt, causing the pebbles from the broken pavers to scatter and roll beneath my boots. Across the street, he peers inside a shop's large picture window, his forehead pressed against the glass surface. "Hey!" I call out to him, hoping my tone comes across as urgent, because it is. "We don't have time for sightseeing!" When he doesn't budge, I shout, "It's a tailor's shop! And the one next to it was a shoe store, and the one next to that was a bakery! Now, can we go?"

He pushes off and takes one last look before returning to my side.

"You've replaced the outdoor market and given the tradespeople their own building. I'm curious, do they live in these shops, too?"

"Some do," I say, stepping over a fallen streetlamp. The streetlamps in this part of the city don't work, their energy yet to be restored. As we weave through the rubble and overgrown weeds, recognition hits me like a slap to the face. Stellara will never be what it once was. This place is nothing more than a page for our history books—a horrific moment frozen in time. How could I have been so naïve as to think twenty-eight angels would be enough to rebuild the city to its former glory?

"Rune? Are you okay?" Elijah asks, waving a hand in front of my face.

I stand in the middle of a patch of tall grass that's sprouted in the middle of the road. I didn't realize I stopped walking. Blinking, I swallow the dread that's lodged itself in my throat. With each passing second, my heart pounds faster and faster, its thumping reverberating beneath my ribs. In my mind, I confess, *Stellara is gone. We can't revive it. I've failed everyone.*

When his warm hand slips into mine, I jerk back. "Don't touch me!"

"I'm sorry," he says.

I long for him to find a connection between us—to save me from sinking deeper into my own internal turmoil. Unavoidable despair, along with the weight of failure, crushing me. I know he's my lifeline, the one who can save me, yet my traditions and my mother's disapproving gaze from the stars above keep me from letting him in.

Taking several deep breaths, I force the rising emotions, threatening to explode, down into the pit of my mind. Focusing on the task at hand, I push aside my tumultuous thoughts, channeling all my energy into why we're here, sneaking around in the dark. "We need to find Loralai's journal," I blurt, then walk past him, stumbling along the debris-filled road. With each step, the weight of despair and failure lessens, replaced by a sense of determination.

These streets and buildings are etched into my memory, despite the decades of neglect, overgrowth, and decay that shroud them. Rounding the corner, making sure Elijah knows we've veered off the main road, I lead us toward the archives building. My mother's private work chambers, which occupied the entire top floor, made this place feel like a second home to me.

After several minutes, he breaks the silence. "It's warmer here than in Harvesgrove."

Quickly climbing the stone steps to the front doors of the archives building, I tell him, "That's because it's the end of our thawing season, right before the blooming season." The blooming season was always my favorite time of the year. *Was* being the key word, since now I rarely have time to enjoy anything.

I push open one of the wide double doors, and it drags along the frame before jamming to a stop. The overhang of the entryway makes it difficult to see where it's catching. Closing my eyes, I rework my internal tethers that control the output for my heightened senses and redirect more energy into my vision. As I open my lids, the world in front of me grows brighter, revealing how the top edge of the door catches on the shattered frame and stonework above it.

Blinking several times, I readjust the energy tethers to their original flow and then say to Elijah, "I'm going to have to break open the door." He steps back, giving me room, and I shove one shoulder into the front of the solid wood door. Wood splinters and breaks away at the hinges. A loud *crack* and the top of the frame snaps too, raining down a thick cloud of debris and dust.

Once everything has settled, Elijah shouts from outside, "Are you okay in there?"

"Yes!" I lower the broken door onto the rug and call to him, "Watch your step!"

There's little moonlight coming in through the dingy windows of the old meeting room. The inside of the archives building, while showing fewer signs of age than the exterior, still bears the marks of abandonment, mostly in the form of a thick layer of dust and grime. We continue around the massive round table in the center of the room.

"The staircase will be at the back. Stay close," I tell him at the same time he bumps into something. Dragging my fingers across the tabletop, I recall my childhood days when Evander and I would hide under it, eavesdropping on our mothers and the other two Star leaders, while they met with city representatives. We couldn't wait to grow up and be the leading Stars, sitting at the table rather than beneath. If only I'd known that the city would be in ruins during my reign, I wouldn't have been in such a rush to grow up.

Once we've made it past the table, I gently nudge my elbow against his arm. "Here, let me lead you the rest of the way toward the stairs." He doesn't hesitate and grabs hold, letting me direct him around furniture and over piles of books scattered on the floor. Even though it's just his arm, my heart flutters from our contact. I instantly feel his absence when we reach the stairs and he releases me. The clouds must have parted because moonlight fills the staircase tower, shining in from the glass ceiling. "Top floor," I say, taking two steps at a time. Four floors later, we're standing outside my mother's private study. The soft light from the stairwell shines over the stone floor but doesn't reach the oak door.

Elijah reaches for the handle and pulls. "It's locked."

A small cubby, positioned at waist height, is nestled within the stone wall to the right of the door. I reach inside and find the sunstone, cupping my hand over it. It's smooth yet has a subtle grainy texture to it, like a river rock, yet it also possesses a springy quality, reminiscent of a freshly baked, warm roll. Withdrawing it, I give the malleable stone a gentle squeeze, activating the light within.

Elijah leans forward, eyes narrowing on the stone. "What is it? And how is it glowing?"

"This is a sunstone. It's unique to the Starlight Realm." I turn it over in my hand, showing him the underside. "Not only do they emit light, but they can imprint on any surface, serving as a key to unlock doors or concealments, but each stone can only do so once. One sunstone for one door or chest or anything else that requires locking." I face the door and press the sunstone to its surface. Once the stone is in contact with the door, I give it another gentle squeeze. The light fades at the same time a succession of rotating *click*s reverberates within the door as the internal components retract the locking pins. Once they're done, I turn the handle and pull. A giant cloud of compressed, dusty air hits us, sending us both into a coughing fit. Waving our hands, we move past the onslaught of stale air and into my mother's private work chamber.

The entire top floor is divided into three rooms, with the study being the largest, occupying half of the space. The other two rooms comprise a private washroom and a sleeping chamber. I cross the dimly lit space and unlatch and open each of the three tall windows; even though their exterior panes are covered in ivy, they still allow warm, fresh air inside. Soft moonlight fills the room, reaching over the dusty furniture and across the room to the fireplace and surrounding bookcases.

With a hand over his nose, Elijah walks the length of the room, inspecting the books and trinkets on the bookcases. "It smells like an old trunk in here."

"The fresh air will help," I say, standing in front of an armchair set beneath the window I just opened. As a child, I would curl up in that chair and read for hours while my mother attended to her official duties. Closing my eyes, I picture the room as it was, warm and inviting.

Shrugging off the memory, I turn and spot my mother's desk at the other end. "We need to find Loralai's journal."

"Loralai? As in Merigoth?"

A thick layer of dust blankets the clutter atop her desk. The arrangement of open books, pens, scrolls, and candles forms a miniature desert landscape, with the dust settling like sand dunes between them. I pick up the top book and use two fingers to wipe the page clean, revealing printed words and an image of the moon's rotation. The page is stiff and resistant to turn as I tell Elijah, "Loralai Songwielder was Merigoth's name before her banishment." After setting the book down, I search the drawers and continue, "Loralai was one of the Star leaders—the South Star. They rarely agreed on matters of the city. Loralai often argued with my mother right here, in this study."

The memory plays out in my mind as I narrate those moments I witnessed for Elijah. "Mom and Loralai would constantly argue about Loralai neglecting her duties as a Star leader," I recount. "Mom's disapproval escalated upon finding out about Loralai's unauthorized excursions. She'd lecture Loralai on how it's not the responsibility of a Star leader to be out exploring the lands and realms; that belongs to the Realmwalkers. But Loralai insisted her duties weren't being neglected, and that her discovery would change everything—make the angels even stronger and more powerful than they were. She promised my mother that she'd never put the city at risk. But that was a lie. Whatever Loralai discovered was the reason everything fell apart. The answers to everything are in that journal."

"Well, maybe not everything," Elijah softly says. "There are some things we may never know the reason behind."

"Perhaps, but at least we'll gain a better understanding of Merigoth's ultimate plan—her true intentions, then and now."

"Don't we already know what her plan was? She wants to rule the Starlight Realm, right?"

"That's what Marcellus believes, but I think there's more to what she wants. I was here when she fought with my mother about making a better world for the angels."

He nods and faces the bookcases again. "Okay, so we'll find the journal and see what answers are inside."

Any regrets I might have had about bringing Elijah fade, and I'm happy he's here with me.

After hours of silence between us, I collapse onto the floor in front of the familiar armchair that once provided comfort during my childhood. The dingy smell assaults my senses, but I push it aside, consumed by thoughts of failure. I'm the inadequate successor to my mother's legacy, and soon chaos will be unleashed upon the Human Realm because I failed to defeat Marcellus. It's only a matter of time before he releases all those Reborns lurking in the cavern beneath the village, and worse, frees Merigoth.

Elijah comes over and lowers himself onto the floor next to me. Warm night air floats in over our heads as moonlight blankets his concentrated expression. He gets comfortable on the rug, his shoulder pressing into mine. With a tender gesture, he hands me a weathered picture frame, its glass cracked but still holding the precious memory within. "I didn't find any journals, but I found this."

Despite the broken glass, I'm still able to recognize the photo. It's of me and Mom, standing on the front steps of the archives building.

"How are you able to capture your reflection on parchment like this?" Elijah holds his hand out, and I pass the frame to him. I was so young, half the height of my mother.

"It's captured with a device that preserves fleeting moments on paper," I explain, my gaze lingering on the photograph. "One day, your realm will develop similar devices."

As Elijah sets the frame aside, a wistful sigh escapes his lips. "It would be nice to have one of these reflection images of you now."

"I'll see what I can do," I wearily say, unsure if I can keep the promise.

We sit in silence until he says, "Rune, I wish I could do more for you. You put so much responsibility on yourself."

"I'm fine," I lie, my eyes shut and my head resting back against the musty cushion.

"You know I'm always here for you, even if..." His voice trails off, as if he's considering his next words. "Even if you only see me as a friend."

The onslaught of suppressed emotions bubbles deep in my core, threatening to surface once again. Every muscle in my body tenses, and I fight to conceal any signs of emotional strain on my face.

As if he can sense my internal struggles, he shifts his position and faces me. "Why don't you let me in?" The second I open my eyes, I find his gaze locked with mine. When he lifts a hand to my cheek, I don't push him away. The warmth from his skin sends a wave of heat rushing through me, causing a delightful shiver to trail up my spine, and in an instant my thoughts return to what they were in the cave when he kissed me. How I wish I could tell him that I think of him every night before bed. How thinking about him helps ease the tension that's accumulated throughout the day from the ongoing challenges of restoring Stellara. I lay there and wonder how he spends his days, what jokes he laughs at, who he talks to, and what thoughts cross his mind while he lies in bed each night before sleep. Does he think of me as much as I think of him? I know the answer to that last burning question. The hunger to do more than rest a hand on my cheek burns in his intense stare.

But no. I can't. I mustn't think about him like that. It's forbidden.

I take hold of his hand and lower it. He slumps his shoulders, clearly aware that I've denied him once more. While it's easy to fantasize about him, acting on those desires is an entirely different matter. My future should be with Evander. It's what my mother would've wanted. I have to stop denying that reality, which means our priority right now should be to find information we can use to rescue my friend. Then, once reunited, Evander and I can lead together and guide the angels toward a state of normality.

"No," Elijah says with determination.

I know I should get up and put more distance between us, allowing my mind to regain clarity, but he continues, and his words have captured my attention so that I can't bring myself to move.

"I've never been in love, so I don't know what love feels like," he admits. His voice is soft and inviting, almost as powerful as Merigoth's lure. I want to give in. I want the problems of the world to disappear. To give me a moment of happiness that I deserve.

"Elijah," I whisper. "We can't." I hold his gaze, leaving him in control to sever the moment.

He slips his hand into mine and lifts it to his chest. "Every morning, I wake and think of you. Every evening, I lie in bed and pray to the stars that you're well and happy. And I know our situation is unconventional—you being an angel and me a human—but my heart doesn't care."

And with those words, my will breaks. With one hand already pressed to his chest, I raise the other to the side of his face. It's enough for him to know I'm granting him access to my heart.

Beneath my palm, I feel the rise and fall of his chest. Then, slowly, he leans in closer, his gaze drifting to my mouth. His voice is barely above a whisper when he says, "I'd like to kiss you now." His words linger in the air, creating a heavy silence between us, rendering my thoughts absolutely powerless. I don't deny him this time. The second I nod, he boldly closes the distance between us, his lips meeting mine in a tender kiss.

My hand traces the curve of his face, then up through his short hair, and finally settles on the back of his head, anchoring him close. The kiss ignites a hunger in both of us, but when he abruptly pulls away and holds me at arm's length, the moment shatters. I won't let him ruin it—a moment I finally surrendered to. Breathless, I reach for him, but he's quick to grab my wrist. Turning my hand over, he laces his fingers through mine.

"Is this a onetime thing, or are you truly ready to let me be with you?"

"Elijah," I whisper, unsure how to explain that this shouldn't even be happening. "Can't we make the world disappear for tonight?"

He smiles, grabs a pillow from the armchair, and sets it on the floor, then lies down, beckoning me with an open arm. "Lie with me."

I oblige, hoping he's only pausing to settle into a more comfortable position before continuing our intimate moment. With one arm draped over his chest, I lean in to kiss him, but he stops me.

"Rune, I don't know if my heart can take having just one night with you. Every part of me is screaming to keep my mouth shut and be with you—to roll you onto your back and kiss every inch of you—but I can't. Not until I know if we're destined to remain friends or—" He stops, as if unable to finish his sentence.

"Or?"

"Or we take the plunge and be together. I know what I want and what I'm willing to do, but it's you, Rune, who needs to decide if your laws and traditions are more important than your happiness."

I have no response that will satisfy him, and I refuse to give him false hope just to ignite the moment again. Even if my insides are aching for him to kiss me again. For a fleeting moment, I was truly happy, filled with overwhelming joy and peace. There's a part of me that wants to do whatever it takes to stay in that bliss. It's the other half, the reasonable half, that asks what cost I'll have to pay to keep that happiness.

My silence speaks volumes. He doesn't let go or leave me to sleep alone. We lie there on the rug, bathed in soft moonlight, slowly drifting off to sleep. Tonight, as sleep envelops me, I don't have to wonder where he is or who he's with, because he's here with me. At some point, I know I must choose: follow my heart or uphold the laws that govern my world.

CHAPTER 18

ADELE

Loud knocking interrupts my peaceful sleep, jolting me awake. I squint, disoriented, and roll over and immediately notice Selene's empty bed. I push myself upright and search for any sign of my friend. Her bed is made, and both her slippers and boots are gone. "Selene?" My voice breaks the silence, contrasting with the quiet ambience of our cottage.

Then I remember our conversation last night. She's left for Fayatin.

After getting to my feet, I grab my socks lying on the floor by my boots and meander out into the main living space of our small home. A shiver runs through my shoulders, and I look over to where a dim fire smolders in the fireplace. She must've tended the fire early this morning before leaving. I pick up the borrowed item, Selene's hairpin, from where I left it last night—on the table.

"Adele!" Kit shouts from outside, beating on the door.

"Hold on!" I yell, setting the hairpin down and slipping on my socks.

Swinging open the door, I immediately wince and shield my eyes from the bright morning sunlight. My voice comes out groggy, and I cough to clear out the congestion. "What is it? And what hour is it?"

"It's well past noon. You missed breakfast." She pushes in past me while handing me a bowl of porridge and some bread.

I close the door with my foot and turn to her. "Is it really that late?"

During my time at Castle Forge, my services were never needed before midday, so sleeping in was normal for me. My life here requires an earlier start to the day, which I'm still adjusting to—with Selene's help, of course.

"It is. Selene's usually the one who wakes you for breakfast." Kit takes it upon herself to throw another two narrow logs onto the fire. Brushing her hands clean, she looks at me and asks, "So, where's your friend?"

"She's returned to Fayatin." I eat a mouthful of warm porridge and savor the cinnamon sprinkled on top. After placing the bowl on the table, I reach for my pants and then slide them on under my nightshirt.

"Fayatin? Like for good?"

"I believe so. Something to do with her uncle and a union proposal."

"Is that right? Selene's getting married?"

I shove another spoonful of porridge into my mouth then roll my eyes. I have no desire to talk about the subject any longer. Finishing my bite, I put down the hot meal and finish getting dressed.

Kit stands there in her long leather jacket, one hand resting on the hilt of her shortsword. "I was about to head out and do a border check. You want to come?"

Taking the last bite, I shake my head. "I have to check in with Aunt Lauren and see how Valor's doing."

"Ah, yes. I hope your feathered friend has a full recovery." She opens the latch on the door but stops and adds, "Oh, and our guests are in their cottage. I escorted them myself after the morning meal. It was an interesting morning at Goslings with everyone whispering and staring at the two the entire time."

I freeze, the spoon halfway to my mouth, porridge dripping off and plopping into the bowl. "Please tell me Aleksandra had her hood on?"

"She did," Kit says with a chuckle. "Though, that would've been a sight for everyone this morning—seeing a young woman with horns growing out of her head! The news of her being here would've spread like wildfire throughout the eastern villages of Harvesgrove."

"That it would've," I scold in a low tone. "More of a reason to send her back to Noviska. Bricen doesn't need that kind of attention."

Kit narrows her eyes. "You'd send her away?"

"If she wanted to leave, I wouldn't force her to stay. She's never been a part of my life, and she's old enough to care for herself. Once we're done dealing with Marcellus, I say let her be on her way." And I mean every word. She may be related by blood, but she isn't my family.

"You don't think she's a threat to the humans of Noviska?"

Shaking my head, I tell Kit honestly, "She's lived a harsh life, and seen how cruelty affects the lives of others. I believe she just wants to live a free life." Something I can relate to. The only thing I ever wanted while living at Castle Forge was to be free. If that's all she wants—her freedom—then who are we to stop her? If she chooses to stay, then I'll deal with that problem when the time occurs.

"Come find me when you're done checking the perimeter."

Kit nods, then heads out, leaving me to finish getting ready alone. I grab the Fayatin dagger and tuck it into my boot, then grab my trusty dagger and tuck that one into my waistband. After changing into my shirt and vest, I grab my cloak and make for the door. I'm already flustered that I wasted half the day sleeping. I pray to the stars that the rest of the day is more productive and that we end our troubles with Marcellus once and for all.

Making my way up to Aunt Lauren's place, I steal a brief glance over my shoulder at the small stone cottage where

Aleksandra and Sayen are staying. One problem at a time. Then, as I arrive at the front door of my aunt's cottage, I give a curt knock before letting myself in.

"Look who's finally awake," my aunt says, already busy preparing tonight's supper rolls.

Also on the table at the other end is Valor, huddled in a makeshift nest of bundled linens. Bending to eye level with the bird, I ask, "How's she doing?"

"Better," my aunt says, then continues to fold and knead the dough. Relief floods through me, and I'm grateful to the stars that she's recovered. My aunt pounds her fist into the dough and continues, "She slept through the night with only a few whimpering chirps. I may not be a healer, but a few drops of my blood mixed with some water was enough to mend her wing." Dusting her hands on her apron, she approaches my feathered friend. "Go on, show her," she prompts the crow.

Valor stands from her comfy spot. Then, after a low *caw*, she spreads her wings and pulls them in with a rustle. Satisfied, I open the front door and wave toward the outside. "All right, off you go! Go find your siblings!"

She takes one more look at Aunt Lauren before launching from the pile of linens.

"Thank you for tending to her." I go to close the door but stop when I spot Mum walking up the hill.

"Not a problem," Lauren responds with a pleasant expression and her usual cheerful tone, then returns to kneading and dusting more flour onto her dough.

Mum enters, and I close the door behind her. "You missed breakfast," she says while removing her cloak and scarf, then hanging them on a wooden peg nailed into the wall.

"So I've been told."

When done, Mum looks at me, eyeing me over, before asking, "How are you doing?"

I'm not sure what answer she's expecting, so I say, "Not sure how today will play out, and—"

She holds up a hand and stops me. "No. I mean, how are you doing with Selene going back to Fayatin?"

Oh. That.

"You saw her this morning?"

Aunt Lauren pauses kneading the dough to say, "We both did. Her and Agnes."

"She explained her sudden need to return to Fayatin," Mum says, pouring herself some water from a small metal pitcher set on the table next to an open sack of flour. "Sounds like she won't be returning."

Shrugging, I say, "No, I don't think she will be returning to Bricen. She made her decision, and now she'll have to care for herself. I can't be there and here at the same time."

"Oh, Adele," my aunt murmurs, wiping her hand across her forehead and leaving a smudge of white flour in its wake. "No one is saying you should've gone with her."

I adjust my cloak over my shoulders, allowing a bit of fresh air to soothe the tension humming along my heated skin beneath my shirt and vest. With a forced nonchalance, I shrug and say, "It's not like we'll never see Selene again. She came to realize that life in a village wasn't what she thought it would be. She's not the 'working type,' even though she wanted to be more hands-on."

Mum comes over and embraces me. The gesture is comforting, and I instinctively want to step away. I find no reason for her embrace. It was Selene's choice to leave. I will miss her, yet there's a tiny part of me that is happy to see her find her own path. Close to my ear, Mum whispers, "It's not easy when someone you care about leaves." When she pulls away, her gaze drifts from me to out the front window.

This time I don't hesitate and step away, knowing her concern has shifted from me to Aleksandra. The darkness swirls with unease, wanting to reach its way into Aleksandra's skull—to find something wrong with her that'll help vanquish Mum's guilt.

"Do you want to come with me? I need to speak with Aleksandra and Sayen about returning to Noviska."

All those years I spent with Mum as a kid, she never looked as old as she does right now. She must've truly felt as if she'd escaped Merigoth and the Under Realm to have been so happy and carefree. Now…now, she's on edge, morning, day, and night, always alert and ready to fight.

Still staring absentmindedly out the window, I snap my fingers in front of Mum's face to break whatever reverie she's fallen into. Blinking, she stumbles over her words. "What? Oh, go with you? No—no, I, uh… I tried talking to her this morning at breakfast. She wouldn't even look at me."

Good. Maybe this wall Aleksandra has put up will make it easier for Mum to let her go. I don't say that, though. "Give her time." It's the best I can offer since my comforting skills are still mediocre at best. Before leaving, I tell her, "Whether she ends up staying or not, take comfort in knowing she's alive. You can't change the past. We can only do better going forward."

"When did you get so wise?" Mum asks softly, barely making eye contact with me.

"Adele…" Aunt Lauren stands straight at the table's edge, a wide smile spreading across her petite face. "It pleases me to hear you speak with such thoughtfulness for others."

I've come to understand the value of presenting a favorable image to my family and friends, concealing the darker recreations I occasionally pursue. They needn't be burdened with the knowledge of my reach yearning to be set free, nor the midnight strolls I sometimes indulge in, seeking wrongdoers who stray through the woods or trespass upon our forest.

"We should decide on the plan once Rune returns. Aleksandra and Sayen will likely want to leave." I linger by the front door, eager to get a sense of the day ahead. "Which we'll consider after we've rescued Evander."

"Aleksandra will have to stay," Mum whispers.

"I disagree," I say, leaving the rest of my reasoning unsaid. She only needs to stay because we need her as bait. What other reason is there for her to stay? Absolutely none. She's not family to me. Mum needs to let her go and live her own life, wherever that may be. If the worst thing she possesses is the physical traits of a demon—her horns—then

I'll take that as a win. I'd think she'd be thrilled to live a quiet, secluded life somewhere she doesn't have to interact with humans.

But there's no need to say any of that out loud and upset her even more. Instead, I tell Mum, "Aleksandra may want to stay with her friend." We can't force either of them to stay. Or at least, once we've rescued Evander, they should be allowed to leave and go wherever they want.

Mum spins to face me, her arms crossed over her chest. In an incredulous tone, she asks, "When was the last time you used your reach?"

The question stings, but I understand she's only lashing out because she's hurting. "I haven't used my abilities in weeks." That's a lie, but it's safer to stay on her good side. Revealing how I attempted to reach into Rhoda's mind yesterday might make her think less of me, especially when she's been urging me to become a healer like her. I'm not skilled at erasing traumatic memories or helping people overcome their phobias. Most of the time, I unintentionally make the distress worse by bringing up unwanted memories and locking them at the forefront of people's minds. One time, I inadvertently overreached and seized control of someone's will—much like Marcellus does—commanding them to forget they'd stepped on a nail. They fixated on the "forget they stepped" part and completely forgot how to walk when they came to. It took Mum nearly a fortnight to help them regain their ability to walk.

"Adele." Aunt Lauren jars me from my thoughts. "Ask the girls if there's anything they need while staying with us.

If they're going to be with us for an unknown amount of time, then we want them to be comfortable."

I nod, then leave, shutting the door behind me. Four crows fly over Goslings and disappear into the forest on the other side of Bricen. Descending the hill, I make my way to where our guests are staying. Somehow, I need to convince Aleksandra to help us save Evander before allowing them to return to Noviska. Groaning and wishing Kit were here with me, I dread the upcoming conversation. I mean, there's no reason for Aleksandra to help us, especially if she's set on leaving and having nothing to do with any of us ever again.

Well, good riddance, if you ask me.

CHAPTER 19

ADELE

With a wide swing, I open the shed door. There's something I must do before talking with Aleksandra and Sayen. While Trevor preferred an empty space, I've used the extra storage to stash weapons I've collected over the months. Some I purchased from neighboring villages, but most come from miscreants wandering the forests late at night. A small collection of daggers and knives, one hatchet, and an ample stash of arrows all hang, meticulously organized, on the walls, and nothing lies on the floor.

But I'm not here to admire my collection. After unlatching and swinging open the wood hatch, I face a wide window that's almost as big as the back wall. I remove one glove, then wrap my fingers over the cold iron bar that crosses the center and whisper, "Come to me, my feathered friends."

As I wait, I slide my hand into my glove. It doesn't take more than a minute before their *caw*s fill my ears. One by one, Olive, Serafina, Barclay, and Valor land on the strong bar. They focus their beady black eyes on me, waiting to hear why I've called them.

Sidestepping, I grab the leather pouch necklace hanging on the side wall, then move to stand in front of Barclay. "Hey, I need to ask a favor." He lowers his head, and I loop the pouch necklace over his head. "Selene left early this morning. She's returning to Castle Forge in Fayatin. I can't be there with her, so I'd like you to keep her company. If there's danger, she knows what to do." I rub the leather of the small pouch. "Can you do that for me?"

Barclay ruffles his wings and releases a string of *caw*s. The others shuffle along the bar, giving their sibling room to flap his wings.

While I've got them here, I face Olive and ask, "Is today the day you reveal your special skill to me?"

She tilts her head and chirps. Next to her, Serafina pecks at her sister's silky feathers, as if urging her to confess. "I think your special skill is being stubborn." I stroke her head with my gloved hand, and she leans into the touch, pressing against my palm.

Barclay releases a loud *caw*, and I look at him. "Be safe in your journey and do well to avoid injuries this time." He turns himself around on the bar before flying out into the afternoon sky. The air is chilly, but the sun shines and makes the day a bit more pleasant. "Stay together, and I'll see you all soon." With that, I dismiss them with a click of my tongue.

The second the remaining three take off, I close up the hatch and lock up the shed.

Now, it's time to go see Aleksandra and Sayen.

As I'm about to knock on the cottage door, it unexpectedly swings open. Aleksandra stands there, her hands holding the door's edge, waiting for me to speak. She isn't wearing her green cloak, and the sight of the horns poking out from her thick curly hair makes me instinctively scowl.

My reaction doesn't bode well with her, and she snaps, "The only reason you should be here is to tell us it's time to leave. I have nothing to say to you or your mother."

She goes to shut the door, but it jerks against my boot that I've wedged between the door and the frame. "I said I have nothing to say to you."

"That's great," I reply, keeping my boot lodged in place. "I'm all for you and your friend leaving Bricen. No skin off my back." Then, cocking my head, I say with a smug grin, "The problem is, you can't leave until we've rescued our friend from Marcellus."

"Not our problem." Her flat tone carries a chilling seriousness, suggesting she means what she says.

"No, it's not. But you owe us… You know, for saving you and Sayen." I let that sink in before continuing, "I'm sure Rune wouldn't have a problem returning you to where we found you."

Aleksandra's narrowed eyes relax, and her mouth gapes open. "You wouldn't."

"Do you know anything about me?" I ask.

She studies my face, then slowly shakes her head.

"Master Ebenus didn't tell you anything about me, Marcellus, or our mum?"

Again, she shakes her head. "I already told you, he forbade me from asking or talking about the past."

I look at her bare hands, still clutching the side of the door. "You don't wear gloves?" She instinctively dips her gaze to my hands—at my gloves.

"I don't like these questions," she snaps. "Maybe Master Ebenus was right to keep the truth from me. All I've ever wanted was to live a normal life. To walk around without being feared or treated like an animal."

This has my insides turning with guilt. She shouldn't have had to live a life with such scrutiny or malice. Yet, I'm powerless to alter her past, or mine. And I'd only allow her to stay if she reconciled with Mum. I don't want Mum to wake up each day with a burden of guilt or to constantly seek forgiveness from Aleksandra.

Sayen softly utters Aleksandra's name from inside the cottage. A gentle reminder for her friend to be kind. Aleksandra's fingers relax against the door, and with a strained smile, she speaks, her words laced with bitterness. "My apologies. I'm still adjusting to this new freedom. To being around people who…" She falters, as if each word causes her physical pain. "…care about us."

I long to assure her that the sentiment is mutual, that she isn't the sister I expected to find. But the words get caught in my throat. Instead, I attempt to reassure her. "Look, I only came to check on you both and to let you know that in due time, we'll let you leave. In the meantime, sit tight." As I withdraw my foot from the doorframe, hoping for a semblance of calm, Aleksandra's anger flares. With a sharp slam, she shuts the door in my face.

"We weren't finished with our conversation," I shout through the wooden barrier, frustration clear in my tone. "Though if you have any helpful insight on how we can save our friend, it'll speed up the rescue, and you'll be able to leave here sooner."

No response.

Fine. Let her sulk like a child.

I turn to leave and am met with Magdala, standing a few feet away. Her eyes are wide and locked onto the cottage door behind me. "Horns. She—she has—"

I don't let her finish. Concern for the child's mental state prickles at the back of my mind. "It's a costume," I say with the hope she'll believe me. "Part of their cult's elaborate ensemble. Pay no attention or speak of the horns and keep your distance. Do you hear me?"

Magdala slowly closes her mouth, her expression still troubled, but she nods in understanding as I take her by the shoulder and lead her away. "What do you need?"

Her feet stumble to keep up, but then she regains her composure, remembering why she sought me out. "There are some kids here, at the front gate, to see you."

"Kids?" I ask, moving farther from the cottage.

Magdala skips ahead, pointing toward the front end of Bricen. "Lauren's feeding them while your mum is trying to get answers, but their leader...some tall kid with bushy hair...he says he'll only talk with you."

"All right, well, let's go see what they want."

She takes off running, and I mosey behind. It's too cold to run, and whatever these kids want surely can't be that important.

Rounding the corner of Goslings, I approach the dirt road leading to the front gate. There's a group of five or six children engaged in a chaotic conversation with Mum and Lauren. Drawing nearer, I pass by the smithy, and Nathaniel's voice calls out, "Oh, hey, Adele!"

My insides cringe. I don't have time for this. Coming to a halt, I face the younger smithy brother as he jogs over. "Hey, sorry we missed you the other night for supper. Selene mentioned you had some pressing matters to attend to."

"Yeah, something like that," I reply, stealing a glance at Mum and Lauren, with Magdala now among them. "Can we talk later? I'm needed elsewhere." With a simple flick of my thumb, I gesture toward the front gate.

His attention follows my thumb, and he sees the group of kids practically climbing on top of Lauren for whatever food she's handing out. "Oh, good gracious. What's going on over there?"

"I don't know. Like I said, I was on my way over to find out."

"Right," he says with a chuckle, rubbing the top of his trimmed hair with a soot-covered hand. "Well, before you go, I wanted to give you something."

Every time General Onica gifted me with something, it was to quell my inner turmoil about the daunting tasks she commanded of me. It was a tactic to ensure my loyalty, one that worked when I was younger, easily swayed by material possessions and comforts. But as I grew older, I saw through her manipulation and the gifts lost their allure.

"You don't have to give me anything, really."

He smiles and retrieves something wrapped in a piece of linen. "It's nothing special, just something I've been tinkering around with."

Curious, I accept the gift and carefully unwrap the fabric. Inside lies a shiny metal hairpin embellished with a carved swirl design along the top. It's a piece beyond the skill of an apprentice. "You crafted this?" I inquire, turning the exquisite piece over in my hand.

With a gulp, he stammers out a hesitant, "I did."

"It's quite the beautiful piece," I admit, genuinely impressed by the treasure.

"And look," he continues, grasping the design with one hand and gently pulling at the teardrop accent protruding from the top. With ease, he reveals a slender blade the length of a finger. Holding it up to eye level, he explains, "I thought if you were ever in a troubled situation and without weapons, it would serve as a handy last resort." He hands over the miniature dagger.

The textured surface of the teardrop hilt provides a firm hold, allowing the blade to slide easily into its protective casing, seamlessly fused to the back of the hairpin's frame. Folding the linen over the hairpin, I thank him. "This was extremely thoughtful of you."

His feet continue to shift along the frozen ground, and he rubs a hand over his chin. "I'm glad you like it."

"I do." A loud cry erupts from one of the rowdy kids. Tucking the gift inside the front of my leather vest, I offer him a rare smile, something reserved for only a select few—Kit, Elijah, Selene. "I should get going," I say, then start to walk away. Glancing over my shoulder, I shout, "Thanks again for the gift!"

"Yeah! Happy to…" His voice fades. "…and, ah, maybe I'll see you tonight at supper!"

I don't indulge him with a response, keeping my attention on the group of kids still clustered around my aunt, scrambling for more food. "Whoa! Hey! Everyone, calm down and give Lauren some space!" I shout, approaching the group. The kids startle and run like scared rabbits, huddling behind the tall boy with mousy hair, their dirty faces peering out from behind.

"Hey, I remember you," I say, walking up to the young boy. "That day we met on the road… You know, you could've been a little more specific with your warning."

"I tried to warn you," he says with a lisp, and when he smiles, I see why. It appears he's lost another tooth since our last meeting. "And hey, you didn't die!"

Crossing my arms, keeping Nathaniel's gift from view, I ask with a raised brow, "Why are you here? Besides to eat all my aunt's bread."

"Oh, it's fine. I can always bake more," Aunt Lauren says, handing out another small roll. A scrawny young girl steps out from behind the boy and snatches the roll from my aunt. She then scrambles back to her spot behind their leader. As she eats it, the other children's tiny fingers reach over her shoulder and tear pieces off.

Magdala tugs on my sleeve, her eyes wide as she gawks at something behind me. I follow her pointed finger to see Aleksandra watching us from the corner of Goslings. Thank the stars she's wearing her green cloak with the hood up, concealing those otherworldly horns. I'll deal with her when I'm done with this gang of kids.

As I return my attention to the boy, I pause because Magdala is still pointing and gawking at Aleksandra. "Hey!" I snap at her, waving a hand in front of her face. "If you're that interested, go see what she's doing." The girl vigorously shakes her head and bolts off in the opposite direction. Meanwhile, Mum and Aunt Lauren are busy handing out extra sweaters and blankets brought over by a villager.

Heaving a sigh, I turn to the kid and ask, "Okay, so what do you need to tell me?"

"You know how I said I used to live in Gailstein?" After I nod, he continues, "Well, every once in a while, I like to visit."

"Sounds great, kid. What does that have to do with me?" My impatience flares, and I'm ready to move onto more important things, like talking with Kit and Mum about our next move in saving Evander and sending Marcellus back to the Under Realm.

The boy leans closer, his voice dropping to a whisper. "I saw a bunch of soldiers going into Gailstein. They wore long blue coats with a fancy embroidery over their hearts. The design was some letter surrounded by blue stars. I can't read, so I don't know what letter it was."

This piece of news commands my full attention. The mention of 'soldiers' has my muscles tensing. Especially after seeing the same insignia yesterday morning after chasing down a man we mistook as a petty thief. Lord Houfston sending a few soldiers into Harvesgrove is one thing, but sending a band of soldiers to Gailstein raises troubling questions. That foul man has no rights to any land in this country.

"How many did you say?"

The boy shrugs. "I can't count either."

With an eye roll, I nod at the boy and tell him, "All right. I'll handle it. You and your friends keep clear of Gailstein for the next few days, hear me?" Mum shoots me an incredulous look, but I ignore it.

"I knew you'd save them!" the boy exclaims, then whistles, calling the attention of his forest gang. "Come on, let's go!" Before Mum or Aunt Lauren can offer them anything else, the lot of them are running out the front gate, carrying whatever goods they were given. Kit strolls in as they rush out, their hoots and hollers echoing in the air for several minutes.

"What was that all about?" Kit asks, approaching me, Mum, and Aunt Lauren.

But instead of answering her, Mum asks me, "You can't be seriously considering going to Gailstein right now?"

"Gailstein?" Kit repeats, her face twisting with confusion. "What's in Gailstein?"

"Fayatin soldiers," I answer. "Rune and Elijah aren't back yet. I say we've got some time to help our fellow neighboring village out."

Mum moves to block me and Kit as we walk toward the stables. Her weary expression makes her appear decades older. Without bothering to brush the loose strands of blonde hair that have escaped her braid and are hanging in her eyes, she firmly states, "Gailstein can wait. We've more pressing matters to attend to."

"I don't disagree, but you don't know Fayatin soldiers like I do. There might not be a village left by tomorrow, or the next day, or whenever we find time to go. We can make the round trip in under three or four hours." Ignoring Mum's protests, I stride past her, heading for the stables. Kit jogs over, silently supporting my decision.

"And what if Rune and Elijah return while you're gone?" Mum's voice carries a note of desperation as she shouts after us.

I yell over my shoulder, "Then send Rune to Gailstein. Or have her wait for us. Whichever, it doesn't matter, but I'm going to deal with this problem whether you like it or not." My reach hums beneath the skin of my fingers, eager to confront the Fayatin soldiers. Although the timing is unfortunate, I cannot abandon those people to whatever is happening there. It's my fault Fayatin invades.

Inside the stables, Kit goes straight to her horse while I pay a quick visit to Bessie. Building stables for the horses was something I insisted on after Bricen was no longer in danger of any future Shade attacks. The winter season was coming, and I wasn't going to have Bessie wandering the village or getting lost in the woods in freezing temperatures.

"How you doing, old girl?" I give my old friend a good rub along her neck, ending with a gentle pat. "You liking it here?" She gives me a subtle whinny, pushing her nose into my shoulder. "I don't have any carrots with me, but I'll make sure to find some for you when I can."

"You can't leave now," a voice I haven't quite gotten familiar with yet says from the stable doorway. Shuffling my boots in the hay lining the cold ground, I meet Aleksandra's narrowed gaze. "The second your angel friend returns, you're to have her open a passage sending us to Sayen's family home."

"And what do you plan to do after that?" I ask, moving past Bessie and over to a young gray mare.

Aleksandra comes closer, holding the edge of her hood with two hands. "I haven't thought about it."

I grab a saddle and hoist it over the horse's back, then start securing it into place. "Well, maybe you should consider moving here." It's actually the last thing I want, but Mum may want her close, and we still don't know if she has any dangerous abilities. I don't really care either way, but acting as if I want her around might help convince her to stay longer.

In a curt tone, she snaps, "Why would I want to live here? You are not my family. *She* is not my mother."

Or maybe it won't.

"True." I refuse to look at her at this moment. She's acting like a spoiled child when she should be grateful to be reunited with her long-lost family. We've all endured harsh living conditions. All the more reason to embrace family and friends when you can. Something I appreciate after escaping Castle Forge. I recall my mindset during my initial return to Bricen to get in, get answers, and get out. I had no intentions of rekindling any childhood friendships or family relations.

Yet, it was exactly what I needed.

After finishing with the saddle, I notice Aleksandra still standing against the stable post at the entrance. "You could come with us?" I'm not entirely interested in forming a sisterly bond. My intentions are purely investigational. I need to know whether she's a threat or not.

Her narrowed eyes soften, and her hands drop from holding her hood to fidget at her waist. "You—you want me to come with you?"

She makes it sound as if I've asked her to embark on some epic journey where we'll battle enemies together, watching each other's backs, then drinking and celebrating our victories in song over a great bonfire.

"I want to give you ample time to consider your options," I tell her.

There's a long pause before she asks, "What about Sayen? I cannot leave her alone."

"Oh, I'm sure my aunt will enjoy her company."

Something I say jolts the tall girl to stand even taller, attention piqued. "We have an aunt?"

This has me smiling. I grab another saddle and hand it to Kit, who glares at me with unsaid words: *We shouldn't be bringing her with us.* "No, not by blood. More like…adoptive. I've known Lauren my whole life." Realizing I've brought up my happy childhood, I grow quiet.

Moving deeper into the stables, Aleksandra tells me, "You don't have to feel guilty about your life here. You, like me, had no say in where we ended up."

Her words catch me off guard because she's right. None of us, including Marcellus, chose where we grew up. Offering some relatability, I say, "These past eight years, I wasn't here in Bricen. Nor our mum."

"Oh." This has her curious, trying to maintain eye contact with me. "Where were you then?"

"Ride with us to Gailstein, and I'll tell you about my childhood here in Bricen, and my life over in Fayatin."

Aleksandra glances out the stable doorway, then nods. "Before we go, I need to speak with Sayen. And then yes, I'd like to hear more about your life while accompanying you to Gailstein."

CHAPTER 20

ADELE

We maintain a steady trot for most of the journey, only slowing to a walk as we near Gailstein. It's then I break the silence and recap a brief version of my life before the Shade attack and my time after—in Fayatin. Aleksandra offers her apologies, a gesture that strikes me as odd since I never once offered my own for her misfortunes.

I also explain how Sara was held captive in Merigoth's prison for all those years. Aleksandra remains silent after that, perhaps contemplating the similarities of our shared experiences.

A mile out from Gailstein, Kit leads us off the main dirt road. "We'll tie the horses up here and go on foot the rest of the way."

We find a tree with a low-hanging branch. After securing the reins around the branch, allowing the horses to drink from a nearby creek, Kit and I retrieve our weapons from the saddlebags.

"Aleksandra, you need to stay here with the horses." I adjust my trusty dagger, making sure it's snug in my waistband, and check that the Fayatin blade is safely tucked into my boot.

"But I don't want to stay with the horses. I want to come with you." She straightens beneath her cloak while checking that her hood is covering her hair.

"Please, Aleksandra. I know you've been subjected to cruel behavior, but you've never encountered Fayatin soldiers. Their demeanor is anything but kind or understanding. They don't care about anyone but themselves. It's too risky to have you with us." My voice comes out harsh yet pleading.

"Fine," she says with a scowl. "I'll remain with the horses. Always out of sight, as usual."

"It's for your own safety," Kit reassures. "We don't even know what we're walking into."

After making our way out of the forest, leaving Aleksandra with the horses, we continue along the road on foot. My bow would've been nice right now, but I've grown fond of the direct approach or sneaking up on people. We're both on guard, which has us walking in silence, ready to jump off the road and into the forest to hide if needed.

The quiet gives me time to think about our next move against Marcellus. If what Rune and Elijah say is true, that there's a massive cavern full of Reborns, we'll need to collapse the tunnel entrance, preventing them from ever leaving and harming the people of Noviska. Then, we'll have to send Marcellus back to the Under Realm and close the doorway. Rune will have to be on the Under Realm side since she can't use her abilities around those monoliths. The truth of what needs to be done settles into my mind—how it'll be impossible for us to get Marcellus through the doorway. He'll need to be unconscious. So, how do we sneak up on him and knock him out?

Loud voices from the road ahead interrupt my train of thought. Kit yanks on my arm, her fingers slipping and desperately grabbing on to my cloak. We duck and take cover behind some trees. Two men, wearing long blue coats with Fayatin insignias signifying their loyalty to Castle Nautica— to Lord Houfston—shuffle to a stop on the road in front of where we hide.

"Looks clear to me," one of them says.

"Agreed. Let's check the west road, then head back. Lord Houfston is about to show a demonstration of his kindness to these Harvesgrove peasants."

He slaps the other in the arm with a wide grin. "We don't want to miss that! Come on, no one will know if we don't really check the west road."

We hold off until they are gone, and then wait for another half a minute before we move. Instead of continuing on the road, we choose to go deeper into the forest, heading toward the north side of the village.

"Once we're inside the village, there'll be a row of homes we can use for cover," Kit explains, her voice barely above a whisper.

As we approach, the village homes become visible through the trees at the northern end, accompanied by increasingly louder voices and screams echoing in the distance. Beneath our boots, sticks snap and leaves rustle. Amid the commotion in the village, I highly doubt anyone will hear us coming.

Gailstein's defenses differ from those of Bricen. Rather than constructing a towering wall, they opted for the security of a moat-like barrier. Strategically, they dug two wide trenches that encircle both sides of the village, forming a formidable barrier to repel Shade invaders. The trenches are ingeniously connected to a northern river, which provides plenty of water. The strong currents provide an extra layer of defense, ensuring the security of the village.

"We're going to have to cross," Kit tells me, and I reluctantly nod. I slide along the embankment, dreading the moment the icy water engulfs my boots. "No, wait!" Kit grabs me. She's holding a long plank.

"Where'd you get that?"

She carries it over to a spot where the trench isn't so wide and drops it across the water, connecting the two embankments. The grass has indents that match the shape of the board, suggesting it's often used in this spot. Kit gives me a smile, and says, "I may have snuck over here a few times to visit Peter."

The shouts and cries from within the village have quieted, which concerns me. Whatever demonstration Lord Houfston is about to show the people of Gailstein, I doubt it involves any form of kindness.

"Who's Peter?" I ask, holding the board steady while she crosses.

She reaches the other side and quickly crouches to hold the board while I cross. "His father is one of the leaders here. I'd accompany Trevor whenever he traveled to Gailstein with furs and meats to trade for grain and herbs. Peter and I would leave them to their meeting, sneaking off to have some fun of our own."

She lifts the board and sets it against the foundation of the nearby home. To the left are three more homes, while to the right are two. Rounding the corner of the home, I ask, "What kind of fun did you and Peter have?"

She stops, staying low against the wood siding of the home. Her gaze searches my face before she asks, "You're being serious, aren't you?"

Unsure of her meaning, I shrug.

"We were in the field, behind one of the hay bales, having—" She stops, narrowing her eyes. "You've never been romantic with anyone?"

Shock rolls through me. "What? No!" I don't mean to be loud, so I repeat in a quieter tone, "No." Lifting my hands, I shake my head. "I can't."

"You can keep your gloves on and still be with someone, Adele." I'm glad to see my misfortune makes her smile. She then adds, "I do believe a certain smithy boy has his eye on—"

"Do not finish that sentence!" I cut her off. Shuffling by her, withdrawing my trusty blade from my waistband, I say, "Let's get a better look at what's going on."

My friend chuckles as she follows me along the side of the home. We find a spot that gives us a clear view to the center of the village. Kneeling, we stay hidden, lurking from within the overlapping shadows of a large oak tree and a small cottage.

Out on Gailstein's green, twenty or more soldiers stand, each one holding a villager—man, woman, or child. One man even holds a small, scruffy-looking dog in his arms, clasping its muzzle tightly. When the man holding the dog looks over at Lord Houfston, who's making some speech about this being his village now, I instantly recognize him. He's the thief Kit, Elijah, and I were chasing from Bricen yesterday morning. The vibrant burn scar running along his chin and down his neck makes that apparent.

"What is that guy talking about—declaring this his village now?" Kit asks, her brows furrowed in a mix of anger and confusion.

I shift my weight, my gaze sweeping over the unfolding scene before us. "I don't know," I reply with a low grumble. "But the man clutching the scruffy mutt is our thief from yesterday morning."

Kit quietly curses, a flicker of realization dawning in her eyes. "Are you sure?" I nod, and she concludes, "Then they must've been scouring the surrounding villages."

"Or perhaps they were searching for me."

Kit drops to one knee. Her posture is tense as she leans forward and rests her arms across her knee. "Not everything revolves around you, Adele," she retorts, her tone sharp. With two pointed fingers, she gestures toward the closest building.

"I say we sneak over there, and then charge out and catch them by surprise. I'm willing to bet most of the villagers out there will fight alongside us."

"Do you see Peter?" I ask.

Kit searches the crowd, her brows furrowing in concern. "No. He's not out there."

Lord Houfston, clad in a long coat and trailing blue cape, strides through the village square. His thick white hair peeks out from beneath a fur cap, and his tanned skin reflects the warmth of his southern coastal origins in Fayatin. Despite his age, his movements are swift and agile as he grabs a boy from one of his soldiers, his grip causing the child to shriek.

"I will not have you disobey me!" he shouts, his voice echoing across the square. "No harm will come to your children as long as you comply with my orders."

The boy struggles against his hold, but Lord Houfston slaps him across the head and leans in to whisper something in his ear. A malevolent smile spreads across his face as the boy's resistance fades. He shoves the boy into a soldier, who promptly restrains the child.

"Return to your homes!" Houfston bellows, his chin held high as he addresses the villagers. "Tomorrow, your men will journey to Fayatin to train for me, while the rest of you remain here to harvest your crops. Your land is mine, and everything that grows here belongs to me."

Kit knocks me on the shoulder, and I flinch instinctively, my body tensing at the unexpected contact. It's not that I don't trust Kit, but I've never been comfortable with physical touch, especially after everything that's happened. Still, I try to suppress my rising anger, knowing it's not her fault. "What?" I snap, my voice tight with restraint.

"We have to stop this," she says urgently, her eyes reflecting the same anger burning within me. "We can't let them trespass into our country and take our villages."

My anger simmers beneath the surface, my reach pulsing with the same intensity, wanting to be unleashed. I peel off my gloves, feeling the cold air sting my heated skin. "Stay here," I say, my tone low and resolute. "I can handle Lord Houfston and the soldiers. If things take a turn for the worse, I want you to go, retrieve Aleksandra, and make your way back to Bricen."

"I'm not leaving you here," Kit scolds, her eyes glaring at me as if I should know better than to argue with her. "I came to help."

I know arguing with Kit is futile. She's as stubborn as they come. "Fine. But you follow my lead and stay close."

Our attention snaps back to the tumultuous scene as a woman breaks free from her captors and steps forward, her voice ringing out clear and defiant. "No!" she shouts, her fists clenched at her sides. "This is our home. Fayatin has no right to Harvesgrove land."

The soldier attempting to restrain her struggles to regain his grasp on her. Lord Houfston's voice cuts through the chaos, commanding attention as he calls for the woman to be allowed to speak. With a single raised eyebrow, he regards her with a mixture of curiosity and disdain, his gaze scanning her disheveled appearance. Strands of her brown hair escape from a once-tidy braid, framing her face in a wild halo, while her simple dress and apron are smeared with dirt, evidence of a struggle or being dragged along the village grounds.

As the woman begins her defiant proclamation, her words are cut short as Lord Houfston withdraws his sword and swings hard. The gleaming Fayatin steel slices through the air with deadly precision, finding its mark at her waist. With a sickening *thud*, she screams then staggers forward as her hands instinctively reach for the blade embedded in her flesh. A collective cry of horror fills the air as many villagers react to the grisly outcome of the woman's protests. Those who are not standing there and screaming have either fallen to the ground, staring in disbelief, or are trying to flee. The soldiers act swiftly and ruthlessly, moving to suppress any hint of resistance. They unleash a barrage of blows upon those who dare to defy their master until all semblance of rebellion has ceased.

I rise to my feet and come out of the shadows to where we're hiding. Flexing my bare hand at my side and tightening my grip on my dagger, I stride purposefully across the brown winter grass, eager to end this situation swiftly and decisively so we can get back to Bricen and focus on Marcellus.

"Hey! Aren't you that pathetic lord from Castle Fishrot?" My voice cuts through the cacophony of cries and shouts, drawing attention to me amid the congested crowd of blue coats and townsfolk.

As I close in on the crowd, the soldiers instinctively part, creating a clear path for me to approach Lord Houfston. His expression, a mix of surprise and hatred, excites the darkness within me. Despite his authoritarian demeanor, I detect a subtle tremor in his hands before he clasps them behind his back, a sign of the fear lurking beneath his façade of confidence.

Good. I'll need to make sure his lesson on proper behavior is one he won't forget.

"Ah, if it isn't General Onica's little pet demon girl," he sneers, his tone dripping with contempt. His attempt to belittle me only serves to strengthen my tenacity. Ignoring his taunts, I meet his gaze squarely, refusing to show any sign of weakness in the face of his insults.

A momentary flicker of uncertainty crosses his eyes but is swiftly concealed by a forced smile. Making sure all hear, he loudly says, "I always wondered why she kept such a frail thing in her company. I guess I assumed it was for…" With a pause, he narrows his eyes and scrutinizes me, leaving his wicked insinuation to be imagined by those around us.

We lock eyes, each playing our respective roles in this deadly game of power and defiance. I feign a nervous swallow, channeling the façade of vulnerability he's always expected from me during his visits to Castle Forge. "Obviously, you know that's not the reason she kept me around. And I never asked for that life."

He emits a noncommittal grunt. "I've heard rumors about you, girl," he says, his gaze flicking to my bare hands at my sides. "Rumors about the Interrogator's touch."

"That's not me anymore," I assert firmly. "General Onica is dead. Go back to Fayatin and squabble over the lands in your own country. Harvesgrove is not to be invaded." The soldiers and villagers on both sides are stepping back, seemingly aware of the increasing tension.

Lord Houfston's attention drifts behind me. "I see you've made a new friend. Tell me, does she know of your past? How you tortured and killed tens, maybe hundreds, of people?"

"You need to leave," Kit interjects, refusing to be drawn into his attempts to think ill of me.

"I told you to stay put," I say with plenty of annoyance in my tone.

"When do I ever listen to anyone?" Kit retorts without taking her eyes off Lord Houfston. Then to him, she yells, "Lower your weapon and leave peacefully!"

"I don't think so," he sneers, and before I can make a move, a sharp pain shoots through the upper part of my arm. Something has pierced through my cloak. Instantly my vision blurs as I try to find the source.

Behind me, Kit's body crumples to the ground. I whirl around to find her lying on the cold grass, her eyes wide and blinking rapidly. A dart with a blue feather sticks out of her neck. She slurs, "Adele, ru—" before her eyelids flutter shut.

I find the dart sticking out of my arm and wrench it free. Holding it up, I examine it briefly before it slips from my weakening grasp. Collapsing to my knees, I curse myself for underestimating Lord Houfston and his resources. Before I can even comprehend the situation, he's towering over me. I reach out instinctively, but the toxin coursing through my veins blurs my vision, making it impossible to discern which of the two Houfstons standing over me is actually him.

Then, a searing pressure clamps down on my forearm, preventing me from trying to grab him. He triumphantly declares, "I've been planning this moment for weeks. You belong to me now. With you under my control, I'll not only rule all of Fayatin, but…" A suffocating darkness envelops me, dragging me into unconsciousness. Before I slip away, I catch his chilling proclamation: "I'll become the first king to reign over all three countries."

CHAPTER 21

RUNE

Behind closed lids, bright sunlight warms my face. I haven't slept this well in ages. It isn't until I hear the door yawning open with a loud *creak*, followed by darkness falling over my closed lids, that I realize someone has entered the room and is standing over me.

"Rune?" A woman's voice floats into my sleepy haze. "What are you doing in here?"

Then, I feel a soft weight beneath my arm, and memories of last night flood back. I jolt awake, sitting upright to find Gianna standing over me. Though her attention isn't on me, but on Elijah.

I've been caught! Jumping to my feet, I hurry and usher her away just as Elijah stirs awake. He stretches his arms and winces at the bright sunlight. "What time is it?" he asks, scratching a hand through his short hair.

As I try to position myself between Gianna and my human friend, panic grips me tightly. My mind races with the consequences of being discovered. She'll surely report this to the others, and they'll convene for my banishment. What was I thinking—breaking one of our most sacred laws? All those years of dedication, all the sacrifices made, thrown away for what—for…for… I don't even know what to call this feeling. Is it curiosity, recklessness, or something else entirely?

Gianna sidesteps, craning her head to look over my shoulder. "Did you have fun last night?" she asks with an amused grin.

I don't even have to turn around to see Elijah's elated expression. I can feel the air shift as he sits up. A soft cough mixed with a chuckle escapes. "Good morning, Gianna."

"Good morning," she says, then shifts her attention to me.

Before she can say or ask anything else, I lead her out of my mother's private study and into the entryway hall. "What are you doing here?"

"The windows were open, and I wanted to see why. No one's been inside your mother's study chamber since returning. I had to investigate."

She's not wrong, and I probably would've done the same. Glancing slightly behind, inside the room, I tell her, "It's not what you think."

Her smile spreads wider. "Well, that's disappointing. I know how much you care for the boy and how much he cares for you."

"He's human!" I say with emphasis yet trying to keep my voice low.

"Rune, does that really—"

"It does. We have laws and traditions that have kept our world safe for as long as our kind has existed. Besides not allowing other-realm beings into our world, forming romantic relationships with beings that are not angels is strictly forbidden."

She tucks her black hair behind one ear. The curve of her feathered wings peeks over her shoulders, and with one brow lifted, she inquires, "So, you're telling me that of all the angels that have ever traveled to other realms, none of them have coupled with people that weren't angels?"

I open my mouth to answer, then slowly close it as Sara's story about Trevor and her forms in my mind. Disregarding the story, I purse my lips and let out a frustrated sigh, feeling the need to shift the conversation. "We were looking for Merigoth's journal."

The second the name *Merigoth* leaves my lips, Gianna's body tenses. She slides one foot back along the stone floor, as if to steady her stance. The fear that I wanted to prevent takes root inside her, and her voice trembles when she asks, "Is the demon queen free from her mental prison?"

"No!" I quickly interject, hoping to correct the panic state I've brought about. "Oh, stars, no! I'm here for my mother's journal, and Elijah offered to come and help me find it. Adele and her mother wanted to learn more about…" How do I delicately phrase this to avoid alarming Gianna about the imminent danger we face in Noviska? "…what happened to Loralai before she became Merigoth."

The tension seems to dissipate. Gianna's shoulders relax, and she nods in understanding. "Well, in that case, I may be of some help. I believe I know where your mother kept her valuables. The journal might be in there."

"How did you come across this information?"

"Someone from my family was close with your mother."

I recall an angel friend frequently visiting her in our home or here in her study. The only friend outside of the council. "Veskor was your father?"

She shakes her head. "He was my father's brother. There was one time I accompanied him while visiting your mother here. We arrived as she was putting something away in a lockbox. I don't know where the sunstone to unlock it would be, but at least I can show you where the box is hidden."

"Yes, please."

I let her go first, and she reenters the study, offering Elijah a small smile. "It's good to see you again."

His eyes meet mine with an apologetic look. He knows my concerns about bringing him here. I expected Gianna, or any other angel for that matter, to show more concern than she did. Her reaction was quite the opposite, for that matter, expressing a keen interest in the potential relationship between Elijah and me.

Elijah stands from his seat on the dusty armchair, and as we cross the room, he follows. "What's going on?"

"Gianna believes she may know where my mother's secret lockbox is located."

"Really?" He stands next to me, and when our arms graze, he steps away, giving me space to watch Gianna. I can't even imagine the confusion I've caused him after trying to seduce him for my own internal cravings. I recall his words, *I don't know if my heart can take having just one night with you*, on repeat in my head. Could I give him more than a fleeting escapade?

"Ah, over here!" Gianna exclaims, saving me from making any hasty decisions. She moves from the desk to a small sitting cove beneath the window. With a strong tug, she lifts the slab seat up, the stone edges grinding against the adjacent walls enclosing the area. After she gently rests the slab against the window frame, we peer down into the secret cubby.

"There's where I saw your mother putting stuff away," she says, pointing to the stone chest nestled within. Along the top, intricate carvings depict a beautiful pair of wings, its feathers delicately etched into the stone. Between the wings, a smooth concave bowl sits, its surface gleaming softly under the ambient morning light. And I know exactly what goes there.

I quickly spin and stride over to the fireplace, where my mother kept her secret stash of sunstones. It's convenient that Gianna knows the location of the safe while I remember where Mother stored her special sunstones. When I press on the center of a stone panel that seems to be part of the fireplace structure, the stone pops open like a small door. Inside lie three sunstones. I gather all three and return to where Gianna and Elijah watch me intently. It's the second sunstone I try that successfully triggers the locking mechanism of the stone chest. Politely, I request Elijah to return the other two sunstones to the secret compartment in the fireplace, ensuring we know their whereabouts if needed later, and he does.

After I remove the lid and set it on the floor, we stare into the safe. It appears empty, but I know the darkness is a trick of the eye. I reach inside and pull out everything—a stack of papers, old photographs, and one leather journal. Loralai's journal.

"This is it!"

The pages are stiff, making it difficult to turn them. The corner of a page breaks off like the fragile edges of a dead leaf. With its pages so brittle, we'll have to be careful while reading.

I face Gianna and express my gratitude. "Will you please not tell the others about Elijah being here? I don't want them to be angry or banish me from my home."

Gianna laughs. "Rune! No one is going to banish you!" She emphasizes the word *banish* as if it's a punch line. "Are you kidding? We need you! You and..." Her laughter abruptly ceases, and her eyes narrow at me. "Where's Evander?"

"He's—" Elijah begins, but I cut him off. "He's helping with a situation in Bricen."

"Oh. Is there anything I can do to help?"

"No!" Elijah and I exclaim in unison. Then, I force a smile, trying my best not to seem as if I'm lying. "Thank you, but it's unnecessary. It's important for you to remain here and oversee the activities in Stellara. I can't thank you enough for your help—both with leading in our absence and with assisting us in finding the journal." I also silently thank her for bringing to light how I've been overreacting with keeping to our laws. Perhaps there is room for change. However, as I glance at my mother's desk, I'm reminded of her unwavering commitment to the laws that have safeguarded our city and its angels. The thought of abandoning them fills me with a sense of betrayal that I know would deeply disappoint her.

Gianna's petite figure straightens, and she appears to gain inches in height. "I'm happy to help in any way I can." I envy her optimism and would give anything to shield her and the other angels from the disappointment I feel, knowing that our beautiful city will never be what it once was without more support. I briefly entertain the idea of leaving the city again to scour the Starlight Realm for other angels, hoping to persuade them to return and aid in the rebuilding efforts.

"I'll leave you to it, then," she says, offering us a curt nod before exiting the study chamber.

Clutching the journal, I glance at Elijah. "It's all in here. The answers to what happened to Loralai, to what she learned from the demons that infected her. We might even find something we can use to save Evander."

Elijah cups his hand over my arm. "We will save him, Rune. With or without whatever's in that journal. We will save him."

Before we return to Bricen, the only thing I can manage without risking a flood of emotions that I've been suppressing is a sincere expression of gratitude. "Thank you."

CHAPTER 22

Rolling over, I slam my temple against something cold and hard. I groan and rub the sore spot, then force myself into a sitting position. My shoulder aches from the awkward position I fell asleep in. Wait, no. Not fell asleep, but poisoned with some sort of sleep serum. My hand goes from my temple to my biceps, where the dart punctured through my cloak and into my skin. That's when I also realize my gloves are still off. After pulling them out from within my vest, I quickly slip them on.

Kit lies passed out next to me. I roll up my sleeve, then hold my wrist under her nose. Soft puffs of warm air blow against my skin. Withdrawing my hand, I silently thank the stars that she's alive.

Looking about the room, I focus on our whereabouts. The cage they've locked us up in is big enough for a grizzly bear, yet not tall enough for me to stand in. Surrounding the cage are rows of long tables and benches. This must be Gailstein's meeting and dining hall. A few rows away, two large barrels with spigots sit at the end of the table. A collection of carved wooden cups and metal tankards surround the barrels. There's nothing else and no one else in the hall but us.

Kit stirs next to me, and I shift against the bars, giving her space to wake. She grumbles and when she goes to sit up, her leg bangs against the iron bars. "Ow!"

"Careful," I say. "We've been locked up in some animal cage."

She stretches her jaw and rubs at her neck. "Are you serious?" After sitting up, she grabs hold of the bars and gives them a vigorous shake. "Well, now what do we do?"

The double doors at the front open. Two soldiers mosey into the great hall, engaged in a friendly conversation. If one didn't know they were here pilfering and murdering innocent villagers, they could've easily been mistaken as benevolent travelers. It isn't until my gaze dips to the bloodstains splattered along the bottom half of their long blue coats that the darkness within grows anxious. That part of me has come to terms with knowing it'll only be set free against those who deserve to be punished, and by their smug expressions and bloodstained attire, I can tell these two meet that requirement.

Both men have swords hanging from their waists and head straight for the barrels. Ignoring us, they fill their cups with water or mead. I can't tell from here.

"Can we get a cup of that?"

They side-eye us before finishing their drinks and slamming the cups on the table, laughing as if I told them a humorous joke. "You get nothing," one says, while the other continues to chuckle, strolling over to the front of the cage. With a hard sniff, he coughs something up before spitting on the ground inside the cage. Mumbling under his breath, he turns on his heels and follows his soldier friend out the double doors, letting them slam shut behind him.

An hour goes by and I'm about to doze off when something scratches at the wood. I search the tables, thinking someone's hiding behind a chair or trying to open a window. But there's no one.

"What's that sound?" Kit asks, also seeking the source.

"There," I shout, and Kit's gaze follows the direction of my pointed finger.

Toward the back of the room, a hatch in the floor slightly bounces, as if someone below the hall is trying to lift it open. Kit moves next to me, and we both watch with anticipation. I curse to the stars when it finally pops open and a green hood peeks up through the floorboards.

"It's Aleksandra!" Kit exclaims.

"I can see that." I'm not as thrilled as my friend is to see the hooded girl. "What are you doing?" I scold loud enough to draw her attention over to us.

Her brows pinch, and she stares at us. "You're in a cage." I can't tell if she's seriously asking us or making a jest. After hoisting herself out of the hole, she hurries over to us. Meanwhile, I give a quick glance over my shoulder to the front doors, making sure we're still alone.

Aleksandra tugs at the iron lock securing the cage door. "Where's the key?"

"It doesn't matter," I tell her. "You're not going anywhere near any of those soldiers—or villagers," I quickly add. "No one needs to know you're here."

"But I can help!" She sits up on her knees, tightening her hold on the front of her green cloak.

"We are in a bit of a bind, Adele," Kit points out.

"No. We'll figure another way out of this mess." I point to the hole in the floor. "You need to return to the horses and ride back to Bricen. Then, tell..." I'm hesitant to say *our mum*, and instead go with, "Sara and the others that we may be a little longer than expected."

"But—"

"No buts... You can't be here right now." I don't let her being on the other side of this cage affect my decision. Yes, she might be the only person here to help us, but I won't risk her getting caught. And not because it's the right thing to do, but because it would destroy Mum if Aleksandra were caught and treated like an animal—like how she was treated up in Noviska.

"We're not in any danger," I lie. "When they come to get us, we'll catch them by surprise. We'll fight our way free and head back to Bricen. But you need to go."

One of the double doors opens, and in walk two soldiers. Not the same soldiers from earlier. They immediately spot Aleksandra in her vibrant green cloak. "Hey!" the taller of the two calls. "You can't be in here."

"Come here," the shorter, paler man demands.

They take a few steps toward the cage, and I turn to Aleksandra, grabbing the soft fabric of her cloak. "Go! Now! Get to the horses and ride to Bricen!"

With a pensive expression, she stands, and for a second I think she's going to listen, but instead she saunters around to the front of the cage, basically doing the complete opposite of what I told her to do. "Aleksandra!" I yell, shuffling on my knees, pushing past Kit to get closer to the front part of the cage.

"That's right, come here," the taller man says. "Let's get a good look-see at your pretty face. Don't be shy."

"Oh, I'm not good with people," Aleksandra says bashfully.

"What is she doing?" Kit whispers. We're both out of reach, unable to help Aleksandra if the men lunge at her.

They're getting closer to her when she asks them, "Do you want to know what happiness feels like?"

Smug grins form on their faces, and they laugh and nod to one another. "Yes, let's have some—" But the man's words are cut short as he stops advancing. The other man does the same. Their jaws drop, popping their mouths open, and their gazes look past us all, up toward the ceiling. Both men appear to be in a dazed stupor. Aleksandra casually walks over to them and giggles as she pokes the shorter, paler man in his round belly.

"What did you do?" I call out, even though I have a good hunch about what just happened.

She faces us, a proud gleam in her expression. "Master Ebenus would be furious with me right now if he saw what I did." This knowledge doesn't seem to diminish her amused giggling. She pokes the man again, but this time on his nose. When he blinks, she shuffles away. "Oh, dear."

"Oh, dear, what?!" I hastily ask. "You can enchant bliss?"

Aleksandra doesn't answer. She's too focused on watching the men slowly stir from their daze. "Are you enjoying the warm happiness flowing over your bodies?" she asks them, and the second she's done, her hand shoots to her head and she wobbles, using a nearby table to balance herself. "Oh, that was too much."

"That's enough, Aleksandra. It's obviously taking a toll on you."

She looks up at me and nods, her hand still pressed to her forehead. "Maybe I will go find my horse and ride to Bricen."

"Tell Sara and Lauren there're at least thirty soldiers," Kit says, grabbing hold of the bars. "Make sure you tell them, so they know what they're walking into if they come."

Aleksandra nods and staggers past the cage. It isn't until two more men walk into the hall and see their fellow soldiers staring off at the ceiling that Aleksandra makes haste for the hatch door. They two men call out, shouting for her to stop. The two dazed men wake from their trance, shaking their heads.

"You two! Go outside and catch her!" a soldier commands. They follow orders and run out the front doors while the two other soldiers climb down the hatch in pursuit of Aleksandra.

"What if they catch her?" Kit whispers.

"There's nothing we can do for her. She's on her own until we find a way out."

Kit slumps to the floor, leaning against the corner bars. "Let's hope she escapes, finds the horses, and rides to Bricen."

The odds of her actually making that happen are not in our favor, but I don't tell Kit that. Right now, we have to focus on how we're going to get out of this cage.

What seems like forever is probably more like twenty or thirty minutes. Kit and I both are lounging about, resting in silence, when the screaming starts. We crawl closer to the front of the cage, eagerly waiting for the doors to fly open so we can see what's going on outside. And when they do, a Fayatin soldier runs inside. But he's quick to close them before we can see what's going on outside.

"What's happening?" I yell.

He flips over and presses his back to the doors. "You brought this, you demon creature!" Seeing his face, I recognize him as the man I chased through the woods yesterday morning. The one with the burn scar along his chin up to his ear.

"I brought nothing here, you incompetent oaf!" I shout.

Kit chuckles beside me.

"This isn't exactly the time to be amused," I grumble.

"Oh, but that's a good one. I'm going to have to use that one on Elijah."

"You do that," I say, trying to stay focused.

The doors behind him shake violently. With outstretched arms he uses his body to hold the them shut. With each hard push, his body bounces against the doors. He looks frantically about the great hall, and I can only imagine he's trying to decide what to do.

"I'd run if I were you!" Kit shouts.

Then, suddenly the rattling stops. With each panicked breath, the man's chest heaves up and down. Then, when something flies by the side windows, he screams.

"How about you let us out, and we'll help you fight off whatever's attacking the village?" I call to him. "Just unlock the cage door."

"I didn't come here to die! I was promised land, and…and a title!" His face blanches as he continues to ramble on about broken promises. He eventually turns and opens one of the doors. "I need to return to Fayatin. They need to know about this!" The second he steps outside, we're able to see soldiers and villagers running every which way, screaming and hollering to move. Then, in a brown blur, something swooshes by and grabs the scarred man in its wake.

I look to Kit, who's also grinning, and we say in unison, "Rune."

CHAPTER 23

RUNE

We don't have time for this. The man's ankle slips from my grasp, and I dip lower in my flight path and release him. He screams and crashes through the thatched roof of a cottage. Circling around, everyone running in every direction, I search out Sara and Elijah. They're at the front of the village, fighting soldiers. I veer left and come at the soldiers from the side, bowling into the line of them, knocking them over. Some lie unconscious while others crawl to their feet, searching the sky for whatever knocked them down.

"Find Adele, Kit, and Aleksandra! Hurry!" I shout, hovering in the air above Sara and Elijah. They take off running toward the large wood structure just behind the open grounds in the center of the village. Across the way, a line of soldiers with their bows drawn are getting into position to fire. A man stands behind them, presumably their leader. His cape flutters in the winter breeze that sweeps through the village.

Drawing their attention away from Sara and Elijah, who have reached the front doors to the hall, I call out to the line of soldiers, "Up here!" When they lift their gazes to where I hold my position high in the sky, my wings beating behind me, their eyes grow wide.

"Kill the demon bird-creature!" the leader bellows, pointing his sword up at me.

Demon bird-creature, I repeat in my mind. How dare he! When they release the first wave of arrows into the sky, I bolt upward, dodging their strikes. Using the sunrays to hide my whereabouts, I hear them all asking one another, "Where is the demon bird?" and, "Does anyone see it?" This has my insides boiling with fury. I am no demon.

"Rune!" Elijah calls to me from the front doors of the hall. From his position, the sunlight doesn't hide me, and he shouts, "We need to find keys! They're locked in a cage!"

"On it!" I yell down to him and swoop low, flying a few feet off the ground, sending a wave of dust toward the Fayatin men. The soldiers gasp and stumble in their offensive positions.

"Get ready!" the white-haired man with the cape yells. "Aim!" I then see the large black iron ring hanging from his belt in front of his sword's sheath. A bunch of keys hang off the ring, and I know those are the keys that will set Adele and Kit free.

I hover in front of the soldiers, wings beating hard, kicking up more dust into the men's eyes. Then, with a forceful thrust forward, I send a powerful gust of wind at them. They stumble backward and fall to the ground. The old man is halfway across the village now, fleeing to save his own life. I chuckle at his pathetic attempt to run. I'll show him what real running looks like. The world around me momentarily blurs and within seconds, I've caught up to him. "Where are you going?" I ask, and before he can answer, I jab the side of my hand into his throat. His hands wrap around his neck as he gasps for air. Eventually, he trips over his own feet and lands hard on the ground. Approaching him, I tuck my wings against my back before reaching down and tugging the iron ring of keys from his belt.

He tries to roll over and get up, but I slam my boot against his chest, forcing him to stay put. "You would be wise to leave this village—this country—and never return." I give a slight push of my boot, emphasizing the threat of my words.

He continues to cough, saliva spilling from his mouth, until he's able to speak. His words are raspy, but he manages to say, "Others will come and hunt you."

A *caw* erupts from above and without looking, I toss the iron keys high into the sky. There's a jingle as Serafina catches them. "Bring those to Elijah," I shout, without looking away from the man's furious stare.

Leaning forward, my boot pressing into his chest, I explain with stern tone, "No one is going to come here and hunt anyone. If I see any of your soldiers, or anyone with that ridiculous *F* on their clothes, I will do far worse than end your life. I will send you to a world where you will feel nothing but pain and suffering for the rest of your days."

The silence between us isn't comforting, but I refuse to take another life—not after the many lives I took while under the enchantment of Merigoth and control of Marcellus. I will not let that life resurface, no matter what.

Slowly lifting my boot from his chest, I look at the soldiers circling us. "You will leave," I shout, "and never return."

The old man staggers to his feet with the help of a few of his soldiers. Clutching his shoulder, he hisses, "This is not over!"

I don't respond and only watch them collect and shuffle their way out of the village. Once they're gone, I turn and make my way toward the long wooden structure. Outside, standing in the doorways of the many homes lining the road toward the hall, men, women, and children all gawk. Their eyes tremble with fear, or worse, eye me over as a threat. Not a single one thanks me.

Adele and Kit stroll out of the hall, Sara and Elijah following. They walk over and I'm about to open a doorway to Goslings when I notice someone missing. "Where's Aleksandra?"

"She was being chased by a group of Fayatin soldiers," Kit explains.

Adele's gaze finds me after she's done assessing the area. "We told her to go to the horses and ride back to Bricen. She may or may not be en route to return."

Coming up next to her daughter, Sara says, "I'll stay and look for her. Where did you leave the horses?"

"I'll stay and take you to the horses." Kit waves a hand for Sara to follow.

"There's a good chance we'll be in Noviska when you return," Adele calls out.

Sara stops, tells Kit to wait before approaching us. Her attention is on all three of us, Elijah, Adele, and me. "You three have been through so much, and I know you'll always look out for one another. No matter what. I see that now. I trust you will do what you need to do to save Evander and come back alive."

"I will protect them," I tell her.

"We'll protect each other," Adele adds.

When they're out of earshot, I open the doorway straight into Goslings, where Lauren and Sayen wait for us. Hopefully within the hour, Evander will be free, and Marcellus will be dealt with once and for all. Dealing with that monster is something I never want to do ever again.

CHAPTER 24

Sayen's eyes plead with me as she repeats her question: "Can you please let me see my family now?" Her gaze flicks to the front door of Goslings, then back to me. "If what you say is true—that Aleksandra has run off—then I'd like to go home…now."

Narrowing my eyes, I question, "But what if she returns?"

Swallowing the lump in her throat, she hesitates but then shakes her head. "My family. I must know they're unharmed—that the master has not paid them a visit. I must know. Aleksandra will understand."

Recalling how Master Ebenus is now under Marcellus's control, I have doubts about him traveling to the girl's family.

Unsure of what to do, I'm silently thankful for Rune stepping over, offering up a distraction. "Here, I brought this from Stellara." She holds out a small leather journal. "It was Merigoth's before her transformation."

Before accepting the journal, I pull off one glove with my teeth while Aunt Lauren sympathetically takes hold of Sayen from behind and ushers her to a chair, giving me space to look over the journal. The leather cover is soft and worn beneath my fingertips, while the paper within is stiff and brittle. When I accidentally clip off one of the corners, Rune reacts with a hiss.

"These pages resemble dead leaves," I mumble, then realize I still have my glove clenched between my teeth. Tucking the glove under my arm, I say again, "Sorry. These pages are as fragile as a dead leaf."

"Then be more careful," Rune says with emphasis.

With caution, I turn each page slowly and deliberately. When I come upon a page that is full of charcoal illustrations, I stop and look more closely. "What are these things?" I wonder aloud as I trace the tip of my finger over the sketched outlines. Most of the drawings depict a peculiar creature, a miniature version of a human or an angel. Its body, limbs, and head bear a striking resemblance to our own. Except the creature has uniquely pointed ears and dark, rounded horns reminiscent of Aleksandra and Merigoth. The horns are surrounded by curly white hair. I struggle to determine the exact color of its skin from the sketch, but she's drawn the creature's face with either dirt or dark splotches, similar to freckles or birthmarks. The most notable distinction, apart from the ear shape, is that Merigoth has filled in the creature's larger eyes entirely using the charcoal writing tool.

"Are these the demons that infected Merigoth?" A wave of revulsion rolls through me at the idea that this creature's blood also runs through my veins.

Rune holds out a hand, and I pass the open journal to her. Immediately once the journal has left my possession, I slip my glove back on while Rune looks over the illustration. With a gentle motion, she closes the journal, and explains, "Honestly, I've only been able to interpret a few pages, but it seems so. Merigoth documented her observations and encounters with the Bocnite, but I can't make out what language she used for her notes."

"She obviously didn't want anyone else reading what she discovered," I mutter.

"Bock-night?" Elijah repeats. He takes a seat around the table where Aunt Lauren and Sayen sit. He looks to Rune and asks, "Do they live in the Starlight Realm?"

She nods, takes a seat at the table, and continues explaining, "From what I can tell from her sketches, these Bocnites live out somewhere in the Shadowlands of our realm."

"Wait," Lauren interrupts, "the demons that infected her aren't from another realm? They're from the Starlight Realm?"

Again, Rune nods. "It appears so." After setting the journal on the table, she crosses her arms and leans back in her chair. "I'd hoped there'd be something in there to help us counter the incantations embedded in the monoliths. But there's no mention or drawing of any symbols. It only documents Merigoth's interactions with these Bocnites."

Leaning on one of the chairs from behind, I ask both Rune and Aunt Lauren, "Has anyone ever traveled to this Shadowland? I mean, surely, Merigoth couldn't have been the first angel to cross paths with these creatures."

The waning sunlight stretches in from the front window across the tavern room, and it's my aunt who answers. "The Shadowlands are a forbidden territory."

The silence between my aunt and Rune lingers, and it's getting on my nerves. "And?"

Rune finally says, "Although my mother, the North Star leader, did not create the law, she strongly enforced it. And if Merigoth was traversing into the forbidden territory, she was doing so on her own accord. A journey like that would never have gotten approved by the counsel."

"It also makes sense as to why she was banished," Aunt Lauren quietly adds. I can't say if the mood has gotten any better between the two of them, but I imagine Rune is still insistent that my aunt leave Bricen and return to the Starlight Realm.

Elijah stands and moves to the fireplace, adding a few logs and stoking the fire while we try and figure out the connection between Merigoth and the Bocnite. After a few minutes, he faces the room and says loudly, "The Bocnite aren't our priority! And since the journal doesn't provide any useful information to help us get past the enchanted monoliths—"

"What about me?" Sayen blurts out, cutting off Elijah while jumping to her feet. Her green cloak billows out around her legs from her abrupt motion.

Aunt Lauren reaches one arm over and pulls the girl in for a comforting squeeze. "The poor child's been through enough and should be reunited with her family."

It isn't Sayen we need to bait Marcellus. I'm not sure how Aleksandra will feel about us returning the girl to her home, but honestly, I don't care. With Rune here, we can open another doorway and reunite the two at any time. I look to Rune and give a shrug. "I say let her see her family."

Rune nods. "Fine by me."

Sayen's smile spreads, and her eyes light up with a revived sense of new life. "Oh, thank you-thank you! Now, quick. Open the doorway!"

A few minutes after Sayen has shown Rune where to open the doorway to, we stand side by side, peering through the passage. I'll never enjoy visiting Noviska. I don't find pleasure in the snowy terrain and frigid weather, but it is pretty to look at.

On the other side of the doorway is a quaint sheep farm. Smoke curls lazily out the chimney of the stone house, and a small herd of sheep grazes peacefully in the late-afternoon sun in a nearby pen. Their thick, woolly coats are a testament to their resilience against the frigid northern temperatures.

After Sayen walks across the threshold, she waves a quick goodbye and runs toward the stone house. We all stare through the passage and watch the girl. She glances behind a few more times, waving each time.

"What is she doing?" I ask, finding the behavior odd.

"Maybe she's just overly grateful that we brought her home?" Rune answers, though her expression mirrors my own confused one. Sayen continues to trudge through the snow toward the farmhouse.

Opening the small wooden gate, she passes the threshold of the small yard and without knocking, enters the home. We all stare in anticipation.

"Maybe I should go make sure she's okay," Aunt Lauren says, stepping closer, her wings now visible along the back side of her blue dress. Then, Sayen pops her head out and gives us one final goodbye wave. Her smile stretches from ear to ear.

A collective sigh of relief escapes from all four of us watching. Elijah turns to Rune and says, "I think that means her family is safe."

Rune agrees, then with a flick of her wrist, she closes the doorway. The fire in the fireplace quickly warms up the room after the brief encounter with the cold country.

"We need a plan," I state, refocusing our attention on saving Evander. "And unless Mum and Kit can find Aleksandra, we have to assume the girl's no longer a reliable pawn to be used in our plans."

Pursing her lips, knowing I speak the truth, Rune slams her fists onto the tabletop. "Marcellus won't give up Evander without a trade."

Elijah jumps in and offers his thoughts. "Let's take a step back and reiterate our objectives. One, we need to stop the Reborns from being set free to cause mayhem in the villages of Noviska. Two, we need to disband the Order. And three, we need to somehow render Marcellus unconscious so Rune can throw him back over to the Under Realm."

Aunt Lauren bites her lower lip, then softly asks, "And how are we supposed to accomplish all of that with only the four of us?" She pauses before adding, "We should wait until Sara and Kit return with news of Aleksandra."

"No," Rune barks. Narrowing her gaze at my aunt, she exclaims with a sharp edge to her voice, "You would do anything—at a heartbeat's notice—if it were *your* family!" She says the word knowing my aunt's true family is not angel born. "So, you'll excuse me if I'm done waiting for all of you to make up your minds about how to save *my* family!"

Elijah steps in to break up the tense stare down happening between Rune and Aunt Lauren. He firmly grips Rune's shoulders, forcing her attention to him. "You are our family too. You and Evander. We haven't been trying to delay the rescue, but to do what we can when we can. We're still at a great disadvantage with you or any other angel not being able to approach the village or use your abilities."

It's nice to see the boy I once knew standing here with the wisdom of a grown adult. He impresses me. Well, sometimes. Memories surface about how he stumbled out of the morning fog, tripping on a tree root and revealing our whereabouts to that Fayatin man. But for the most part, he means well with his good-natured heart.

"We can draw him out of Bluskyn? Get him to come to us," Aunt Lauren suggests, a proud smile replacing her tense expression from earlier.

"Okay," I say, even though I doubt Marcellus will fall for any ploys we throw at him; as of right now, it's our best option. "How do we draw him out of the village and away from the protection of the monoliths?"

The room falls to silence. I already know the answer, and I'm assuming everyone else does too. No one wants to say it out loud, so I do. "We use me as bait."

Then, before anyone can agree or protest, the front door to Goslings swings open, slamming against the wall. Startled, all four of us spin to see who it is that's rushed into the tavern.

Aleksandra is out of breath, as if she ran all the way from Gailstein to Bricen in record time. Her gaze searches the room until she finally stops and stares at me. "Where is Sayen?"

CHAPTER 25

*A*DELE

Aleksandra storms farther into the tavern toward us. I crane my neck to look out the open front door, wondering who's out there that saw her because her hood's drawn back, allowing anyone a clear view of the black horns curling out the sides of her head. I rush past her, because I need to know, and stand on Goslings' porch. No one. Not a single soul outside. The stars must be in our favor. No one saw her. Not even the smithy boys are out working.

After returning inside, I close the door and ask my aunt, "Where is everyone?"

"Probably cleaning up for supper." With her hands raised in a gesture of peace, she approaches Aleksandra. "What happened? Where's your horse?"

"You first," she hisses, keeping one eye on me as I move to stand next to Elijah. Aleksandra repeats her question: "Where's Sayen?"

Without hesitating, Elijah explains, "She was distraught and wished to return home. We didn't see a problem since Rune could easily take you there if you wished to go too."

At the same time Aleksandra says, "I wish to go," I ask, "Where are Sara and Kit?"

Aleksandra's fury points at me. "How am I supposed to know?"

"They stayed behind in Gailstein. To search for you," Elijah explains before I can. He's inching closer, as is Aunt Lauren.

"Well, I never saw them. Now"—she waves a hand through the air, mimicking Rune's hand gesture when she opens doorways—"take me to Sayen's home."

Rune glances at me, and I nod. She flicks her wrist and reopens the doorway she opened earlier for Sayen.

"You should put your hood up," I say.

With a scowl, Aleksandra tugs at her green hood, pulling it up over her hair and horns. She goes to step through the doorway but stops. "That is not Sayen's family home."

"What?" Rune peers through the passage at the sheep farm blanketed in snow. The small herd is no longer sunbathing in their pen, but the smoke from the chimney still rises. "You're mistaken. This is the home Sayen showed me."

"She's right," I confirm. "We saw her enter that stone cottage, right there."

Aleksandra steps through, her boots sinking into deep snow right next to Sayen's footprints embedded in the snow. She bends down and traces a finger along the edge of the impression, her finger coming up with melted snow on the end. "She has misled you. This is not her home."

"And why would she deceive us?" I ask.

Lauren walks through the back door of the tavern with a pile of cloaks and furs in her arms. I didn't even see her leave. "We'll need these if we're going over there to find Sayen."

Aleksandra stands and starts walking, following the deep footsteps left in the snow. I grab a thicker cloak and quickly swap it for the one I have on. Elijah does the same, then wraps a scarf around his neck and crams a fur hat over his head.

"Let's hurry. Aleksandra's gaining ground and we can't lose her too," I say, stepping through and trudging into the ankle-deep snow. Elijah is on my heels while Rune and Lauren take to the sky.

We finally catch up to Aleksandra, who's panting, holding on to any tree she passes for momentary support. I call to her, "You're going to pass out before we find her, and I'm not carrying you, so slow down and catch your breath!"

"No, we're almost there! I know this place!"

Glancing past Aleksandra, through the pine trees, I spot what appears to be a door blending in with the forest. The closer we get, I can see it's a home, but only the front side is visible, as the rest of the house appears to be buried in the side of a hill. When we reach the front of the home, there's a stump with an axe embedded in the center, some fish hanging on a rope between two slender trees, and two barrels next to the front door.

"Adele!" Elijah jogs over. "Is this Sayen's true home?"

Lauren lands nearby. "Why would Sayen show Rune the wrong house?"

"Because she doesn't trust you," Aleksandra answers loudly, not hiding the truth from us. "You are not her family, and you don't understand what either of us have lived through." She opens the door to the home and disappears inside. Elijah and Lauren follow Aleksandra into the hillside home.

Rune beats her wings, slowly descending until she's standing next to me. "Something's not right," she tells me.

"What did you see from the sky?" Glancing up, I shield my eyes from the blinding sun with one gloved hand.

"A wagon traveling down the road from the north. It'll be here momentarily."

"How many passengers?"

"One, maybe two," she says with a shrug. "We can only hope this isn't their destination and that they continue along the road."

"Let's hope." I keep a concentrated glare on the road between the sparse stretch of pine trees. Once the wooden wagon becomes visible, it swiftly disappears again, hidden by the trees. I pray to the stars that the horses keep moving forward. However, either my prayers are too late, or the stars are not in our favor today, as the horses halt abruptly on the road ahead, causing the wagon to rear up on the uneven ground before finally coming to a complete stop.

"It appears this is their destination," I point out. With a swift motion, I lift the edge of my cloak and draw out my trusted dagger from its concealed spot within my waistband.

Rune tucks her wings behind her shoulders and conceals their existence. Someone jumps down from the wagon seat, but I can't see who. What I can see is the color of their cloaks—a russet brown. Whoever they are, they don't belong to the Order.

They approach us, sticking close to the pine trees. As the dark figure reaches the final line of trees, my heart plummets into my gut at the sight of his smug expression. It's Marcellus. He confidently strides toward us, never breaking eye contact with me. "Hello, sister."

Seeing him yesterday while Kit and I were spying on him at the Bluskyn meeting hall was one thing because he was unaware of our presence. But now, he sees me. His hands are just twenty paces away from me. Rune tenses up and swiftly positions herself two steps ahead of me. Suddenly, she unveils her wings and stretches them out wide, making herself appear twice as large and intimidating.

Every muscle in my body freezes as if the temperature in this frigid country dropped another ten degrees. Without looking away, Rune whispers to me, "He's out in the open. I can take him. There are no monoliths here to prevent me from throwing him back into the Under Realm."

My mind is racing because this is too easy. Why would he risk exposing himself like this? "Wait!" I grab her arm, my gloved hand clutching the fabric of her white shirt. "Something's not right."

Shrugging my hand away, she seethes, "I'm not letting him get away. Not this time. This time, we say our goodbyes for good. This time I throw his lifeless body back to the Under Realm where his corpse can rot."

"Rune…" The rest of my words don't come. I want to tell her *no*—that he's a lost soul, he's been used as a weapon the same way General Onica used me. That we might be able to save him. But the words are stuck in my throat, refusing to leave my lips.

She takes another step, ready to lunge at him, when a blur of reddish-brown feathers swoops across my vision, stealing Rune off the ground and into the air. I trip backward, nearly falling into the snow, but manage to steady myself by grabbing on to the handle of the axe, which is stuck in the cutting stump. Gripping the hilt of my trusty dagger, I also wrench the axe free from the stump, ready to fight if Marcellus advances. The more weapons, the better because I refuse to let him touch me—to claim my free will.

But he doesn't move. He only has eyes for me, and I can't tear mine from his. His smile falters, and he crosses his arms behind his back. "I will not force you to accompany me unless I have to." He pauses, and I can't think straight. Then he gestures to the hillside home. Someone yells from inside. He says with a bit of triumph in his voice, "Think of your friends' well-being, Adele. You can save them if you just follow me to the wagon."

A crashing sound booms from inside the hillside home, followed by a giant plume of dusty debris and smoke. I'm torn between running into the home and helping Aunt Lauren and Elijah fight whatever's in there or going with Marcellus. Undecided, I hold my ground, ready to fight if he takes a step closer. Without moving, I yell, "Elijah! Lauren! Everything okay in there?"

More crashing and pounding erupts, accompanied by grunts and shrieks. Unsure of what's happening inside the underground home, I have to trust that Aunt Lauren can handle it.

"You can make it stop," Marcellus states calmly. "All you have to do is climb into the wagon and return to the village with me."

Shaking my head, wanting to run inside the house and help them, I shout, "I don't believe you! You'll kill my friends and claim my mind."

"You have my word that I will not. I actually want to talk with you—something we haven't really gotten to do, have we?"

This is most definitely a trick. More shouting and wood cracking come from inside the home. For a brief second, I look to the sky. *Where is Rune?* The only one who would be able to swoop down and steal her off the ground is Evander. So, she's no good to me right now. My breathing grows heavy with uncertainty, and not wanting to give in yet, I demand, "Tell me who's in there." I throw out my hand and point to the small door leading inside the home. Packed dirt and patches of grass trail up the hillside that doubles as the front exterior wall of the home.

His reply seems unnervingly casual. "Alister."

No, no, no. That unearthly brute almost killed me and Aunt Lauren the last time we faced him. Another scream erupts, except this one comes from the sky. Holding up the axe and dagger, I look up to see Evander holding Rune by the shoulders, pushing her through the air. She's trying to escape his clutches, but her wings are struggling to gain control.

"One word," Marcellus says, my attention returning to him, "and I can make it all stop." His words come out in a pleasant manner, as if he knows he's won.

And he's not wrong.

"Fine! I'll come with you, but if you so much as flinch in my direction, I'll do whatever it takes to end you—even if it means ending me, too."

His grin grows, and he gestures with a wide sweep of his arm to the wagon.

"You first!" I snarl.

He turns and leaves, walking toward the wagon.

"No! I mean, you call off Evander and Alister!"

"Not yet," he shouts without turning around.

It takes me a long moment to decide what to do. Should I ignore Marcellus and run in to help fight Alister, or go with Marcellus and trust that he'll keep his word and call off the Reborn man?

The first step is the hardest, and I practically have to force my foot to lift off the ground and move...in the direction of the road. Marcellus holds open one of the double doors to the back side of the wagon. Not wanting to get too close, I tell him, "I'm not coming within an arms-length of you. If you want me to get inside that wagon, you need to be over there." I point farther down the road, about five or six paces from where we stand.

"I gave you my word," he insists.

"Your word is as good as the mud under my boots." Then I glance down and see dirty snow under my feet. "Well, the mud back in Bricen. Oh, you get what I mean. Your word doesn't mean anything to me. I don't trust you."

With his chin held high and a confident stride, he takes three steps back, all the while expressing, "I'm aware of many individuals who consider the mud you mock to be a reliable mortar for binding their stones and wood when constructing their homes and structures."

Eyeing him with caution, I shuffle closer to the wagon. "If you wish to compare yourself to *reliable mud*, then so be it."

He shakes his head, tsking at me. "You will learn to appreciate what we're trying to do here, one way or another."

My reluctance to climb into the covered wagon vanishes as he approaches, and I hurry into the empty back and settle on the side bench. Once I know he's not within reaching distance, I make it perfectly clear how I feel about him and his cause by cursing and spitting on the floorboards of the wagon.

Marcellus shakes his head and sighs with disappointment. He also doesn't join me. Rather, he remains standing on the road, holding open the double doors.

"Call off Alister," I demand, breaking the silence lingering in the cold air between us. He doesn't respond, only stares at me. My voice quivers as I repeat my words, now louder and with a stronger plea, "Marcellus, call off Alister!"

His grin fades, replaced by a cold, hard stare that takes me back to that day in the throne room of the Under Realm. The pleasantries appear to be over. I can see it in the way his eyes narrow, locking onto me with a predatory intensity. My heart races while the darkness in me stirs, yet it doesn't itch to be released. Does it sense we cannot win against Marcellus?

"You should've woken her when I asked you to."

Whispering, I say with defeat, "You promised me you wouldn't lay a hand on me."

"I always keep my word, Adele."

Something scuffs against the wood off to my left, except there's no one else in the wagon with me. Suddenly, a necklace made of leather with a flat stone at the end slides along the floor in front of me. When it stops, I stare at the strange symbols etched into the stone. Familiar symbols. As I turn to see where it came from, a shiver runs the length of my spine as a broad figure suddenly appears at the other end of the wagon, clad in a vivid green cloak with the hood concealing their face.

My heart pounds inside my chest, and I press my back against the wall of the wagon. My gaze swivels between the Hood and Marcellus. It isn't until the man withdraws his hood that my breath catches. Before I can react, Master Ebenus presses a different stone, also attached to a leather necklace, to my cheek. "Sleep, child."

CHAPTER 26

RUNE

There's no getting through to him. Evander's mind is not his own. Wet snow and pine needles brush against my wings as he propels me through the tops of the forest trees. His vacant gaze is fixed over my head, focused on our path through the dense woodland. His fingers grip the muscles of my shoulders and upper arms tightly, pinning my arms to my sides. We're hurtling at such speed that I'm anxious about colliding with a tree, and it feels as though we must be miles away from Sayen's cottage, rooted in the forested hill.

"Let me go!" I yell, clawing at his arms, desperate to find anything to hold on to. "Evander, please! Listen to my voice! You know me!"

Nothing. It's as if I'm shouting into the void. He obeys his commander's orders, showing no recognition or empathy. I'm worried that the only way I'll be able to break free is to fight him—and I hesitate, uncertain if I can bring myself to hurt him.

From beneath the collar of his shirt, I see a leather string around his neck. He continues careening us through the forest, my attention now drawn to the strange symbol carved into the stone, smeared with dirt or oil… No, it's blood.

After wriggling my arm free of his grasp, I try to reach for the leather string—to remove it from his body, but the second I get my chance, he shoves me hard, and I crash to the ground. My body lands hard on a snowy slope, tumbling for a long stretch before I finally stop. My elbow slams into a rock, while my hands protect my head and face. Rolling onto my back, I lie there and catch my breath. In the sky above, Evander banks sharply to the left, executing a wide arc between the clouds, momentarily disappearing from view.

With only my hurt pride and a few bruises from the brunt of my fall, I quickly get to my feet and launch into the sky. My wings beat fast in order to clear the forest as I brace myself to confront him once more. Because no matter what it takes, I refuse to give up on him. He is my oldest and dearest friend, and he'd do the same for me.

In anticipation, I shout, "You are Evander of the West Star family!" My voice carries through the air. Searching the sky, unable to see him, I continue my efforts to get through to him. "We grew up together, running through the streets of Stellara as children and later as adolescents. You are my closest confidant and—"

Before I can finish, he slams his fist into my spine, just below where my wings connect, forcing all the air from my lungs, and I fall. With each passing second of free fall, the weight pressing into my lungs becomes more suffocating, leaving me breathless and gasping for air. Once again, I'm plummeting to the ground, sharp pine needles lashing my face and hands. A tingling numbness trails the lower half of my spine, and I'm unable to find the strength to spread my wings. The collision is much more brutal this time, as there is hardly any snow to soften the blow. Rolling about on the forest bed, gasping for air, I struggle against the pain pulsating through every muscle.

Though my vision is blurry, I see him hovering in the sky above.

"For Merigoth! The Queen of Realms!" he proclaims, then takes off, flying in the direction we'd originally come.

As I attempt to get up and go after him, my limbs tremble and falter, leaving me unable to follow. Tears fill the wells beneath my eyes as I can no longer suppress the inner disappointment of my failure. I release it into the forest with a resounding scream.

I give myself time to heal. Once I've regained enough strength to stand up, I test my wings. They extend without pain, and when I give them a strong flap there's only a slight ache at the base where they meet my spine. Inhaling deeply, I take flight, then retrace the direction I think we came from. I know I wasn't there, but I have to hope that Adele prevailed against Marcellus and that whatever Elijah and Lauren were fighting inside Sayen's home was defeated as well. I search for the road, hanging on to the hope that everyone is safe.

The forest seems to go on forever as I scour the ground below. Eventually, I spot Elijah waving his arms along the road, trying to catch my attention. I descend and land in front of him. It's not my best landing, but at least I didn't fall flat on my face.

"Hurry!" he shouts, and runs between the pine trees toward the hillside underground home. "It's that Reborn guy who almost killed Adele!"

Oh no! Alister.

I run fast and intercept Elijah in his path, forcing him to stop before we reach Sayen's home. "Stay out here," I command, pressing a hand to his chest. "I'll send the others out to you, but be ready to run." He nods, and I move to the front door of the underground home. Ducking my head, I enter the home and stand in the main living area. It's dark and only the light from a few small round windows and the open doorway provides enough light for me to see the chaos that's been unleashed. Quickly, I rework my inner tethers to boost my visibility in the dim room. Once adjusted, I can see the room is much bigger than I anticipated from the outside. Off to the right, one of the ceiling joists from the domed ceiling has fallen and crashed on top of Sayen's legs. She's crying, but that's okay. Crying means she's alive. Sitting next to her is Aleksandra, holding her friend's hand and trying to comfort her.

Lauren comes out from around a fallen cupboard and stands between the girls and the Reborn. Blood trickles down the sides of Lauren's face.

From what I know, Lauren was a fighter back in her days at Stellara. She trained and fought as one of the Starlight Guards, but then volunteered to explore other realms for the counsel. That's how she ended up in the Human Realm. She gave up the armor for a life of baking bread for humans.

"You will not be victorious today, demon slug!" Lauren yells, throwing another burst of wind at the Reborn. Her breathing is heavy, and I'm not sure how much more she can take.

The Reborn steps out from the shadows at the rear of the room. Alister. His pasty skin isn't looking too healthy and sags along his jawline and under his eyes. The skin around his black eyes is full of red, bulging veins. Those evil eyes are focused on Lauren. And I'm not sure how much more of a beating she can handle.

"You will leave this place!" I yell with every bit of pent-up anger and frustration I have at the Reborn man.

"Rune! Get them out of here!" Lauren shouts, then ducks when Alister's meaty hand swings wide to try and catch her.

With a flick of my wrist, I open a doorway behind his massive figure. With everything I can muster, I run straight for him and shove one shoulder into his side, sending us both plummeting through the doorway. The passage is high off the ground, hanging in the air, and we both land hard on the dusty ground of the Under Realm. Behind him, Lauren staggers to her feet. He must've grabbed her as I shoved him through.

Getting to my knees, I yell to Lauren, "Go and help the others!" while keeping one eye on Alister. Holding one arm across her waist, she stumbles and winces, shuffling away from us.

With a groan, Alister rolls over and slowly gets to his feet. The months haven't been good for the human body he inhabits. I don't know if it's because of his time in Noviska, or just his human body decaying from the powerful demon spirit inhabiting his body. Whatever the reason, his skin has torn in spots along his arm and cheek, and where there should be red blood and pink flesh, there is nothing but inky liquid and gray mush. Darkness engulfs his eyes.

Alister spits on the packed dirt and groans before saying, "You'll pay for that." I swear the veins surrounding his eyes pulse with fury.

Lauren extends her wings, ready to fly up to the realm doorway floating above. But the moment she bends her knees to launch up into the air, Alister grabs her by the arm. I try to slam my shoulder into his side to assist her escape, but he throws a hand out, which sends me staggering backward. With a firm fist, he punches Lauren in the stomach, and she doubles over, unable to flee. He then grabs her by the throat.

"No!" Lauren cries. Her pale gray wings flutter desperately, like a bird caught in a cage.

Until he releases her, I'm unable to create a passage and send him somewhere…to his death. Once I gain my footing, I try again, sprinting at full speed toward him, my heart pounding in my chest. Reaching him, I unleash a rapid succession of punches at his side, each one landing with a satisfying *thud*. He might be a strong Reborn, but from his groans, I can tell he feels the brunt of my angel strength.

With a forceful swing, he tosses Lauren across the dirt, over the gravel path, and out into the barren wasteland. I'm about to lunge at him again when I hear her screams. She's dragging her body out of a wide crack in the ground, filled with glowing red magma.

"Lauren!" I scream, needing to help her. Both of her wings are on fire, dripping with molten lava as she crawls away. Her wails grow louder with each agonizing drip landing on her body, sizzling through her clothes and flesh. Soon her dark hair catches fire and she frantically attempts to extinguish it by brushing her hands through the blaze consuming every strand of hair. Eventually, she digs her hands into the dry ground and throws dirt over her body and head.

I go to run to her, but Alister intercepts me, grabbing one wing and tossing me in the opposite direction. Tumbling, I fall into one of the sleeping pits. He stands over the hole. Lauren's whimpers and pleas for help grow softer in the distance.

"You are a monster! I'm going to kill you!" Filled with boiling rage, I open a passage beneath his feet with a flick of my wrist. He tumbles into the void, his hands flailing as he desperately tries to find a solid object to grasp. I hoist myself out of the dirt pit and peer over the edge, watching Alister splash into the stormy waves of the Yasmin Sea. It doesn't take long for the stormy waves to claim him, giving him the death he deserves.

I run to Lauren's side, closing the doorway in my wake. My knees slide along the packed ground. She's barely moving.

Carefully, I roll her over and pull her into my lap. The molten lava has hardened, burning away her wings. All that's left are two bony stubs covered in a charred residue. The skin on her back, shoulders, and neck is gone, revealing raw flesh that's burned and blistered. Smoke curls off her dirt-coated scalp, between the few remaining patches of singed hair.

"Rune." My name on her lips sounds foreign. As if she only just learned it. I didn't have enough time with her—to get to know her. "You must promise me…" She coughs, struggling to keep her body still. I can't even imagine the pain she's enduring with each slight movement.

"I'm here," I say, letting the tears come. We may have had our differences, but Lauren doesn't deserve this.

"Promise me, Rune, that you'll make a new future for the angels." Her vibrant brown eyes stare up into the midnight sky of this dark realm. Not until I say, "I promise," does she look my way.

"Oh, it hurts…everything hurts," she cries out, her charred fingers wrapping around my arms. Then, a sudden stillness overtakes her as her body trembles uncontrollably, her muscles tautening with each passing moment. The air is dry and hot, filled with an intense silence that's broken solely by the sound of her struggling breaths. "I can't see you."

"I'm here," I say, tears streaming down my cheeks and nose.

Her eyes flutter, and her muscles tense again. As if she's fighting to survive. She isn't ready to go. She opens her mouth and struggles to say each word as she whispers, "Tell Sara…Adele…Kit…and…" her voice is growing quieter, and I can barely hear her when she says Elijah's name. "Tell them I love them. Tell them…"

I nod, wet eyelashes blurring my vision.

With a sniffle, I quietly say, "I will tell them all you love them. I promise," at the same moment Lauren exhales her last breath.

I don't move, holding Lauren's body in my lap. The dark world blurs around me, and I let everything that's been building up inside come pouring out. It's all too much. My failure at rebuilding Stellara, letting Evander get taken by Marcellus, breaking Elijah's heart, and now losing Lauren.

Eventually, I hear Elijah's voice calling to me and try to regain some semblance of control. Sniffling, I look up to him.

"Rune!" he shouts from the doorway high in the sky. "It's Sayen! She needs—" He doesn't finish his sentence as he stares down at me, holding Lauren. "Oh no. Is that…?"

"Move away from the doorway!" I shout. He does, and I flick my wrist to close the doorway, only to reopen it at ground level. He comes running out and falls to his knees beside me.

"No, no, no!" His eyes are wide, taking in every inch of Lauren's mutilated body. "What happened?" His voice is pitched and cracking, and tears trail over both cheeks.

I give him the truth. "Alister threw her, and she rolled into the magma." Glancing into the Noviskan hillside home on the other side of the doorway, I ask, "Where's Aleksandra?"

"With Sayen. She's in a lot of pain, the beam is pinning her legs, but at least she'll live. We need your help lifting the ceiling beam. Aleksandra eased some of the pain with her ability to induce bliss."

My brows pinch and the muscles of my face tense. "Like Merigoth can?"

He nods, and even though he's talking to me, his attention is solely on Lauren. "We need to get Sayen to Bricen where we can heal her with…well, I guess now your blood."

Normally, Lauren would heal the physical wounds. I slowly lower Lauren's body to the ground. "We can't leave her here."

"I know, and we won't."

Standing, my left wing tender from where Alister yanked me, I open another doorway next to the Noviska one directly into Goslings. Immediately, Sara and Kit are there, sitting at one of the tables, waiting for us to return.

"It's about time!" Kit says as Sara walks through.

Sara gasps and runs over to us, then falls onto her knees next to her friend. "No!" Her hands hover inches over Lauren's body, as if she's trying to decipher what killed her. Shooting a furious glare at me, she asks, "What happened?"

"The Reborn, Alister, happened," I answer.

"Where is he?" Sara stands, her hands at her sides, fingers splayed wide. "I will turn his mind into soup!"

"He's gone. I tossed him into the Yasmin Sea to drown." My energy is dwindling, and I have no more tears to give.

Tearing her eyes from Lauren, Sara asks, "Where's Adele?"

My answer won't make our situation any better. And Sara can tell what I have to say isn't good.

"Tell me!"

So I do. "The last I saw her, she was outside Sayen's home with Marcellus."

Her eyes grow wide, and she pushes past me to run through the doorway into Sayen's home. Meanwhile, Elijah and Kit help carry Lauren's body from the Under Realm over to Goslings.

"We'll be there shortly," I say.

"I'll be waiting with a pitcher of water for when you bring Sayen," Elijah tells me, then continues to help Kit with Lauren.

Once they're through, I close the passage, then proceed through the doorway into Sayen's home. Before helping Sayen, I quickly close the doorway to the Under Realm. Loud sobs fill the quiet house, and I turn to find Aleksandra with her head in her friend's lap. Her shoulders are trembling, and when she looks up at me, I see not only that she's been crying, but also that Sayen's gone vacant-eyed and still.

"What happened?" I ask, crouching next to the two girls. "Elijah said she'd live. He said you helped her with her pain, using…" I pause, then force the words out. "…providing the girl with bliss to help numb her until we could heal her legs."

Shaking her head, the tears coming faster, Aleksandra cries, "I don't know what happened! I did help her. She told me the pain had stopped, and then she stopped breathing. I tried to help, but I don't know how to help someone who can't breathe!" The girl turns away, bending over her friend once more, sounds of crying filling the home.

I give Aleksandra a moment to grieve her friend. Then, I rest a hand on her back, and she sits up and says, "She was my only friend." The poor girl's eyes are rimmed red. "Now, I'm all alone."

"You are not alone," Sara says from the open doorway, then looks to me. "Adele is gone."

Helping Aleksandra up, I ask if she wants us to bury her friend. Aleksandra nods, and the three of us carry Sayen's body out front. Since the ground is frozen, we pile rocks over her. It takes longer than I expect, but when it's done, Aleksandra thanks us both. "You didn't have to do that. Stay and bury her."

"Yes, we did. It's the least we can do," Sara offers, still maintaining an arm's length from her daughter.

I open a doorway and tell them, "We need to go. Because now we need to save not only Evander, but Adele too."

CHAPTER 27

RUNE

I can't help but avert my gaze from Lauren's lifeless body resting on the floor of Goslings in front of the fireplace. Instead, I stare out the front window of the tavern, the late-evening sun setting behind the treetops. Sara sits on her knees by her friend, hands clasped, muttering prayers to the stars that her friend has a place among them. Sitting and quietly talking with Elijah, Aleksandra recounts what happened to Sayen.

Outside, more villagers congregate by the village's front gate. My heart aches for them as Lauren's presence will be missed. She showed kindness and generosity to everyone she encountered.

I recall my promise to her. I must do better for the angels. Ever since I returned to Stellara, my concern has been to restore everything to the way it was before Merigoth's attack. I wanted nothing more than for angels to feel safe and free to live their lives as they please, whether it be here or elsewhere—but only after we worked together in rebuilding Stellara. I'm starting to see the damage is far too great. I can't help but wonder if I've been wrong this whole time—if we've misdirected our efforts—if we should've taken this opportunity to establish a *new* Stellara.

I turn away from the window and look at Elijah with Aleksandra. His hand rests on top of the Shade girl's hand. He's exactly the kind of character Stellara needs—someone who sees the good in everything and never gives up fighting for what he believes is right.

It's quite an ambitious idea, and I'm not sure how the other angels would react if we were to open our city gates to visitors or potential new residents. When Elijah gets up and quietly leaves the tavern through the back door, I shift my gaze from him to the angel lying on the floor. I realize now that I wasted so much time arguing with Lauren about her responsibility to go back to the Starlight Realm and contribute to its reconstruction. I should've listened to her right from the beginning. It was foolish of me to let my pride and stubbornness take control, holding on to the old ways when it's clear that times have changed. Lauren and many other angels have not only built homes but also formed tight-knit communities of family and friends in the Human Realm. A sense of shame swells inside as I recall all the countless fights we had, where I neglected her happiness and insisted that she return to a city that no longer held any significance for her.

And even though it saddens me that the memory of Stellara only lives on through bedtime stories and campfire tales—I know all is not lost. I refuse to abandon the city, leaving it in ruins, and will do whatever is necessary to see it thrive once again.

"Where did Elijah run off to?" I ask Sara, who's still sitting on the floor next to her friend.

She sits up straight and wipes her cheeks, though they remain damp and flushed. "I believe he went to help Kit and a few of the villagers set up the pyre." A sniffle follows, and she uses the cuff of her sleeve to dab under her nose.

"What's this?" Aleksandra withdraws a hand from beneath her cloak and reaches across the tavern table for the old leather journal.

I snatch it up, telling her, "It's Merigoth's journal." Then, with care, I set it on a table away from her. "Even though there's nothing of value to our cause in rescuing Evander or Adele, I promised Adele she could have the journal."

Beneath the edge of her green hood, Aleksandra's eyes go wide. "You mean to tell me that's Merigoth's journal from her days before she was infected?" She pushes the chair away, wood scraping along the planks of the floor. Coming around the table, closer to me, she eyes the leather-bound notebook. "Can I see it?"

"Maybe later." I can't help but notice the eagerness in her eyes. "Let's give our attention to our fallen friend, and then figure out how we're going to save Adele and Evander. Then you can read the journal."

There's something behind her eyes—confliction, maybe? Whatever it is, the moment passes, and she eases into her seat again. "Of course. Whatever I can do to help."

Elijah peeks his head inside the tavern, this time from the front door, and gives me a nod before exiting again. I'm about to walk over to Sara when I notice Aleksandra still eyeing the journal. Needing to remove temptation so she can focus, I open a small passage along the tabletop. Then I pick up the journal and store it on a shelf on the other side. Then, with a flick of my wrist, I close the passage.

"Where did you put it?" she asks in an unsettling tone.

"Don't worry. I put it somewhere safe. It's old and fragile—the pages can easily turn to dust if mishandled."

This seems to appease her curiosity. "Oh, that's smart. Keep it safe."

Leaning closer, I tell her, "It's natural to want answers to your past. Sara and Adele also want to know more about Merigoth's life before her time in the Under Realm. Have patience, and stay focused on what's important."

"Oh, I always do," she says under her breath. When I raise an eyebrow, she reacts by pressing the tips of her fingers to the bridge of her nose. "My apologies. My fatigue is catching up to me, and Sayen's death is taking a toll on my wits."

We're all exhausted, both in body and mind. We turn to Sara when she blows her nose in a cloth before pocketing it. Leaving Aleksandra's company, I cross the room and crouch next to Sara so we're at eye level. The muscles along my back ache with a dull throb from the downward motion. Then, resting one hand on Sara's forearm, I say, "It's time."

Pressing one hand to the side of Lauren's face, she says her last goodbye. "May you live a fulfilling afterlife among the stars. I'll miss you, my friend."

Sara stands, wiping her eyes and cheeks clean while I scoop up Lauren's body. There's barely any weight to her body, which is a good sign that her spirit has ascended to her next life. It is believed that individuals who die with burdensome bodies are tethered to their physical forms, condemned to wander the mortal realm as restless spirits due to their wickedness and self-centeredness.

Looking to Aleksandra, I instruct her to stay and wait for our return.

"No. It's okay," Sara says. "I want her there. She's part of our family now." Sara offers Aleksandra a small smile.

Aleksandra returns the gesture and says, "Thank you." Though, her expression appears somewhat conflicted, and I can't tell whether it's because of Sara's kind words or if she's wanting to stay and look for the journal.

But in the end, Aleksandra accompanies us. I let them go out first, then follow. The entire village is outside waiting, either standing and staring at me walking down the steps or crying while embracing someone next to them. Kit and a few villagers I recognize but can't recall the names of lead the procession out the front gates of Bricen. We slowly walk toward the pyre they've prepared in a small clearing by the creek. I vaguely recall the area, as it's close to the spot where Adele and Elijah brought me to wash up that morning after they captured me.

With ease, I set Lauren's body on top of the large log pyre stacked in a table-like way.

Kit hands Sara the torch. Sara clears her throat and says, "Lauren wasn't only loved for her freshly baked breads and rolls. You welcomed her into your lives and into your hearts because she was compassionate and devoted to protecting everyone here. She will be remembered and missed." After collecting her composure, Sara steps closer and wedges the torch between the logs in multiple places around the stack. The fire takes to life, slowly claiming the angel's body. Her skin begins to shimmer, becoming almost transparent. Tiny specks of light, like glowing dust, float up, intertwining with the orange flames before rising higher into the evening sky.

"The stars have accepted her," I whisper to Sara. I already assumed from her weight that she wouldn't have been one of the damned. "She will be there waiting for you when it's your time."

Tears streak her cheeks as she watches the last of Lauren's brilliance blend in with the waking stars. She tells me, "The stars will never accept my soul. They will only ever see me as tainted with evil."

"You are wrong," I say. "You are not tainted with evil. You've chosen a better path—as a healer. And you can teach your children to follow in your honorable path."

She drops her gaze from the sky to me. "And Marcellus. What of him? His actions are my fault."

I have no answer for her regarding Marcellus, and my hesitation is all she needs to know my opinion on the matter. Turning, she whispers something to Aleksandra, and they start the walk back to Bricen.

"Are you okay?" Elijah comes up next to me. Kit walks by us, following Sara and Aleksandra.

"When will it end? Merigoth… Marcellus… The pain that comes with anything they touch or create."

"Well, that's what we're going to see about, right? Making sure Marcellus is dealt with once and for all."

I don't ask to what end. Do we send him to the Under Realm again and hope he doesn't find another way out? Or does he deserve the same fate as Alister? Shuffling my steps over the packed dirt of the road, I make my way toward Goslings, Elijah walking by my side.

Before we enter Bricen through the open gate, I confide in him, telling him, "The fight isn't over."

"No, it's not," he agrees.

When I slip my hand into his, he stills before relaxing and clasping his fingers over mine. I say, "I promise you, we will not lose any more friends."

He gives my hand a gentle squeeze. "Yes. We will overcome this—together."

Inside, Sara and Aleksandra are shouting at one another. Kit leans against the bar counter, letting the two verbally go at it. Elijah immediately jumps between them, arms spread wide.

"What's going on?" he barks, eyeing them both.

"She wants to use me as bait!" Aleksandra shouts. "And I refuse! If Master Ebenus or his goons take me, I'll never see daylight again!"

"I won't let that happen!" Sara counters in a volume that matches her daughter's. Then, in a more calming tone, she explains, "We have no other way to draw them out. Rune can't get close enough to the village to open a doorway, fly, or use her strength to fight."

"Sara," I cut in, "Marcellus has Adele. There's no reason for him to want Aleksandra any longer."

"Well, he may!" she shouts, then looks to the ceiling, her eyes glossing over. With a shaky voice, she says, "If only we could disarm the enchantment. Somehow take out the monoliths, allowing you your full strength and abilities."

Aleksandra hesitantly says, "I may be able to help with that."

The room goes silent. Everyone's attention shifts to the girl. Sara pushes past Elijah, stepping closer to her daughter, and asks, "You can do that? Why didn't you say anything sooner?"

Aleksandra answers with a weak shrug. "I'm still adjusting to the idea of working collaboratively with others. My whole life it's been about looking out for myself, which includes not sharing valuable information."

Sara lets out a deep sigh through her nose, likely preparing to berate Aleksandra for keeping secrets from us. Scolding the girl won't help us, though, so I'm grateful for Sara's restraint.

I cut through their glaring stares and ask, "How do we disarm the enchantments imbued into the monoliths?"

Scratching her scalp in a spot right beneath one of her horns, Aleksandra explains, "If you don't have special permission, which would be one of the symbols carved into a small stone and hung from around your neck, then I believe all you need is a drop or two of your blood. Smearing it over the symbols on the monolith somehow makes the enchantment recognize you as an exception."

I try to think back to when Marcellus claimed Evander out in front of the village. There was a moment when Marcellus looped a necklace over Evander's head. That must've been how he was able to enter the village.

"What do you think?" Sara asks me.

"I think she's right about the necklace part, but I have no idea about the blood smearing theory. But it's also our only option." Then, pondering the question of what we would do if it did work, I ask, "How long is the trek from Bluskyn to Sayen's home?"

"Half a day's journey," Aleksandra answers.

"Okay, we've got probably half of that to get into the village and search for Merigoth's body. It's the only leverage that'll work to get our friends back." My confidence rises. This plan might work, provided that Aleksandra isn't misleading us about disabling the monoliths' enchantment.

"We'll also have to collapse the tunnel leading into the cavern where the Reborn horde waits," Kit adds. "Anyone have any suggestions?"

"If I have my strength, I can collapse the tunnel," I offer.

"Good." Sara nods, pleased with the plans being laid out. "We'll start with disarming the monoliths, then I'll go with Aleksandra and Kit to search for Merigoth while you and Elijah take care of the Reborns."

Hope builds within, but I'm also keeping an open mind about if Aleksandra is wrong about the monoliths. If she is, then there's a high chance we're going to fail. And failing isn't an option when losing to Marcellus.

CHAPTER 28

RUNE

A gust of northern air sweeps past the five of us, carrying powdery snow. We move from monolith to monolith, smearing my blood on the front across the symbols until we've reached the last one at the village's entrance. I cut into my palm again, then quickly drag the open wound across the carved symbols before my skin heals itself.

"There," Aleksandra says. "You should be able to enter the village now."

Sara, Elijah, and Kit stand close behind, watching as I approach the wide opening in the wooden fence. With an outstretched hand, I walk forward. A sense of dread floods through me when my hand presses up against a solid surface, invisible to the eye.

Lowering my hand and facing the hooded girl, I say, "It didn't work."

"What? No! It should. I know what I overheard Master Ebenus say… He said, 'There. It's done. Now no angel shall enter without blood consent.'" Leaning closer, she examines the last monolith I smeared with blood. "The blood should alter the enchantment, making it recognize you and exclude you from its effects."

"Should?" I repeat with annoyance. "You said you knew how to get me into the village."

"I did… I mean, I do! I was here when he imbued the monoliths. I overheard him speaking to the man with the shaved head from a distance."

Kit mocks the situation with an annoyed tone. "Well, it looks like you overheard wrong."

"Now what?" Elijah asks, looking at Sara.

"We go home." Sara turns in the high snow and walks away. "We can't face Marcellus without Rune's help. It's a death sentence."

"Look what we have here!" a gruff voice calls out from within the village. Everyone's attention shifts to see five Hoods making their way out of the village hall right toward us. They move into formation, three Hoods in the front while two linger in the back.

Kit shifts her hand, tightening it on her sword. "Ah, man. Not these guys again."

"Rhoda! You can choose a different path!" Aleksandra pleads. "Master Ebenus has been lying to you—to all of you! There is no promise of eternal life or endless powers!"

"Because you took him from us!" Rhoda screeches with her deep, masculine voice. "Where is he?"

My heart races, and I know I'm no good in a fight, especially if the fight occurs inside the village. I was only able to access the village before because the doorway connecting the Under Realm and Noviska was within its boundaries.

"Aleksandra, we could really use Rune's help right about now," Elijah prods the girl.

"I did what I thought we needed to do! Blood on stone!"

Blood on stone or one of those stone necklaces. Scanning over the three, I see one of the Hoods is wearing a similar necklace. A palm-sized river stone around his neck. I don't know what the symbols represent on the small, smooth rock, but we have to try.

"We need that necklace!" I say, pointing toward the Hood standing at the rear. Looking to the treetops, I release a loud whistle, calling for our feathered companions that insisted on coming. All three had persistently pecked at the tavern's front window, displaying their determination to get inside. Responding to my call, three dark silhouettes appear from within the pine trees, soaring toward us. "Serafina, I need that stone from around his neck!" I shout, pointing toward the Hood inside the village. With angel-like speed, they fly by and take aim at the Hoods.

Rhoda and the man wearing the stone necklace I need reach down their shirts and draw out small vials hanging from leather strings. Kit shouts, seeing what I see, "They've got blood vials!" She takes a few steps back, and the others follow suit.

After consuming the blood from the vials, both Rhoda and the man let their empty vials dangle against their shirts. Rhoda then circles a hand through the air, throwing a wave of power at the crows. They tumble in the air, but before they hit the nearby stone home, they regain control and fly up onto the roof.

"We can get it," Sara insists. "If that's what you need to get inside the village, we'll get it." She points to Kit and Elijah with a nod, and they charge into Bluskyn.

"Kill them!" Rhoda commands, her deep voice resonating louder with the power of Aleksandra's blood coursing through her veins. The three green Hoods at the front obey and run toward Sara, Elijah, and Kit.

I watch with nervous anticipation, knowing I'm helpless if any of them get hurt. Sara swings her daggers, one in each hand, at the lead Hood, who unexpectedly reveals a shortsword from beneath his cloak. Metal clanks and sparks arc from their collision. Kit is off to the right, fighting against another female cult member, their blades barely missing deadly strikes for each. I silently pray to the stars that Kit isn't the one to receive a deadly blow.

Elijah slides on his knees, ducking the incoming swing from the Hood charging him. Scrambling to get up, he doesn't turn and face the Hood but runs farther into the village. I hate that I can't see where he's going and the attacker chasing him.

Rhoda and the other blood-infused man watch the two run off, unconcerned about their outcome. The brawny woman laughs, and I fear she knows something I don't.

"Kit! Sara!" I shout. "Hurry!"

Kit sighs and heaves a deep breath before nodding. She twirls her shortsword in her hand and then slams the tip down into the ground, the Hood's foot caught in its path. The woman screams, clawing at her boot to remove the impaled weapon from her foot. Kit rips her sword free and steps away.

Aleksandra isn't paying attention to Kit and stares over at Sara, who has her hand pressed to the man's face beneath his hood. "What is she doing?" the girl asks me.

"Probably doing something she swore she'd never do again. She's only ever used her abilities for healing since her escape from the Under Realm—or so Adele has told me."

We both watch as Sara releases her hand, and the man crumples to the ground. Stepping over his body, she approaches the next Hood. "I do not fear death," she bellows, reaching her hand out to the Hood's face. "If anything, you should fear me. One touch and—" Sara's words are cut short. She drops to her knees, grasping at her throat.

"No!" Aleksandra cries. Her hands clasp over her mouth and her eyes tremble as her mother struggles to breathe.

The man holds his hand up, fingers curled in the air as if choking the wind. Kit's only able to take a few staggering steps toward Sara before Rhoda raises her hand and throws it out to her side, the magic within picking up Kit and thrusting her body through the air. She slams hard against the stone wall of a nearby home. A painful cry escapes Kit's mouth as Rhoda splays her fingers wide, causing Kit's arms and legs to stretch.

"Do something!" I demand of the three crows perched on top of the roof. They chirp and caw, but it's Olive who reacts. Rustling her feathers so her petite frame looks twice its size, she opens her beak wide and releases a strange guttural knocking sound from her throat. The sound resonates through the air. A few seconds later, a small murder of crows appears from the east. They fly over and into the village, distracting the two green Hoods by circling their bodies and heads. The Hoods, startled by the attack, momentarily release Sara and Kit. They fall to the ground, gasping for air and rubbing their wounds.

"Now!" I shout up to the roof again. This time, Serafina takes flight and dives toward the hooded man, her intent focused on her mark. With an unnatural force, she seizes the leather cord in her beak and swoops upward, breaking it free from around his neck. When he realizes what's been taken, he throws his arms out with a forceful thrust, sending a powerful wave of energy up into the air. The crows Olive called all go flying, hitting random things in the village. Some of them stagger up and wobble away, while others lie still in the snow.

"You shall pay for that trick!" the man seethes, then resumes his assault on Sara. His invisible reach grabs her once more by the throat. Kit's eyes go wide, and she crawls through the deep snow, trying to retreat from Rhoda's attention, but it's too late.

"Where do you think you're going?" the burly woman growls. She swoops her hand up into the air again, dragging

Kit's body along the ground before stopping only to stretch her limbs once more.

Serafina lands on the monolith nearest us, stone necklace in her beak. I rush over and grab it from her.

"Clean off the blood!" Aleksandra shouts. "Before you apply your own!"

I do as instructed and cover the small stone in fresh snow, then wipe it clean before cutting the tip of my finger and smearing my blood over the carved symbols. The creases of the symbols absorb most of my blood, leaving a dirty smudge behind. Tying the leather string around my neck, I glare at the two Hoods torturing our friends.

I don't question the imbued symbols' meaning, only thank the stars when my energy and abilities return. My wings spread wide, and I sense my inner tethers once more. I'm more than ready to join the fight.

"You better stay where you are!" Rhoda threatens with a laugh. "The second I see your feet leave the ground, I'll snap her neck."

Instead of launching myself at them, I open a doorway next to me with a flick of my wrist. The forest outside of Bricen comes into view. "Olive!" Before I can shout out a command, it appears the small crow has picked up on my intentions. She repeats her special skill and calls forth more crows. The guttural knocking she makes from her throat releases into the air with an unnatural level of sound. And as I hoped, it carries through the passage and into the Harvesgrove forest. Within seconds, a dark cloud appears in the sky, over the treetops. When they reach the doorway, the crows funnel through and fill the entire village of Bluskyn, circling both of the green Hoods. Once again, Rhoda and the man release Sara and Kit, trying to wave gusts of power at the onslaught of birds wrapping them in a whirlwind of black feathers, sharp beaks, and razor claws.

I scream out an encouraging battle cry as I launch myself off the ground, spearing toward the two remaining Hoods. Olive releases another round of knocking sounds, and the crows part, making a clear path for me. I grab the fabric of the green cloaks and toss them into a doorway I opened a second before grabbing them. They both land and roll along the packed black dirt of the Under Realm. Not waiting for them to gain their footing and use their mystical powers on me, I quickly close the doorway.

The hundreds of flying crows settle, perching on rooftops, wagons, barrels, and anywhere that isn't too snowy.

Lowering myself and tucking my wings against my shoulders, I thank Olive. "You did well!" Then, to the other crows, I say, "You all did well. But you can't stay here. It's too cold and I can't be sure of what's going to happen next. I need you to be safe for when Adele returns home."

Olive, Serafina, and Valor all caw and take the lead, flying through the doorway back into the Harvesgrove forest. Once the last of the crows has returned home, I close the doorway and help Sara and Kit to their feet.

"That was amazing!" Kit says with a smile while stretching her arms over her head. "Not the almost dying part, but the crows coming to our rescue."

"Did Adele know they could do that?" Sara asks, her voice raw from being strangled.

"No," Kit answers. "We've been waiting for Olive to reveal her talent."

"And what a talent that is," Aleksandra says with admiration.

I walk over to the nearest stone home and push the front door open. A stream of dark gray smoke wafts out. Glancing at the three of them, I say, "I can get to the Reborn tunnel this way." They follow me inside. Against the far wall, where the fireplace should be, is a sizable hole smashed through the floorboards. Smoke rises up from beneath the ground, but instead of filling the stone house, it flows up and out through the chimney.

Rustling my feathers, getting ready to fly again, I say, "Give me two minutes." Then I drop through the hole and enter the cavern. The groans and shuffling of the Reborns down on the cavern floor echo up through the dark space. Only the fires from the pillars illuminate the top half of the cavern.

I circle the cavern, searching for the tunnel. I spot it along the far end and dive. When I land, some of the Reborns notice me and some continue to shuffle about. With an assertive tone, I command them, "Marcellus has sent me to tell you to stay put. You will be released upon this world shortly!" The lie works and they stare at me, believing that Marcellus has taken control of my will. Then, before they figure out my falsity, I lift myself off the ground, just above the cave tunnel entrance. Redirecting my internal tethers, I boost more energy to my muscles. The power infuses my arms and hands, and when I strike the rock wall above the tunnel, the whole cavern jolts. Debris and dust cascade from above. As I hit it again, and again, eventually the wall cracks and large pieces of rock break free, collapsing over the entrance tunnel. The Reborns behind me realize what I'm doing and start grabbing at my feet, their angry groans growing louder. Once I know the cave is secure, I give a hard push, flapping my wings and flying up through the hole in the ceiling.

Inside the house, Sara, Kit, and Aleksandra wait.

"Was that you?" Kit asks, in awe.

I nod. "The tunnel into the cave has been sealed. We don't have to worry about the Reborns getting out now."

"Good work," Sara compliments, then exits the house. We all follow, and out in the fresh air, she asks, "Where'd Elijah run off to?"

"I'm here!" he cries, winded, warm breaths of air pluming from his mouth. "And I found her!"

"Who?" I ask, brushing the last of the cave debris off my sleeves. If he means Adele, then we're about to face off with Marcellus.

To my relief, he shouts, "Merigoth!" He turns and jogs toward the gathering hall while waving for us to follow. "I found the staircase you mentioned, Sis, and you were right. It took me down into the tunnels where Rune and I were after we crossed over from the Under Realm."

Following him, I can't help but revel in our victory. We have Merigoth. Let's hope it's enough to win back our friends.

CHAPTER 29

ADELE

Coming to, I feel a strange sense of familiarity in the way my body moves, the sound of wagon wheels creaking, and intermittent bursts of bright sunlight on my closed eyes. My mind searches for an explanation, recalling Marcellus.

I'm trapped in a memory.

The one where I've been taken and transported across the Fayatin countryside as an unclaimed child, ready to be sold into servitude. I've faced many scary opponents and situations before, but this right here…the naïve little girl who thought the world was kind to everyone…was on her way to become Fayatin's infamous Interrogator.

I force myself to sit up, and when I see Marcellus sitting at the far end of the covered wagon, I rub my eyes and blink several times. His legs are stretched out, crossed at the ankles, and his eyes are peacefully closed. He's sleeping.

I'm not trapped in a memory.

This is real.

And he's right here for the taking.

Slowly, I get to my knees. After removing one glove and tucking it into the front of my vest, I lean forward and crawl toward him at a snail's pace. As I reach for his face, the wagon jostles as if catching a divot in the road. My body goes stiff, and I remain perfectly still, waiting to see if Marcellus reacts. He doesn't. After counting three deep breaths, I reach closer. It isn't until I'm inches from his face that he says, eyes remaining closed, "I was wondering when you'd wake."

I'm caught off guard as he reaches up and grabs my arm. Holding my breath, my heart pounding against my chest, I fear the end. But then, as he tightens his grip, I see his fingers clasp over the linen of my sleeve. He hasn't made contact with my skin.

He slowly opens his eyes, and asks, "Should I show you the same kindness you were about to show me?"

Wrenching my hand free, I retort, "I'm not holding you against your will."

"Nor am I," he says condescendingly. "You're free to go whenever you please."

That's a lie, but I don't take his argumentative bait. "How long was I out?"

"A better half of the day. It seems, dear sister, that your body needed sleep."

"What I need is to be let out of this wagon!" I pound a gloved fist against the planks of the covered wagon. Bright light shines in through the cracks between breaks in the forest, exactly how the sun shone into the freight wagon when I became an unclaimed child. My heart pulses beneath my chest, because I fear if Marcellus lays a hand on me, I'll be forced to relive that horrible day over and over again.

"I know it was Master Ebenus who induced me into that slumber state. I just can't figure out how?"

He gestures to a stone necklace resting on the bench where he sits, just at the other end. "Did you know that Master Ebenus is our father?" He stares at me, as if gauging my answer to be truthful or not.

I have no reason to lie to him. And a slim part of me wants him to realize the path he's chosen is wrong—that Merigoth has tainted his view on what a good life should be. "Yes, but I only recently learned that truth."

Despite his ongoing antagonism, he maintains a calm and nonthreatening demeanor, leaning forward with his arms on his knees. "Hmm. Interesting. Did Sara willingly share this information with you?" he asks, a hint of pain lacing his tone. "Or did you have to force her to face her past and pry the truth from her traitorous mouth about what she did?"

The silence lingers between us, and I wait to see if he's done with his childish outburst before saying, "Our mum has many regrets."

"Hm, I bet she does." He scoffs, then clarifies, "And she's your mum, not mine."

"Sara"—I emphasize Mum's name rather than argue about who she is to him—"did, in fact, explain what happened all those years ago. It was Merigoth who forced her to stay in the Under Realm, and it was Merigoth who took you from your crib the day *our mum* was to escape."

The muscles in his face tense. "And yet, she still left."

"How easy do you think it was for her to escape with two babies in her arms? Imagine three?" I pause, letting that visual form in his mind. "She told us it was nearly impossible for her to leave you behind, but she needed to escape. Her plan was to escape, hide Aleksandra and me, then return for you. However, as you may already know, not all plans unfold as expected."

A smug grin breaks through his stony expression. "Is that what she told you? Because that's not what I was told. Merigoth told me she chose you and our sister and left me."

"And you believe that conniving, evil woman who has done nothing but control and manipulate you your entire life!" I snap. I want desperately to believe there's a part of him I can reach—a part I can convince that his devotion was misplaced. He doesn't have to live this life. He can live a peaceful one without being controlled by anyone or anything other than his own free will. But he's making it extremely difficult for me to hold on to this hope.

Continuing my efforts to thwart his hate for our mother, I say, "Sara said that after she escaped through the doorway to Noviska, our father was on the other side, waiting for her. She believed it was a miracle—him being there. Ultimately, he tricked her and induced her into a forced slumber." I wonder if the imbued stone was how he forced Mum into that sleep. No. She said it was after her last cup of tea. He put something in it, causing her to slowly lose consciousness.

Glancing toward the front of the covered wagon, I say, "You can't trust him."

"Who?" Marcellus asks, then answers his own question, "Master Ebenus. I already know that. He's been torturing our sister for years. If I'd known about the doorway sooner, I would've come and pierced holes into his flesh, draining his blood for those hungry devotees to consume rather than the blood of one of our kind."

I'm torn between praising him and gagging at the thought of Master Ebenus bleeding out while others drink from his wounds. "How did you know about Aleksandra?"

He eyes me wearily, then says, "Is that her name?" Him confessing he didn't know is bold. He's sharing something personal—something he didn't have to share.

"Yes, and she's scared and alone."

His smile spreads. "I'd be happy to provide her a loving home." He crosses his arms over his chest. "You have no idea what's happening here, do you? Merigoth let you into her home, trusted you enough to welcome you into her arms. And the second you had the chance, you turned on her—without even knowing why she's out for vengeance."

"I do know why. I saw it when I trapped her."

"Ah. I understand now," he says softly, then closes his eyes and tilts his head back to rest on the wall of the wagon. "All this time, I thought Merigoth was in danger. But she knows exactly what she's doing."

His words are not comforting. If she knew I would make an attempt, then showing me that memory was intentional.

My thoughts are jostled by a forceful *thud* that rattles the topside of the covered wagon. Through the cracks, something blocks out the sunlight and moves across the top.

"Evander has returned," Marcellus tells me.

"Where are my friends?" I ask.

He doesn't answer. I'm about to ask again, but the wagon comes to a stop. "Ah, we're here." He turns away from me and unlatches the rear doors. They swing open, and I expect to be blinded by bright sunlight reflecting off the snow, but instead the setting sun glistens through the pine trees. Marcellus hops out and stretches his arms before turning to me. "I'd offer you a hand, but you know…"

"I can get out myself." Then, so he doesn't leave my question unanswered, I ask, "My friends…are they alive?"

With his hands tucked into the front pockets of his leather jacket, he swivels and faces Evander, who stands a few feet away from us. "Well?"

"I believe all are alive but one, possibly two. The fight was taken to another realm."

All are alive but one, maybe two, I repeat in my mind. I chose the wrong path. I should've stayed and helped. Now, someone is dead. Who? Who will I never speak to or have supper with again? Who is gone from my life? The dread of not knowing starts to eat at my insides. I need to know. "Who? Who lost their life?"

Evander opens his mouth to answer, but Marcellus holds up a finger. "Ah, let's leave the suspense lingering in that treacherous little brain of yours. I mean, that's valuable information I can use."

"Use to force me to wake Merigoth!" Blood boils beneath my skin while the darkness in me surges with fury. The tips of my fingers throb, my reach eager to be let free. "I will never wake that monster!"

He ignores my shouts as he walks away. Evander pushes my shoulder, urging me to follow along the snowy path. We continue through the pine forest, and Bluskyn comes into view. We've made it back to the village. As we pass the monolith and approach the first stone house, something appears off. The snow along the path and in the surrounding area is disturbed as if multiple fights took place, and…are those black feathers everywhere?

We walk past one dead man in a green hood while another lies nearby. I'm unsure if that one is alive or dead by the red snow around her boot.

Master Ebenus comes up from behind, not even acknowledging me or Evander…or his devoted followers lying dead in the snow. Marcellus tells him, "Go and check on our queen! Guard her, and if anyone tries to come near you or her—kill them!" The man nods and hurries off toward the hall.

Marcellus then tells Evander, "You. Go and check the Reborns."

Evander enters the closest stone cottage. Within a few minutes, he returns. "They're all in the cavern."

"Good. Take the tunnels through the mountain and meet me in Merigoth's chamber." Then to me, he says, "You're out of time. I swear, my patience is wearing thing. I've kept my word, Adele, but one move against me, and I will claim your mind. Do you understand?"

Evander disappears into the cottage again while Marcellus and I follow the path toward the meeting hall at the rear of the village. Every part of me wants to scream at him that he doesn't need her. But I can tell in his eyes that any chance I had of trying to talk civilly with him is gone. He's raging about what's happened here.

Needing to ease his anger, I try to strike up another casual conversation. "What good will come of Merigoth returning to the Starlight Realm?"

Muttering, he answers, "She will rule over that realm and every other."

"And she's spoken these words to you? She's told you that's her goal?"

My question is met with silence.

I slow, but he slams a hand against my back, below my shoulder. "Keep going."

Inside the village hall, we continue into the storage room where Kit and I first interrogated Aleksandra. We descend the stairs and instead of another room, there's a door-sized cave entrance leading into a dark, looming tunnel.

"You're not afraid of the dark, are you, Adele?" Marcellus taunts.

"No," I say with a sharp tone before entering a tunnel that seemed deceptively tall yet surprisingly short. I imagine Alister's oversized body barely fitting through this stretch of passage. I'm grateful for the faint light ahead, which as we get closer, I see is an iron torch wedged into one of the cracks.

It isn't long before we approach a split. One path veers off to the right, and the other makes a sharp turn to the left. That's the one Marcellus has me go down. At the end is a cozy, open cavern, transformed into a bedchamber. One candelabra has candles in it, but they aren't lit. The second, located across the room, making the bed area dim, only has a few lit.

"Come here!" he demands.

I step closer, unsure how I'm going to escape this.

Marcellus leans over the bed, drawing the fur pelt blanket down, only to startle when Rune surges out of the bed and lunges—not for Marcellus, but for Evander, who I didn't realize had caught up to us and was standing behind me.

Rune pushes her angel friend out of the bedchamber and down the tunnel. Marcellus watches, but only for a fleeting moment before swinging his gaze to the bed. "*No!* Where is she?"

With fury burning in his eyes, he reaches for me. Before his fingertips can graze my skin, a *swoosh* slices through the air, and he screams. Clutching his bloody hand to his chest, he stares down at the four fingers lying on the cavern floor.

I pivot on my toes to see who has saved me. "Kit!"

She tightens her grip on the hilt of her shortsword. "That's for taking control of my mind! And this…" She raises her blade high over her head. "This is for my mother, and Alya, and all the other villagers you stole from Bricen!" But before she brings her wrath down for a second time, Sara and I yell out in unison, "No!"

Mum comes around from behind Kit and says to him, "You deserve the truth, my son." She reaches up and before he can swat her hand away, she presses her palm over his forehead. We all stand, ready to take action against Marcellus if he breaks free from Mum's hold. His eyes tremble, darting left and right as if he's watching scenes flash before his eyes—visions we can't see. Soft gasps and whimpers escape, reactions to whatever Mum is showing him.

"Please choose a different path," she begs him. "You were taken from me. You and Aleksandra. I made the mistake of not going after you both. That regret will weigh on me for the rest of my life. But you—you didn't choose your path. Merigoth chose it for you." She glances over at Aleksandra, standing in the shadows where the candlelight doesn't reach. "And Lukah, your Master Ebenus, he decided your fate." Looking back to Marcellus, she says, "Well, now it's time you both chose your own paths. From now on, you are accountable for your own actions."

"I choose to make my own path," Aleksandra announces. "I don't want to be controlled by anyone ever again."

Mum takes a deep breath, releasing a portion of her hold on Marcellus, returning a few freedoms. He blinks and looks about the small bedchamber. "Why can't I move my arms or legs? What did you do to me?"

"You think you're the only one who can control others?" Mum says like a stern parent. "You may look about the room and speak, and that is all I grant you."

His whole body shakes, as if he's resisting her hold, fighting to break free. Blood from the four finger stumps seeps into the fabric of his shirt.

"Doesn't feel so good, does it?" Kit asks, her words as sharp as Fayatin steel.

"I will never choose you, if that's what you're wanting to hear," he seethes, saliva spraying over his lips, dribbling along his chin. "Merigoth is my mother. She has plans for you!" His gaze travels past me. "And you!" We all turn to the tunnel leading out of the makeshift bedchamber. Rune stands there.

"Where's Evander?" I ask.

"Restrained for the time being." She steps into the bedchamber. "And me, what?"

A vein bulges in Marcellus's neck, like a snake beneath his skin. "Merigoth will return to the Starlight Realm and rule as is her right! Your mother stole that from her when she banished her!"

"I think we've heard enough. It seems you've made your decision," Mum says, defeat lacing her words. Then to Rune, she says, "Return him to the Under Realm."

With a flick of her wrist, Rune opens a doorway to the dark world. "Are you sure?"

Mum nods. She raises her hand, about to press it against his forehead again, which I'm going to assume is to release her hold over his mobility, when he says, "When you come to the Under Realm and seek my help, and you will, just know my help comes at a price that you won't want to pay. But you will because the darkness that comes for you—for all of you—is far greater than what you fear in me or Merigoth." To my surprise, my brother starts laughing. A deep, delusional laugh.

"You and Merigoth are the epitome of evil," Rune asserts, her voice unwavering.

"No, you are not evil, my son. I will hold onto the hope that you will rethink your ways because I love you." Instead of using her hand to release her hold over him, she leans in and plants a kiss on his forehead. Then she gives him a forceful push, propelling his body backward through the doorway. As he falls, I can barely believe what I see. A tear trails down his cheek.

He lands against the charred, packed dirt of the Under Realm with a loud *thud*. We all stare and wait. Slowly, his eyes close and his smile goes limp.

"Is he dead?" Kit asks, coming around to my side to get a better look.

"No," Mum says.

"Good riddance," Rune says then closes the doorway.

"What about him?" Elijah calls from behind. We all turn to see he has Master Ebenus by the shoulders, escorting him into the room.

Mum approaches him and presses her hands to his temples. After a minute, she lowers her hands. His face relaxes, and he takes in his surroundings.

Curious, I ask Mum, "You can break Marcellus's compelling hold?"

"I can." She then faces her once husband. "It's been a long time, Lukah."

"Sara?" he questions, his attention landing on her. "Oh, Sara! You're alive!"

"You can stop pretending you care about me."

Aleksandra steps out of the shadows. "You don't care about anyone but yourself."

His eyes narrow beneath black brows, and his tone reflects everything Aleksandra told us about him. "Mind your tongue, child."

"No," Mum interjects. "You don't get to speak to her like that anymore. In fact, you don't get to speak to her at all anymore. I think you need some alone time to think about your actions." She sounds like she's scolding him for stealing some bread rather than starting a cult and draining my sister for her magical blood. Mum looks to Rune. "Send him somewhere that he'll have to work hard to survive."

"No, Sara…please, don't do this!"

"I know just the place," Rune says with a grin, then flicks her wrist, opening a new doorway. Beyond is a lush world with oversized plants that occupy the entire view beyond. "One world full of animals that are as big as a house."

Mum smiles. "Perfect."

Master Ebenus throws a few swings, resisting what's coming, but eventually Mum pushes him through. A deep growl reverberates from somewhere in the forest, and Ebenus screams for us to save him. Rune doesn't wait for anyone to have doubts and closes the doorway.

With all the portals closed and only a few candles lighting the cozy space, we all breathe a sigh of relief that it's over. We've sent Marcellus back to the Under Realm and removed the cult leader from the Order.

Strong hands grab my shoulders and pull me in. I don't resist Mum's embrace and wrap my arms around her. Another pair of arms comes from behind, and I don't shove them away. Then another. Both Kit and Elijah have joined in our victory hug, while Rune stands aside with Aleksandra. When they finally free me, I ask, "Where's Merigoth?"

"I've hidden her somewhere safe in the Starlight Realm, where I can keep a close eye on her," Rune explains.

"But isn't that exactly where she wants to be?" I ask. "It's a little risky."

"She's locked away in a secure location that is only known to me. A family secret." Rune then shifts the subject. "Everyone's gathered at Goslings to mourn…" Her words fade and she doesn't finish.

Someone died. That's what Evander said. "Who did we lose?" I'm unsure if I want to know the answer, even though I know I'll learn the truth eventually.

"Sayen," Aleksandra says. "There was one of those demon-inhabited men at her house. He killed her family and her."

"I'm so sorry to hear that." Then, my heart races as I recall who else was there at Sayen's home: Rune, Elijah, Aleksandra, and… I realize who isn't here. A lump forms in my throat, and tears build behind my eyes. *Please, no. Don't let them say her name. Please, no, no, no.* After swallowing the lump, I ask shakily, "Where's Aunt Lauren?"

Mum raises her chin, as if she's trying to hold it together. Her eyes gloss over, and she pulls me in for another hug. "I'm so sorry, Adele."

"It wasn't her time!" I push Mum away. "And she's strong…and fast…and—and how did—"

Rune finishes with one word that tells me everything I need to know. "Alister."

Trembling, I try to control my anger. That brute. That insufferable Reborn creature! "Where is he now?"

Again, Rune answers, "I tossed him into the Yasmin Sea. The storm waters consumed him, pulling him beneath the waves."

"And you're sure he's dead?"

Blinking several times, as if unsure, she nods. "I saw the waves crash over him, claiming his life for the sea. No man can survive that."

"He's no man," I remind her. "But for now, I'll take your word."

Elijah comes over, easing the tension in the room by saying, "Can we go home now?"

"The doorway that Marcellus initially used to come to Noviska. It's closed?" Mum asks as Rune opens a doorway into Lauren's cottage rather than Goslings.

Rune nods. "It is. Neither one of them will be returning to the Human Realm anytime soon." She stands there and guards the doorway as everyone passes through. Once we're all back in Bricen, Rune raises her hand to close the doorway but stops to ask, "Aren't you coming, Aleksandra?"

The group turns to face the passage. Still standing on the Noviska side is my sister. Her hood has collected around her shoulders, letting us all get a good look at her horns. Stepping closer, Mum tells her, "You don't have to decide right now.

You're more than welcome to stay in Bricen...with us, or go your separate way. Though, for tonight, I think it's best that you shouldn't be alone."

"You promise Master Ebenus won't find me—he won't harm me ever again?"

I step up next to Mum. "He's never leaving that realm without the help of an angel. And I promise not to let anyone else hurt you. You have my word." And with that, I hold out a gloved hand to her.

"Okay, then," Aleksandra says, slipping her hand over mine. "I accept your protection, sister."

CHAPTER 30

ADELE

After Elijah builds a fire, bringing some life into Aunt Lauren's home, I look around, wanting to savor the memories of my life here with her and Mum. It's hard to believe she's gone. I keep expecting her to walk in at any moment. The flour sack that's always open at the end of the table has been closed and moved to the floor by the cupboard.

Aunt Lauren stayed in Bricen even after Rune demanded she return to her rightful home in the Starlight Realm. Her determination to stay here with her family might have upset Rune, but the people of this village, including me, loved her for it.

"Bring him here," Mum says, setting up two chairs facing each other. "Sit him down. I've never tried this on your kind before. So, I'm not making any promises."

"I appreciate you trying," Rune says, easing Evander into the chair. He's not resisting her lead. He's not anything. It's as if he's sleepwalking.

Mum presses her hands to the sides of his head. Her expression twists, as if she's struggling to reach his mind. After several minutes, she drops her hands and heaves a sigh. "He's too strong. He's resisting me."

"Resisting you?" Rune asks. "What does that even mean?"

"Hey, it's okay." Elijah comes over and tries to console Rune, but she's not having it, gently pushing his hands away from her.

"We finally rescued him and now he's, what…stuck like this?"

Moving closer, I offer my help. "Let me try." Mum stands, and I take her seat in front of Evander. As I roll my neck and inhale a deep breath, the darkness stirs within. I reel in the excitement and try to focus on the task at hand. Silently, I tell myself we're helping Evander, not harming him. My reach is eager and ready to be released. I remove my gloves and set them on the table. Then, with practiced ease, I slide the tips of my fingers over his temples. Letting my reach flow from me into him, I snake my way into his mind. To my surprise, I'm met with that same large oak door that Rhoda had.

"There's some kind of door preventing me from reaching his mind."

"I saw that too." Mum's voice floats into my head while I inspect the giant door. "Lukah…or Master Ebenus…he also had one, but it was easier for me to open. Evander's not so much."

I wind the tendrils of my reach around the handle and try twisting it open, but it doesn't budge. I even try slamming my reach's energy against it like a battering ram, but still…nothing. "This door isn't from Marcellus. I've seen it before, on one of the Hoods from the Order."

"The stone necklace!" Rune's voice floats into my mind. She sounds so far away, even though I know she's only a few steps from where I sit. There's a rustling sound, and after a few moments, Rune's voice returns, much louder. "Did that help?"

The door slowly fades from existence. And I confirm, "It did! The door is gone!" In its place is a giant translucent bubble, just like the ones I construct when trapping someone's mind in a mental prison. I extend my reach over the entire bubble, coating it like spilled black ink. Then, slowly, I pull at its threads until it dissolves, freeing his thoughts and memories.

It's not the first time I've done this, released someone from their captive state, but it has rarely happened. Discretion was more important than mercy when it came to General Onica and those she sent to me for interrogation.

Once the last thread has dissolved, I'm flooded with memory after memory from Evander's early childhood years up until moments before Marcellus claimed him for the second time.

Opening my eyes, I lower my hands and say, "Done."

Evander blinks his eyes open and looks about the room. His focus lands on Rune and he smiles. "I knew you'd save me."

With arms open wide, she hugs him where he sits. Then, releasing him, she tells him, "It wasn't just me."

Standing, Evander thanks everyone in the room. "I am in your debt, all of you. Thank you."

"Can we go eat now? I'm starving!" Kit pushes off the wall and heads outside. "I'll see you all at Goslings."

Elijah cups Evander's arm. "It's good to have you back." Evander nods, and Elijah follows his sister out the door.

"Come on, let's get you something to drink," Rune says, leading Evander out of Aunt Lauren's cottage.

It's just me, Mum, and Aleksandra left. Mum walks over to me. "I'm proud of you."

"What did you guys do that made the door disappear?" I ask, curious to know.

Mum holds up a necklace with a small gray stone hanging at the end. "It's one of Lukah's enchanted stones." She then turns and tosses it into the fire. "Aleksandra, you must be hungry, too."

"You want me to come where all the villagers will see me?"

"You can keep your hood up if it makes you more comfortable. Though, if you decide to stay here in Bricen, they're going to learn the truth one way or another. And these people have seen their share of unearthly encounters. You'd be surprised at how welcoming they can be."

Aleksandra offers Mum a smile, but still raises her hood over her honey-blonde curls and black horns. "I'm not ready for that yet, and I think tonight should be about your friend." Then, to me she says, "Tonight should be about your aunt and not about the night the girl with the horns decided to move to Bricen."

Her words have me grinning because I think I'm okay with her staying. "So, I guess that means the cottage you're staying in is your new home."

"Yeah, I guess it is," she says, then follows Mum out the door.

As we make our way up the front steps to Goslings, I slow when I spot Nathaniel leaning against the porch railing. He sees me and stands tall, a smile spreading on his face. Mum and Aleksandra don't wait and head inside.

"I've been waiting for you. Worried, about whatever big battle you and the others went off to fight."

"Oh, you've been waiting for me," I say, slowly making my way up the stairs. When I reach the top, he makes room for me on the porch. We stand there, leaning on the railing and staring out at the night sky. "I miss her already."

"I'm sorry about your aunt."

"Thank you." Heat flushes beneath my skin. I had assumed his reasoning for making conversation with me was because he was too shy to talk directly to Selene. But recalling the beautiful hair pin with a secret dagger he made *for me* has me thinking his feelings are for me. This is all unfamiliar territory, and I wish Selene were here to tell me if I look like a fool.

He leans farther over the railing, and it creaks under his weight. Not wanting to break the support beams, he quickly stands upright. And when he crosses his arms, I find myself staring at his arm muscles.

What is happening to me?

"Can you fight?" The words escape before I realize he may be insulted by such a personal inquiry.

Shaking his head, a smile forming, he confides, "I can handle myself, but I've never been one to win a confrontation. I leave the physical arguments to Brandulf."

A small chuckle escapes, and I have no clue what's gotten into me. "I can teach you. I mean, if you want, and if you have the time."

His smile spreads wider. "I'd like that."

I inch closer to the front door of the tavern, and he catches me by the arm. My muscles go stiff, but I don't flinch or pull away. *Am I ready to let others get this close to me?*

He releases me and says, "I was wondering if you'd like to sit with me and my brother."

Inside, the villagers gather around the tables, stand in groups, and converse by the fireplace. Their voices carry out into the night air. Most are talking and sharing their memories of Lauren, while others are singing songs about her. It's a sad occasion, but the celebration of Lauren's life is to be carried out through good times and happy stories. Across the room, at a table near the back bar counter, Mum sits with Aleksandra, Kit, Elijah, Rune, and Evander.

"Thank you for the offer, but I think I'll sit with my family."

"Oh, of course. How absurd of me! You should sit with your family."

Just then, a familiar string of *caw*s fills the evening air. One by one, the crows land and perch on the porch railing. I move past Nathaniel over to—all *four* crows! "Barclay! What are you doing here? Is everything okay at Castle Forge? Is Selene in danger?"

The crow caws the loudest *caw* I've ever heard from him. Then Valor pecks at the leather satchel hanging from her brother's neck.

"Right. Let's see what the message says." I open the small piece of paper, which is folded several times. Then, I remember I'm still learning to read. Facing Nathaniel, I politely ask, "Can you read this to me?"

His brows pinch, and he accepts the note. Without making a fuss about my lack of reading skills, he says, "You teach me to fight, and I'll teach you to read. Deal?"

Something warm ignites in my chest. Something I've never felt before. A spark of heat that brings me joy. Though, not the same kind of happiness I get when Kit asks me to go hunting with her, or when Elijah tells a funny joke. It's something different.

Holding my gloved hand out, every part of me screaming *What are you doing?*, I gesture to seal our deal with a shake. "It's a deal then."

He slides his hand over mine, curling his fingers around my palm, and gives it a gentle squeeze. "Deal." Then he opens the note and reads it. He's quiet for a moment, then folds the note up and hands it back.

Unsure of what just happened, I ask, "What does it say? You were supposed to tell me what the note said!"

"It says you've been invited to a wedding."

Though I should be excited to see Selene, my shoulders slump and dread fills my once-joyous core.

"You don't want to go to a wedding?" he asks, taking in my reaction.

"I don't want to go to Fayatin."

"Ah. That's understandable. I grew up over there. My brother and I swore we'd never return. It's a horrible country."

A strange urge has me wanting to ask him more questions. Not like interrogation questions, but I want to know him better. I think Aunt Lauren would've appreciated me stepping out of my comfort zone and befriending more people.

Gesturing to the front door, I say, "We should go inside." He nods, and before he gets too far, I ask, "Would you like to come sit with us?"

He rubs the back of his neck, his hand trailing up the shaved part of his head to the short, trimmed hair. With a sheepish smile, he politely says, "Ah, normally I'd jump at the chance to sit with you and your family. But I think you should be with them tonight remembering your aunt. We can catch up tomorrow. I'm not going anywhere, and hopefully you aren't anytime soon."

"Okay, see you tomorrow."

We part ways, him heading over to his brother, whatever his name is, and me weaving through the tables to where my family sits. It's loud and I feel as if everyone from the village is stuffed inside Goslings tonight. They're all laughing and talking about one time or another with Aunt Lauren. Kit pulls out a chair and I take a seat.

"Nathaniel, huh," she says with a snicker.

I roll my eyes, then face Mum. "If you want to leave…if it's too much, we can take our leave."

"No. It's fine. This is what I need. To hear how much everyone loved and appreciated her."

Magdala comes around with a basket full of rolls. "These are the last ones. I made sure no one ate them, thinking you'd want to have them."

We all know her meaning.

These are the last rolls made by Lauren. We all take one and hold it rather than eat it. I want to keep this roll forever. The young girl then faces Aleksandra and holds up a hand to whisper something in her ear.

Unsure of what to do, Aleksandra hesitates at first, but then leans in closer to hear the girl's secret. A grin forms on her face and remains as Magdala continues to the next table.

"What did she say?" I ask, curious eyes all on her to know.

Heat blushes along her cheeks. "She apologized for her initial reactions after seeing me with my hood down, and then asked if we could be friends."

Oh, that kid. She's got a good heart. Everyone in Bricen does.

More people have joined in the serenading around the fireplace, and soon everyone is singing. Mugs and tankards clank with each mention of Lauren's name in the lyrics.

Kit stands, her chair scraping and almost tipping over. I grab it and steady it as she moves around the table. "I have a bottle of wine I've been saving. Let's open it!"

"I can help gather some cups," Aleksandra offers, and when Kit nods, she hurries to follow Kit over behind the bar counter.

Rune stands and clears her throat. "Can I have everyone's attention, please?" she shouts, and when the songs die down and everyone stops talking, all eyes are on her. "You all know Lauren as the kindest woman who baked the sweetest breads and treats." She pauses to admire the roll in her hands. "But I know her as one of the bravest angels to ever live. She'll be remembered not only here in your world, but also in mine. Her death is untimely, but it has opened my eyes to our commonalities. And with that, I want to open a permanent doorway between our two realms, here in Bricen, directly to Stellara, our beloved city in the Starlight Realm. Whomever wishes to come and live there is welcome. We could sure use the help in rebuilding our home."

"And we can come and go, between worlds?" one villager asks.

"Can I bring my whole family?" another asks.

"Yes, and yes," Rune answers. "I won't force you to help us rebuild but having you there to help us clean up and rebuild our city would be a tremendous help. And it would become your city too."

Elijah stands. "I'd be honored to be one of the first from our realm to move to Stellara and help you any way I can." An unsaid declaration between Rune and Elijah fills the air between them.

"Thank you."

A few other villagers stand, pronouncing their services and help. Then, slowly, the song picks up again and the villagers' voices fill the tavern. Rune and Elijah take their seats while Kit and Aleksandra pass out cups of wine.

"I am so proud of you," Evander says to Rune. "We will build a new Stellara with new laws and new ways."

"Yes, we will." Rune's gaze barely leaves Elijah's.

"I'd like to come too," Aleksandra says, clasping her cup of wine with two hands. "As much as I think Bricen would accept me, starting a new life where no one knows me sounds thrilling."

Everyone looks to Mum, who looks to Rune. "It's your call."

"Aleksandra, you are more than welcome to come and live with us. And if you decide you want to return to Bricen, the doorway will be there for you to travel through. I'll make sure that anyone can pass through without a Realmwalker nearby."

I lean in close and quietly ask Rune, "Can I speak to you in private?" She nods and we make our way out onto the front porch of Goslings. With the door closed, once it's just the two of us, I ask, "Are you sure about leaving a doorway open between our two worlds?"

She nods. "I want to welcome humans into the Starlight Realm, but I don't want them to feel like they're stuck there. Having the doorway here in Bricen with you, Sara, and Kit here gives me assurances that it'll be guarded and safe."

"Can I confide in you about something?" I quietly ask, still holding the roll.

Without breaking her gaze from the dying light through the forest trees, she says, "Of course, friend."

"I've been trying not to use my ability, especially in front of the others. I don't want them comparing me to Marcellus."

Standing tall, she rests a hand on my forearm. "No one compares you to Marcellus. Everyone knows when you use your ability, it's to protect yourself, your family, or your home. Do you want my opinion?"

Nodding, I wait for her to speak her mind.

"Don't be ashamed or hide who you are. You don't need to tell people one thing, then do another in secrecy because you fear they will judge you. Your ability is a weapon, just like a sword or a bow and arrow is. Yes, you can use it to heal or help, but if you prefer to use it as a weapon, then do so. Protect those you care about. And don't hide it. Let the world know your name and what you can do. Your family won't love you any less. They trust you and your judgment."

Her words sink in, and she's right.

"Thank you, Rune. You're a good friend."

She holds up her roll. "Savor this night. For with the bad rises the good."

I raise my roll and tap the edge to Rune's in a cheers gesture. Then we both take a bite and smile. "No one will ever be able to bake like Aunt Lauren."

Rune nods. "These are quite delicious."

We remain out on the porch, looking at the night sky above Bricen for some time. I've been so worried about what everyone thinks of me, I haven't been able to be my true self—which makes me feel incomplete. And I want to feel complete. Going forward, I'm going to embrace the darkness, as Rune said, and show people they don't need to fear me. Especially if Bricen will be the gateway between our two realms. I'll need to be more protector than healer—more vigilant around those who travel to our village. Learn to read people on the outside and widen my circle of trusted friends. There's much to be done in the coming days.

But first, I have to go to a wedding.

EPILOGUE

ALEKSANDRA

"And this will be your room," Rune says to me. "I hope you don't mind staying in my home until we can find you a suitable place of your own." She pushes open the door and crosses the room, turning on a light. "We only cleaned up and restored power to the homes we needed. But now, with so many coming over from Bricen and other villages, we'll need to focus on fixing up more homes sooner rather than later."

My heart is pounding. I'm actually here—in the Starlight Realm. "It sounds exciting, and I appreciate you letting me stay with you," I say with all the pleasantries I can muster.

"It's nice that you're here. And you don't need to worry about wearing your hood. The angels living here were excited about opening the doorway and allowing others to come over and live." Rune makes her way to the bedroom door, her speckled brown wings tucked behind her shoulders. "I'll leave you to settle in."

"Thank you, again," I say out loud, and then in my head, add *Oh, please just go and let me be.*

She closes the door and leaves me in solace. "Finally," I mutter under my breath and quickly approach the door, needing to know if it locks. Unable to find a locking bolt, I curse, then turn to my bag, resting on the floor up against the bed. I reach into the bag and pull out a bunch of leather string necklaces. The stones dangling at the ends clatter together as I lay them out on the quilt. Then, returning to my bag, I pull out a slender iron stick resembling an oversized threading needle. I'm grateful for the fireplace in my room, and heat the tip in the flames until the end glows red. I quickly begin carving a symbol in the stone, and when the heat subsides from the tip, I repeat the process of heating it up again until I've successfully etched two imbuing symbols into the stone.

I return to the door and drape the stone necklace with its newly embellished enchantment on the door latch. Then, I test the enchantment and try to open the door. It doesn't budge. Satisfied, I collect the remaining spare necklaces and hide them at the bottom of my bag. While my hand is in my bag, I search for my large stone. Withdrawing it from the bag, I set it on the bed. It's black like onyx and perfectly round. The symbols carved into it are hard to see, and when I prick my finger with the carving needle, I rub the blood over the symbols, activating the stone.

"Hello?" I ask, seeing if my mysterious friend will be there tonight.

Several minutes pass, and I'm about to clean up and call it a night when I finally hear a reply. "Hello, Aleksandra?" The woman's voice is calm and pleasant.

Holding the black stone closer to my mouth, I say, "Yes, it's me. And I have news that will please you."

"Oh, is that so."

It wasn't until one year ago that I discovered this black stone. It was one of the trinkets locked up in Master Ebenus's cabinet of gifts from the Under Realm queen. I stole it and kept it secret, loving a good puzzle to solve. And eventually I did solve it, discovering the almost undetectable symbols etched into the surface. But it wasn't until a smear of blood touched the symbols that the puzzle was solved.

"And what news do you have to share with me?"

Lifting one knee onto the bed, I say with delight, "I'm here. I'm in the Starlight Realm." My news is met with silence. Not the reaction I hoped for. "Did you hear me? I said—"

"And now you can begin your search for the journal?" the girl asks, her voice carrying a slight echo, as if she's traveling through a cave or standing on the edge of a cliffside.

"That's the second thing I have to tell you." From the side pocket of my bag, I retrieve the stolen item I took. It's wrapped in a linen cloth. With delicate fingers, I carefully unwrap the cloth until the leather notebook is revealed. Holding the stone to my mouth, I say, "I've already obtained Merigoth's journal."

"Then you only have one more task before coming to the Shadowlands, and all your questions will be answered. Can I ask what happened to your companion? The girl, Sayen? You were supposed to bring her, as part of our deal."

"Sayen was becoming difficult. I was presented with an opportunity and so I took it. But don't worry, I will find someone to take her place."

"Good."

"I look forward to finally meeting you," I say. Then, from outside my door, Rune calls me to come eat. I shout in response, "I'll be right down!" I spit a small amount of saliva on the smooth surface and wipe clean my smeared blood from over the symbols, ending our conversation. I return the black stone ball and the iron threading needle to my bag. Then, I remove the necklace from the door latch, thus removing the locking incantation. Before heading downstairs to eat with Rune and Elijah, I hide the necklace under my pillow. I'll find better hiding spots later when I unpack all my belongings.

Heading out the door, I remind myself that my purpose here is not to make friends or rebuild their city. Instead, I'm determined to uncover the truth about the demons that have infected Merigoth. It's through this pursuit that I hope to discover my true calling.

Throughout my entire life, I've been treated as a mere creature with the potential to bring destruction and chaos. But perhaps, deep down, I'm a powerful being deserving of fear and worship.

If everything goes according to plan and I successfully complete the final task assigned to me, I'll no longer be regarded as an animal. Instead, I'll be revered and worshipped across all realms.

As I descend the stairs to join Rune and Elijah for supper, a chuckle escapes me, because no one even suspects their freedom is coming to an end.

THANK YOU FOR READING

A VENGEFUL SHADE

BOOK TWO IN THE THREE SHADES TRILOGY

If you enjoyed this book,
please consider sharing your thoughts in a review on:

GOODREADS   AMAZON

And if you really, *really* enjoyed this book, please consider
sharing your thoughts on your social media pages and with
your friends and family.

To learn more about my books, where to find me online,
sign up for my newsletter, visit my Etsy shop, and more visit
www.kimberlygrymes.com/links or scan this QR code:

BOOK THREE: SHADES AND BLOOD OATHS
COMING FALL 2025

ACKNOWLEDGMENTS

I didn't grow up as a reader. Through school, high school, and even into my twenties, reading never captivated me. My reading disability made it difficult to comprehend what I was reading unless I was fully focused. It wasn't just about reading the words—it was about understanding them. If I wasn't interested in the book, focusing became even harder, and for years, I avoided reading altogether.

Then, in my late twenties, the young adult fantasy fiction trend took off with the release of *Twilight* by Stephenie Meyer. Curious about the hype, I went to Target and bought my first book (yes, the first book I'd ever owned!). If my high school English teacher, Ms. Narkis, had seen me, she might have asked someone to pinch her! But once I started reading, I was hooked. Something about the young adult writing style and fantasy genre clicked with my brain. I could finally follow along—word for word, sentence by sentence. It was such a joyous experience that I wanted more. Soon, I was reading (and listening to audiobooks) two or three at a time.

A few years later, I tried writing a book of my own. It was a grueling experience—grammar, punctuation, and all the rules of writing were lifelong struggles for me. But I was determined. I wouldn't let my ADHD brain get distracted. Eight years later, I finally hit the publish button on my debut young adult science-fantasy book. What an exhilarating experience! But after releasing that book, I realized I'd barely learned anything about the business side of self-publishing.

I'd been so focused on writing that I assumed everything else would just fall into place—like dominoes. Boy, was I wrong.

Every writer has their own methods, but we all learn from each other. After releasing that first book, I expanded my understanding of the many hats a self-published author must wear. Not only did I want to continue improving my writing, but I also needed to learn more about marketing and maintaining financial records.

This is where the Acknowledgments section comes in. So many wonderful people in the book publishing industry have supported and encouraged me, helping me grow as a writer and author. Each book I release is special to me because it shows my determination and dedication to succeed. I will never stop learning and improving my craft. It's knowing that I'm doing everything I can to overcome my comprehension disability by learning from others and working with professionals.

Before I thank those who directly helped make this book the best it can be, I'd like to express my deepest gratitude to my husband, Jim, for his unwavering support and encouragement. He's been there for me since I decided to write and publish my own stories. I'd also like to thank my three kiddos, Kayla, Abby, and Chloe, for their constant love and support. They're always there to celebrate with me or give hugs when I'm burned out from writing or marketing. I couldn't do what I do without their love and encouragement.

Every writer should have one or two friends to share milestones, project details, or morale boosts. I'm lucky to have so many writer friends to talk shop with: Liz Delton,

A.E. Kincaid, and the many wonderful and supportive members of Sacha Black's Rebel Author group.

A special thank you goes to the beta readers of *A Vengeful Shade*—Fatima, Brook, and Liz—who provided invaluable feedback before professional edits began. Your early reader comments and insights were tremendously helpful in highlighting scenes that needed more detail and confirming that others were as impactful as I'd hoped.

Next, the manuscript went to Nikki at NAM Editorial for a round of line edits. Given my struggles with grammar and punctuation, Nikki's expertise truly worked its magic, elevating my story to the next level. Her educational approach to line editing has been invaluable, teaching me so much over the years and significantly improving my writing. There's something fascinating about how my teenage brain was so reluctant to learn and retain these things, whereas now, I eagerly embrace and apply what I've learned.

Once all the line edits were applied, I was excited to hand off the manuscript to Aime at Red Leaf Word Services for the final round of edits—the proofreading. Aime's meticulous attention to detail and the insightful feedback she provided during this last read-through ensured the book was polished and ready for publication.

The last step was sending the finished manuscript to my audiobook narrator, Amanda Davidson. Amanda's ability to bring a story to life with her exceptional storytelling and diverse voices was the perfect finishing touch for the project.

I'd like to thank Angeline Trevena at Step-By-Step Worldbuilding for hand-illustrating the map of the *Three Shades Trilogy* and Yves Muench for the character illustrations on the cover and in the color interior of the special edition hardcover. I'd also like to thank Gab (Gabryella Ferreira, @gabsgabx) for her beautiful illustration of Rune and Elijah, which is exclusive bonus artwork included in the color interior of the special edition hardcover.

My gratitude extends to Sarah at Behind The Pages author services for her invaluable assistance with promotional tours during the pre-launch months. Marketing can be challenging, but with Sarah's help, it was an enjoyable and rewarding experience.

Last, I'd like to thank you, the readers, for picking up book two in the series. After finishing book one, *Shade of Light*, I had a moment of panic, worried about delivering an engaging and exciting story that would entice you to read book three. However, after writing the first draft, I felt confident that I had crafted the best possible middle installment for this trilogy. I cannot wait for you to dive in and read the epic finale. Thank you again for your support and for taking the time to journey with me through this series.

About the Author

Kimberly Grymes is drawn to the imaginative realms of science-fiction, fantasy, mystery, and the paranormal. Her passion lies in crafting original tales within the young adult fantasy genre, where she explores worlds of magic, adventure, and the supernatural. In addition to her storytelling, Kimberly supports fellow writers through her direct shop, where she provides a range of checklists and worksheets designed to guide writers through the brainstorming, outlining, and writing process.

When she's not immersed in creating resources or weaving narratives, Kimberly enjoys spending time with her family, indulging in movies or TV shows, and delving into captivating books. She and her family reside on the outskirts of Wichita, Kansas, accompanied by their two lively miniature pinschers, Cori and Jubilee.